THE

ORIGINAL

OWLAM

Dara J. Carr

THE ORIGINAL OWLAM

Dara J. Carr

Harrison House Publishing

Harrison House Publishing
www.theharrisonhousepublishing.com
info@theharrisonhousepublising.com
ISBN: 9780986128561
Library of Congress Control Number: 2015960348
Harrison House Publishing and the "HH" logo are trademarks belonging to
Harrison House Publishing.

PRINTED IN THE UNITED STATES OF AMERICA

TXu 1-910-146

1

The large spacecraft finally arrived at the edge of a new star system. It slowed to sub-light speed as it neared the furthest planet from the central star.

The Captain of the ship turned on his log recorder. "Computer, annotate the date and time." He waited for a moment as he stared at the planet on the monitor. "Deep Space Explorer ship *Discoverer* has finally arrived at the outer planet of the star system that we have labeled 'NZ-3591'. We will begin scanning this planet, NZ-3591-14, and work our way in. The Science Officers will record the findings as we go."

He leaned back in his chair. "Helmsman, establish a standard equatorial orbit. Science Team…do your scans."

Captain Ronald Milch, of the exploration ship *Discoverer* was a tall lean man with gray eyes and graying hair. He looked somewhat tired and bored as he contemplated the screen again.

He looked over at the five personnel on the Science team as they were all looking over the data that was coming in from the sensor readings. "Commander Gomez, anything spectacular about this planet?"

Gomez snickered. He was a very short man with a rough ruddy complexion. He looked as if he should be a gaucho on some ranch taking care of cattle. "It may not be a planet at all. So far, all we're getting is massive readings of frozen methane. There are minute traces of hydrogen, helium and nitrogen…virtually nothing else. The frozen methane crust, is registering as being at least 1350 meters thick…throughout the entire planet. For some reason, our sensors don't seem to be able to penetrate any further than that. We've found no geological formations at all. So far…we're looking at one great big ball of frozen methane, with a surface temperature of twelve degrees Kelvin."

Milch chuckled. "Is that equatorial or polar?"

Gomez rolled his eyes and clicked his tongue in frustration. "So far, it seems to be the entire planet."

Milch looked back at the monitor. "Really," he replied softly.

Gomez cleared his throat. "Another oddity about this planet…is the fact that it is orbiting that…or any star…at all."

Milch looked confused. "What's that supposed to mean?"

Gomez shrugged. "The distance…it is just…so *far* away. It has a normal spherical orbit, but…it would take…according to our examination…somewhere between 710 and 715 years for one orbit, we haven't been able to nail it down to any specific time…yet. I don't see as how it is…caught in any kind of gravitational pull from the star…at all. Possibly the gas giants in the sixth and seventh orbits have something to do with it."

Milch chuckled. "We *have* seen some very strange things out here. It seems that no matter how many we find…and think that we've seen it all…we always seem to be able to find something else that…defies logic or…the laws of physics."

Gomez shook his head and smiled. "Yes, Sir."

"Anything else we can find out about this planet?"

"Not from here. If we launch a planetary crawler and let it do some exploring…we might find something else when we come back and retrieve it…later."

Milch stretched his arms out and yawned. "Okay, go ahead and launch one. As soon as we know that it has safely landed, we'll go to the next planet."

Gomez shook his head. "Fourteen planets. Five inner planets. Then that sixth orbit - that's a strange one. There are three gas giants in that orbit. The seventh orbit has two more gas giants. Then there's the four outer planets."

Milch snickered. "That's a real puzzle. Finding two planets in the same orbit…what a rarity. Then we find that this star system has two planets in one orbit and three in another." He smiled and smoothed his hair back. "Incredible." He looked over at the science monitors. "Does this planet, that we're orbiting, have any satellites?"

Gomez turned to his aides. "Riley?"

Riley shook his head and chuckled. "The only thing that I

can find is chunks. The largest one…so far…is fourteen meters in length. Sensors have picked up about 250 of these chunks. Nothing spectacular…just mundane space rocks and asteroids."

"So, Commander Gomez, do we need to stick around here much longer?"

"No, Captain, once the crawler's on the planet, and set on the exploratory program, we can head on to the next one."

"Status on the crawler?"

Gomez turned back to his team. "Salisbury…what's the status?"

"I'm working on it," she said. "This planet's got a heavy gravity and it is rather tricky trying to get that thing down safe. I'm having to use a lot of retro rockets to do it safely."

Milch sighed. "Okay, let me know when it's down and set."

Salisbury worked a joystick and was hitting several control buttons as she was fighting to keep control. She finally let out a sigh of relief and leaned back in her chair. She looked a little exhausted from the ordeal. She took in a deep breath. "It's down…safe."

Gomez looked over at another aide. "Burkowski, why don't you program it? Make sure that the internal heater is working. 12 Kelvin could freeze the system up…real quick."

Burkowski went to his keypad and started feeding in the data. After a few moments he stopped and shook his head. "Okay, the thing is set. I don't know how long that battery's gonna work, because that heater is gonna suck a lot of power out of it. It'll go until the battery quits."

"That's all we can ask for," said Gomez with a shrug.

"So," said Milch, "are we finished here…for the moment?"

"Yes, Captain," said Gomez.

Milch turned back and looked at the big monitor. "Helm, onward and forward to…NZ-3591-13."

The Helmsman looked back at the Captain. "I don't think that that is prudent…at this time, Sir. According to the charts, planet number 13 is clear on the other side of the star in the orbital path. At sub-light speed, it would take about eight weeks to get there. We're so much closer to planet number 12…about eleven hours."

"What a mess," muttered the Captain. "We can't go into light speed, inside a star system." He grunted. "All right, Lieutenant Rabb, on to planet NZ-3591-12."

"Aye-aye, Sir. ETA at planet twelve is ten hours, fifty-four minutes."

The big spacecraft broke orbit from the methane planet and was steered towards the closest planet to their current location.

Captain Milch stood up and stretched. "Exec Officer, you have the bridge!"

"Aye-aye, Sir, said Commander Hiroko Kasaki. The small Japanese woman walked up to the Captain's chair. She watched as Milch headed for the exit.

Milch turned back to his Executive Officer. "I'm going to the Officer's Mess, Hiroko, Alejandro, join me."

"Aye-aye, Sir," said Gomez as he followed.

Just before exiting the bridge, Milch turned back again. "Hiroko, let me know when we're getting ready to establish orbit at number twelve."

"Aye-aye, Sir." Again she watched. As soon as he went through the exit, she sat down. "Captain's off the bridge!"

Milch and Gomez headed to get something to eat.

Milch shook his head. "Five planets in two orbits...what *do* you make of that?"

"It's quite a puzzlement, Sir. According to long range scans, the three in the sixth orbit are all about the same size and they are in exactly the same orbital path. Planets six and seven are a mere 106,000,000 kilometers apart, while number eight follows in the same path, over 2,500,000,000 kilometers away. Planets nine and ten, in the seventh orbit, are within 5,000,000 kilometers of being on the exact opposite sides of the star, however, still being in the same orbital path."

Milch chuckled. "So they're symmetrical as far as their orbit, but not their placement."

"Correct, Sir. These five gas giants have a lot of gravitational pull, by themselves, and that's one of the reasons why we think that planet number fourteen stays where it is. As I said, it's just way too far away from the central star to be...held in place by that alone."

"Will you be able to...confirm that theory?"

"Oh, yes, Sir. Now that we're in the system itself, we can get far greater accurate readings on all the planets." Gomez shook his head. He wondered how someone as ignorant, of astronomy, as Captain Ronald Milch had been allowed to obtain a Captaincy and command of his own ship...especially a scientific space exploration vessel. Maybe it was just so that he would be more interested in the day to day running of the vessel and not being sidetracked by scientific studies of his own.

Milch felt a hand on his shoulders. He opened his eyes and looked up at the Chief Yeoman, Elliott Matthews. "What...uh...is it?"

Now that Milch was awake, Matthews stood up straight. "We're about ten minutes away from establishing orbit at planet twelve, Sir."

Milch stood up rubbing his eyes. He sniffed hard and blinked several times, attempting to get fully awake. "Thank you, Yeoman." He yawned.

"Yes, Sir."

Milch headed to the bridge, shaking and stretching kinks out of his body. He arrived at the bridge.

"Captain's on the bridge," shouted Yeoman Matthews.

Normally everyone would snap to "attention" for a moment. They did not. All of the attention of the science team was on one monitor at the science station. Almost everyone else was looking over at the science team as they jabbered about the planet. Milch was hearing words like: Incredible, unbelievable and someone even said - Impossible!

Milch made his presence known by shouting. "What's all of this excitement?"

Gomez looked up a little startled. "Uh...yes, Captain." He turned back to his team. "Ensign Martin, put it up on the big screen."

"Yes, Sir," said the tall flaxen-haired woman.

Milch looked up at the main screen. All he saw, for the

moment, was the northern hemisphere of the actual planet - NZ-3591-12. After Ensign April Martin finished punching a few buttons, a grid pattern appeared, overlaying the planet. Then the entire picture spun a little as the scanners zeroed in on a specific location. Next, there was a large red area and a green area overlaying a part of the planet and the grid disappeared.

"Okay," said Milch, "what am I looking at?"

Gomez pointed at the screen. "That red area, Sir...it's a mammoth vein of high grade platinum. The green area, is an equally mammoth vein of high grade gold. This planet is absolutely reeking of mineral wealth...if we still went on a gold-standard system. Since we're not, that platinum and gold...there is enough in just these two veins...to supply all of the electronic needs for...our entire military and scientific fleet, with...thousands of kilotons to spare."

"It looks like a large vein, but I don't see how there could be that much there. What makes you think that it's that rich?"

Gomez grunted. "Sir, you're thinking along the parameters of our home planet. There the equatorial circumference is roughly 38,400 kilometers. This planet has a circumference of 224,000 kilometers - almost *six* times that of home. So those veins are about six times what you would imagine...back home."

Milch almost collapsed into his command chair. He stared at the screen for several moments. "So...whoever gets...mining rights...to this planet...they're going to be *very* busy, for a *very* long time."

"That's a reality...but we also have a...very strange anomaly."

Milch put his left hand over his eyes and moaned. "Why can't anything ever be normal or...semi-normal?" He sighed dropped his arm to the armrest. "Okay, what's the anomaly?"

"First, let me give you a prelude. Up at the northernmost sections of the veins, they're over 6,000 kilometers apart. You can see, as the veins go south, they get closer to each other. Just north of the equator, that one part there, the veins are only 115 kilometers apart. In that area...someone has already been there...and tapped the veins."

Milch felt a little shocked. "Someone...has already been here!

Someone is already mining that...those fields of precious metals."

"Yes, Sir...they *were*."

Milch gave Gomez a, somewhat angry, sideways glare. "Were?"

"Yes, Sir. Whoever tapped these veins...they took some of it...and then they departed...taking *all* of their equipment...with them...when they left."

Milch frowned. "That's stupid! You leave *some* equipment... pre-staged, for when you return. The only reason that you take all of your equipment, when you leave, is because...you're not coming back. Who would take...just a small portion...of veins, that large... and then just skedaddle?" He looked at Gomez helplessly. "How much do you estimate was taken...in those previous mining operations?"

"Less than .002%...of each."

Milch placed his index fingers against his temples. "Veins that rich...and you...just take...a smidgeon?" He looked at the screen. "Dumb!"

Gomez shrugged.

"So...how much - in kilotons - do you think was taken?"

"We don't know how much of the mined area was surrounding rock and how much was ore, so our best guess is that they took approximately 150 kilotons of each."

Milch's jaw dropped. "150...kilotons...of...platinum...and that was less than .002%...of the overall vein?"

Gomez nodded. "Yes, Sir."

"Same...with the gold?"

"Yes, Sir."

Milch leaned back in his chair. "Are there any other... precious metal veins...anywhere on the planet?"

"Yes, Sir," said Gomez with a smile. "On the other side of the planet, there are over 1,000 small veins of silver and copper. In the southern hemisphere, there are even larger deposits of molybdenum, tungsten and tin."

"I wonder if the high command will want to come back here and obtain mining rights."

Gomez chuckled.

Milch gave Gomez a sideways glance. "Were the deposits of copper and silver…tapped?"

"Yes, Sir. Around 200 kilotons of silver and 250 kilotons of copper was taken."

"Still…no equipment left behind?"

"No equipment, Sir. Just large voids in the deposits."

Milch sighed. "Any satellites around this planet?"

"Two large moons…that have nothing spectacular to report…about them."

"Okay, Science Officer, let me know when you've finished with this planet."

"Yes, Sir."

Milch turned his attention to the maintenance reports. He was reading how they were still having trouble with one of the doors on cargo bay 4. It had been giving them fits for almost two months now and they still could not figure out why it would not function properly. He kept on reading the reports from the section chiefs until Gomez informed him that they were ready to go on to the next planet. He stretched, blinked and looked at the big screen. "Helmsman, which is the next closest planet?"

"That would be NZ-3591-11," said Lt. Washington. "About sixteen hours away, Sir."

Milch grunted and nodded. "Proceed!"

"Aye aye, Sir," said Washington.

Planet 11 was nothing special. It had three satellites that were rather mundane as well. Planet 10, one of the gas giants in the seventh orbit, turned out to be a rather normal gas giant, with thirty-one satellites. Planet 9 was on the other side of the star, so they headed to orbit six where there were three more gas giants. Gas giants 7 and 8 showed no new anomalies except for the fact that number 7 had 452 satellites orbiting it. Three of the satellites orbiting number 7 were large enough to have an atmosphere.

The only thing that the Science team found interesting here, was the fact that while the planets were in a virtually identical orbit, they were moving at different speeds. 8 was moving at .012

kilometers faster than 7 and would catch up to number 7...in about 8,500,000,000 years.

Again planet 6 was on the other side of the solar system, so on to planet 5.

Planet 5 had a plethora of volcanoes that were spewing all kinds of noxious fumes into the atmosphere. After examining what they could here, they determined that it would be suicide for any living form to attempt to go to the planet's surface. The temperature was an inferno, because of all of the magma and there was no oxygen at all. It had one mundane satellite.

"Planet 4 is inhabited!" LtJG Burkowski looked up from his screen. "It *is* inhabited by a sentient life form. Just over 4.5 billion and if I'm reading this correctly, there might just be more than one, if not several, sentient species on this planet."

Milch nodded and put down his cup of coffee. "Can you make any estimate - going by our history as - as to what time frame they might be in?"

"From the initial indications, I would guess that they are close to or around...early to mid-Renaissance."

"Someone needs to get Montalvo out of his studies from that last solar system," said Milch. "We've got a new species for him to look at here."

"Yes, Sir," said Burkowski with a grin. "Especially since that last bunch, in that other star system, was in the Stone Age...and numbered less than 300,000. Not much to learn about there."

"I've already contacted Montalvo," said Lt. Daywood, the communications officer on duty. "He's on his way up here, Sir."

"Thank you," said Milch. He turned to Gomez. "Are there any of those aggravating anomalies...anywhere on this planet?"

Gomez chuckled. "We're looking, Sir."

"Anomalies, yes," said LtJG Fletcher. "...but not on the planet. The anomalies are on the two moons."

Salisbury huffed. "Anomalies on the moons?" She laughed and chided him some more. "What'd you find...little green men?"

Fletcher looked at Salisbury angrily. "Watch your mouth, you..."

"HEY!" Milch glared at both of them. "Whatever your problems with your personal lives...I don't care about. Don't bring your problems to the bridge! Is that clear!?"

"Yes, Sir," said both Salisbury and Fletcher, both looking a little guilty.

"Okay," said Milch. "What's so special about some anomaly on the moon...either one of them?"

"Most of the data, from the smaller moon, was picked up as we approached this planet. It appears that there is some kind of technology on the far side of the small moon...however, it appears that it's more wreckage, rather than ruins from...some form of abandoned planetary colonization. It's hard to check on from here, because all of it is on the far side of the moon...from our current position."

Milch grunted. "Since it seems that most of our attention is going to have to concentrate on the main planet...someone needs to take a shuttlecraft and do some separate investigating there."

"Yes, Sir," said Gomez. "Ensign Martin, get with someone from Engineering and go take a look."

"Yes, Sir," said Martin as she got up and headed off the bridge.

Milch watched her leave and then turned back to Fletcher. "Okay, what's the deal with the larger moon?"

"I'm finding a lot of strange subterranean voids."

Milch grunted. "What's so special about a cave?"

"No, Sir, not a cave - a void. These voids are manufactured. Every one of them has 90 degree angles."

The entire Science team now was looking with great interest at Fletcher's findings.

"That's...weird," said Gomez. "Someone done gone and made some underground rooms...on a moon that has no atmosphere. Why?"

"Hard to tell from here," said Fletcher. "As far as I can tell, all of the voids...or rooms are approximately the same size. They're roughly 109 meters long, 55 meters wide and 12 meters high. All eight of them are exactly 135.24 meters below the surface...in their respective area and they...wait...uh..." He leaned closer to his monitor. "...there's a ninth one."

Milch sighed. "Sounds to me like we're going to need to send another shuttle to the large moon, for some closer observations."

Gomez chuckled. "I fully agree, Sir. This is far too interesting a puzzle to ignore."

Milch looked at the big screen frowning. "Do you think we need to send anyone from Engineering to the big moon?"

"No, Sir," said Gomez. "More likely we need to find someone on board who's an architect - and someone from geology. That's who I'd like investigating those...voids. You know, how were they constructed, what are they used for and how do you get in and out... without any atmosphere?"

Milch leaned back and sighed. "Again, it appears that the vast majority of our attention is going to be on this planet and the two moons orbiting it. Someone needs to take a third shuttle and go check out the remaining planets that we haven't looked at, closely, yet."

Gomez smiled. "Aye aye, Sir."

Milch leaned back in his chair. The thought of scattering his personnel and resources all over this solar system was aggravating even though it appeared to be necessary. They had discovered a new sentient life form. There was some strange wreckage on the small moon that orbited the inhabited planet. Someone had constructed some kind of vaults on the large moon. Mining projects on one of the far planets. Not to mention the fact that they still had six more planets to investigate.

Someone with technology, above that of the planet's inhabitants, had been here before. They had mined one planet, crashed on another and built vaults for storage on another...and departed without leaving a trace as to what they were doing...or why...and took all of their equipment with them...other than the things that had crashed on the small moon.

Milch called down to the shuttle bay. "Don't have anyone waiting around for any reasons. As soon as they're ready to launch - go!"

"Yes, Sir," came a reply over the intercom.

Milch looked back at the big screen. "Okay folks…let's start counting the continents, counting the islands, counting the people, counting the animals, counting the flora and fauna, bugs, fish, birds and then we'll count the counts…and see what we've got."

A voice came over the intercom. "Shuttle 2 is already on the way to the small moon, shuttle 1 is launching to the large moon."

Milch keyed the intercom. "Thank you," he said nonchalantly. "Gomez, who's going where…among your people?"

Gomez came up to Milch. "I'm sending Ensign Martin to the small moon, Lieutenant Fletcher to the large moon, Lieutenant Commander Riley and Lieutenant Burkowski to the other planets. Lieutenant Salisbury and I will remain here and coordinate the information coming in from the shuttles."

"What's taking so long to get that third shuttle going?"

"They're going to be gone a *lot* longer than the other two. They need additional personnel and equipment…to check out the other planets, Sir."

"Good, good…where's Montalvo?"

"He's at his station in the Science office."

"Get him up *here*. I'd like to get current information about these people…as he gets it…especially since we may be talking about a planet with more than one sentient race."

Gomez activated the intercom. "Lieutenant Manuel Montalvo, please report to the bridge."

An affirmative response came back over the intercom.

"Thank you," said Milch.

The bridge crew kept on with their normal chores while Milch stared at the planet on the screen. There were several routine conversations from Engineering, and Security going on over the intercom.

Montalvo showed up on the bridge. "Lieutenant Montalvo, reporting as ordered, Sir."

"Good," said Milch. "I want some current news on the indigenous residents of this planet. I was told that there's a strong probability that there is more than one sentient race."

Montalvo chuckled. "*That*…is a *tremendous* understatement,

Sir. While I was at the work station in the Science lab, I was able to isolate and identify twenty-eight different sentient species…and I'm only talking a portion of *one* of the continents. According to the quick scan that was taken earlier…the computer has possibly identified…well over one hundred different sentient species."

Milch's shoulders sagged. "That could be a huge nightmare for the Linguistics and Anthropology department. If each one has their own language, plus several dialects, as well as habits, rituals and religions that are peculiar to only one species, it could take months to figure everything out."

A call came in from one of the shuttles: "Shuttle 1 calling *Discoverer*, do you read?"

"Go ahead," said the communications officer, "we read you, loud and clear."

"This is shuttle 1, we took an orbit around the moon and we've found that there are twelve of these strange voids…or vaults… or whatever you wish to call them. We're going to land and try to get some kind of reading from the surface on these things."

"*Discoverer* copies, shuttle 1. Please keep us informed of any new data."

"Shuttle 2 calling *Discoverer*, do you read?"

"Go ahead, shuttle 2, we read you, loud and clear."

"The back side of this moon is littered with debris. At first we thought that it was just one rather large spacecraft. Now, from what we can see, it's scattered too far and wide to be just one craft. The initial scans indicate that there are over one hundred crash sites… from varying time frames and also different origins of the spacecraft."

"*Discoverer* copies, shuttle 2. Please keep us informed of any new data."

Milch grunted. "This is getting awfully redundant. Every time we get some kind of answer about something, it just raises all kinds of new questions…both intriguing and frustrating…and somewhat baffling."

Shuttle 1 and 2 were the first ones to return. The third shuttle was still on the other side of the system, identifying, checking and mapping the other planets.

The people gathered in the conference room. Captain Milch called the meeting to order and turned the recorder on. "This is Captain Ronald Milch, calling this meeting in regards to some strange wreckage found on the small moon orbiting NZ-3591-4. Lieutenant Brian Justice, from the Engineering section and Ensign April Martin from Science section were dispatched on a shuttle craft to examine this wreckage closely. We are now going to get their full report...computer, please annotate the date and time."

Lt. Justice stood up. "What we have, it seems, is more questions than answers. We count 354 crash sites. From what we saw of them and were able to examine, 105 of these sites were large exploration...or hostile attack mother ships. The other 249 crash sites were, either shuttle craft or small, one-seat fighters, from the mother ships. In each and every case, it appears that the space ship, in question...did not just crash land - every one of them *slammed* into the moon - or more properly put - augured in, going at an estimated speed of over 4,000 kilometers per hour...upon impact."

Milch shook his head. "How...how can you...estimate the speed...?"

"Depth of penetration into the crust of the planet. The faster you're flying, if you were to slam into the moon the way these ships did, the deeper the nose of your spacecraft penetrates into the ground. The larger the ship, the more penetration...and how widespread the debris field becomes from the impact."

"And there's absolutely no doubt that they all...*impacted*?"

"None at all, Sir."

"At over 4,000 kph?"

"Somewhere between 4,000 and 4,200 kph, yes, Sir."

Milch sat there contemplating for a few moments. He turned to his Chief Medical Officer. "Doctor Lewis...start looking at the personnel on board...all of the personnel...for any form of erratic behavior. What ever caused all of those people to slam their craft into a planet...at that speed...that was *not* the act of someone who was thinking rationally."

Lewis cleared his throat. "And what happens if I start acting erratic?"

"Have your second - Doctor Randolph keep an eye on you."

"Yes, Sir."

Milch looked over at Martin. "Ensign Martin, what about the ships themselves?"

Martin shook her head. "From what we found, I would say that the 105 major vessels, came from 95 different places throughout the galaxy...judging from construction and formation of the ships."

"Are there any...bodies...in any of these wrecks?"

She scoffed. "Pulverized! When the ship impacted, any form of a humanoid body would have been just about vaporized, because of the sudden stop at that speed, and the *very* fast change in pressure."

Milch held his arms out as if asking a question. "Was...there some sort of...massive battle?"

Martin chuckled nervously. "That's another...anomaly."

Milch clapped his hands together and he looked up. "Oh, goody!" he said sarcastically. "Just what we need - another anomaly... as if we didn't have enough already. Okay, what's this one?"

"From what we can tell, from accumulation of meteorite dust, and other space debris that lands on that moon...the oldest crash site...is somewhere between...13,000 and 13,500 years old." She let that piece of information sink in. "The newest of the crash sites...is around 3,500 years old. When we look at the estimates of each crash...there was always a span of, at least, 150 years between crashes."

Milch contemplated again. "So...they didn't know each other...but somehow or for some inexplicable reason, they *all* pulled a kamikaze mission on that moon." He looked very worried. "Engineering section, start running a trouble-shooting test on *all* systems. Even though it's been a long time since the last crash...I don't like what I'm seeing...or hearing." He bit his lip. "It seems... very disturbing."

"Yes, Sir," said Martin. "All those crashes, occurring at different times over a period of ten millennium...does raise all kinds of questions. Unfortunately, the only ones who could tell us what happened...were blown to atoms when their ships crashed."

"Did you try getting some form of…ship's log…from any of them?"

"All that data has decayed completely. We found no form of written log and all of the computer data banks have been totally corrupted, decayed or just…smashed," said Justice.

Milch growled nervously under his breath. "We came out here to explore and learn. I don't have any desire to meet the same fate as all of those others." He looked at the chief of the Science division. "Gomez…can we send a…drone or something back…to one of our deep space locations? We need to let someone know… what has occurred here and if we disappear - God forbid - then they might have some kind of clue as to why and also tell others to…stay away from here…at all costs."

"Sure, Captain," said Gomez. "I can have it set up…in about five minutes. It'll have all of the minutes of this meeting and all of our findings, about this system…so far."

Milch sat back and folded his arms across his chest. "I hate to just…sit here, waiting to…involuntarily commit suicide and take the rest of the ship with me. We have to…find out what happened… and why. That way…anyone else will know…whether or not to come here as explorers or just…avoid."

"Yes, Sir," said Gomez. "We need to find out…a *lot* more information."

Lieutenant Commander Emerson, Chief of Security, spoke up: "My best thought, on this situation, would be to send a team to one of the crash sites…preferably the newest one. Go there on a sort of search and rescue mission. It'd be more of a search and *investigate*, but, maybe we *can* get…some form of a clue as to what happened."

Milch shook his head. "I can't think of anything else that would be more useful. Go ahead, take a team down there…and investigate."

"Who should I take, Sir?"

"Take, at least one person, from each section - take the Executive Officer from the Command section if you think it'll help…I don't care. Investigate and…find something…*anything* that will, could or might help."

"Yes, Sir," said Emerson. "I'll start assembling a team immediately."

Milch sighed. "Okay, Lieutenant Fletcher, is there any good news from the big moon?"

Fletcher sighed. "No, Sir, just more puzzles."

Milch grunted in disgust. "What a surprise," he muttered sarcastically.

Fletcher continued: "We have established that there are definitely twelve of those vaults. They *are* manufactured, they *are* being used to store something, there *is* some kind of atmosphere inside them…we just haven't figured out a way to get inside of any of them."

Milch frowned at him. "Uh…how about…through the entrance?"

Fletcher cleared his throat. "We…can't find…any entrance…in any of them."

Milch's shoulders and jaw sagged. He sat there for a moment speechless. "You have my attention," he said softly.

Fletcher sighed and took in a deep breath. "To begin with, we can't figure out the walls. It appears that…somehow…someone was able to find a place…in the bed rock, open up a…gap of some kind and push the rock out, making an interior void. The way it was done…defies logic, technology or any other thing that we can think of. As the void was made larger, the rock around it was condensed… in every direction. The top, sides and bottom are all made of this highly concentrated, condensed rock. We have a tough time seeing through it, we can't get through it…we can get a drilling probe down close to it. That's where it ends. The rock is so hard…a drill bit, even a diamond drill bit just breaks off…and doesn't even scar the rock. All of the surrounding bedrock is…completely undisturbed. There's no evidence, whatsoever, that any form of tool was ever used on it and we can't find any tunneling system. Whoever did this, did it without digging any tunnel. They were able to do it from the inside and not leave any way of getting in. We tried a few things with energy transfer…but again…nothing goes through."

"You said that you have a tough time seeing through it…

what are you seeing…if anything?"

"Shapes! There's definitely something inside each one…that was manufactured. We can see angles and curves that don't appear in any natural formation. We can tell that there are many metal objects and wooden objects inside each one. We just can't see what they are."

Milch continued staring, totally flabbergasted. "The enigmas in this system…are enough to drive you nuts! Mining operations… with no equipment…or equipment left behind, storage vaults… with no way of getting in or out…hundreds of space craft that flew across…who knows how many light years distance of space, only to all crash into the same planet. An inhabited planet with numerous sentient species on it…where there is no form of technology that could have caused anyone to migrate to this planet. I can't think of one scientific department that won't be baffled by this system and its history."

Someone shyly said: "Botany?"

While the third shuttle was still out charting the remaining planets, several of the scientists, on board, were kept very busy categorizing all of the species on the inhabited planet. Mammals, fish, mollusks, reptiles, birds, insects, arachnids, crustaceans, amphibians, as well as a few creatures that almost defied classification. Botanists, microbiologists and geologists were also having a lot of fun doing some mapping. Archeology and Paleontology were coming up with a few enigmas of their own.

The entire Anthropology section was getting one headache after another. They were positive that there were at least eighty-one separate species of sentient creatures…at first. The possibility of cross breeding and certain types being very isolated just threw their count completely off. They gave up trying to use the sensors to do the classification. They needed to get down to the planet and, in some subtle way, get some DNA samples in order to properly differentiate any of the species.

The third shuttle came back and reported their information. There did not seem to be anything very interesting about the other planets - nothing as interesting as the inhabited planet, the two moons orbiting it, or the strange mining operations from planet 12.

Lt. Montalvo sat at the conference table looking as if he had not had any sleep in days. "Captain, we absolutely *must* go to the surface of the planet and figure out a way to get DNA from these people. We've found some isolated and rare types as well as the very common and abundant species…as well as unique oddities. We're not sure if some of them *are* an independent species…or a half-breed - and if a half-breed, which two are they from? We *need* this DNA to determine…any relation of these people as to how they evolved. Two sentient species on any planet is an incredible find, but this… takes most theories…and many facts…and blasts them right out through the window…the door, the walls, the cellar and the ceiling."

"So…how?" Captain Milch sat there looking a little disgusted. "You say that some of them are uncommon, rare or unique. These… rare ones - are they isolationists that are completely xenophobic? Are they suspicious? Are they friendly? Are they brutally territorial? Are they cynic, stoic or epicurean? We may not be able to obtain what you want…without killing them. We don't want that at all. We're here to investigate and observe…not conquer…or turn any sentient creature into a lab rat."

Montalvo chuckled nervously. "I didn't say that it was going to be easy. Some of them…we may just have to…classify from observation. Many of them we'll be able to obtain DNA with very little problem. The ones that we can - we can. The ones we can't… we'll just have to be mystified."

Milch hung his head low. "Make whatever preparations you need…and we'll see about getting most of them classified…" He raised his head and looked sternly at Montalvo. "…*without* any fatalities and as few injuries as possible!"

"Yes, Sir," said Montalvo.

The meeting broke up. Milch left the Third Officer, Lt Kent in charge as he headed to his quarters for some sleep. This system was proving to be the most fascinating system he had ever been to. It was also the biggest headache.

2

Lt Paulette Burke, of the Engineering section, was doing one of the extra (redundantly boring) checks that been ordered. It was getting extremely tiresome, however, no one wanted to be the on the next ship that torpedoed that small moon. LtJG Aaron Brooks passed behind her as he was checking something on the other side of the aisle. Brooks stopped and was doing some very close scrutiny on a repaired section of a conduit.

Burke sighed and laid her scanner down, next to a console, as she rubbed her tired eyes. She leaned her head back and flexed her shoulders, attempting to get some of the fatigue out of her system. She took a deep breath and then let it out. She opened her eyes while she still had her head tilted back. She reached down...and found no scanner. She looked down a little startled. She looked all around for the missing scanner. It was nowhere within her immediate vicinity.

Getting a little miffed, she called to Brooks: "Hey, Mister, what'd you do with my scanner?"

Brooks looked back at her completely confused. He said nothing.

"I had a scanner and I put it down..." She pointed at the spot. "...right here. You went by and now it is gone...what'd you do with it?"

Brooks looked back at what he was scanning. "I didn't touch your scanner. I'm busy with the one I checked out."

She started stomping her way over to him. "You're the only other person in this area. I didn't hide it and it couldn't possibly walk away...that leaves you! Which scanner is the one that you've got in your hands? I checked out number 5, which one is that scanner?"

Brooks pointed the bottom of the scanner at her. "This is the one that I checked out - number 18! See? I don't have time for pranks...not with all of these confounded extra checks."

"I'm having a tough time believing that," snapped Burke. "I

know you and I'm aware of all of the pranks that you've pulled in the past..."

"That was when we had nothing to do. NOW, we have all of these extra checks to do...I don't have time for any...extracurricular activities." He looked back at the spot that she had just come from. "Is that your scanner...the one on the console?"

Burke looked back to where he was pointing. She did a double take. She had a bit of a terrible feeling of panic as she saw the scanner sitting...right where she had placed it. She swallowed hard and walked slowly back to where the scanner was sitting. She was thinking to herself: 'Am I losing it? I was just there...and the scanner...was not there. Where...? How...?' She reached the scanner. It was still running. Without touching it she slowly bent down and looked at the bottom. The big yellow, number 5 was on the scanner. She was thoroughly confused. She had put it down and then could not find it...in the exact spot where she had placed it. 'Am I losing my mind? Is this how it starts?' She swallowed hard again.

She took a deep breath and let it out slowly. "I'm gonna be fine," she whispered. She picked up the scanner. Then she had a thought - 'if someone did grab it...from here and momentarily hide it...the thing was still running and actively scanning...it would show...who, or what had happened to it - in the last few moments. She hit the button to review the scans over the last five minutes... and nearly lost her lunch. She stared at the readings in horror. She turned towards Brooks. "Broo...Brooks...uh help. Brooks...could you...come here...please."

At first Brooks was ready to start chewing her out. Then he saw the fear on her face and heard the panic in her trembling voice. He cautiously walked towards her. He shut his scanner off and placed it in a holster on his side. As he advanced, he could see huge beads of sweat on her forehead. Her expression of terror had not changed a bit. "What...what's the uh...problem?"

Her hands were shaking like a leaf in a windstorm. She slowly faced the scanner at Brooks and held it closer to him. "Would... please...can you look...at...the..." She closed her eyes and tried to think. "...the...review portion? I...I'm either losing my mind...or something...really freaky just happened."

Her hands were shaking so badly, he had to pull it out of her grip in order to do the review. His jaw dropped as he looked at the information on the display screen of the scanner. He cleared his throat and did the review again. He looked back up at her. The fear and panic that he was feeling was not quite as bad as hers...however, he was feeling very uneasy. He hit the intercom. "Cap...Captain... this is Buh...Brooks. I'm in the...engineering section...uh...Echo 12. I need you to...come here...Sir. Something...very strange...Sir."

Milch heard the voice on the intercom and responded. "Why can't you just tell me, from where you are? Why do I have to come down there?"

Brooks cleared his throat and tried to sound as calm as possible. "Please...Sir, the...thing...happened here...in Echo 12. I need you to see it here...where it happened."

Milch growled a little, more to himself than anyone on the bridge. "Where...what happened?"

Brooks came back. "I don't want to sound...crazy...or anything like that, Sir."

"Too late," said Milch in an irritated manner.

"Please," pleaded Brooks. "You must see it here...Sir."

Milch saw that the Chief of Maintenance and Engineering, Lieutenant Commander Boris Komodowski was on the bridge. He thought for a moment. "All right Mister Brooks, I'm on my way." He pointed at Komodowski. "Boris, you're with me." He looked around the bridge for the ranking individual. It was Lieutenant Commander Ivan Emerson, Chief of Security. "Mister Emerson, you have the bridge."

Emerson headed for the Captain's chair. "Yes, Sir." He watched as Milch headed out. "Captain's off the bridge!" He sat down.

Komodowski gave Milch a strange look. "Why am I needed... to go with you to see Mister Brooks?"

Milch grunted in disgust. "I have no clue whatsoever where... on this big flying tin can, this...Echo 12 is. I thought maybe you'd know."

Komodowski laughed all the way to the lift. "Yes, Sir. I have a clue. Maybe…if this thing, that Brooks found, is big enough, we should have Gomez or someone else from Science meet us there…as well."

Milch pondered for a moment. He hit the intercom. "Commander Gomez, this is the Captain. Please meet us at Echo 12."

Gomez heard it from the station he was working from. He shrugged, stood up and yawned. He hit the intercom. "This is Gomez, I understand and am on my way, Sir."

Milch looked at Komodowski. "I said that I needed to know about any strange thing that happens…some of these people are carrying it a little too far. This thing that Brooks found had better be good."

"Right," said Komodowski. "One thing that I've noticed… that I hadn't told you about…yet…was the CO2 levels."

Milch was confused. "Is there something wrong with the levels?"

Komodowski shook his head. "They're way too high. The filters are able to handle the problem, with a little bit of tweaking, but, it's almost as if there were twice as many people on board than… normally would be. I've got my people checking for leaks…nothing so far, but we are getting an awfully high reading."

"How high?"

"236% above normal…for the number of people that are currently on board."

"You don't think that that would have caused those ships to crash, do you?"

"Carbon dioxide poisoning wouldn't cause the engines to make the ship target towards, and slam into a specific planet…over 100 times. It would just kill the entire crew…if that was a problem… that happened aboard the other ships. The ships would then just… fly blindly around the area until they hit something. All of those ships…purposefully targeted that small moon."

It took a lot more time than Milch imagined to get to Echo 12. By the time they got there, he was completely lost. He was in a part of the ship that he had never been in before.

As they approached the troubleshooting station where Burke and Brooks were waiting, Milch whispered to Komodowski. "Boris, if you leave here without me, I swear, when I finally find my way out of this maze, I'll demote you to a cook's aide."

Komodowski chuckled again. "Fear not, my fearless leader."

Gomez showed up just about the same time coming from another direction. "What's the big fuss?"

Brooks held the scanner up. "The readings that are on this scanner. It seems that this scanner took a little…uh…side trip…off of the ship, as well as out of this realm…Sir."

Milch, Komodowski and Gomez chorused a: "What?!"

Burke had settled down quite a bit after her initial shock. "I was doing some of that extra preventive maintenance that you ordered. I stopped here by this console. I set my scanner down, without turning it off. After rubbing my eyes and stretching a few tight muscles, I reached back down to pick it up and…it was gone. I thought, at first, that Brooks here was playing some silly little prank on me. He passed by about the same time that I was stretching. I went after him, because I thought he had it, to get my scanner. He showed me that he had a different numbered scanner than the one that I was using. He then pointed back to the console…and I saw my scanner…sitting right where I'd left it." She stopped and cleared her throat with a guilty look on her face. "When I saw it…sitting there, for a moment I thought that I was just *losing* it. Then I came back here and picked it up…saw that it was still actively scanning, I figured…I'll catch the perpetrator who swiped it…by reviewing the last few minutes of scanning. When I saw the readings…again I thought that I was losing it. I had Brooks…confirm the review. He agrees with me…and you'll have to see it for yourself…in order to believe it. I think if I told you what the reading was…you'd think that I *have* lost it." She held the scanner out to Milch.

Milch raised his eyebrows, looked at Gomez and gave a quick little jerk of his head, signaling Gomez to check the scanner.

Gomez took the scanner with a little sigh and started looking at the readings. His eyebrows went up and his jaw went down. He looked at Burke, totally stunned. She nodded. He looked at Brooks. Brooks nodded. Gomez pulled an umbilical line from the console and plugged it into the scanner. After a few seconds the console beeped. Gomez then ran the review through the console. He shook his head. "It happened…just the way the scanner…recorded. You can't…fake this."

Milch was looking from face to face. "Okay, folks, tell me what I'm looking at."

Gomez shook his head. "According to the readings…this scanner was picked up…" He looked at Milch. "…by someone who was…not only *not* on the ship…this person…or creature…is *not* even in this dimension."

Milch looked skeptical. "You can tell this…from a very bad picture, on the screen, and a bunch of squiggly lines?"

Gomez fought back the desire to chastise the Captain's lack of knowledge of science. 'Either he's testing me, or he's completely ignorant of…all the sciences,' he thought. "Those…squiggly lines… represent different frequencies. Each and everything in the universe has or gives off a frequency…even in the other dimensions. These are all frequencies that we can pick up with our scanners. We see here that there are five, radically different, frequencies. Four of them registered for .3 seconds. That means that the scanner, while actively gathering data, was moved through these different dimensions. It measured the frequency of each one as it went through. Four of the frequencies each measured for .3 seconds. The fifth dimension was scanned for 29.7 seconds…while…whoever…or whatever pulled the scanner through was looking at it. He…or it…then, after 29.7 seconds, sent the scanner back through the same other four dimensions, each for .3 seconds again, on the way back to putting the scanner back…from where he took it. As you can see the four short duration frequencies are now in reverse order."

Milch licked his lips. "That…explains the different dimensions. The scanner picked up something…if nothing other than a smidgeon of that dimension. Why don't we have any form of a clear picture of the entity that took it...on our screen?"

Gomez sighed. "Unfortunately...the entity...had a finger... or a talon or a tentacle...or some portion of the anatomy...partially obscuring the optical sensor. Something that close to the sensor made it impossible to focus clearly on anything. We can see some black blur...some red blur...some brown blur. We have no idea what is what...whether it's clothing or fur...or skin...or exoskeleton. We don't have any clear picture or idea...what this entity is."

"Can we follow him...through those dimensional changes?"

Gomez grunted in frustration. "Nope!"

"Why not, we've had some of our ships go through to other dimensions before, why can't we just follow the same path that he did?"

"Because each time one of our ships broke a dimensional barrier, we knew, technologically, how it had occurred. If someone else came through, we were able to find the technological path that they took to come across. If we...accidentally went through, we use our scanners to find out what happened and in each case, we have been able to recreate the same circumstances, with our technology, to copy and use the same scenario. Here..." He threw his hands up in frustration. "...there is no...technological path...that this entity used...that we can comprehend...or see...with our technological gadgets to mimic that same set of...paths."

"Can you tell me...anything...about this entity...other than the fact that he...or it exists?"

Gomez sighed in frustration again. "We would need...some kind of a specimen...of DNA...if nothing more than a trace. We've all handled this scanner...so any foreign DNA might have been badly compromised. It would be so small, as well as tainted, we might not get anything usable."

"What about the optical sensor?"

"Sir?"

"You said that we don't have a clear picture of the entity, because some portion of *its* anatomy was covering the optical sensor. Have any of the three of you, or any other user, been pawing the optical sensor...since *it* did?"

Burke and Brooks both shook their heads.

Gomez was looking at Milch in complete shock. 'He isn't a scientist, but he can look at something in an analytical way...to obtain the needed information,' he thought. "I guess...we can take the scanner...to the forensic lab...and have them check the optical sensor for the presence of any...alien DNA."

Milch smiled. "Sounds like a plan to me."

Gomez gave him a weak smile. "I'll get to that right away, Sir."

"Good," said Milch. He looked at the other two officers. "I want you to make a full report on this and get it into the ship's logs. You may not have *much* to say, right now, however, what you have to say is at least a start to...who knows what."

Burke and Brooks both nodded and gave a "Yes, Sir."

"Fine," said Milch. "Let's all go do what needs to be done." He looked back at Komodowski. "Boris, Let's get back to the bridge."

"Yes, Sir," said Komodowski with a smile.

Gomez walked away with the scanner, heading to the forensic section. He was shaking his head. 'That man...Milch, is a complete mystery to me,' he thought. 'He is totally ignorant of most of the sciences that we use on a scientific discovery ship, but he knows how to analyze and utilize it. He's a good administrator...and maybe that's why they have him leading a scientific explorer - he's not a scientist so, again, he can't get sidetracked, trying to get deeply involved in one or more of our experiments. He just leads the expedition.' He quickened his pace to Forensics.

After two days of looking over the alien DNA and the dimensional puzzles found on the scanner, once again, there were more questions than answers. Several people were gathered in the conference room to discuss the "*Borrower*" of the scanner.

Milch sat down. "Computer, annotate the time and date of this meeting. We are going to go around the room and get a roll call of everyone who is attending. I'll start with myself - Captain Ronald Milch, Commander of the *Discoverer*." He pointed to the next person.

"Commander Henry Lewis, MD, Chief of the medical section of the *Discoverer*."

"Lieutenant Robert Schmitz, Chief of Forensic Pathology."

"Lieutenant Manuel Montalvo, Anthropology section."

"Lieutenant Joyce Upton, Zoology."

"Commander Alejandro Gomez, Chief Science Officer."

"Lieutenant Commander Ivan Emerson, Security."

"Lieutenant Commander Samuel Jones, Physics"

"Lieutenant Paul Smith, Astrophysics."

"Lieutenant Paulette Burke, Engineering."

"Lieutenant JG Aaron Brooks, Engineering."

After getting the roll call, Milch took in a deep breath and let it out slowly. "Okay, people, what do we have? Who wants to start?"

Gomez shrugged. "Start with the people who first found this anomaly." He looked at Burke and smiled. "Paulette?"

Burke shrugged. "I don't know what else I could add. I was scanning, I stopped to get some kinks out of my back and the *Borrower* grabbed my scanner, took it off the ship, out of this dimension, looked at it for a few moments and then put it back. I checked the review on the scanner to find out why I hadn't been able to find it and discovered that it had been…momentarily borrowed. I called Aaron, and had him look at the review section. He confirmed that I was not going nuts and that…someone or…something had borrowed it…for a few moments."

Gomez looked at Brooks. "Anything to add to that, Aaron?"

Brooks sighed and thought for a moment. "She asked me to review, I did, I found an anomaly, and I called the Captain for guidance."

Milch grunted. "We already know this. We don't need the redundant. We need new information. What have the scans on any trace DNA come up with? Robert, you're the one in Forensics - whatcha got?"

Schmitz smiled. "More questions." He sighed. "Yes, I did find some foreign traces of DNA around the optical portion of the scanner. I also found some strange…contaminants on the exterior of the scanner. The DNA obviously came from the *Borrower*. The odd contaminants…I would need to know *every* place that this particular scanner has been used…in order to determine where these oddities came from. I absolutely cannot tell if they're a result of the actions of the *Borrower*. Until then, the contaminants are irrelevant or misleading. All that I have to work with is the strange DNA."

Milch leaned forward. "Strange? Do you mean something that we've never come across before…or strange in another way?"

Schmitz sighed again. "Uh…both! I'm trying to think of a way to describe this conundrum, without sounding like a complete idiot."

"Break it down, one piece at a time," said Milch.

Schmitz pursed his lips. "We humans, have 23 chromosomes, from each parent, making a total of 46. This creature, the *Borrower*, appears to have 41 from each parent, making a total of 82." He cleared his throat. "However…they all appear to be…somehow… mutated…damaged…or synthetic."

Everyone in the room was silent. Either they were waiting for the next statement or they did not even know what question to ask for any form of clarification.

Schmitz continued. "It appears…that there must have been something in this creature's past, where it underwent some kind of… strange or catastrophic metamorphosis. I've come across people who have gone through some strange things, especially out here in outer space. The mutations that have happened to them…usually only… foul up one or two of their chromosomes. This one…" He shook his head. "…it appears that *all* of the chromosomes were somehow radically altered. Normally, a massive change like that…would cause…horrendous, if not fatal, trauma. This creature…survived it and…is able to function…and to my best guess…*is* intelligent and sentient."

Milch frowned. "Why do you say that the *Borrower* has to be sentient?"

"Lower life forms…non-sentient creatures, don't do what this one did. Some creatures, like the packrat, if they are interested in something, they trade for it. Other creatures are attracted or curious about either shiny things or noisy things. They'll pick the item up and play with it, or sniff at it or move it around with their nose, or appendages. If they like it, they might keep it...for a time. If they don't like it, or their curiosity is satisfied, they drop it and leave it. Only...a sentient creature...that is not a thief...will put the item back where they got it from. Having to cross five dimensional barriers, indicates some rather sophisticated capabilities, intellectually. A non-sentient creature that can move across dimensional barriers... at will, would be one huge headache...a monster that could cause all kinds of problems...anywhere and everywhere."

Milch looked around. "Does Anthropology agree with this analogy...Manuel?"

"Yes, Sir," said Montalvo. "The *Borrower* is sentient. He borrowed something out of curiosity and because it wasn't his...he politely put it back from whence he took it."

Milch nodded. "How about Zoology...Joyce?"

"Definitely not animal," said Upton. "Definitely a sentient form of life. No creature of animal intelligence, would have put it back in the exact spot they took it from."

Milch grunted. "So we haven't solved a thing except to decide that this is a sentient creature, somewhat mutated, probably humanoid in appearance and probably bipedal...and for the most part...honest. Are you sure, or is there a possibility that this is a... clone?"

"No, Sir. No chance of it being a clone. If someone were to clone themselves and had this many...mutated genes...the clone wouldn't have had a chance of survival."

"Could it be...just some kind of difference...between dimensional creatures?"

"It would be the most unique situation that we've ever come across...if that were the case."

"You used the word - synthetic. Is it possible that someone has been able to create...scientifically...a living creature?"

Schmitz bit his lip to keep from laughing. "If we had the proper equipment...there is the possibility that we could - with all of the correct chemicals - make a human body. Once done...that's all we'd have. We could make the body...but...how do you create the spark of life and animate this body? The only option for us would be to transplant someone else's brain into our...creation...and hope, HOPE, that something positive happens."

Milch sighed. "That kinda leaves us with - as you said - more questions than answers."

Milch looked around. "Does anyone else have anything to add?"

"I do," said Jones. "This thing about...*it*...whatever it is, going through the different dimensions...this information has knocked over a huge apple cart."

Milch chuckled. "How so?"

Jones cleared his throat, trying to think. "Centuries ago, it was thought that there was only one dimension. Then came the theories and some *questionable* proof that there were others. As new discoveries led to good, hard evidence, we found that there were at least seven other dimensions. Since then, we have added thirteen more." He leaned back and sighed. "This...little show...that the... *Borrower* has put on...this gives us five dimensions...that were not on our list of twenty."

Milch sat there chuckling. "So he just upped our list of different dimensions, from twenty to twenty-five and all we have of the new ones is...what...just .6 seconds of four others and 29.7 seconds of a fifth." He shook his head. "If you didn't laugh, you'd be crying."

Smith decided to get in on the conversation. "One of the scary things about this creature, is that it was somehow, obviously, capable of watching us...from another dimension. It reached through four other dimensions - why, we have no idea - just to pick up a scanner and give it a quick once over. This kind of dimensional travel where it can jump from one to another to another in less than a second...it just boggles the mind as to what kind of technology this thing has."

Schmitz shrugged. "Until we have a face-to-face meeting with this person, or someone else from his race...we're currently stuck in neutral."

Milch sighed. "Then...until we have more...meeting adjourned."

At that moment, Lt Salisbury walked in looking very pale and scared. "I...I...I...don...don't think...the meeting...is...over... y-yet."

Milch cleared his throat. "And...why not?"

Her breathing was erratic. "That...that planet...crawler... that we set down...on the fourteenth planet...uh...when...uh... when did we retrieve...it?"

"We haven't," said Gomez in an irritated manner.

She looked around as if she were about to lose her lunch. "Then...why...is it in the...equipment...storage bay?"

Gomez growled under his breath. "Which one did you send down?"

She gave a helpless little laugh. "I...sent...uh...crawler number 1."

Milch spoke up. "Are you saying that crawler number 1 is in storage bay?"

"Yes, Sir."

Gomez scolded her a little sternly. "Well, maybe, just maybe, you sent one of the other crawlers, when you thought you sent number 1."

She swallowed. "Uh...no, Sir...that's not what happened. I know, because...I was just in the storage bay...and all four crawlers are in their places...in the storage bay." She looked frightened and concerned. "All four!" She took a deep breath. "All four are there. I took the memory bank, of number 1...out, just in case...there was some kind of...mistake. I checked it...for data...and...uh..." She held the gray box up. "The...the information...on it...is...uh... weird."

Milch sighed. "At least she didn't say it was an anomaly."

Gomez walked over to her and yanked the memory bank out of her hand. He took it to his seat, pulled an umbilical cord from the computer hook-ups in the conference table and plugged it in. He tapped a few spots on the computer keypad. Monitors came up out of the table, one at each seat, for all to see what was in the memory bank of 'planet crawler #1'. Within a few seconds, the expression on the faces of every person changed from interested to shocked, stunned surprised, confused or fearful.

Jones was the first to find his voice. "Am I seeing…what I think I'm seeing?"

Gomez tried three times to get an answer out. He croaked twice, cleared his throat and finally said: "Yuh…it is."

"Okay," said Milch. "What am I looking at…specifically?"

"According to this…." Gomez shook his head helplessly. "… that crawler…uh…number 1…it was on the planet. It was there for 16 minutes and 9 seconds. It was doing its job. It recorded a little bit more than what we got. According to these readings, that planetary wide, frozen methane ocean…is at least 1500 meters thick… before there are any geological formations. Uh…it started doing the business of moving around…and someone…or something… grabbed it, brought it back to the ship…and turned it off…and put it back in the storage slot…where it belongs."

Milch sighed. "I'm…seeing some of those…squiggly lines… like I saw from the scanner. Are you telling me that this gadget went through a couple of…different dimensions…just like the scanner… and recorded its little trip…through the…unknown?"

Gomez gave him a helpless smile. "Yes, Sir. That's…exactly what happened. This one…however…did not go through…uh… five different dimensions. This one only went through…two."

"Did it go through any different dimensions, or are they two of the same dimensions that the scanner went through?"

"A moment, Sir." Gomez made another entry on the keypad. The readings from scanner #5 came up. He sniffed. "Dimension number 1 and 3! Same dimensions that the scanner went through… only this one skipped three of them."

"Someone…or something…is fooling around with us," said Emerson with a little irritation and concern in his voice.

Milch sat back and rolled his eyes. "Really!" He gave Emerson a sour look. "What could possibly make you think that?"

Emerson closed eyes. With very little movement of his lips (and clenched teeth) he growled. "Okay, so I said, out loud, what everyone else is thinking."

Smith gave a little helpless chuckle. "At least, whoever it is…

they haven't done anything…offensive…or destructive."

Milch looked at Smith. "Yet!"

Emerson let out a deep breath. "So…Captain…now what?"

Milch hung his head for a moment. He looked back up. "Full crew! Start a ship-wide inventory. Everything! Everything on board…including all personal items. Let's see if there are any more…" He nearly choked on the word: "…anomalies."

3

Milch read one of the reports from the Botany section about a plant that seemed to be able to move around. There was an argument between Anthropology, Botany and Zoology as to what this *thing* actually was - plant or animal. Was it a plant that was somehow animated, or was it an animal that was so heavily camouflaged as to appear to be a plant? According to the Entomology section, there were insects, on several different planets that had been explored, that were camouflaged in that manner, so why would it be impossible for some animal - somewhere in the cosmos - to have the exact same capability?

He put the report down and headed in to take a hot shower. After showering and doing all the necessary stuff to go to bed, his head hit the pillow. He sighed in contentment. This frustrating day was thankfully over. He closed his eyes…then the intruder alarm went off.

Milch was out of his bed immediately. He grabbed a pair of pants, his robe, his intercom and some slippers. He headed for the bridge, shouting through his portable intercom: "Security, this is the Captain, report!"

"Lieutenant Carlucci here Sir, we've detected an unknown intruder on deck 3. We're attempting to corner and apprehend at this time, Sir."

Milch burst onto the bridge. "Captain's on the bridge and I want to know exactly what's going on."

The current on-duty Communications Officer, Lt. Frank Overton was attempting to clear up all of the chatter from the Security personnel as they all headed for deck 3. "An unknown intruder has been detected. We're steering all of the Security personnel to cargo bay 1, on deck 3. At this time, Sir, we have absolutely no idea how he got there or how long he's been on the ship. One *big* question is…where did he come from? We've detected no other ships in the area…except for the wrecks on the small moon."

A voice came over the intercom: "This is Lieutenant Eli… where's the intruder?"

Overton growled. "He's in cargo bay 1 on deck 3."

"No, he's not! I'm in cargo bay 1…I, along with eight other personnel. No one's in here who isn't authorized on the ship…I repeat - WHERE IS HE?"

Overton stammered a little. "He…uh…I'm looking. He was in there…just a moment ago. What? Uh…sensors have just detected him…in the head, next to the cargo bay."

Another voice came over the intercom: "How'd he get in there? There's no doorway between the cargo bay and the head."

"I don't know," said Overton. "The sensors are showing him in *that* specific head…WAIT…the sensors just picked him up…in the maintenance storage bay…on the other side of the head."

The voice came back. "Are you sure? There's no doorway there either. How did he get from one to the other? He had to have gone out in the hallway…"

Overton shouted. "I don't know how he's moving around! All I can tell you is that he's going from room to room…through the walls…some…how." Overton shook his head. "That's impossible," he mumbled. He looked back at his monitor and shouted: "That's the readings!"

Milch sat back in his chair and growled. "We're chasing a cotton-pickin' ghost!"

"Ghosts are non-corporeal…even if they do exist…Sir," said Overton. "This one knocked a few things over and that's what set off the alarm. We've seen him…on the screen…moving around in the cargo bay."

Milch let out a small growl. "Why don't you describe him to those people down there?"

"We did, Sir, just before you arrived. He's medium height, wearing a black cape, black pants and boots and has long, dark brown hair."

Milch calmed down a little. "So where is he now?"

Overton let out a grunt of frustration as he continued pressing buttons. "I…don't know. He's…disappeared…again." He enlarged the search pattern. His shoulders sagged. "He…he's on deck 2… how…?"

"If he can go through a confounded wall, he can easily go through the floor," muttered Milch.

Overton shouted at the intercom. "He's gone down to deck 2, how I don't know, but he's no longer on deck 3."

There were several mutterings coming over the intercom as all of the security personnel started heading for the different ways to the lower deck.

Milch sat there frustrated. "Try…somehow…to keep a lock on him. I don't know how, but…try!"

Overton tried to respond as he kept pressing buttons. "That's…what I've been…trying to…do….Sir! He…just…keeps going…through walls. Hard to…track…or follow."

Lt. Cecelia Daywood came on to the bridge. She was the Communications officer from a different shift. With the intruder emergency going on, she came in to help. "Where is he now?"

Overton did not look up. "He's still cavorting around…deck 2…I think."

"No…he's not," said Daywood.

Overton snarled in frustration. "Well…where…?"

"Expand your search perimeters," shouted Milch.

"I have," said Overton as he continued scanning his monitor.

"Deck 1 is clear," said Daywood.

"Deck 2 is clear as well," said Overton.

Lieutenant Commander Cynthia Watkins had entered the bridge as well and was looking at a screen of her own. "He's not on deck 3!"

Milch had a white-knuckle grip on the armrests of his chair. "This is ridiculous!"

Overton looked up at Milch and opened his mouth as if he were going to say something. He froze, for a moment, and had a rather stupid look on his face. "I…found him…Sir."

Milch glared at Overton and snapped at him: "WHERE!?"

Overton swallowed hard and stuttered a little. He cleared his throat. He looked up at Milch, and with a smile that looked more like nausea, he said: "He's…standing…about…one and a half…meters…behind the Captain's chair."

Milch felt a cold chill run down his spine. With the exception of almost everyone turning their head to look at the spot designated by Overton, all activities ceased. The only one not looking behind the Captain's chair, was Milch himself. He looked at the eyes of all of the personnel on the bridge. They were all looking, staring at a spot, just to the left and above Milch's left shoulder. Milch saw no fear in any of their eyes. He saw some looking confused, some frowns, a few open mouths and Overton's weak smile. The only sounds were the voices of the Security personnel coming over the intercom and a few beeps and buzzes from the computer as it ran some redundant operations.

With a rather weak smile of his own, Milch looked at Overton. "Is…are the Security personnel…aware of your…discovery?"

Overton cleared his throat again. "I…believe that they heard it…over the intercom. It *is* currently…an open line…throughout the entire ship."

Milch nodded and sniffed loudly. "Thank you." He stood up slowly. He reached down to straighten out his tunic. He felt the robe and his face flushed. He realized that he was wearing only his trousers slippers and robe. He closed the robe, tied it and slowly turned to face this mysterious intruder.

Milch was a tall man, just under two meters. He looked down at the intruder. The stranger appeared to be very close to something that was human. He was shorter than Milch, about 17 ½ decimeters. He was wearing a black cape that had a bright red lining. His pants were black and he was wearing black boots. On his right leg was a scabbard, with a rather ornate hilt sticking out of it…that appeared to be chained into place in the scabbard. His shirt appeared to be made out of silk that was a bright red and matched the inner lining of the cape. Around his neck was a golden chain. There was what appeared to be a broken piece of translucent, red glass or rock that had originally been part of a globe. He had a little paunch around his midsection. He had long brown hair, a very carefully groomed short beard, steel blue eyes and a face that did look very human. His ears took away the human look though. He looked more elfin than human. What would normally be the top of the ears for a human, was where the ears went back and then took a sharp turn up. The top of his ears went above the top of his head to a very small point. The back of his ears were wide and tapered to the point as it went up. His skin color was what a human would call caucasian. He was standing there, with his arms crossed across his chest, looking Milch over with no readable emotion showing on his face.

He spoke with a baritone voice and no form of an accent. "You are not dressed the way that you have normally been attired… Captain Ronald Milch."

Milch gave a wan smile. "I…was getting ready to go to bed… when you made your…sudden and shocking appearance."

The intruder's eyebrows went up. "Bed?" He looked thoughtful for a moment. "Oh! A bed! Yes one of those things?"

Milch was momentarily taken aback. "That…is where one sleeps. Don't you…sleep?"

The intruder looked puzzled for a moment. "Not…often enough that I would have a…bed…just sitting there…waiting to be…used."

Milch cleared his throat. "Don't you get tired and have to go to sleep in order to refresh yourself?"

The intruder looked thoughtful. "Sleep…sleep…only…after an occasion where I've really exerted myself. Again, that doesn't happen very often."

"Uh…when was the last time…you awoke from sleeping?"

His gaze went up in thought. "I…don't remember. It has been quite some time…since I needed to…sleep." He looked off to the side contemplating. "It has been…at least ten months."

At that moment several of the Security personnel came running onto the bridge, panting, puffing and sweating from their run.

The intruder looked at the Security people. "There is no reason for any form of force…Lieutenant Commander Ivan Emerson."

One of the other Security men spoke without thinking. "You…know *his* name?"

The intruder sighed. "I know your name too…Lieutenant Marcus Eli."

Milch was getting a little miffed. "How many other personnel do you know the names of?"

The intruder started looking around the room and stating the names of everyone on the bridge…correctly, along with their primary duty. As soon as he finished he looked up at Milch. "Did I miss anyone?"

Milch cleared his throat. "You have us…at an extreme disadvantage. You seem to know all of us…and we don't have the slightest idea…who you are…or where you came from."

The intruder nodded and chuckled. His arms dropped to his sides. He bowed his head slightly. "I am Soolchakan, Drey Sssorg of the Owlam. That is who I am. I come from the planet that you are now orbiting…we call it…Hardooth. If I were to translate that, it would mean…Heart!" He smiled. "What you call - the small moon - we call: Niygool. What you call - the large moon - we call: Zhagool."

"Okay," said Milch cautiously. "You can answer the question about our immediate vicinity. How long…have you been watching… and studying us? I mean…you can't learn all of our names…in an instant."

Soolchakan looked around the bridge. "I've been with you… and studying you…ever since you dumped that contraption…on Denhahbon."

Milch felt a little foolish. "Den…what?"

Soolchakan looked a little impatient. "Denhahbon! The planet that you have designated as…NZ dash 3591 dash 14. I was also there, when you discovered the mining operations…on Bri. Bri is the planet that you call…NZ dash 3591 dash 12."

"So…if you have been with us…all of that time…why did we not see you…until now?"

"Because I didn't let you see me."

"Really? Uh…how do you do…that?"

Soolchakan instantly vanished. He reappeared less than a

second later, approximately a half a meter left of where he had been standing originally. "By willing myself to go through the different dimensions. There are two of them...where I can walk among you... aliens...or anyone else without being seen. I can see you, I can hear you, and I can watch your every move. *You* have no idea that I am there. It is quite convenient...for observing you and determining whether or not you are...hostile."

Milch felt a few beads of sweat trickle down his spine. "And... have you...determined...whether or not...we are...hostile?"

Soolchakan smiled. "If I thought that you had hostile intentions toward my home planet...we would not be talking. You would be wondering: Why is the ship flying, totally out of control, at over 4,000 kph, directly toward one of the gas giants?"

Milch's eyebrows went up. "You...would not crash us...on the small moon?"

Soolchakan grunted. "Niygool has been littered with too much debris. We now hide the wreckage on either Ragath or Rogoth."

Milch smiled helplessly. "And those...are...?"

"Ragath is what you call: NZ dash 3591 dash 8. Rogoth is what you call: NZ dash 3591 dash 7. We also call them the running twins. Ragath is the runner, Rogoth is forever chasing Ragath across the night sky."

"So...now you hide the crash sites...inside two gas giants?"

"Oh yes, there's *so* much more room there. I can send it there, they can't send out a distress call, they don't know what's happening and any corpses are...stuck in the gas...forever."

Milch now looked at the intruder with a questioning frown on his face.

Soolchakan noticed this and with a smile asked: "Is there something wrong?"

Milch grunted a little. He was trying to think of the best way to word his question. "From what we have observed...of the planet - *Heart*...there is very little...sophisticated technology - or more correctly - practically none. For someone who comes from a planet like that...you have an amazing knowledge...of astronomy... and it seems that you know...quite a few things about the workings of…spacecraft."

"Our planet…was not always like that."

"You mean…there was technology…and you…digressed… back to what it is…now?"

Soolchakan stroked his beard. He looked up at Milch and smiled. "Do you have time…for a *long…long…long* story…of our history?"

Milch put a big smile on his face. "Absolutely! That's why we're here. We are here to find out…everything…that we can about this planet."

Soolchakan chuckled. "Aren't you wanting to…bed…for a while before hearing…any of my history?"

Milch smiled back. "I am way too excited, right now, to be able to go to…*sleep*. I would love to hear…something…that explains your knowledge of…astronomy, engineering, spacecraft…and whatever other things that seem just…*way* too far ahead of what we see down there on the planet. I also am curious about why you're talking to us and not killing us."

"Shall we go and sit down in your conference room and discuss it, for a while?"

"Oh, by all means, yes. I'd love to have a long, long, long chat…with you."

4

They went, together, into the conference room.

Milch sat down at the end of the conference table. "Computer, annotate the date and time. This is Captain Ronald Milch. We are having a first contact meeting with one of the inhabitants of NZ-3591-4. These people call the planet: 'Hardooth' or translated into our language: 'Heart'. While the inhabitants of this planet appear to be in the time frame of the Earth Renaissance, the individual who has identified himself as 'Soolchakan' seems to be very familiar with advanced sophisticated technology. He is also very capable of coming and going…just about anywhere he pleases…without the aid of any technology. We are going to have a nice long conversation with this person and find out a few things about him and the history of the planet that we are currently orbiting. We will start with the roll call of personnel in the room…starting with our guest."

Again a chuckle. "I am Soolchakan, Drey Sssorg of the Owlam."

"Commander Alejandro Gomez, Chief Science Officer."

"Lieutenant Manuel Montalvo, Anthropology."

"Lieutenant Joyce Upton, Zoology."

"Lieutenant Commander Ivan Emerson, Chief of Security."

"Lieutenant Richard Avery, Security."

"Lieutenant Marcus Eli, Security."

"Lieutenant Mark Angelo, Security."

"Lieutenant Robert Schmitz, Forensic Pathology."

"Lieutenant Commander Samuel Jones, Physics."

"Lieutenant Paul Smith, Astrophysics."

"Commander Henry Lewis, Doctor, Chief of the Medical section."

"Commander Hiroko Kasaki, Executive Officer."

"Yeoman Alani Aua."

"Now," said Milch. "You, my friend…Soolchakan…you have

our complete attention. Do you wish to start telling us about your planet and its history, or would you prefer that we ask questions… about what we are interested in the most?"

Soolchakan smiled. "I suppose that I could start by making a long, boring oration. I feel, however, that answering questions about things that *you* are the most curious about…first…is appropriate. What do you want to know, first?"

Gomez spoke up. "I have heard you call your home planet - Heart. You said that it is *Hardooth*, in your native tongue. May we know what you call all of the other planets…in this system?"

Soolchakan smiled. "The star at the center is called: Holgotho. It is the giver of light and heat. The planet closest to Holgotho, is Malitay. The second planet is Krog. The third planet is Olotoosh. You know my planet. The fifth planet is Bygloto. There are the three gas giants in the sixth orbit. As I told you before, the two that are close to each other are the running twins - Ragath, the leader and Rogoth, the chaser. The one that is on the other side of the system is called Chabayo. The two gas giants in the seventh orbit are: Weeloow and Makatindi. The twelfth planet, where you found the mining operations is Bri. The thirteenth planet is Afkoth. The last one…soooo far out there is Denhahbon."

Gomez nodded. "What is the significance to these names?"

Soolchakan folded his arms. "They're the names of…heroes and gods…of civilizations…that are long dead. Civilizations that existed…over 20,000 years ago. The only story that stayed with us… is the running twins. Other than that, I don't remember most of the history of the names. Kiyalee might be able to help you there."

Gomez frowned. "Kiyalee? Who's that?"

"One of my wives," said Soolchakan. "She…kept track of some of that…ancient history."

Milch cleared his throat. "*One*…of your wives?"

"Yes," said Soolchakan. "I have three wives."

Montalvo spoke up, looking a little miffed. "So you openly practice polygamy?"

"We…don't really have much of a choice. It seems…and it has been consistent throughout our history, the history of the

Owlam people, that 75% of the Owlam population…is and always has been…female. If we did not practice polygamy…there would be a rather large population of…lonely women."

"So there is a practicality to this…practice," said Montalvo, looking a little less upset.

Soolchakan simply smiled.

"I'm Lieutenant Joyce Upton…and my specialty is Zoology. I'm very curious as to how…all of these different races…of sentient beings evolved on this planet."

Soolchakan looked a little baffled. He slowly turned his head towards Upton. "E…evolved? What is evolved?"

Now she looked a little baffled. "Evolution! You know…how the higher life forms, over several million years and several million generations, evolved from lower life forms, into the beings that we are today."

He looked a little sick. "Is this…an attempt…at humor? What makes you think that…*your* ancestors were…what did you say…lower life forms?"

"Are you trying to tell me…that, what did you call yourself - an Owlam? You and your kind…just appeared on the scene? Did all of the other races, on your planet, just appear out of nowhere? I'm sorry, Sir, but you had to come from somewhere. You can't just…pfffft from out of nothing…and there you are…a fully grown Owlam…with this 25% male and 75% female. Your ancestors had to come from somewhere…or something."

Soolchakan stared at her totally bewildered. "You're… serious?" He looked around at the other faces. "You people…are serious…about this…evolved?"

Upton looked a little upset. "Whatever you are, your ancestors had to be just like you…for several generations. They had to come from somewhere or something. Are you going to try to say that your people, the Owlam, have always been Owlam, ever since time began?"

"Are you saying that your people…the human beings… were…*not*?"

"All creatures, great and small, evolved from some lower

form, at some time in the past - that is evolution."

Soolchakan raised his eyebrows, closed his eyes and shook his head. He sighed. He opened his eyes. "When I was born...I was born into the race of the *Heyyah*." He looked at Upton. "This is the race that is the most prevalent on the planet. I am no longer a member of the race of Heyyah, because of a weapon. This weapon... changed me...and everyone else of my...race...when it went off. I don't know what the original builder of this weapon called it, but I... we call it...a genetic bomb. When it went off, it changed...me and my Owlam colleagues. It made...many new species...all over the planet."

Milch shook his head. "We're gonna need a *lot* more information on that particular incident. It sounds incredible."

"Yes...," said Soolchakan staring down at the table. "...I'm not surprised...that you would want to hear that...time of our history. Before those...genetic bombs...went off...we were all one race - one species - the Heyyah." He looked around the table at all of the faces. He knew he had their complete attention. "Before I start telling you about what happened, maybe I should introduce you...to my wives. They'll confirm what I'm saying."

Milch smiled. "Oh, by all means, let us meet them. How can we get them aboard the ship?"

Soolchakan smiled. He tilted his head back and closed his eyes. Just seconds later, a woman...whose ears and hair looked very similar to Soolchakan's was standing behind him, looking a little surprised and upset. As soon as she appeared, the intruder alarm went off. She was dressed almost identically to how Soolchakan was dressed, except the lining of her cape and her shirt were blue. The rock hanging from the gold chain around her neck was blue as well. She also had a scabbard on her right leg, with a hilt that was chained into the scabbard.

Milch ordered the intruder alarm to be turned off.

Another female Owlam appeared. Again the intruder alarm went off. Again her dress was the same except for the fact that she had on a green shirt, green lining in her cape and a green rock hung from her neck.

Again, Milch ordered the intruder alarm to be turned off.

Another female Owlam appeared. Again the intruder alarm went off. Again her dress was the same except for the fact that she had on a yellow shirt, yellow lining in her cape and a yellow rock hung from her neck.

Again, Milch ordered the intruder alarm to be turned off.

The one in blue started chattering in a foreign language. Her words were not understood, however, her angry manner was very evident.

Soolchakan glared at her and she stopped talking. He closed his eyes and sat there very still. All three women jerked their heads and stood motionless with their eyes closed. After about thirty seconds, all four opened their eyes.

Emerson leaned over to Milch. "I believe that they are communicating telepathically. We won't be able to find out anything from that."

Milch looked at Emerson. "We found out that they can communicate telepathically."

The one in blue, still looking upset, took a deep breath. "May we have a place to sit?"

"Oh…yes," said Milch as he stood up.

Milch signaled to Lt. Angelo who quickly produced some chairs for the three women. He pulled them up to the table trying to smile and be as polite as possible. The three women sat down, glaring at their hosts.

Soolchakan stood up. "Let me introduce my wives. The one in blue, is Bonarain. The one in yellow is Kiyalee and the one in green is Chyning." Each one of the women nodded as she was introduced. He looked down at the three women smiling. "Be sweet…or else!" All three snarled back. He sat down. "I don't know if the words translated or not…if they didn't, let me do some translation for you. My name is Soolchakan. In our language, that means: Scholar. Bonarain, her name translated is: Beneficial. Kiyalee is Stormy and Chyning is Cunning. I notice that all of you have…more than one name. After looking at some of your history, I understand why. We don't do this practice…any more. We used to…but…it became irrelevant. I used to be known as: Scholar, son of Treecutter and Nice. Now...Scholar is enough."

Montalvo frowned. "Why did you drop it?"

"Because...no one...of this day...and age has any clue who Treecutter and Nice were."

"They're still your parents."

"Yes, but they were Heyyah. I am not."

Montalvo looked around at the other people at the table. "This conversation...is getting a little strange. You say that you were born into one species...and now are another species - how could this...possibly happen?"

The four Owlam all looked a little saddened and somewhat disgusted.

Bonarain looked at Soolchakan. "Should we each tell our own rendition of what happened, or are you going to tell it all yourself?"

"I'll tell it," he said despondently. "It's something that we haven't thought about...in a very long time." He looked at Bonarain and scoffed. "Maybe if we tell them what happened to us...they'll give up this ridiculous ideology of...evolved."

Milch cleared his throat. "You have our undivided attention."

Soolchakan took in a deep breath and let it out slowly. "A long, long time ago...before this age of empires and countries...we were all one race: The Heyyah. We were very divided...in different City-States...all over the planet. One hundred twenty-seven different major City-States and four hundred fifty-five minor City-States. Each and every one warred against all of the others. If two or more had ever merged...then they could have possibly done some massive conquering. No one did...so for a few dozen centuries, before I or my three wives were born, the different City-States just continued their endless battling against each other, accomplishing virtually nothing, as far as obtaining new lands. There were no... governments...as you know them, or as they are today.

The four of us were born in the major City-State of Owlam. Since we were born there, we were obligated to be in the Owlam army...some time during our lifetime. We all did join the army, at a young age, all four of us. Each one of us got assigned to the defensive forces. We would sit in the watch bunker, searching the area in front of us, in our sector, for any enemy activity...that might be headed our way.

At that time, we did have...sophisticated technology. We had technological offensive weapons and technological defensive devices as well. As the offensive artillery became more destructive and... capable of much longer firing ranges...our defensive technology had to increase as well, if we wanted our city and our way of life to survive.

Even though the technology had increased and destructive capabilities had increased enormously, one of the main forms of defense was still a...large wall. The wall that we had built...around Owlam was...so wide...so wide and thick, that you could drive 25 vehicles, side-by-side on the top of the wall and there was a comfortable amount of room in between each vehicle." He smiled. "The only wall that's left...that looks anything like some of those massive walls, from days of old, is the Turgon wall."

Emerson perked up. "Turgon?"

"Yes." Soolchakan sat there contemplating for a moment. "Later on, we'll show you that wall. It doesn't ring a city, like the Owlam wall did, but it does, mercifully, keep us separated from the Turgons.

Anyway, let's get to that fateful day...so long ago. That day when we ceased to be Heyyah and became...Owlam Elf...we are called Owlam Elf because that is where our race...began. The Axswain Elf came from the city of Axswain, the Kalash Elf from the city of Kalash, the Galsino Elf from the city of Galsino...and so on."

"Excuse me," said Montalvo. You use this word "elf" as if it means something. We use that word as well, but, maybe it means something different...in our respective tongues. What exactly does...elf...mean in your language?"

Soolchakan looked puzzled. He looked up contemplating for a few moments. "It means...something that has mutated: An animal, organism, cell, or gene that has mutated. Something resulting from mutation: undergoing or resulting from genetic mutation. Why, what does the word mean to you?"

Montalvo pulled out his pad and made an entry. "According to our definition, of the exact same word, it means: Small supernatural mischief-maker: in folklore, a small lively imaginary being resembling a human with pointed ears, often considered to have a mischievous nature and magical powers."

Soolchakan looked a little perturbed. "Imaginary?"

Bonarain looked at Chyning in a patronizing manner. "Mischievous?" She cleared her throat and shook her head.

Kiyalee just sat there giggling.

Chyning looked up at the ceiling, sucked her lips in and blushed.

The crew of the ship sat there wondering for a few moments why the reactions by the three women. Apparently it had something to do with the history of those women, however, diplomacy dictated that they should not ask.

"Yes," said Montalvo. "The word is pronounced the same, in both of our languages, but, the definition is *so* different. Mutation in your language, and a mythical sprite in ours."

Soolchakan cleared his throat. "We may have to do some other comparisons…later on."

Montalvo nodded with a smile. "Yes, we will."

The oration started:

Soolchakan was on his way to work. He took the wall-rail shuttle from his home to the place that he was assigned to, this evening. He watched the signs as he rode along. Watch Sector 585 was where he was supposed to be tonight. Each day the ride was getting longer and longer. For some reason they kept on moving him to Sectors that were further and further from his home. Such is the way of one of the lower echelon Officers. Maybe once he got up in rank, he could do some of his own choosing as far as which station he would be…and which shift.

He did not know who else was going to be assigned there tonight, so he wanted to make sure that he was not late. He had been late one time and that wretch, Officer Grade 3, Balshaga had caused him no end to grief, that evening, and kept the heat on by reporting it and telling the tale repeatedly to anyone and everyone. He had no idea who the Red Shirt was today…just some hope and prayer that it was not Balshaga.

He saw his sign and pressed the stop button. The shuttle slowed as it approached the platform. Once it stopped, the door came open and he got out. He looked up at the big black and white sign that marked 585, yawned and stretched. He slowly walked up to the control panel, while glancing off to the side at the clock. There was plenty of time. As the transport pulled away, he punched his control number on the keypad and waited. A small panel opened up and a small armature came out with a fresh white pad on the end of it. He licked the pad and hit the retract button. The machine analyzed the DNA in his saliva. Once it had confirmed his identity, the big door to the elevator came open. He walked in and fed his secondary control number into the keypad in the elevator. The door closed and down he went.

The door came open and Soolchakan was looking at the face of a man, wearing the Red Shirt, who was looking a little surprised.

"You're quite early!"

Soolchakan smiled. "Officer Grade 5, Soolchakan reporting… early. I'm reporting early, so that *H'oolyach* Balshaga can't add to his stupid lies."

The man scoffed. "Officer Grade 3, Whallek is grateful that you're early and will make sure that Balshaga cannot add anything to his orations." He looked off to the side. "Since you're early, I know that I'll be able to go home on time." He picked up the roster sheet. "Tonight, my friend, you are the Red Shirt."

Soolchakan was shocked. "WHAT? ME? A Grade 5? How did that happen?"

Whallek smiled. "We have word, from the Intelligence Network Officers, that this area should be quiet tonight. It seems that the city of Galsino is getting enough headaches, from a major offensive, put on by the city of Kalash. They've been going at it for…" He checked the Intelligence report. "…three full days now. There doesn't seem to be any let up, so they don't have time to launch any offensive, major or minor, or even a reconnaissance against us."

"So why don't we launch something against Galsino… ourselves?"

"Because of that other problem…to the north…you remember, that walking pestilence, the city of Axswain?"

"Oh…yeah…are they…?"

"When have they not?"

"So, we're expecting total quiet tonight…here?"

"Before the Kalash offensive against Galsino started, there was a normal amount of harassment from the Galsino troops. The day after the offensive started, the harassment dropped to…less than minimal. Yesterday…absolutely nothing. They're expecting the same again tonight."

"How nice of the city of Kalash," said Soolchakan sarcastically. "Bless their rotten non-existing souls." He went to the uniform locker and pulled out the Red Shirt of Command. He chuckled to himself. This was the first time that he had ever been allowed to touch - let alone wear - the Red Shirt. "Who's the rest of the team?"

Whallek looked at the roster. "Your Blue Shirt, tonight is Officer Grade 6, Bonarain. The Yellow Shirt is Officer Grade 6, Kiyalee and your Green Shirt is Officer Grade 7, Chyning."

Soolchakan froze in shock. "Are you joking? One Blue… doing all of the ground surveying? One Yellow doing all of the motion monitoring? One Green back up…and the backup is a… Grade 7…rookie?"

Whallek growled at him. "AGAIN…the Galsino are very busy with the Kalash! Most of our attention *has to be* directed towards Axswain!"

Soolchakan went back to buttoning the shirt. "I've never seen…less than…eight people…in one of these bunkers before." He shook his head in wonder. "That must really be some big fight, between Galsino and Kalash."

"NOW, you've finally got the picture," said Whallek.

"So…all of the extra personnel are heading over to watch the Axswain…just in case they try something against us…like Kalash is doing to Galsino."

"Hopefully it will be *real* quiet tonight…hopefully. You can never tell with those Galsino people. They're…just *too* sneaky. Keep alert anyway."

Soolchakan gave him a salute and a smile. "Yes, Sir!"

The elevator door opened up. A woman stepped out…or rather stumbled out. She looked as if she had just awakened a few minutes ago. She walked past the two men as if they did not exist. She opened the closet and pulled out a Green Shirt.

Whallek snickered. "Excuse me! Who are you?"

She turned and looked at him dull-eyed. "Why…Sir? Does it really matter that much to you?"

"I need to know, so you can be assigned the correct dress for tonight."

She grunted. "I *always* get the Green."

Now Whallek was a little irritated. "Officer! What is your name!?"

She gave him a nasty look. "Officer Grade 6, Bonarain," she mumbled.

"Tonight, Officer Grade 6, Bonarain, you get the Blue Shirt."

She looked as if she had been slapped. She looked at the two men totally slack-jawed and shocked. "Blue? Me? Uh…why…uh… Sir?"

Soolchakan walked closer to her grinning. "Because there are only four of us on tonight, here, and one of the ones showing up is a Grade 7. Since you are *not* a Grade 7, you got the Blue Shirt."

She was staring slack-jawed again. Her shoulders sagged and she looked around confused. She then shrugged. "Yes, Sir. Tonight… Blue." She grinned and put the Green back. She moved over to the Blue Shirts and found one in her size. She grinned as she put it on and checked herself in the mirror. She talked to her reflection. "Blue Shirt, Bonarain, ready for duty…as soon as I get some kwatha juice." She went to the dispenser and got a steaming hot mug of kwatha. She walked over to the Blue Shirt that was currently on duty, slowly sipping the kwatha, getting ready to get her shift briefing.

"Well," said Soolchakan. "I hope that the one who gets the Yellow is just as happy."

Whallek chuckled. "We'll see."

Soolchakan took his time looking over the briefings from the previous shift reports. Most of them were redundant and boring. He had not realized just how early he had been until he looked at the dates on the reports and found that he was reading reports from twenty days prior.

He looked up at the clock and was now wondering when his other two personnel were going to show up. At that moment the elevator door opened and both women walked in. They both looked up at the clock and let out a sigh of relief. They both headed for the closet.

"Made it on time," said one.

"Not by much," said the other.

They opened the closet and both pulled out Green Shirts.

"Hold it," said Soolchakan. "Which one of you is Officer Grade 6, Kiyalee?"

One of the women looked at him fearfully. "Wha...what'd I do? I just got here, I can't be in trouble already. I mean, I got here in time...didn't I?" She looked back up at the clock.

"You are *not* in trouble," said Soolchakan adamantly. "Are you Kiyalee?"

She swallowed. "Yes...Sir...yes I am...why?"

"Because tonight, you, Officer Grade 6, Kiyalee...you are wearing a Yellow Shirt."

Now she stood there stunned. She looked around confused. "Me? I'm...wearing a...Yellow...tonight?"

"There are only four of us on duty, in this bunker. To our southwest, Galsino is being kept *very* busy by the city of Kalash. To our north, Axswain is doing some buildups and our main attention is on them. Since we, in bunker 585, are not facing north...we should have an easy night...even with only four people. So...I, Officer Grade 5, Soolchakan wear the Red, Officer Grade 6, Bonarain wears the Blue, Officer Grade 6, Kiyalee wears the Yellow and Officer Grade 7, Chyning...she gets the one and only Green."

Chyning started silently mouthing obscenities as she went to the dispenser to get herself a mug of kwatha.

Kiyalee grinned as she put on a Yellow. She primped, for a few moments, looking at herself in the mirror. She then got a mug of kwatha for herself and went to get her briefing.

Whallek smiled. "Your crew is here. Are you going to relieve me and my crew…early?"

Soolchakan looked over at Bonarain and Kiyalee as they were getting their briefings. "As soon as those two are satisfied…I'm satisfied, Officer, Whallek." He looked back at Whallek. "You've already given me a briefing…so I don't really see any reason for any of your crew to stick around…unless they want to."

Whallek turned to the workroom. "Day shift Greens…you are relieved." He watched as a man and a woman went to the closet to retrieve their personal shirts and put the used Greens in the laundry. They went to the elevator, entered and the doors closed. "Blue and Yellow, you are relieved as soon as your relief is satisfied."

Soolchakan looked up at the shelves where the library of military regulations were kept. "Are there any new directives…that the Supreme Officer has thought of up there?"

"Not yet," said Whallek. "I hear that someone has demanded a very large new writing of Regulation 3. There is a *big* rumor that it desperately needs some major clarifications."

Soolchakan chuckled. "Someone got in trouble. Whoever it is, they're trying to say that the Regulation is…*unclear.*"

"Do you know who that someone is?"

"No, Sir, do you?"

Whallek leaned in close. "Master Officer, Jahong"

Soolchakan grunted in disgust. "Not him again!?"

"Oh yeah, him again."

Three men wearing Blue headed for the closet. They shed their Blues, donned their personal shirts and headed for the elevator.

Whallek smiled. "Five down, two to go."

It was only a few moments later that two women, in Yellow, headed for the closet. While they were changing, Whallek went over there and changed out of his Red. The last three day shift personnel entered the elevator and waved at the oncoming swing shift as the doors closed.

Soolchakan got himself a fresh mug of kwatha and got ready, for what he hoped would be, a long boring shift.

After a short time the last remaining rays of the sun started going down on the horizon. Soolchakan was having a miserable time trying to stay awake. The three women were not very talkative and he needed something to keep him alert. He did not want to fall asleep on his first assignment as a Red Shirt.

He pulled up the roster for the people who were supposed to be relieving this shift. Once again it was only four people. He was only familiar with one of the names. That reading took all of about two moments.

Bonarain leaned closer to her scope. "Did you hear that?"

"Yes," said Kiyalee.

Both Soolchakan and Chyning headed for the monitors to find out what it was.

"Looks like a herd of one of the larger bovines," said Kiyalee.

"Yeah," said Bonarain, "but...what spooked them...to stampede?"

Soolchakan looked at one of the vacant monitors, next to Bonarain. "Where'd they come from?"

"They're heading in a northeastern direction...*there it is...* behind the herd." She directed her scope to a certain spot and magnified.

One of the big predators of the plains was currently ripping the throat out of one of the slower members of the stampeding herd.

Kiyalee turned her head away, covered her mouth and groaned in disgust. "I gotta throw up." She got up and ran to the bathroom.

Chyning immediately took the chair, while Kiyalee was in the bathroom losing her lunch.

Bonarain looked toward the bathroom. "She's not gonna last very long, in the military, with a weak stomach."

Soolchakan grunted in agreement. He headed for the bathroom to check on her.

At that moment, all of the power shut down. According to the safety protocol, the weapons locker came open and all of the weapons were ready for easy access. Soolchakan ran to the locker and grabbed one of the larger caliber weapons. Bonarain and Chyning were right there, looking for one of the weapons that they were proficient in. It was a little difficult in the dim light.

That was when Soolchakan noticed that the emergency lighting had not come on. The emergency lights were completely independent of the city power and the emergency generators. They were on a battery that turned the lights on, whenever there was a power failure.

Kiyalee was feeling her way out of the bathroom. "Nothing's working! The lights didn't come on in the bathroom and the flusher isn't working either."

Soolchakan was at the communication panel. He hit the emergency button in an attempt to get in contact with headquarters. That button was the easiest to find because it was larger than your hand and took up most of the right side of the panel. He looked at the big button, waiting for the light to come on. "Nothing! We're dead here! We're cut off without any communication! Let's hope that someone in headquarters is monitoring this and can get us some help…soon."

Chyning gave out a growl of exasperation. "These wretched night vision goggles aren't working either!"

Soolchakan was getting a little scared. "How could someone… shut off everything…including the battery powered stuff? That's… impossible!"

"Well, somebody did it," said Bonarain condescendingly.

Soolchakan had to show some leadership in this mess. "If nothing electrical is working, we don't have to worry about someone coming through the elevator. Let's focus on the big windows."

All four of them took cover and started looking out the windows for any movement that they could see in the dimming twilight.

Suddenly they were all blinded by the most brilliant light they had ever encountered. They all clenched their eyes shut and took cover under desks and consoles. Just as suddenly as the light hit, it quickly dimmed to something a little more tolerable.

Chyning looked around fearfully. "Whawuzzat?"

Soolchakan scoffed. "How should I know? I've never seen anything like that…ever!"

"Look at the trees," said Bonarain.

Kiyalee pointed out the window. "Yes…the trees."

Soolchakan held his arms out questioningly. "What about the trees?"

Bonarain grunted in frustration. "There's some kind of… bright light shining on them…from behind us…I mean the station. Look at those long shadows…that are going the other way."

Chyning spoke up. "Whatever *it* is…*it* is behind…the station. How are we gonna find out when we can't get out by the elevator?"

Soolchakan growled and looked up at the manual handle. "We'll have to use the escape ladder." He climbed up onto the console and yanked on the manual handle. A trapdoor, in the ceiling, swung open and a ladder came sliding down to the floor. All three women looked up at Soolchakan.

"Red Shirt first," said Bonarain with a jeering smile.

Soolchakan tried to hide his disgust (and fear). He slung the rifle over his shoulder, got down from the console and went to the ladder. He looked up through the dark hole in the ceiling and huffed. He started climbing. He heard the clanking of the footsteps of the three women on the aluminum rungs as each of them started climbing after him. As he climbed, he could see almost nothing in the pitch black of the escape shaft. He kept on going up into the dark.

He remembered that they had prepared for escapes in the dark. The last ten rungs at the top of the ladder were all round instead of flat. He knew that as soon as he felt the round rungs he was almost there. He kept climbing. He was a little amazed at just how deep down the station was, compared to the transport platform.

He finally found a round rung. Up just a few more and he felt for the trapdoor. He felt the keypad on the door and growled. No power! The keypad was worthless. He felt around the edges for the five knobs that he had to move in order to manually open the door. He found the first and pushed it to the left. Then the next. When he pushed the fifth one a spring of some type helped open the trapdoor a little. He pushed it up the rest of the way and finished the climb out onto the top of the transport substation.

There was a strange glow coming from the inner city. He looked in total horror at the spectacle in front of him. All of the city was in flames. Near the center was a huge column of dark smoke that rose up to a giant black cloud that was overhead. The cloud was easy to see from the glow of the burning city.

He stumbled several steps away from the trapdoor and fell to his knees. Chyning was the next to exit the trapdoor and her reaction was similar to his. Bonarain came up next and nearly passed out when she saw the city.

Kiyalee came out last and started crying immediately. "Momma! Momma! My momma is…somewhere in that…fire!"

Soolchakan shook his head. "Could…Axswain…possibly have…had some weapon…capable…of…*that*?!"

There was a sudden brilliant glow that came from behind them. Again all four had to shield their eyes because it was so incredibly bright. When the brightness subsided, they turned and even though it was quite a distance away, they saw another giant black cloud with a column of smoke.

Bonarain let out a gasp of horror. "Whatever…hit us…they hit the city of Galsino as well. That…that mess is…approximately where Galsino sits."

Chyning pointed off to the northwest. "There's another one!"

They all looked where she was pointing. That horribly brilliant glow was not so painful to the eyes at the distance that this one was.

Bonarain again did some quick geographical figuring in her head. "That's the city of Kalash!"

Soolchakan was finally able to find his legs. "Are…the Axswain that powerful?"

Bonarain turned her attention off to the north. "OH! Oh, my…there's another one…and it's about where Axswain should be. They just got hit…by one of those things…too."

Soolchakan was almost in tears himself. "Who else…is close

enough…for us to see…another one of those…?"

At that moment another one went off, far to the east.

Bonarain swallowed hard. "That…that's Teltermak." She turned her gaze to the southwest. "The only other one that we could see would be…" At that moment, far to the southwest, another one of those glows went off. She stood there staring helplessly. "…the city of Zee-Altha."

Soolchakan fell to his knees again. "Owlam…Galsino…Kalash, Axswain, Teltermak and Zee-Altha. How many…more of the…City-States are…gone…that we can't even see from here?"

Small and large white particles started slowly floating down on and around them.

Kiyalee looked at the sudden shower of white. "Is that…snow? There shouldn't be any…snow…for another three months."

Chyning picked a piece up. "It's…ash of some type. Its ashes from the city…raining down on us. It's whatever…is burning…in the city."

Bonarain fell to her knees. She was in too much shock to cry. "Whatever…or who…ever," she said in a dead monotone.

They heard some popping, buzzing and humming start up. Emergency generators were kicking into gear, lighting up the area and turning all of the power on in the area. Soolchakan was the first to get back to the trapdoor. He went down as fast as he could. Bonarain was next followed by Chyning and Kiyalee.

He immediately headed for the radio. There was some chatter and static going on already. He listened at first, trying to hear if there was any answers. So far it was just questions and no one seemed to have any answers. All of the chatter was coming from the perimeter Watch Sector locations. Nothing was coming in from Command Central.

He looked back at the three women. "I don't know what to say to you. This is my first command…and it may be my last. We'll just have to wait and see…until someone from the Command Section calls us with instructions…if there's anyone from the Command Section who's still alive."

Kiyalee looked at him with worry on her face. "What happens

if you're the only Officer Grade 5 left?"

"They had to have someone…on the…northern perimeter… facing the Axswain area who…is at least a Grade 3…at least. If they don't, then we'll see what happens from there." He sat down and tried to listen to some of the chatter.

The three women sat down as well.

Chyning sighed and looked over at the dispenser. The kwatha was still hot. She went over and poured a fresh mug for herself. She looked back at her colleagues. "Does…anyone else want a mug?"

Bonarain scoffed. "How can you think of eating or drinking at a time like this?"

Chyning shrugged. "Go ahead and starve if you want to. It may be a while before we get any more of the good kwatha. I…don't wanna miss this opportunity."

Kiyalee sighed and went to pour herself a mug. She looked over at Soolchakan who was listening intently to the radio. She poured another mug for him and took it to him. Chyning poured another mug and offered it to Bonarain. Bonarain sighed and accepted it with a nod of her head. They all sat back sipping kwatha and listened to anything on the radio that might give them a clue as to what had happened and what was going to happen.

Soolchakan stopped his oration at that moment. He looked around the room at all the faces. Bonarain was sitting there sniffling. Kiyalee had her jaws clenched tight. Chyning had a tear run down her cheek. She wiped it away and cleared her throat.

Soolchakan took three long breaths before going on. "We later learned…that all of the minor City-States had been completely… destroyed. There was nothing…at all left of them. The fires that resulted from this…*weapon*…had incinerated everything within their walls. Four hundred fifty-five minor City-States…gone…along with their entire population. Of the one hundred twenty-seven major City-States…only one was untouched. This was our main clue as to who did it. Algothon was intact…while all of the other one hundred twenty-six major City-States were…in flames."

"What you're describing…is what we call a…nuclear bomb,"

said Milch quietly. "The electromagnetic pulse...that shuts off anything electrical. The intense light from the initial fireball. The firestorms on the ground that spread out from the center. The giant mushroom shaped cloud. The ash fallout of alpha and beta particles."

Soolchakan looked confused. "What's mushroom? What's alpha? What's beta?"

Milch cleared his throat. "The cloud that comes out of a nuclear blast, is shaped like a mushroom. A mushroom is a fungus that grows all over the place, on our home planet." He turned to a monitor on the wall. "Computer! Call up from video archives. We need to see a video of a nuclear detonation."

The monitor came on and beeped a few times. An electronic voice said: "Ready."

"Show the video," said Milch solemnly.

Soolchakan stared at the monitor with sagging shoulders and jaw.

Bonarain looked away and sniffled.

Kiyalee stared with her jaws still clenched tight.

Chyning looked as if she wanted to be somewhere else.

After the video of the mushroom shaped cloud ended, Milch quietly spoke. "Monitor off." He turned back to Soolchakan. "Was that what you saw?"

"Yes," said Soolchakan quietly. "Is that the shape...what you called a...mushroom?"

"Yes," said Milch.

"So...you're familiar with that type of...weaponry and warfare?"

"My ancestors...developed that thing...centuries ago. Unfortunately it was used...in warfare. Fortunately, they only used... two of the nasty things. The enemy...who got hit...surrendered... unconditionally."

Soolchakan sighed. "We...didn't know...for a while...who it was, exactly, that used that thing...on us and the other cities."

Gomez crossed his arms and grunted in disgust. "You liar! What makes you think that I should believe that...*story*?"

All three women looked up with anger and hatred in their

eyes. They were ready to stand up and do...who knows what. Soolchakan closed his eyes and bowed his head slightly. All three women suddenly looked at him and then sat back down. Their gazes of sheer hatred went back to Gomez.

Soolchakan leaned forward a little. "What makes you think that I'm fabricating this incident?"

Gomez scoffed. "You said that four hundred fifty-five minor cities and one hundred twenty-six major cities were all hit by... nuclear bombs."

"Yes! That's what happened. Why are you calling ME A LIAR?"

Gomez snickered as he shook his head. "Five hundred eighty-one nuclear bombs, all going off, within a very short time frame, inside the planet's atmosphere...all over the globe...the residual radiation would be devastating to the entire ecology of the planet. Every form of life...plant, fish, mammal, avian, mollusk, reptile...insect...all of them would suffer for years, if not centuries...*if* they survived. The weather patterns would be disrupted. Plus, we'd be able to measure that kind of residual radiation - which *would* be around for a bare minimum of seventy-five years - on our sensors...*nada!* We would *see* the devastation that it would do to all of the living creatures on the planet, for at least three hundred years...again *nada!*"

Soolchakan cocked his head to the side. "Three...hundred... years. Is that all? Just three hundred years?" He snickered.

Gomez was momentarily slowed by the reaction. "Yes. At least three hundred years. I see no sign of any form of devastation, the likes of which you're describing. I see an ecology that's not suffering from any form of that kind of nuclear cataclysm. I find no residual radiation."

Soolchakan snickered again. "Three hundred years." He leaned forward with a somewhat sinister look on his face. "How *old* do you think I am?" He quickly held up his right hand to stop Gomez. "Before you answer that question, I want you to think of something - don't measure my age, by the way that *you* age...measure it by the way *I as an Owlam* age...if you have any clue as to how...I age. I'll give you a clue...each orbit of our planet around the star, Holgotho, equates to one year. Now...how old am I?"

Gomez did not look quite so cocky. He thought of how they had come across several different species who aged very slowly and lived a lot longer than any human could imagine. The way that Soolchakan had presented the question made Gomez worry a little. He needed to stall a little. "Can you give me any other clues?"

Soolchakan smiled. He looked at the three Owlam women. "Chyning, my third wife...she's the youngest of the four of us." He glared back at Gomez with an even more sinister look.

Gomez decided to give up. "I...don't have a clue...how old you...are, or how old Chyning is. You don't look...very old."

Soolchakan leaned back in his chair. "I was born in the eighth year of the tenure while Shongorath was in command of the City-State of Owlam. He was in command for five more years, after my birth." He looked at Bonarain.

Bonarain leaned forward. "After Shongorath stepped down from command, it was Olbiy who took command. I was born in the seventh year of the administration of Olbiy."

Kiyalee leaned forward. "I was born in the eleventh year of the administration of Olbiy."

Chyning cleared her throat and just sat there looking smug. "I was born in the twelfth year of the administration of Olbiy."

Soolchakan chuckled. "Olbiy stepped down from command after fifteen years. Then there was Nontoor - who took command and his administration lasted for sixteen years. I joined the military, just as Nontoor took over. I was twenty years old."

Bonarain broke in. "I joined the military in the twelfth year of Nontoor's administration. I was twenty at that time."

"I was thirty-two when she joined," said Soolchakan.

Kiyalee now took her turn. "Nontoor stepped down just before I joined the military. Joonatha became the Supreme Officer when I joined. I was twenty."

"I was now thirty-six," said Soolchakan.

"I was now twenty-four," said Bonarain.

"I joined the military, when I turned twenty," said Chyning. "It was just about one year after Kiyalee came in. Joonatha was just about to start her second year as the Supreme Officer. She was diagnosed with a disease called: The Red Death. She died and Nagasoom became the Supreme Officer."

Soolchakan gave Gomez another condescending glare. "It was about three months after Nagasoom took over that…the bombs…those…weapons of mass destruction…hit. You said that the cataclysmic devastation would be evident…for three hundred years…after the bombs hit. You see no devastation. You find no… residual radiation. Now…how old do you think I, and my wives, are?"

Gomez licked his lips. "From what you're saying…you have to be at least…three hundred and thirty-seven years old…or more."

All four Owlams got a good giggle out of his response.

Gomez felt his dander rising. "What…too much?"

Soolchakan turned to Chyning. "You like keeping track of that. Why don't you tell him? I don't think that he'll *ever* come close to guessing the correct answer."

Chyning leaned forward looking really smug. "We have two time factors. One is the 'Unknown Times'. Everything that happened in the…'UT', was not and has not been recorded…accurately by any historian, of this day and age. The next one is called: ATUT…After the Unknown Times. That's when the historians started recording what was going on where…and when…and to whom it happened. The current year…is now 5599 ATUT. The four of us…we were born…during the…UT."

Gomez had been attempting to show his best poker face, with his arms folded high across his chest. Now he sat there stunned. His arms dropped to his sides and he sat there staring in shock.

Chyning's smile got bigger. "I was born in the year…9027… UT. 9027 plus 5599…equals 14,626. *That*…is *my* age."

"I am 14,627 years old," said Kiyalee merrily.

"I am 14,631 years old," said Bonarain flatly.

"That makes me…14,643 years old," said Soolchakan. "I was a mere…37 when that horrible…*incident*…took place. You people said that the first crash, of those spaceships, on Niygool, took place approximately 13,500 years ago? It was exactly 13,414 years ago. I was there. I was one of the ones who brought it down on Niygool... at over 4,000 kph. I was involved in *all* of the crashes on Niygool." He put his elbows on the table. "Is fourteen...*millennium*...long enough for the...ecology to come back...from a...nuclear cataclysm?" He gave Gomez an innocent smile.

Gomez swallowed hard. He felt his face flush. He looked around the table at some of the other people. They all seemed to be waiting for his response. "I...apologize...for my...inappropriate remark. It is...very rare that we come across a...race that...lives as long...as you...do."

Soolchakan stared up at the ceiling and started his oration again. "When we were Heyyah, our lives would have been just as brief as yours. Since that genetic bomb...or weapon of mass destruction... went off, we...don't seem to be aging at all. We just keep...going on. No Owlam has ever...died from...old age. Murder, war wounds, or suicide...those are the only ways that any of us...Owlam...have... died...in the last 14,000 years."

Milch cleared his throat. "How...did you...survive the initial blast? I mean, when a nuclear bomb goes off...it covers a massive area. It should take out...an entire city."

Bonarain looked at him sadly. "The perimeter of those... horrid firestorms...didn't reach the outer wall...of Owlam. It completely...burned everything...and everyone...in the inner part of the city. The outer farming and livestock areas...were not really touched...by the blast or the firestorms. All of the people who were...outside the firestorms were changed...genetically. Anyone who was on duty at the perimeter watch bunkers and in the homes in the crop and livestock areas survived...but changed."

Upton looked at her in shock. "Changed...to...Owlam?"

The look that the four Owlams gave Upton answered her question.

Montalvo leaned forward. He wanted to change the angry attitudes that he was seeing on the faces of the four guests. "I heard you say that the outer...farming and livestock areas were unaffected... by the firestorms. Are you saying that the area, inside the walls, had crops and livestock...farms and ranches?"

"Yes," said Bonarain. "It was necessary. If someone came along and took over any farmlands or ranches that were outside the wall…you lost them. We had to have some form of food sources…inside the walls…just in case there was a siege."

Montalvo's jaw dropped. "You're telling me that the walled in area was…that big?"

"Yes." Bonarain smiled. "The Trams that were on the rail, going around the perimeter wall…if you got on one at…oh say, station one, at sunup…and you rode in that same Tram all the way back around to station one…it would be well past sundown before you got back to station one. There were two hundred sixty Tram cars on that rail and they were never close to each other."

"That's quite an area," said Milch. "Were all of the major City-States that big?"

Soolchakan shrugged. "In most cases…yes."

Gomez spoke up, trying to get back 'in the good' with the Owlams. "So…anybody who was in Owlam…who was outside of the area of the destructive firestorms, ended up being changed genetically…to what you are…today. How many of you were there?"

"There were 7,016 survivors," said Bonarain. "5,262 women and 1,754 men. And yes…we *did* just pffft out of nowhere."

Milch looked a little skeptical. "How soon were you able to establish any form of hierarchy? I mean…if your main command center suffered a direct hit from the bomb, and was incinerated…who was in charge?"

Soolchakan smiled. "It was immediate. Our Supreme Officer, Nagasoom wanted to do a visual inspection of the perimeter watch bunkers himself. Instead of being at Central Headquarters in the middle of the city, he was in one of the bunkers…facing north…towards the Axswain when the bomb hit. As soon as the power came back on…he let it be known that he was still alive…as soon as all of the panic chatter ceased." He shook his head. "He became the very first Drey Sssorg."

5

Commander Kasaki, the Executive Officer shook her head. "Could you please tell us your rank structure? I'm hearing... Supreme Officer and Officer Grade 3 and 5 and 6 and 7...now I'm hearing this...Drey Sorg..."

All four of the Owlam stood up with fire in their eyes. With his teeth clenched, Soolchakan growled at Kasaki. "If you're going to say it...pronounce it correctly!"

Kasaki looked a little frightened. "Uh...what did I...miss?" She was very defensive in her speech and actions.

Soolchakan leaned forward and put his fists on the table. "It is pronounced...Drey SSSSSorg," he snarled.

Yeoman Aua leaned over to Kasaki. "He's talking about an elongated S. That's the only part you messed up."

Kasaki swallowed hard. "Okay...uh...Drey...Sssorg."

All four Owlam sat down. "Thank you," said Soolchakan, still looking a little upset.

Kasaki cleared her throat. "Okay, so it is...Drey Sssorg. You have that and you also called him the Supreme Officer. Which is which and what puts whom at the higher end of the rank structure?"

Soolchakan bowed his head forward. Bonarain jumped slightly as if she had been surprised by something.

She looked at Soolchakan and then started talking in an automated monotone. "There are ranks and rank structure. In our rank structure, the highest ranking Officer was called the Supreme Officer. The rank just below that was the Master Officer. Then the Senior Officer. Then Officer Leader. After that was Officer Grade 1 through 7. The higher the number, the lower your rank. When you're talking about Drey Sssorg...you are not talking about some... hollow title. Drey Sssorg...is a power. It is a power that somehow goes to the eldest Owlam. Don't ask me how...we have no idea how it happens. It just happens." She stopped talking and bowed her head.

Kiyalee started in the same monotone manner. "As was said before…Supreme Officer or Officer Grade 7, these are hollow titles. These are ranks that you earn by doing whatever it takes to obtain that rank. In the case of Drey Sssorg, we have no idea how it started or why. We only know that it goes to the eldest living Owlam. If that person dies…then whoever is the next eldest Owlam obtains the power. Again…we don't know how or why." She bowed her head.

Chyning started talking - in monotone. "Right now, Soolchakan is using the power of Drey Sssorg. He is making us tell what we know about the power…which isn't much. All we know is that it exists and we have no power against it. All that Soolchakan has to do is think of something. He doesn't have to tell us to do it, he just thinks it…and we do it. We do it whether we want to do it or not." She bowed her head.

Milch looked horrified. "Are you saying…that if he wanted you to commit suicide…all he has to do is…think it…and you'd do it?"

Bonarain looked up. "That is exactly what it is. That *is* the power of Drey Sssorg."

Milch swallowed hard. "Well that…that's…just…"

"Terrifying," said Soolchakan flatly. "I have to be…so…so… so careful of what I'm thinking. I can't have any form of…vicious or vindictive thought…towards any of my children. If I do…the consequences could be…" He closed his eyes and bowed his head.

"This is the power of Drey Sssorg," said Bonarain. "It is *not* just some useless, hollow title. It *is* the leadership of the Owlam."

Milch was intrigued by this new revelation. "Did any of the other…new races get this same kind of…power?"

"We don't know," said Kiyalee. "We don't think so…or at least we've never seen anyone else manifest that sort of thing."

Montalvo jumped in. "Okay, so this power of…Drey Sssorg, it might be something that is strictly a characteristic of the Owlam. What happened after the attack? How did you come together? Why are you still here? Why did the people who attacked you not come in to finish the job?"

Soolchakan sighed. "Nagasoom was the first Drey Sssorg. He started issuing orders. We were obeying them, but we thought that it was just because he was the Supreme Officer, we were subordinates and the city had just been attacked. We started organizing, finding out who was left, how much weaponry and getting together to make a counterstrike."

Emerson, the chief of security, jumped in. "Counterstrike… against who?"

"Nagasoom had decided that the attack had come from Axswian. We were getting a force together…to attack them," said Chyning dejectedly.

"But…you saw them get hit…as well," said Emerson.

Kiyalee scoffed. "According to Nagasoom, *that* was a diversion. It really hadn't happened to Axswain. According to Nagasoom, no one could have attacked us…that horrendously, except the city of Axswain. He had a little problem with prejudices. His parents, his siblings, all of his uncles and aunts…all of his cousins…and two of his children…had all died in attacks from Axswain. It was more of a blood feud with him. Kill all Axswain…*no matter what.*"

Emerson sat there confused. "So…you attacked?"

Bonarain snarled at him. "We didn't have a choice! The Drey Sssorg had made a decision. We cannot go against the Drey Sssorg. We've tried…when we knew that the Drey Sssorg was making some mandate. We obey it, no matter how much we disagree with or hate it."

Milch butted in on Emerson. "So…what happened?"

Soolchakan looked at him sadly. "We didn't try to put out any fires. We didn't try to find any survivors in the rubble of the inner city. We got the weapons all together at one place on the north side…and we attacked. Nagasoom was in the lead vehicle. He was standing in the upper turret with a high powered weapon, ready to fire…at the first sign of any of the Axswain military." He shook his head. "His vehicle was the first one hit…by a pulse cannon. Blown apart by somebody…from Axswain that was looking for us as well. As soon as Nagasoom was killed in that blast, Master Officer, Plothok took over as Drey Sssorg…instantaneously. He was in total disagreement with this offensive. There were just over 7,000 of us and that does not make for a decent attack force. It doesn't even make a barely good defense force. As soon as Nagasoom was blown away, Plothok made the decision, in his head, without telling anybody, and we all immediately retreated."

"So this…Plothok got everyone back to Owlam safely," said Milch. "What then?"

"Yes, everyone…that was left, got back to the city wall," said Soolchakan. "Now, Plothok, being a little more level headed made us start looking for any survivors in the rubble. We of course left about 150 in the watch bunkers, checking for any incoming activity, while the rest of us searched for survivors. We found none. The heat had been too intense. We found nothing but…charred remains…if we found anything at all."

Bonarain shook her head. "Once it was finally decided that no one could have possibly lived through that inferno, Plothok went on to talk about building up our defenses. If it hadn't been for the power of Drey Sssorg, we wouldn't have done it. It was a joke. 7,000 of us trying to defend a huge area like that? If it had been one of the smaller City-States, it might have been possible, but…some of the top strategists had stated, several times, that it would take a force of over 500,000 to properly defend the entire city of Owlam."

"Plothok made the decision and we did it," said Kiyalee. "The real ridiculous thing about defending Owlam…we were defending a gargantuan pile of charred rubble. There was no real city left." She sighed. "There was an alarm. It came from the direction of the watch bunkers that faced Galsino. As big as the city area was, we had very little transport that could get us from one end to the other, and so most of us were late getting to the location where the Galsino had been spotted. Plothok and several others…tried to defend that area. The Galsino were breaking through. They had breached the thin line that we had. When the rest of us arrived, we were able to beat the Galsino back. But…now Plothok was dead. He and ten others died…in the attempt to defend that area."

Chyning started up. "The next in line was Master Officer, Neenatha. She was now the Drey Sssorg. She came up with a way to put the entire perimeter watch line on automatic. It was not the best, but it was a lot easier than what few of us were left trying to keep people at all the stations all the time. This time the attack came from Teltermak. Neenatha tried to get us to keep going on against… incredible odds. During that attack, we had to retreat into the rubble. That was the only way we survived that one. The Teltermak were just too powerful…militarily. Neenatha died in that attack…along with nineteen others."

"Now…Master Officer, Jahong was the Drey Sssorg," said Soolchakan. "He had been noticing that he was capable of doing some strange things. Instead of warring on others, he decided that we should learn things about ourselves…before we went after others. The capabilities that we suddenly had were being slowly discovered. We found that we could communicate…telepathically. We could use kinetic energy to…make things move. We were moving…from one place, where we knew where we were, to another place…that was…so strange and different. We were then able to come back to the familiar. It took a while to understand that these were different dimensions that we were going to."

"Some of them were friendly, others hostile…others… we hadn't found a way to describe them," said Bonarain. "We had different ways that we referred to them."

"We found two different dimensions where we could go to and observe our dimension…without being seen or heard: Tanani Pay and Tokshoom Kel," said Kiyalee. "These are most useful, when spying on…strangers." She looked up with a sly grin. "…any strangers."

"We were watching you and your ship…ever since you first arrived at Denhahbon," said Chyning.

Milch cleared his throat nervously. "So…why haven't we been crashed into…Niygool?"

"Because of what we found out while we were spying on you," said Soolchakan. "This is an exploration ship. We got into your computer banks and looked at your laws and rules. You leave people alone…for the most part. You come in and study them. But you try to keep from injuring…or conquering. If we thought for one moment that you came here as conquerors, your ship would have been crashed into Ragath or Rogoth...and no one would have known how or when you disappeared. Your drone would have never been launched. Your people would never know what happened to you."

Bonarain snickered. "It was under the studying eyes of Jahong, that we also discovered one of our strange racial traits: Scales on the back of our necks. There is a mucus that is excreted out of these scales. We didn't know for some time that this was significant. We just cleaned ourselves and tried to figure out a way to get rid of these strange scales."

Kiyalee sighed. "Jahong was out...not paying attention one day. He was assassinated...by an Axswain. Using our dimension shifting talents, we got that Axswain...and his three accomplices."

"Now, Senior Officer, Nakalak became the Drey Sssorg," said Soolchakan. "This one was a real winner. He was very despondent most of the time and because of him being Drey Sssorg, the despondency spread...no choice in the matter by us, it just spread."

"210 Owlams committed suicide because of his...depression and dull-normal attitude," said Chyning through clenched teeth.

"He finally committed suicide himself," said Kiyalee.

"Now, we got Senior Officer, Holla, as the Drey Sssorg," said Bonarain. "She was different in that she wanted us to clean things up. She did not like any kind of mess and so...we started cleaning up the inner city...after almost 21 years. It was now...under Holla that we found out one of the most remarkable things about us that had happened as a result of the genetic bomb...we are completely immune...to what you call 'residual radiation.'"

"Some of the survivors from Galsino or Axswain or Teltermak came inside our walls to...kill what remained of the Owlam," said Chyning. "We would shift to the dimension - Tanani Pay. We would watch them searching through the cleaned up areas. We would watch them, very quickly, start to get weak and have strange sores appear on their bodies. Most of them died before they got out of the inner city area. We shoved the bodies into the dimension Serani Tan."

"That's not very nice," said Doctor Lewis. "You could spread all kinds of diseases…in this other dimension, from dumping all of those dead, radioactive corpses."

"Not to worry," chuckled Soolchakan. "There's nothing in Serani Tan…except for one gargantuan star. We've taken some of the ships, before we crashed them, into Serani Tan, in order to see if there's anything there…usable. We used the sensors of those ships to determine what is in Serani Tan. There's nothing - no dust, no comets, no asteroids, no planets…and no other stars. One dimension…one entire dimension with NOTHING…but one tremendously large star…and a little debris that we've dumped in there."

"Holla figured, after about five of the disastrous attacks by the enemy, that they would learn a lesson and leave us alone," said Bonarain. "They didn't. Because of her lackadaisical attitude about putting up guards and stressing everything on cleanup…we were attacked. She died in that attack. There were 64 others who died with her."

"Senior Officer, Wilfadge, became the Drey Sssorg," said Kiyalee.

Soolchakan looked at the three women. "We could bore them with all of the ones who were Drey Sssorg…before me. We don't need to. Just recite the remembrance."

The four of them stared at a point in space and started reciting: "Nagasoom, Plothok, Neenatha, Jahong, Nakalak, Holla, Wilfadge, Hadathoo, Till, Wymini, Jeejow, Xadorm, Plykatha, Booxo, Kloob, Zebenee, Junrud, Pextow, Thes, Gorral, Sleea, Eeleeg, Panatorm, Malapi, Sheekog, Melming, Yod, Salgim, Stra, Chreeker, Banbora, Sumik, Londarid, Manifana, Nepnep, Snewap, Umeso, Kenchom, Shaffani, Tachtor, Klup, Seetaya, Halalua, Pirem, Voostoo, Wunteer, Groff, Porompet, Joogdam…and now…Soolchakan."

"Those are the names of all of the Owlam who have had the power of Drey Sssorg. I am the fiftieth Drey Sssorg," said Soolchakan. "During the administration of each of the other forty-nine Drey Sssorg…other Owlams died. Today…there are only the four of us… from the original 7016 who survived that initial blast. We do have children…but no colleagues. So, we are doing everything we can to assure that they are not murdered, slaughtered or…abused in any way. We've made a few mistakes along the way, however, we have also discovered a few…wonderful things about ourselves and what we can do." He leaned forward. "We will protect our family. We will protect them…without any concern for anyone else. Try to hurt any of our family…and we will fight you in the only way we know how to fight our enemies…genocide."

"Others tried to fight us," said Bonarain. "They are now… extinct. The Axswain, the Cacktash, the Sodle, the Teltermak, the Gabeesh-Or, the Maka-Or, the Rakab-Rosh, the Zee-Altha, the Bising, the Twakon, the Noga-Or, the Parash-Zanab, the Neksheth-Or, the Towlayaw-Or, the Yagalom-Ayin, the Beetsik, the Perfor… and the Heyyah of the City-State of Algothon."

"I didn't hear anything about those Galsino or Kalash," said Emerson. "You've mentioned them several times as far as geographically close enemies…but you didn't say anything about wiping them out."

Soolchakan gave him a sinister smile. "They stopped attacking us…before we started the ultimate campaign of destruction against all enemies. If they ever start it up again…we will not hesitate…to rid ourselves of those pestilences…forever. The Kalash…they seem to be like us, though. They're more interested in just…live and let live…find out what we are and leave all the others alone…while we are discovering ourselves. The Galsino…they could be a problem… someday…we will take care of any problem that comes along…when it comes."

"Including those from outer space," said Milch flatly.

"Yes," said Soolchakan with a smile.

"Going back to that one thing you referred to," said Montalvo. "…this thing about how you could make someone do something…by just thinking about it and they would unconsciously do it. According to what I heard, you could make someone commit suicide. How do you control your temper…that well?"

Soolchakan took in a deep breath and let it out slowly. "Believe it or not, I am in contact with all of the other forty-nine Drey Sssorg. They have all said that they don't want to come back…

but they do help advise me...on many things. I know that's difficult for a lot of others to believe and I can't really prove it. You'll just have to take my word for it. They do help with controlling my temper... even the ones that committed suicide themselves."

Emerson cleared his throat. "Excuse me, but...I'd like to hear about the...first time you crashed one of those alien outer space ships. The technology that you had...could not have been anything close to a ship that could travel across light years to get to your planet. You did have technology, but...how?"

"That was during the administration of Till," said Soolchakan. "He...had long believed in...the existence of creatures from other planets. He instilled this belief in us...even though most of us didn't want to believe it. We started looking at the other planets in our solar system...closely." He looked up at Milch. "*We* discovered those mineral deposits on Bri as a result of his outer space explorations. We decided to take just a little bit because we didn't know what would happen if we brought too much...foreign weight...home to Hardooth. We were filthy rich...but we couldn't get anyone to trade with us. So we stored a lot of the stuff on Zhagool...in vaults that we made...using our dimension travel capability."

"That explains those...voids...on the big moon," said Milch with a weak smile.

"Yes, it does," said Soolchakan with a smug look. "Anyway, while we were sweeping the outer perimeters of our star system, we did encounter a spacecraft coming in. We informed Till and we were all immediately assigned tasks aboard the vessel. We went to the Hoyani Kel dimension, boarded their vessel, went to the Tanani Pay dimension and observed them as they got closer to our planet. Learning a new language - even an out-world language - we found it to be unbelievably simple. We learned their language, learned that they were a scout ship that was sent there to search out a system to conquer...so we took over their ship."

Bonarain let loose with an evil laugh. "Yes, we took over. We started stealing just about anything and everything that we thought we could use. They were absolutely mystified as to how all of their systems were going crazy and all of their equipment was disappearing…then they were no longer in control of the ship…and we flew it on a suicide flight…directly into Niygool." She chuckled again. "Boom," she said quietly. "It was somewhat satisfying to see the look of horror and fear on their faces. Fearless conquerors who were losing control of their bowels…as the ship got closer and closer to the moon. Moments before impact, we all went back to Hoyani Kel…and departed the ship."

Milch tried to ask something and had to stop and clear his throat first. "Uh…where…did…these people come from? Who were they?"

Soolchakan laughed and shook his head. "Who cares? They came here to search out an inhabited planet that they could conquer. They found an inhabited planet and started mapping it. We took over and got rid of them…before they could do any damage."

Montalvo was a little curious. "What about others of their race? Did others come…at a later date…and try searching this system…again?"

Soolchakan shrugged. "Who knows? We've never taken an inventory of the would-be-attackers, to see if any of them were second timers…or third timers. Anyone who comes here as a conqueror, gets to visit one of our planets…the wrong way."

Again Emerson came in. "All of those different species… coming from all kinds of different places…how were you able to figure out all of the different…technological systems…without any foreknowledge of that or any system like it?"

Soolchakan smiled. "Learn the entity, learn the language, learn the system…take over…simple."

"But…just the four of you…" Emerson stammered. "How?"

Soolchakan looked up and closed his eyes. "Bikaropin… Shalam…I need you to show yourselves."

Two new Owlam men were now standing in the conference room. Again the intruder alarm went off.

Milch ordered the intruder alarm to be turned off completely…until further notice.

With a big smile on his face, Soolchakan addressed the two newcomers. "Do you think that you'd have any problems, taking control of and flying this ship?"

"Not a problem," said one.

"Very easy," said the other.

"Thank you," said Soolchakan.

The two newcomers disappeared.

"There's a lot more than four of us," he said with a big smile.

Milch let a small growl come out of his throat. "Just…how many of you…are on board?" He cleared his throat nervously.

Soolchakan chuckled. "Let's go back out on your bridge."

Soolchakan, Milch and Emerson all walked out to the bridge.

Again Soolchakan chuckled. "My children…show yourselves."

Immediately the population on the bridge, more than doubled. There was at least one Owlam standing near every crew member on the bridge. Some of the female Owlams had small children with them. All of the crew members were staring at all of the new comers with stunned silence.

Soolchakan looked at Milch with a smug smile. "You can tell Boris that you found the source of all that excess carbon dioxide."

Milch gave Soolchakan a weak smile, turned his head away and groaned.

Soolchakan looked back out over the bridge. "You may go back to your chores, my children."

All of the Owlam disappeared. All of the crew members were looking around - some with apprehension, some with fear, some with disgust, some with gloom - all with some form of trepidation.

Again Soolchakan looked back at Milch. "You have absolutely no secrets from us. The fact that we have not found any… conquering ways in your logs…is the only reason that you people are still alive. You came here to watch us, and during that operation, we are watching you. I believe that you have a legal term…what was it…oh yes, *Quid Pro Quo*."

"Yes, we do," said Milch. "Yes, we certainly do."

They went back to the conference room.

Once they were back and seated, Montalvo spoke up: "You say that the four of you…are over 14,000 years old. If you are that old…the population of your race should be…in the multi-millions… but I don't find any of you…anywhere on the surface."

"We hide rather well," said Soolchakan. "We don't want to be found. All of the conquerors…be they local or from somewhere else, have been fooled by the fact that we hide. We also hide because we have been hunted. In each case, once we figured out who the hunter is…we destroy them, without hesitation. Whether or not it's an individual or an empire…we destroy them."

"I can understand that, however, your numbers…how do you hide that many people so completely?"

"I've told you why we hide. How and where is none of your business. I will tell you that our…*numbers*…are not as high as you may think. Because of our longevity, we don't practice procreation very much."

"How do you stop them? I mean, young people of almost every race that we have encountered…they start maturing and their hormones go wild and they want to experiment…with sexual encounters."

"I don't allow them to…experiment."

"How do you stop them?"

"By the power of Drey Sssorg!"

"That…power…that power is that strong?"

"All Owlam obey the power. Whether they like it or not - they obey!"

"What's the earliest age that…you allow them to…wed and procreate?"

"None of them are allowed to mate until they reach a minimum age of 95 years old."

"You're telling me that this Drey Sssorg power…can keep their raging hormones under control…for 95 years?"

"Their hormones don't start getting…in a rage…until they're at least 65 years old. We age very slowly…even as children. We also require an outside stimulation, before any hormones can start raging."

Gomez started snickering. "No youth needs any outside source to get interested, sexually, in the other adolescents around them." He shook his head with a sneer on his face. "Plus, you're telling me that they're not interested, in any way, shape or form, until they're 65 years old, that's pure nonsense. They *all* start getting interested after they hit twelve years old."

Soolchakan scowled at Gomez. "Maybe among your species, but NOT with mine."

"What," scoffed Gomez? "Is it because you tell them not to? Is that Drey Sssorg that powerful?"

Soolchakan sat there with his eyes shut for a few moments. Suddenly a female Owlam with three younger girls appeared in the room.

The adult newcomer looked around rather confused. "What's going on? Why did you want me...and these three of my children?"

Soolchakan calmly looked at the ceiling. "Please introduce yourself...and your three children."

She grunted in exasperation. "I am Mahanee of the Fourth." She placed her hand on the head of the tallest girl. "This one is Anahaya of the Fifth." She placed her hand on the head of the middle one. "This one is Yanvani of the Fifth." She placed her hand on the head of the smallest. "This one is Xahayi of the Fifth." She placed her fists on her hips. "Now, what's going on?"

Soolchakan snickered. "They don't believe us...about certain things."

"What things?"

Soolchakan closed his eyes. Mahanee stood there staring at him. Her expression changed several times as he was updating her, telepathically. She had a condescending look on her face as she glanced around the room at each one of the crewmembers of the ship.

She scoffed. She looked up at the ceiling and started scratching her chin. "Oh really," she said in a disdainful manner.

"Yes," said Soolchakan flatly. He turned his gaze to Gomez. "Okay Mister Know-it-all, take a look at the three girls and tell me how old you think each on is."

Gomez looked at Soolchakan and shook his head in disgust. He turned to the three girls. "The youngest one...I'd say that she's just past the toddler age. She's probably four years old…at best."

All three girls fought hard to keep from laughing out loud.

Gomez looked a little confused, however, tried to keep his composure and go on with the guessing. "The middle one…she looks to be about…oh say seven or eight…nine at the most."

All three girls were now having an even more difficult time at attempting to not laugh out loud.

Gomez figured that is was some trick so he kept on. "The oldest one is…probably twelve or thirteen, fourteen at most."

The two youngest now did laugh out loud. The oldest turned aside, and giggled with her hand over her mouth.

"They don't agree with you," said Soolchakan flatly. "Again you've made the mistake of thinking in terms of how *your* species ages." He looked at the three girls and smiled. "Xahayi, how old are you, my dear?"

Xahayi clasped her hands in front of her, puffed her chest out and proudly exclaimed: "I'm fifteen years old."

All of the ship's crewmembers gawked in shock at this revelation.

Soolchakan chuckled slightly. "What is your interest in boys…at this time?"

Xahayi looked a little confused. Her arms dropped to her sides. "Uhm…as far…as…what?"

"A mate," said Soolchakan flatly.

Her shoulders and lower jaw sagged. "I…I…I'm only… fifteen! "A mate? That won't…that's not…at least eighty years from now! I'm only fifteen…I won't…" she looked at her older sisters a little confused. She turned back to Soolchakan. "Why?"

"We have someone here who does not believe certain things about our race."

Her brow furrowed. "Like what?"

"We'll explain it to you later, my child." Soolchakan now turned to the middle one. "Yanvani, how old are you?"

With a big grin on her face, she said: "I'm thirty-eight years old."

It did not seem possible, however, Gomez now had his eyes

and mouth open even wider.

"What do you think about boys...as far as mating?"

She giggled and shook her head. "That don't happen...not at my age...not for another..." She looked up thinking. "...fifty-seven years...at least."

"Thank you," said Soolchakan with a smile. Now he turned to the oldest who had her lips clenched tight in a grin. "Anahaya, he said that you look about fourteen...what is your age, my child?"

She snorted through her nose, attempting to stifle a laugh. She stood tall and sniffed. "I'm sixty-three years old."

Gomez leaned his head back with his eyes closed and just shook his head, still slack-jawed.

"What have you thought about, so far, with boys and mating?"

She stood there with her mouth wide open. She threw her arms out. "I...I'm not ready...my body...not ready. I need to mature...physically and mentally...before I think anything about... mating and...having a baby!"

"Thank you," said Soolchakan. He turned to Gomez. "Hey! Mister brilliance! How old do you think their mother is?"

Gomez looked as if he was nauseous. He took in and let out a deep breath. He shrugged. "I...dunno." He took a look at her. He looked back at Soolchakan. "1000? 2000? I dunno."

Mahanee stood there with her fists on her hips and a smug look on her face. "My oldest daughter - Hisang - was born in the year 599 ATUT. *She* is now 5000 years old."

Gomez looked off to the dejectedly. "Of course she is," he said gloomily. "Why not?" He sighed and hung his head.

Milch turned to Mahanee. "Excuse me, Ma-am, but you said that you are...Mahanee...of the...fourth? What is the fourth?"

Mahanee looked at him as if he was a complete idiot. "Of the Fourth, means that I am of the fourth generation...from Soolchakan. Soolchakan, Bonarain, Kiyalee and Chyning are all of the First generation. My children are all of the fifth generation."

Milch smiled. "Thank you for that explanation."

The zoologist, Upton, decided to try to get some of the tenseness out of the room. "Uh, excuse me, but...I'm noticing something about your ears."

Soolchakan gave her a smug look. "Yes?"

"Well...your ears...the four of you...first generation...your ears are...much larger than any of the other...Owlams that have come into the room. Is there a...reason for this?"

Kiyalee chuckled. "Our ears never stop growing. They grow *very* slowly, however, they do grow. The larger the ears, the older the Owlam."

"Oh, I see," said Upton. "Would it be...possible to see a... newborn? That'd give us a real good example of this...growth."

Bonarain sucked in deep breath, glared at Upton and then at Soolchakan. Her eyes darted back and forth from Upton to Soolchakan, while her breathing was coming in and out quickly through clenched teeth.

Soolchakan stared at Bonarain with no emotion on his face at all. "Like any mother, my dear wife Bonarain is very protective of her children. Especially the newest ones."

Bonarain's expression got even angrier. "You're not..."

"Yes I am," said Soolchakan firmly. "They just want to see the ears. If these people, even attempt, any harm to your babies...I give you permission to wreak havoc aboard this ship."

Milch put his hands up in a form of surrender. "No one...is even going to think about harming any babies! Absolutely no one on this ship wants to harm babies...not at all. Your children are safe... here on this ship. If anyone tries to...or even looks as if they're going to harm your babies, I will wreak havoc on that, or those, persons... myself...without hesitation."

Bonarain still glared at Soolchakan. Her fists and her teeth were clenched tightly. She closed her eyes for a moment. Three female Owlams appeared, each holding a small sleeping baby in their arms.

Soolchakan spoke quietly. "I would like to introduce you to three of our newest additions to our...extended family. Two girls, Nabtami and Nabtemi, and the boy Nabovon."

"They're beautiful," said Kasaki.

"They're so cute," said Aua. "How old are they?"

"Yes," said Upton, "I can see the difference in the ears. Very narrow at the base and much smaller lobes. So…later in life all that grows out?"

"Yes," said Bonarain looking around for any threat at all. "Like all Olwams, their ears will get larger…and they're exactly fifty-five *days* old." Her gaze went to Doctor Lewis. "What are you doing?"

Lewis cleared his throat. "I…uh…it's my duty…to do a quick…scan, uh…medical scan on anyone new arriving on the ship. It doesn't hurt them, it just…looks for any…sickness in them, or possibly a…parasite on them. I assure you, they are *not* being harmed."

"Stop scanning," snarled Bonarain in a threatening manner.

Lewis shut the scanner off and put it away. He gave her a bit of a guilty smile as he did so. "My apologies, dear lady. I absolutely meant no harm of any sort. I'm a doctor and one of my sacred vows is: First of all - do no harm. Uh, whose…babies…are they?"

Bonarain still glared at him. "They're all three mine!"

Kasaki looked at Bonarain with admiration. "Triplets?"

Bonarain glared back at Soolchakan. "All right! They've seen them! Can I send them back now?"

Soolchakan gave her an understanding smile, closed his eyes and nodded assent. The three newcomers, with babies, vanished.

Milch yawned involuntarily.

Soolchakan noticed the yawn. "Why don't you go to your bed? Get some rest. We'll continue this discussion…later, after you're…bed."

"Thank you," said Milch through blurry eyes. "I appreciate that."

All of the Owlams in the room vanished.

Milch yawned again. "We all have a little something to contemplate - from this first encounter. Go contemplate, while I go get some sleep. Everyone, *except Gomez,* is dismissed."

The other people filed out of the room. Gomez sat there staring off into space. Finally it was just the two of them.

"You're an idiot," growled Milch.

Gomez looked at Milch with surprise and anger on his face. "I'll have you know that my IQ is…"

Milch leaned towards Gomez and yelled as loud as he could. "Shattup!" He sat back in his chair glaring at the surprised face of Gomez. "IQ is meaningless. You have all kinds of book sense, but you have absolutely no *common* sense. What kind of stupidity was that, calling someone who could, without us even knowing it, take over this ship and slam us into a…grave where no one could find us in a gas giant?"

"From the information he had given us and the readings that we had, he was not telling the truth…I got the truth out of him!"

"There are more tactful and diplomatic ways of saying it!"

Gomez was getting angry as well. "Like what?!"

Milch held his arms out in thinking. "Oh, something like: Excuse me, but the readings that we're getting tell us that this mass detonation of all those nuclear bombs…had to have happened a long time ago - how long ago *did* this battle take place?" He leaned forward. "And you say it in a nice manner. You don't accuse!"

Gomez got even angrier. "What's your problem?! I got the truth out of him…don't you like the truth? Don't you…?"

Milch stood up and leaned towards Gomez with his fists on the table. "QUIET!! I don't want to hear another word out of you! This has just become a one-way conversation. You keep your big mouth shut and listen! Everything that you're doing and saying is defense and justification for attacking that man needlessly. From now on, while we are dealing with these Owlams, you keep your mouth shut! If you have a question, you submit it to me or someone, with a little more diplomatic capability, in writing." He sat back down. "You have almost as much tact as…as a rabid wolf! When we are dealing with a species like this…who has all kinds of…strange and unknown capabilities…tact and diplomacy…these are very necessary. You are a wonderful and very intelligent scientist. That's why you're in the position that you're in. You're a good scientist, but, as a diplomat, you *stink*…out loud. Stick to your science and leave the diplomatic discussions with foreign species to those who can talk to them without sending them into some vengeful rage."

Gomez sat there with his teeth clenched. "You mean: Kissing their collective butts?"

Milch leaned forward and tried to look as sinister as possible. "If that's what it takes to get this ship and the entire crew out of this system, alive and intact…YES! You will be on your knees and you will be placing a big wet, sloppy one…fanatically…to whichever part of their anatomy they want kissed…however many times they want it kissed! Is that clear?"

Gomez glared back. "Yes, Sir," he growled through clenched teeth.

Milch leaned forward a little, looking even more sinister. "Dismissed," he whispered.

Gomez got up and stomped out, not moving his arms, with his fists clenched tightly at his sides.

Milch hung his head and let out a long sigh. He did not know if he was being watched, at this time, by some spying Owlam. He knew that it was unlikely this would not be under scrutiny. He hoped that his display would satisfy any kind of suspicions that the Owlams might have towards his motives and the motives of the governments that he represented.

"Uh…Captain…excuse me?"

Milch looked up a little surprised. "Doctor Lewis…what…did you need?"

"I was wanting to tell you something…while it's still fresh in my mind. Something about…these Owlams."

"You want to tell me something…extraordinary…about a species that has shown themselves to be extraordinary…already?"

Lewis chuckled. "Yes. It is…" he cleared his throat with a bit of a sour look on his face. "…an anomaly."

"That word has been used *way* too much, lately."

Lewis chuckled again. "Amen! What I have is that… Soolchakan was…is the entity who borrowed that scanner. The DNA is identical. He and the three women that were here…all four…did go through some kind of incredible metamorphosis. How they survived is beyond me, but, they did. The others that showed up…are something altogether different."

"How so?"

"They are definitely Owlam, I have to admit that. The difference is that...whatever happened to the originals...they were able to somehow repair the damage. The later generations show... no sign of this genetic damage that the originals went through. Somehow...in one generation, they fixed...everything."

"How can you say something like that?"

"Those three babies. Bonarain said that she was the one who was the mother of those triplets."

"Yes."

"They're...perfect!"

"What...do you mean? Newborns that are healthy...that's really nothing very new."

Lewis looked up with his eyes closed, trying to think. "Healthy! Yes, healthy." He opened his eyes. "The problem is... healthy is one thing...*perfect* is something altogether different. Perfect babies from...what I could only say...they came out of parents that are...nothing but genetic garbage. What I mean is that...while some of the children that I have seen born...they've been healthy, but, somewhere in their body, there is...one or two...non-perfect things. There's a bone that is slightly disfigured. There's a sinew or tendon or muscle or vein or artery...some part of the body... somewhere that's...*not*...perfect. It can be possibly too long or too short or twisted or too skinny or too fat...or some...imperfection. Those babies...don't have that problem. None of the other Owlams that showed up have any imperfections either. Some of them have scars...but that could be expected, of just about anyone over the age of two. That has nothing to do with the fact that they have figured out a way to bear children...that are 100% totally perfect. No flaws at all. I mean...if a couple were to come to me and they were talking about infertility...and I checked them out and found that they were as flawed as...those four Owlam...I would discourage any form of procreation. In my professional opinion, any...offspring would be...nothing but an amorphous mass that...would have no chance of survival...or a normal life." He shrugged. "But their children... they show no signs of any of the mutated mess that their parents are and…I have no rational explanation for that conundrum at all."

Milch stared at Lewis through bleary eyes. "I'm so tired that I can hardly stand up and you had to hit me with something like that…now. Excuse me, but, I'm going to bed right now. Remind me of that…rather odd and interesting information…later! Good night, Doctor."

Lewis backed out of the doorway smiling. "Good night, Captain."

Milch headed back to his quarters. He did not bother taking the pants or robe off. He just flopped down on the bed. For a few moments he thought of the information that had just been dumped in his lap, in regards to this super race of beings that had undergone this transmutation. Words went through his tired mind. Words like: Interesting, fascinating, incredible…terrifying. He closed his eyes, yawned and let the exhaustion take over.

6

Milch walked into the conference room. He was surprised to see Montalvo already there scrutinizing notes. Upton was there, as well, reviewing notes while sipping a cup of tea. Gomez was the next one to enter the room. He looked around and averted his eyes from Milch, looking a little irritated. He sat down and pulled a keypad and monitor up (so he could write his questions down).

Doctor Lewis, Physicist Jones and Astrophysicist Smith came walking in, each with a cup of coffee in hands. They acknowledged each of the people in the room with a friendly nod.

Yeoman Aua came in rubbing sleep out of her eyes and stretching some of the kinks out of her body. She went to the food dispenser and ordered a large glass of orange juice, pulled it out and went to her seat, guzzling as fast as she could.

The three security personnel came in, Emerson, Avery and Eli, and took their stations.

Emerson walked up to Milch. "When do you think our…"

At that moment, Soolchakan, Bonarain, Kiyalee and Chyning all appeared in their seats.

Emerson's expression turned to one of aggravation. "…guests will arrive?"

Milch answered with a wan smile, a shrug and a mild chuckle. "About now."

"We never really left," said Soolchakan smugly. "Bonarain was the only one who left the ship…a couple of times…to take care of her triplets."

The pathologist, Schmitz, came rushing into the room. He looked around with a bit of a guilty look on his face. "Sorry, I'm a little late…I was doing…" He cut himself off shook his head and took his seat.

Soolchakan looked around. "Aren't we missing someone?"

Milch scanned the room. "Everyone who needs to be here is

here."

"What about that other woman…Kasaki?"

Milch smiled. "She does not *need* to be here. She's currently on the bridge. She is the Executive Officer, or second in command, and the first to take over…if I am not available."

Soolchakan grunted. He licked his lips. "All right! What needs to be covered…today?"

A small light came on, directly in front of Milch. He looked down at his small monitor - Gomez had a question. Milch quickly read the question. He looked at Soolchakan with as friendly a face as he could muster. "We put a planet crawler on…the fourteenth planet. It suddenly showed up, back in the storage bay. We were wondering if you…were the one who put it back there."

Soolchakan smiled. "No, that…was Kazil and Falchon. They…were being a little mischievous. Normally, we would have thrown that thing into Serani Tan. They decided to put it back… from whence it came…until we had a better look at you people and determined your exact policies…in regards to our home world."

"I was wondering," said Montalvo, "…you talk about some of the technology that you had…during your…wars of the past. A lot of advanced offensive and defensive technology. Now, we see none of that. What happened…if you don't mind my asking…to all of that technology? Why did you digress?"

Soolchakan lowered his head, closed his eyes and let his breath out slowly. He looked up and took in a deep breath. "We made up our minds, a long time ago, that nothing…NOTHING… like those…genetic bombs, would ever happen again. We took all of that technology and either destroyed it…or hid it. We watch over our planet. If we find anyone who starts developing, or looking into the advancement of science…we stop them. There will never be another…what did you call it…nuclear bomb? *Not* on this planet."

"That's also why we stop any…out-world intruder from bringing that stuff here and…changing our world," said Kiyalee flatly. "We saw what those things do. We don't want another… nuclear cataclysm."

"But…" Montalvo looked a little perturbed. "You are

denying…all of those other people…any kind of advancement. How do you justify that?"

Soolchakan looked thoughtful for a moment. "I once heard someone say: Everything happens for a reason. If *that* is true… then there was a reason that we - the Owlam - have been selected… for a reason, to be what we are. We have…what most species would consider…an incredible longevity. We have powers where we can stop others on our planet from developing any new…nuclear devices. We also have a tremendous capability of protecting our planet… from species whose technology is far beyond anything we ever had here…initially. Even after 14 millennium, we're still learning new things about ourselves. We are protectors and watchers. We have successfully stopped…over 400 different out-world intruders from claiming our planet as part of their empire."

Montalvo was adamant. "You still deprive the others, of any advancement."

"We protect ourselves…as well. Some of those…who have come up with…*advancements*, have tried to use these things against us. It always seems to be the smartest, most inventive, most creative…most arrogant and ambitious…who want to go after *us*… the Owlam. A lot of them…don't even know that we still exist. The ones who find out…we become their first target, in an effort to obtain global domination. If somebody attacks us - we fight back - with everything that we have. I have had to bury some of my children. *That*…will *not* happen again. Anyone who attacks my children…I kill! I kill without any thought to the survival of the enemy or their culture…or…*their* children. If they feel that the only way that they can survive is to try to kill me…I kill them. Then, I and my children, are safer."

Montalvo looked down and grunted. He looked back at Soolchakan. "Like…who?"

"The Teltermak," said Kiyalee through clenched teeth. "We had a war with them…once. In defeating them, we were merciful in the aftermath, and allowed them to continue to exist. Centuries later…they came after us again. So, the last time, we handled them in a way that it won't happen again…genocide!"

Chyning added her opinion: "They were attacking and killing us...the Owlam...to obtain certain of our internal organs... for some appalling experiments. They didn't ask, they didn't explain, they just killed some of us...without any conscience. They carved out these *chosen* organs...and left the body to rot. All for profit."

Montalvo shook his head. "But...wasn't that the children of the ones that you defeated? I mean, why didn't you try to make a... merciful peace with them?"

Bonarain spoke in a scolding manner. "It wasn't their children! The Teltermak...like us have...uh...*had* a longevity that had not been established as to how long they actually live. While our hair has not turned gray, the Teltermaks, that we warred on the second time, were the same ones, only with gray hair. They didn't learn anything from their defeat in the first war...except how to be a lot sneakier."

Emerson let his curiosity get the best of him. "So...who were all of these people...that you destroyed? Did they all commit the same...outrage against...your race?"

Soolchakan looked thoughtful for a moment. "The Heyyah of Algothon were the first to go. They were the ones who invented that...thing! They also invented the rockets that carried the bombs to each of the cities. We found out that when they launched all of those rockets, they waited for a very windy day. That way, all of the smoke would be blown away...from them, towards the city of Shan-Ad." He chuckled. "A lot of the different Elf races said that that is why the Shan-Ad have such a nasty attitude...towards everybody - they were breathing all of the smoke from all of those launches *and* they got hit with one of the bombs as well."

Montalvo finished making a few annotations on his pad. "Did all of the others make war on you?"

"Yes," said Soolchakan looking off into space angrily. "They came at us and tried to kill us...or claim our guts...or property...or they were mad at us because we had a skill that they didn't have...or they were just plain hateful as well as overly ambitious."

"Some of them thought that *we* were the troublemakers and needed to be eliminated," said Bonarain with disdain. "They said that we were too dangerous and should not be allowed to live. Since they passed that judgment on us, without really knowing us...we took them out."

Montalvo sat there in shock. "You mean...someone just... came up to you, announced that they thought you were a danger and started...just killing?"

"No," said Soolchakan with a little disgust of his own. "They came to us and said that we should all line up, in a neat and orderly fashion and that they would be merciful in the way that they exterminated us."

Bonarain gave a loud grunt of repulsion. "At first, we thought that it was just one race of Elf. We found out as we were exterminating them, mercifully or not, that it was two different species. It was the Beetsik and the Towlayaw-Or. They looked similar. They both had skin that was a brilliant scarlet. That's why, at first, we thought that they were identical. Then we found out that the difference between the two races was height. The Beetsik were about...what do you call it - decimeters?"

"Yes," said Milch. "We usually talk about a person's height in decimeters."

Bonarain nodded. "So the Beetsik were about thirteen decimeters in height and the Towlayaw-Or averaged about seven decimeters."

Several jaws dropped in shock.

"*Seven...decimeters?*" Milch looked around visibly shaken. "That is someone...that would just come up...to about my knee! Thirteen decimeters is somewhere just above my waistline. How could they be such a threat...to you?"

Kiyalee cleared her throat. "Short size doesn't necessarily mean weakness. They came in a large group. There were not that many of us...at that time. They came and *commanded* us to line of for extermination. No trial, no questions...no thought of our feelings whatsoever. Just line up and...die!"

Emerson could not hold back. "Were there any other judgmental jerks...like that? It seems rather stupid to just walk in and order an entire civilization to just...surrender to be slaughtered."

Chyning snickered. "A few years later, the green-skinned Bising showed up. They claimed that the Beetsik and the Towlayaw-Or had every right to come in there to kill us and that we were totally unjustified in turning it back on them. That's when we found out that it *was* two completely different races. We told them that we had a right to live, just like they did and since we gave no one the right to pass judgment like that, over us, we had the right to fight back. They had unilaterally decided that we were wrong and didn't have the right to make any decisions. They were, now, going to slaughter us...so we destroyed the Bising."

Bonarain scoffed. "Yes, the Bising. Next came the Rakab-Rosh, another green-skinned bunch. This bunch, though, had shiny skin. It seems that they had been friends of the Beetsik, the Towlayaw-Or and the Bising. Once again, another bunch who decided that they had the right to decide our fate and that we had no say in the matter. They condemned us all to death, for destroying those others. They commanded us to all line up for execution. They were dispatched...in the same manner as the others."

Milch felt a little troubled. "How...were you able to... completely get rid of all of them...without suffering too many casualties among yourselves?"

"Simple," said Soolchakan whimsically. "We went to Tanani Pay. We reached through Serani Tan to Tok. We grabbed them by the back of their belt and pulled them, from Tok to Serani Tan... and let go. They die in the void of space, in Serani Tan, and their splattered remains slowly float towards that one big star."

Montalvo was trying to take notes as the conversation went on. "I'm a little confused...about the names that you keep calling... these different dimensions. How did you come up with the names... for each one?"

The four Owlam looked at each other a little confused.

Soolchakan shook his head. "What...do you mean?"

"You call one of them, Serani Tan, another is Tanani Pay... how did you come up with these names?"

Bonarain looked at Montalvo as if he were an idiot. "They're numbers!"

"Num...what? How could they be numbers?" Montalvo now looked thoroughly confused. "But...they're not...translating." He looked at Gomez. "Is there something wrong with our translator?"

Gomez looked at Milch. Milch nodded.

Gomez cleared his throat. "It's not the translator, where we're having a problem. The problem is with speech patterns and nouns. When they're saying the name of one of those dimensions, it comes through as a proper noun and the translator doesn't translate proper nouns." He sighed. "Give me a moment, I'll see what I can do...to remedy this problem." He started tapping on his keyboard, while looking at the monitor, with several different expressions on his face. He looked up at Soolchakan. "You said that this dimension...with the one star is called Serani Tan?"

Soolchakan nodded.

"Okay, just tell me the number."

"45," said Soolchakan flatly.

"How about the one...where you can observe us?"

"That's 53."

"What do you call...this one, the Home dimension?"

Soolchakan rolled his eyes. "1."

Gomez nodded. "Could you please...count for me?"

"How high?"

"Just one through ten...for the moment."

Soolchakan sighed. "Tok, saw, pay, ser, tan, hoy, nak, kel, hig, tokani."

Gomez made an entry through the keyboard. "Again please."

Bonarain counted this time. This time, however, they came through as numbers that the crew of the ship could understand.

Gomez nodded in approval. "Are there...any other...ones that you visit...on a regular basis...that you might share with us?"

Soolchakan shrugged. "108 is another one where we can observe from. That one, though we can see you but not hear you. 68 is a very strange one, in that distances are irrelevant. Then...if we want to give someone a lesson...of some kind...where we are trying to stop you from fooling around with us...we take you to 92."

Milch huffed a little. "What's so special about this...92?"

Kiyalee wrinkled her nose in disgust. "It *stinks!*"

Schmitz, the forensic pathologist chuckled. "I've come across some pretty bad smells in my time…what's so bad about this…92?"

Kiyalee looked at Soolchakan. He closed his eyes. Kiyalee got an evil grin on her face. She loudly sucked air into her lungs and vanished. Schmitz let out a surprised squawk and vanished. Several moments later, the two of them reappeared in the conference room. Kiyalee let the air out of her lungs and breathed a little heavily for a few moments.

Schmitz had a look of complete revulsion on his face. He got up, walked over to a small door on the wall (that was a trash chute), opened it, put his face in the opening…and vomited. He walked over to the food processor and ordered a cup of mouthwash. He poured the mouthwash in his mouth and sloshed it around as he walked back to the garbage chute. He spat the mouthwash into the chute. He turned back to the people in the room. "I will never complain about the smell of a rotting corpse…again."

Doctor Lewis chuckled. "Come on, Bob, it couldn't be that bad."

Chyning sucked air into her lungs. She vanished. A moment later Lewis got a surprised look on his face and he vanished. Several moments later both Chyning and Lewis reappeared. Lewis looked a little stunned. He got up and did a staggering penguin walk over to the garbage chute. He opened the chute…and threw up. He spat a few more times into the chute.

Lewis sighed. "I have just experienced something…that I hope I never come across again. I have just…re-defined…the word…*stench!*" His entire body shuddered as he walked over to the food dispenser, and got himself a dose of mouthwash. "I don't really think that it was the smell that made me…lose my lunch. I think that there's some kind of…natural ipecac in the air…or some other…thing…that'll make you regurgitate…in gaseous form. One good whiff…and it's…heave ho! It's still…very shocking." His entire body shuddered again.

Soolchakan looked around the room with a big merry smile on his face. "Anybody else?"

Milch held his hands up. "On, no, no, no, no, no. If two…doctors, who deal with cadavers…all of the time, have that kind of reaction…I don't want to know."

"That one," said Emerson, "…the one you called '68' - you said that distance is irrelevant…what do you mean by that?"

Soolchakan disappeared and reappeared right next to Emerson. He grabbed Emerson's arm and both of them vanished.

Emerson was shocked at first because he was seeing a very unclear blur of colors. The blur only lasted for a few seconds. When his vision cleared, he was looking at… "No, that's…impossible," he said in a shaky voice.

Soolchakan was still standing next to Emerson, still holding the arm. "I looked for a structure…that appeared to be…unique. This one was one of several that are…rather unique. Do you recognize it?"

"Uh-huh," said Emerson weakly as he nodded. He looked at Soolchakan, stunned. The blur of colors went past his eyes again. When his vision cleared, he was once again in the conference room. He looked at Soolchakan, a little frightened. He swallowed hard. He went back to his post, still with that look on his face.

Milch stood up. "Ivan, what's wrong…where'd you go?"

Emerson gave Milch a weak smile. "Paris…I was standing on a rooftop…looking at the…Eiffel Tower."

Milch now looked shocked. His gaze went to Soolchakan. "You were only gone…about ten seconds. Are you telling me that you went over 750 light years…and back…in a matter of…seconds?"

Soolchakan looked smug. "As I said - distance is irrelevant… in that dimension."

Milch sat back down. "Uhm…are there any other dimensions…that you go to…frequently?"

"Not really," said Soolchakan. "Those are the most…useful. Most of the others are too…unfriendly or…of very little use…to us."

Emerson, still with a confused look on his face, spoke up. "Have you found anything…living…in that…stink?"

The four Owlam looked at each other with questioning and thoughtful expressions.

Soolchakan shook his head. "No, nothing that I can remember."

"The only thing that I remember seeing it moving…" said Bonarain, "…was a strand of some kind of…hanging hairy stuff…that was being blown in those nasty breezes."

Lewis smiled weakly. "Foul smelling breezes?"

Bonarain smiled. "Very foul smelling."

Milch let a small sound come out of his throat. "All right, let's get back to these…enemies."

Kiyalee scoffed. "Which ones?"

"The…uh…ones that you say were trying to say that they had the right to just come into your homes…and order you to line up for extermination."

Chyning waggled her head a little. "We did have a short, friendly agreement with the Kalash and the Sodle…for a very short time. It was when we…were trying to figure out what to do about the Turgons."

Montalvo perked up. "Turgons?"

Chyning looked at the other Owlams. They were all staring back at her so she continued her oration. "When that genetic bomb went off in the city of Turgon, it turned them into…mindless, destructive, carnivorous…big nasty animals. They still stand up on two legs, they run like the wind…they have clawed hands, they have long snouts, with big sharp teeth…and a very large appetite for anything…living…that is meat. We saw them attack and kill one of the big plains predators. Only two of the Turgons were killed in the fight. The remaining Turgons ate the predator…and their own dead…and injured colleagues."

Emerson was shocked. "How could you cope with them?"

"We were still under the impression, at that time, that we should live and let live, while we discovered ourselves. The Turgons were not letting anything…live." Chyning cleared her throat with a look of disgust on her face. "While the Sodle and the Kalash were trying to build a wall, to keep those monsters in, we used our dimension shifting capabilities to lead them way out into that northern peninsula on the North Chilamte continent." She shook her head. "They were taking *far* too long to build that wall, so after we got the Turgons all out there on the far western end of the peninsula, we went back and finished the wall...*our* way."

Montalvo cleared his throat. "How were you able to keep away from them...even with that dimensional capability?"

Chyning giggled. "We would let them see us...we would run a little. When they started catching up to us, we would shift to 53. We would then move a short distance away, come back to 1 and the chase would be on again. Occasionally, we'd accidentally come across some indigenous creature...and that animal would become a meal for the Turgons. After they finished...lunching...the chase was on again. We kept moving them west. When we got to the far western shores of the peninsula, we had the vast majority of them there...we went back to the wall and, again, we finished building the wall...*our* way."

Montalvo raise his eyebrows. "*Your*...way?"

Soolchakan gave him a rather nasty grin. "Our way!" His body became transparent. He reached down and touched the table. A section of the table separated from the rest of it and he moved that section forward, into another part of the table.

As he was doing his magic, Bonarain narrated. "We go to dimension number 207. We bring a section of the rock...or in this case a section of the table with us. We move this disembodied section to another part of the table and then bring that section back to 1. Now, both of the sections are *joined* - as one. Now, he's taking that double section and putting it into another section of the table. Once he brings it back to 1, again, you now have a section of the table that is three times as strong, three times as heavy, three times as much mass, therefore three times as much weight...but it doesn't take up any more room."

The monitor in front of Milch beeped. He looked down - at a question from Gomez. He looked up at Bonarain. "Is that how those twelve vaults, on the big moon, were made?"

Bonarain smiled. "Of course!"

"So," said Emerson inquisitively, "you build the wall and trapped those Turgons. You said that there was a short agreement with the…those others…what, if anything, went wrong?"

With bitterness in her voice, Chyning answered. "That *Sodle* trash decided that they were going to take full credit for herding the Turgons and building the wall. We - the Owlam and Kalash - were just their slave labor. They now decided that they were going to feed all of the Owlam and Kalash to the Turgons…then no one would be able to dispute *them*. As it turns out, the Kalash were in complete agreement with us…the Sodle were not going to get full credit. Between our dimension shifting capabilities and the *very* deadly shooting accuracy of the Kalash…the Sodle were now the ones…on the west side of the wall…feeding the Turgons."

Upton shook her head. "Uh…didn't you say…that all of the Turgons were at the far western end…of the peninsula?"

Chyning smiled. "We weren't able to get the wall built instantly. By the time the wall was finished…a lot of the Turgons had found their way back…to the wall. They were probably looking for food."

Kiyalee scoffed. "We found out, once the Turgons had finished dining on Sodle bones, that those beasties were very capable of climbing the wall."

Emerson looked horrified. "How…how'd you stop em?"

"Fire and bullets, mostly," said Bonarain.

"I thought you got rid of all that technology," said Emerson.

"That was about 13,900 years ago," said Soolchakan with a shrug.

Upton sat there with a weak smile. "Are there…still Turgons…even today?"

Soolchakan gave a small disgusted grunt. "Unfortunately, yes! They seem to be a very resilient species. 13,900 years and they're still attacking the wall."

Emerson was in shock. "Who…defends the wall?"

Soolchakan leaned back in his chair and clasped his hands across his chest. "The Turgon Wall has become…a giant prison. On the west side - the Turgons. On the east side, every country throughout the world, sends their criminals…those who are sentenced to either life in prison or at least 25 years imprisonment. They are sent to the wall from all over the world to serve their sentence there...fighting the Turgons. A second wall was constructed, behind the first, to make sure that the prisoners could not escape."

Milch scratched his head. "How...how do you get...the prisoners to fight? I mean...just because someone is sent there for... oh say - 45 years...why should he risk his life, fighting the Turgons... for 45 years?"

With a rather nasty grin on his face, Soolchakan answered. "If you refuse to fight the Turgons...*you* become Turgon food."

Emerson looked off to the side a little perturbed. "That's a pretty good incentive."

Jones, the physicist opened up. "You say this wall has been there for some 13,900 years...how does it remain intact...with all of these attacks?"

"The wall does have to be repaired...occasionally," said Soolchakan matter-of-factly. "One thing to remember though, is the fact that the Turgons...don't know how to use any form of sophisticated weapon. They're not mentally capable of utilizing any weapon...even one that's as complicated as a club. They fight with their teeth and claws...and usually in very large groups."

Upton looked horrified. "13,900 years...how could there... possibly be any form of...other indigenous life...on the west side of the wall? What are they eating? After all of this time...the only thing that they could possibly have left is cannibalism. What are they eating?"

"I don't know," said Soolchakan with a chuckle. "Do you want to go in there and check?"

Upton still looked concerned. "No, we can...take a look from up here." She picked up a pad and punched in a few entries. "I'm going to make sure that we do check. This is...incredible."

Emerson seemed a little amused. "These...Turgons are so dangerous, yet you...haven't pulled one of your genocidal attacks on them. Why have they been allowed to survive, while you eradicated other species?"

"The wall went up, before we became targets," said Chyning. "Since they're trapped on the other side of the wall - they're no threat to us. Plus that area is used to keep felons busy...very busy."

Montalvo looked over a few notes. "You gave us a list of the races that you...exterminated. Did *all* of them come in and just try...to erase you?"

"No," said Kiyalee. "The ones that have tried to erase us - after we got rid of the Sodle - the Yagalom-Ayin and the Maka-Or... these people decided that we needed to be eradicated. They came in to attack, conquer and destroy. We didn't let them. We destroyed them."

Bonarain snickered. "The Gabeesh-Or came in and *informed* us that since we were mentally inferior to them, that they were *self-appointed* masters over us and that we should not argue or interfere with their plans. We proved to them, the hard way, that they could not rule us...without our permission. They fought back...we won."

Soolchakan shook his head. "The Perfor came in with... basically the same attitude. They thought that they were so superior and we should bow down to them...as gods. We proved to them that they were *not* any form of a divine being."

"The Cacktash were next," said Kiyalee flatly. "That wretched bomb that hit their city gave them a tail...with a deadly stinger on the end. They could whip that thing around and kill someone... if they refused any order...with lightning speed. We - as a group - had to all go to 53 and figure out a way to get rid of them...without getting killed."

Kiyalee snickered. "We came up with a plan that just irritated the *peewoden* out of them. While in 53 we would come up behind them with a plate...or a bowl...or anything that we could hold up near their butt...where that infuriating tail was attached. We then moved the plate to 1. It fused with their tail, where the plate was and they lost control of that foul thing. With the plate there, it cut off all blood circulation to the tail - as well as control - and they became... *very* helpless. Then we got rid of them."

Bonarain grunted. "Then came the Noga-Or. They tried to sneak up on us. Sneaking up on anyone...especially at night...when your skin glows in the dark...is rather difficult for anyone. They were under some...idiotic ideology that *they* were the only ones who could see that glow." She got a huge smug smile on her face. "They learned, the hard way, that they were wrong and we got rid of them."

"Then came those dreadful Teltermak," said Chyning through her teeth. "They were the most successful...at killing Owlam. They would hunt down an Owlam...kill...and harvest some of the internal organs...for their ghastly experiments...or mixing of an equally ghastly potion. They were killing us...for profit."

"We thought we killed them off," said Soolchakan sadly. "We didn't. A few centuries later...they came back. They enslaved, or enlisted others to help them with their dirty work."

Bonarain sat there with her eyes closed. "The Teltermak were the brains of the conspiracy, the Axswain were the enforcers and reconnaissance - who kept the others in line. The Teltermak and the Axswain sent in the Neksheth-Or, the Parash-Zanab and the Twakon to do all of the *really* dirty work...while they sat back and reaped the profits."

Soolchakan got a really grim look on his face. "When we finally figured out...who was doing what...we destroyed all of them."

Milch interrupted. "Uh...I can...somewhat...understand this eradication...of the bosses and the enforcers...but you said that there were others who were enslaved...why didn't you just free them and let them go?"

Kiyalee leaned forward. "Dimension 53 is extremely useful. We found a den or two of the...enslaved. They were trying to concoct some plan where they would revolt against *their* captors, conquer them...and take over the organ harvesting operation...with themselves as the leaders."

"The Neksheth-Or, the Parash-Zanab and the Twakon, all found out how valuable our guts are," said Soolchakan. "They decided that they wanted to be the profiteers...instead of the workers. The eradication of those monsters was just as necessary as the extermination of the Teltermak and the Axswain."

"Excuse me," said Emerson, "I've been hearing about some of this bickering and battling between City-States...but I haven't heard anything about any *air* warfare. With the technology that you had... before you were changed...didn't you have any military aircraft?"

Bonarain chuckled. "The big pulse weapons rendered, just about any form of aircraft, as insignificant. There were a few cities that tried to develop some kind of air power...but they had no chance against the big defensive weapons. In order to manufacture a shield, strong enough to defend the aircraft from being shot down... the physical shield was so heavy that the thing couldn't get off of the ground. The electromagnetic defense that could have been put inside the aircraft, to ward off the defensive pulse weapons, gave you no room for anything else to put in the aircraft, as far as offensive or reconnaissance equipment.

Emerson scratched his chin. "Okay, but, you have given us the impression that...the people who attacked you, with the thermonuclear weapons, did so...with some kind of airborne weapon."

Chyning shook her head. "The missiles that the Algothon developed were a complete surprise. The nasty things flew so high that they were - for the most part - completely undetected, until it was too late. Our defenses were designed to take out any airborne attack...that was coming from an altitude that we could see. These went *way* up there and...by the time they were coming down, they were over the central part of the city...and all of our defenses were aimed...out."

"We were completely defenseless...against that...attack," said Soolchakan looking glum.

"So," said Emerson, "there was no other form of useful aerial weaponry?"

Bonarain looked up grimly. "None! After that attack, when we had all been changed...the destruction of the Algothon...ended that threat completely...until things started coming in from outer space. We just used our capabilities to...eliminate our enemies on the land and sea."

Kiyalee looked at her fingernails. "The last bunch that we eliminated was the Zee-Altha. They weren't causing us any personal...grief. They just decided that they were going to be world conquerors. They were going to enslave the entire planet...under their dominion. When they started their attempt at conquest, they had procreated themselves into a huge population. They would go to a village, a city, a town…an area…they would whip the people down and anyone refusing to be subjugated was tortured to death. We ended their campaign…very quickly."

Soolchakan chuckled. "By the time the Zee-Altha tried their stunt…we were using Ragath and Rogoth as a dumping ground, for all of the refuse that was bothering us. We dumped over two million of them…in those two gas giants."

Montalvo looked horrified. "Two…*million*?"

"When you can find them in groups…" Bonarain gave an evil grin. "…it becomes much easier to…move them."

"I can understand that…but…" Montalvo looked around trying to think. "How could you do all of that…without…becoming some kind of psychotic savages yourselves?"

"Self-preservation is a powerful thing," said Kiyalee. "We had very little choice. They wouldn't listen."

Montalvo's shoulders sagged. "That's true, but…two… *million*! How long must that have taken?"

"We don't have to do it one at a time," said Bonarain with a smile. "We have the capability of moving…some rather large amounts of things."

Milch looked a little confused himself. "Like…what? Or should I say how much?"

All four Owlam closed their eyes and started concentrating. An alarm went off in the ship.

Milch immediately got on his intercom. "Bridge, this is the Captain, report!"

Kasaki came back: "We…are suddenly not where we were before. The navigational computer is trying to ascertain where we are…but…it's very confusing."

Milch gritted his teeth. "How so?"

"We can only find one star…and it…I can't believe these readings."

Milch got up and headed for the bridge. He walked in and shouted: "Captain's on the bridge! What is going on?" He looked up at big screen. There was a star on the screen that almost filled the entire thing. "Why are we focusing on that star?"

Lieutenant Leonard Truax was the one currently on duty at the helm. "There's nothing else to focus on…anywhere! That star is the only thing that we can find."

The four Owlam walked onto the bridge.

"Welcome to dimension number 45," said Soolchakan smugly. "Now you can see how we were able to move an entire population… without them being able to do anything about it."

Kiyalee snickered. "People…you are looking at *the* largest single object in all of the 239 known dimensions. The one and only star of dimension number 45."

Milch cleared his throat. "How…uh large is that thing?"

"Extremely hard to determine, Sir," said Truax. "There's so much radiation coming off of that thing…even at this distance it seems to be messing with our sensors."

"How far away are we?"

Truax gave Milch a helpless look. "Again, I can't be exact… but that thing is at least…35 light years away."

"What?!" Milch was flabbergasted. "35 light years…and the thing is filling the entire screen? What's the current magnification factor?"

Truax swallowed hard. "The current magnification is…1."

Milch stood there gawking, slack-jawed, at the screen. He slowly turned his gaze to Soolchakan. "You…pulled the…entire ship…into this dimension? How?"

"The bigger the object, the more concentration and effort it takes…however it can be done…since all four of us were working at the same time."

Milch stared helplessly. "Okay. You've shown us…how you got rid of those…Zalthas."

"Zee-Altha!" said Bonarain impatiently.

Milch smiled. "Thank you…Zee-Altha. Would you be so kind…as to take us back…to our regular dimension?"

The four Owlam all bowed their heads. Moments later the screen blurred with static and then cleared to show they were in orbit again.

"Standard orbit…around the…Owlam home planet…Sir," said Truax with a shaky voice.

Milch looked back at Soolchakan. "Thank you." He let out a big sigh. "Shall we…go back to the conference room?"

"Moving the ship, back and forth, took some effort," said Soolchakan. "We need to go…get a little rest. We'll come back later."

"All right," said Milch nodding his head. "We will anxiously await your return."

All four Owlam smiled and vanished.

Milch shook his head. "Egad!"

"Really," said Truax.

Milch looked to some of the other people on the bridge. "Science section…did you record how that was done…I mean moving from one dimension to the other?"

Lt. Salisbury shook her head. "Sir, we recorded that it happened. The computer is still trying to…compute…*how* it happened. From what I'm seeing of the results…so far…I don't expect anything…positive…any time in the near future."

Milch just hung his head and grunted.

Salisbury giggled. "One thing that we do know about them now…they do get tired…from something."

Milch just looked up and nodded.

Dara J. Carr

7

The group was back in the conference room. They were all going over their notes again. A few looked at some of the notes taken by others. They talked quietly, sipping tea or coffee.

The four Owlam appeared in the conference room.

Soolchakan smiled. "We're back...for whatever questions you wish to ask at this time."

Doctor Lewis cleared his throat. "I have...a question about you...it's something that...is really puzzling me."

Soolchakan chuckled. "What?"

"I...scanned you - all four of you - and each one of the other Owlam - as each one came into the conference room. I...find that it's rather strange that the four of you...seated here...your DNA it appears as if it is..." he looked off to the side trying to think of the right word. "...corrupted. The DNA of all of the other Owlams...it seems as if it is...somehow corrected - even to the point of them... all being so...perfectly healthy. I don't understand how...all of these other Owlamites could be related to you...if their DNA is so clean and yours is..."

Soolchakan raised his eyebrows. "Dirty?"

Lewis grimaced. "I don't...mean to sound insulting...it's just that I don't...quite understand...how. All of the markers line up, which gives me ample proof that you and they are all Owlam. The problem is...how did their DNA get corrected and so perfect and they're so healthy...and yet they came...from what appears to be something that was...so corrupted by those genetic bombs?"

The four Owlam looked back and forth at each other. All four bowed their heads and sat silently for a few moments. Soolchakan looked up. A new Owlam appeared in the room looking a little surprised and suspicious. The new one was female and appeared to be very late in her third trimester of pregnancy. She frowned as she looked at Soolchakan.

"Please introduce yourself to these people," said Soolchakan quietly.

She put her fists on her hips and huffed. She did not look at anyone in particular. She stared off into space. "I'm Jonokee of the Seventh," she said in a rather irritated tone. "What else do you want?"

The other Owlam women looked up at her.

"The ship's doctor is going to scan you and your baby," said Bonarain.

Jonokee looked at Bonarain in anger and shock. She vanished.

Soolchakan sat there with his teeth clenched. "Get back here!" His voice sounded as if it were much louder, deeper and coming from a completely different person…in a cave.

She immediately reappeared looking a little frightened, with her fists covering her mouth. She stared at Soolchakan looking like a guilty child.

Soolchakan went back to his normal voice. "He is not going to hurt you. He just wants to use his instruments to look at your child."

Jonokee stammered a little. "But…wh…what if…he…hurts…my baby? Wh…what…then?"

"If he does anything…stupid or harmful…you toss him into 45," said Soolchakan with a smile.

Kiyalee and Chyning got up, walked over and stood on each side of Jonokee with their hands on her shoulders.

Soolchakan smiled at Lewis. "You may start your scans."

Lewis looked a little nervous. "Yes," he said anxiously. "Just scans…uh…nothing more." He walked up to Jonokee and turned his medical scanner on. He held it near her abdomen as she glared back at him. "I'm seeing that the fetus…has a defective kidney…the left one…I…"

At that moment Kiyalee, Chyning and Jonokee all closed their eyes and bowed their heads a little. Their heads moved a little every few moments as they were communicating telepathically. The expressions on their faces did not change as they continued their chore. Lewis, on the other hand, was gawking at his scanner in complete shock. He was so engrossed at what he was seeing on his scanner that some spittle came drooling out of his mouth. After several moments, the three women all opened their eyes and looked at the doctor. He gave his scanner another look, chuckled helplessly, shut his scanner off and walked back to his seat. Kiyalee and Chyning went back to their seats. Jonokee vanished.

Milch cleared his throat in a very loud manner. "What's going on? What happened?"

All four Owlam looked at Doctor Lewis, smiling.

Lewis looked very rattled. "I...I...scanned...the fetus... and...and I found that...the left...uh kidney was...very defective. Now...I...could help and...and...and repair the...kidney...with my medical instruments. I...uh I, however watched as...those three... did something...and the kidney was completely...repaired..." He looked at the Owlam with fear and awe in his eyes. "HOW?!"

Kiyalee just started giggling. Chyning looked towards the ceiling with a big smile on her face.

"One of our...*acquired*...talents," said Bonarain. "We found that we can...repair...our children while they're still in the womb. When I had my first pregnancy, with Shalam, I discovered this talent. I just thought about what was in my womb...and somehow...I don't really know how...I was able to see him...and everything about him. His...legs were not developing right. They were badly deformed. I started thinking about his legs...how I wished they were...correct. Next thing I knew...his legs started...getting..." She looked up thoughtful for a moment. "...straightened out. His feet had been deformed as well...and I just thought the repairs on them...and it happened."

"This is intriguing," said Lewis looking at Bonarain with child's wonder in his eyes. "What...happens if the child...is born *with* the deformities?"

"We don't know," said Bonarain with a smile. "We've never allowed any child to be born *with* a deformity...or defective organ. We make sure that they're healthy - and perfect - before they're born."

Lewis cleared his throat. "Uh...you said that you...were alone in that first pregnancy...uh figuring out how to repair the fetus. I just observed that it took three…to repair the child of that one…just now…how were you able to do it alone?"

Bonarain looked up and pondered a moment. "I accidentally figured it out…on my own. I did *not* leave the others wondering… how to do it. The first time Kiyalee got pregnant - I showed her how to look the child over and repair anything that was wrong. When Chyning had her first pregnancy…I did the same for her. Now, every new mother…we show her how to do it…during her first pregnancy. After that, she can do it on her own…now that she knows what to do and how to do it." She smiled.

Lewis sat there, still open mouthed. "Incredible!" He looked down and shook his head. "You have a gift that…every mother… throughout the milky way…would love to be able to have - repair a child before birth…to make sure that the child is perfect…when born." He looked back up at Bonarain and shook his head still awed. "Incredible!"

The monitor in front of Milch beeped. He looked down at it. Gomez - who appeared to be pouting a little - had a question. Milch read it quickly. "In the observations, of your planet, we saw that there is, what appears to be, a mobile plant. We're not sure whether it's a plant or animal…or just how to classify this…" He nearly choked on the word. "…anomaly. We were wondering if you know…what this plant, or creature, is and how to classify it."

Chyning chuckled. "That sounds like the Roistee."

Kiyalee looked at Chyning. "Yeah…I was trying to remember that. The Roistee! It is the Roistee."

Milch looked at them expectantly. When he got nothing more, he smiled and cleared his throat again. "Okay, you call this… phenomenon, you said Roistee. What we want to know…is it plant or animal…or what?"

"It just happens to be another Elf race," said Soolchakan. "They have rather dark green skin. They have, what appears to be, leaves growing out of all parts of their bodies. They are…somewhat mischievous…in that they try to hide all of the time…in forests. They don't really hurt anyone or…seem to mean any harm. They are…much like us…they just want to live and be left alone."

Again the monitor in front of Milch beeped. He looked down and his eyes opened wide. He looked at Gomez with a smile. He turned to Soolchakan with a bigger smile. "Would you be so kind as to...give us a list of...all of the different Elf races...and how to recognize them?"

Soolchakan looked a little perturbed for a moment. He looked at his three wives. All three of them shrugged. His eyes dulled and that strange voice came out of him again: "Bikaropin, come to me!"

Once again, Bikaropin was on the ship. He looked a little frightened. "Yes, Drey Sssorg, what is it?"

Soolchakan gave him a smile. "Our...guests...from another world, would like to know about...all of the different races on Heart."

Bikaropin looked confused. "Uh...is that all? I mean you... used the voice...Drey Sssorg...and usually...when you do that...I'm in trouble."

Soolchakan leaned back in his chair. "Really?" He frowned and contemplated the statement. "I didn't..." he looked back up at Bikaropin. "...think that...I did that." His eyebrows went up. "Hmph! Something for me to consider." He chuckled. "Anyway, our guests would like to know about all of the different Elf races."

Bikaropin looked a little fearful. "Do you...want a complete history of all of them...or...what?"

Milch's monitor beeped again. He looked down and read quickly. "No, any complete history can wait. All we were wondering, at this time, is just how many Elfin races there are...and how to identify...the differences between them."

Bikaropin sighed in relief. "Oh, just something...brief...to identify. That's rather easy." His reached out at something with his right arm. His entire right arm disappeared momentarily and then came back with a rather large scroll in his hand. He looked around. "Uh...do you mind...if I could have a place to sit down?"

Lt. Eli came up with another chair and placed it at the conference table for Bikaropin. Eli and Bikaropin exchanged smiles and Bikaropin sat down. He laid the scroll on the table and untied a string that was holding it shut. He started unrolling it. He looked around at all of the people at the table and smiled. "Are you ready?" He smiled and looked down at the scroll. "Let's see, we'll start with the Af-Ad. They're species has very dark brown skin and a very, very long nose. The adult is usually about 18 decimeters in height. They're a very common race and they're usually nice, however they can be pranksters." He looked around the table. "Is that enough of that one...or do you want more?"

Milch smiled. "Yes, just a brief physical description...that is used to identify that race...and commonality, along with a few things about attitude - just fine."

Bikaropin smiled back at him. He sniffed and looked back at the scroll. "Okay, next is the Af-Kawder. Their skin is..." He looked at Milch. "...I believe what you call - caucasian..." he looked back at the scroll. "They are usually about 13 decimeters in height. Their noses are black...and flat. They're not as common as the Af-Ad, however, there are a lot of them. They like to live by their own set of rules. They don't like anyone telling them what to do.

"Next is the Af-Peh. Again, caucasian. They are rather rare. They usually stand about 18 decimeters and they also have very, very long noses. They are very unpredictable in how they act around others." He shook his head. "Very frustrating trying to figure out what they're going to do next."

He looked around again. "Number four on the list is the Akraneth-Ozen. Again caucasian, and somewhat uncommon. Their height is about 17 decimeters. They have pointed ears that grow straight back. They are another bunch that is unpredictable.

"Number five, is the Arba-Kara. They're a very rare species. Their skin is..." He looked up in thought. "...somewhat like the sand in a desert, or on a beach. They're usually very nice people. They stand about 17 decimeters. When they are still, they stand straight up. When they walk or run...they do it on all fours." He looked up thoughtfully. "When they run on all fours...they can outrun some of the equine species." He shook his head. "Very fast!"

He looked back down at his scroll. "Number six - Aree-Ayin. Another caucasian race. Rather uncommon. They stand about 16 decimeters. They're rather nice people, however, somewhat unpredictable. Their eyes…are like reptilian eyes. The pupil is like a slit…up and down. I don't know about their ability to see at night, because they're very reclusive…at night."

He adjusted the scroll in order to continue. "Number seven… Aree-Pawneh. Very rare, very dark tan skin and they stand about 10 decimeters. They have feline faces and they see *very* well in the dark and are usually only out and about…in the dark."

He scratched his nose. "Number eight - Argaman-Or. Another very rare Elf. Their skin is…" He looked up with a helpless smile. "…lavender in color and their hair is…pink!" He snickered. He cleared his throat. "They are about 16 decimeters in height and… they are very strict…about laws. They will recognize your laws, unless that law disagrees with theirs…then they ignore it completely."

Milch noticed that Gomez was rapidly tapping on his keypad, taking all kinds of notes. It seemed rather redundant, seeing as how the computer was recording everything that Bikaropin said.

"Number nine - Arom-Sar. They are one of the most common Elf races. They have pale brown skin, stand 18 decimeters in height…they have absolutely no hair *anywhere* on their bodies." He clicked his tongue. "They will *not* commit to any side…on any discussion…with any person…outside of their race."

He looked around again, then continued. "Number ten is the Atachoy. They are not too common, they are…" He smiled. "… caucasian, they stand a little over 18 decimeters, they're usually very nice people…and they have curly horns growing out of their heads."

Upton the zoologist looked up. "What? Horns? What kind of horns?"

"Uh…they curl back…the base is very thick and they curl back and around."

"Just a moment," said Upton. "Let me show you something." She looked down at her monitor and started tapping on her keypad. She looked up at the big monitor on the wall as a picture of a ram showed up. "Are their horns anything like that?"

Bikaropin looked a little surprised and amused. "Yes, they're almost exactly like that."

Milch interrupted. "Joyce, why do you need specifics on the

horns?"

She looked up at Milch. "Because, I've seen several different Elves with horns. I want to make sure which species has which type of horns."

Milch shrugged and nodded approval.

Bikaropin looked back and forth from Upton to Milch. "Do I continue now?"

"Please," said Milch with a cordial smile.

Bikaropin looked down opened his mouth and then frowned. He looked up at Soolchakan and then to Milch. "The next one...is extinct. They warred on us...and we...got rid of them."

Montalvo, the anthropologist spoke up. "We would like to know about all of them, even if they don't exist any longer. They were still a part of the history of your planet."

Bikaropin shrugged. "Okay." He took in a breath. "Number eleven is the Axswain. They stood about 21 decimeters in height. Don't know what their skin color was, because their entire bodies were covered with short, coarse hair that was red and white striped. Very nasty, evil people. Good riddance to them."

He adjusted the scroll. Number twelve, that's the Ayawl. They're uncommon, they're caucasian, they stand a little over 18 decimeters they are rather nice people...and they have horns." He looked at Upton. "These horns are rather tall they're very thin and they go straight up. Do you have some animal to compare to that?"

Upton smiled and made a few strokes on her keyboard. Several different pictures went across the monitor.

"That one looks about right," said Bikaropin.

Upton smiled again. "Gazelle."

Bikaropin frowned. He shrugged. "They're your animals... you can call em' whatever you like." He went back to the scroll. Number thirteen is the Ayby-Sar. They're uncommon, their skin is...pale brown. They stand about 15 decimeters...and their hair is very curly and very *blue*. This is another race of unpredictable people."

He took in a deep breath and let it out. "Number fourteen is the Barratokefin. They are another uncommon race. They have ebony skin and black teeth. They stand a little over 17 decimeters." He got a sour look on his face. "They are nice people, but they're picky, picky, picky, picky, picky, picky, picky about obeying each and every law, of the land, to the nth degree."

He grunted. "The next - number fifteen - is another extinct species. The Beetsik. A bunch of - so called do-gooders - who had Scarlet hair and skin. They stood about 13 decimeters."

He looked up at Milch. "Number sixteen, is another extinct species." He looked back down at the scroll. "They were the Bising. Emerald colored skin, with *tremendously* large heads. They were usually about 19 decimeters."

He adjusted the scroll again. "Number seventeen is the Bloynid. Unfortunately they're an abundant species. They have dark tan skin, retractable claws, on their hands and feet. They stand about 15 decimeters high and they have the *nastiest* attitude towards…just about anybody."

He looked around. Next, number eighteen…" He took in a deep breath. "…the Bohereth-Rahanan-Or. They're rather common, they have bright green skin, they stand about 18 decimeters and they're almost as nasty as the Bloynid."

He cleared his throat. "Number nineteen - Boyto. Abundant, with pale brown skin…and a forked tongue. I don't think that your scanners can see that…from up here. They're nice enough people though. They stand a little over 15 decimeters."

He reached out with his right arm again and it disappeared again. When he brought it back, he had a mug. He took a long drink from the mug and then continued. "Number twenty…" He snickered a little. "…the Braquarsian. They are somewhat rare, they have medium brown skin, they stand about 18 decimeters, and they're another bunch that's very picky about following the rules…" He giggled. "…and they have these ridiculously long, floppy ears. If they didn't hear what you said, they reach up, hold one of their ears up and ask you to repeat what you said. If they attend some meeting, they usually tie some cloth around their head…in order to hold the ears up, so they can hear everything." He giggled again. "Looks ridiculous."

"Number twenty-one! The Brodiff. They are rather rare, they have tan skin, they stand a little over 16 decimeters, they're rather nice people...it's those...eyes! Their eyeballs are...pure white! There is no iris, no pupil...just white! They're rather difficult to look at...uh...I mean, directly in the eyes...because you don't know what they're looking at."

He shook his head. "Number twenty-two - Byencheel. Yellow skin, rather common race, about 16 decimeters...and they're difficult to look at in the eyes as well. They have eyes that glow...very bright...especially at night."

He looked around. "Is anyone getting bored yet? I mean, other than the Heyyah, there are still 103 races left to cover."

Montalvo looked at him in shock. "You mean to say that there are 126 different sentient races on this planet?"

"Not really," said Soolchakan. "Don't forget...we have had to eradicate seventeen different species...that tried to eradicate us."

"And they're not really all that sentient...especially in the case of the Turgons," said Chyning.

"All right," said Milch looking concerned. "Make the descriptions even...more...brief."

Bikaropin smiled. "Number 23, Cacktash - extinct, poisonous stinger on a tail. Number 24, Chebok, Red skin, about 17 decimeters. Number 25, Cowpa, pale brown skin, 15 decimeters, with very dark blue hair. Number 26, Crobtag, rare, dark brown skin, I think, 18 decimeters and covered with fur...all over. Number 27, Dardsrom, brown skin and pure white hair. About 18 decimeters. Number 28, Dawm-Or, 16 decimeters and dark maroon skin. Number 29, Deserth, caucasian, 17 decimeters, they have pointed ears that point... anywhere - no particular direction. Number 30, is the Destleed. Pale gray skin and brilliant scarlet hair. About 13 decimeters. Number 31 is the D'Hibwar. Brown skin, 18 decimeters and very little hair on their bodies...mostly fuzz. Number 32, Dowb. Brown skin 19 decimeters, and a huge body, that had a very large chest and legs and arms. *Big* body! Number 33 is the Etsba-Tafas. Pale green skin. They can climb anything, because of their very long and prehensile toes and fingers. About 16 decimeters. Number 34 is the Fastern.

They're abundant, dark brown skin, usually over 19 decimeters, nasty people with long fangs. Number 35 is Feeror. Caucasian, 13 decimeters, rather common, another bunch with a nasty attitude... possibly because they're teased about their flat, brown noses. Number 36, Fewedota. Light brown skin, very common, a little over 18 decimeters, and they are all...genetically obese. Number 37 are the Filkont. They have pale brown skin, stand about 14 decimeters, another nasty attitude...they have large ears that actually have bony ridges running from top to bottom." He stopped to take another drink from his mug.

Montalvo was sitting there looking up with almost child-like anticipation as he was getting more and more information on all of these people.

Bikaropin sniffed and adjusted the scroll. "Number 38 is... extinct. The Gabeesh-Or. They had...bony pearlescent skin." He grunted as he looked at the information. "Number 39..." He had a look of disgust on his face. "The Galsino. Nasty, ugly people. They're skin is dirty white, they have red bulging eyes...they have clawed hands, they stand about 19 decimeters. Never trust a Galsino. Even their women don't trust the men. They have to be imprisoned...and procreation is usually a product of forcible rape." He shuddered. "I hate those people!" He took a breath. "Number 40...the Grod. Dark tan skin, about 17 decimeters..." He looked up at Milch. "This is another one that you won't be able to identify from outer space. You have to get these nasty attitudes to smile. They have pointed teeth." He looked back down at the scroll and cleared his throat. "Number 41 are the Gru-Evia. Caucasian, uncommon, about 16 decimeters, rather nice attitudes...huge bulbous eyes. Number 42 are the Hospaltik. Very dark skin, about 19 decimeters, nice attitude, uncommon... they stand about 19 decimeters and their wrists are usually even with their knees. Number 43 are the Ibka-Sar. Uncommon, tan skin, 16 decimeters...they don't have hair on their heads...they have quills... which they can shoot at you...if you really irritate them. Number 44 are the Ikogo." He chuckled. "According to the first generation, they had to move from their original homeland...after the bombs went off. They became amphibious. They can breathe underwater just as easily as out of the water. They are rather rare, very dark skin, 16 decimeters…and another bunch with a nasty attitude. Number 45 are the Itsakan. Pale brown skin, 18 decimeters, never commit to anything…publicly…" He gave Milch a sideways glance. "Their racial marker…they have two rows of teeth. Number 46 are the Kafal-Rooak. Rather rare, ebony skin, 16 decimeters…with a four meter wingspan. They're wings look just like their skin…no special markings. Rather nice people. Number 47 are the Kafal-Shan. Common, brown skin, 15 decimeters, nasty attitude and they have big ugly tusks. Number 48 are the Kalash." He paused and looked up thoughtfully. "We can get along with them…even though they can be a little unpredictable. They're caucasian, somewhat uncommon, about 17 decimeters…and they're another tall-eared race. Number 49…" He took in a deep breath. "…Kalawb-Rahanan-Or! They have a milky-green skin, 15 decimeters, *really* nasty attitude. Number 50 are the Karob-Karaw. Rather rare, dark brown skin, very picky about politeness and protocol…they stand about 12 decimeters because they have very stubby legs. Number 51 are the Kawdar-Ayin. Very rare, dark brown skin, a little over 16 decimeters, rather nice people…with totally black eyeballs. Number 52 are the Kawneff-Arbeth. Common, brown skin, unpredictable…this is another race with wings…these wings, however, are totally transparent. It's not understood how…those fragile wings can keep them in the air. Number 53 are the Kawneff-Ataleff. They're common, pale brown skin, 17 decimeters, really nasty attitude…they have leathern looking wings. Number 54 are the Kawneff-Ebraw. They're very common, caucasian, about 14 decimeters, and they have feathered wings."

Milch interrupted. "These people that have wings…were they all in the same area…when the bombs went off?"

"Not even close," said Soolchakan. "They weren't even on the same continent. As you can see, the…genetic changes were completely random. Some are similar…others…somewhat…to very unique."

Milch nodded in understanding. He looked at Bikaropin. "Please, continue."

Bikaropin adjusted the scroll. "Number 55 are the Kileshon.

They are abundant in population. Pale brown skin, 15 decimeters, nice enough people." He grinned at Milch. "Their racial marker is a black tongue." He looked back at the scroll. "Number 56 are the Kowak-Or. Very rare...we think. They can disguise themselves... against any backing with their chameleon like skin. They're about 16 decimeters and rather nice...when you can find them. Number 57 are the Laubane-Ayin. Very rare, medium tan skin, 16 decimeters, nice people...dark blue eyeballs...and tongues. Number 58 are the Laubane-Or. They're uncommon and they're a race of 21 decimeter albinos. Number 59 are the Leban-Sar. Their faces are a medium brown and the rest of their bodies are covered with long white hair. They're common, 18 decimeters and rather nice. Number 60... extinct...the Maka-Or. They were covered from top to bottom with black fur. Number 61 are the Merkab-Kara. Very common species. Shiny ebony skin 12 decimeters, nasty attitude...probably because of the weird way they look. Their feet and hands are...*extra*-large. Number 62 are the Moplytak. Rather rare, dark tan skin, tallest one of them is 11 decimeters, they're easy to put up with and they have a large protruding forehead. Number 63 are the Mountarn. Common, about 17 decimeters, unpredictable and they have four arms. Number 64 are the Mukgat." He shook his head and chuckled. "They have light tan skin, stand about 16 decimeters...and they have four sexes."

Montalvo looked up in shock. "What?!"

Bikaropin smiled at Montalvo. "*Four*...sexes."

Montalvo was now thoroughly confused...and fascinated. "But...what's...in between the male and female?"

Bikaropin looked at Montalvo, grinning. "The first sex, we will call a normal male. He supplies the semen. The second sex is... what we call the Ovarian. She has ovaries and supplies the ovum. Those two...copulate and the egg is fertilized. About nineteen days later, the ovarian grows...what looks like a blister on the abdomen. They have some kind of...different form of copulation...between the ovarian and the third sex: The Uterine. The very young fetus is somehow transferred from the blister into the uterus. There it gestates for another forty to forty-five days. The Uterine gives birth to a very underdeveloped child. This child is then *given* to the fourth sex...the Mammary sex. This one has a pouch on the abdomen. Inside the pouch is a mammary gland. The undeveloped child attaches itself to the gland and then continues gestation, in the pouch, for another seven months...before detaching itself from the gland...and becoming a full-fledged, independent being."

Upton snickered. "It almost sounds a little like the kangaroo on earth."

Bikaropin looked at her skeptically. "A...little?"

Upton smiled. "The kangaroo only has two sexes. The male and female mate, shortly after conception, the fetus climbs out of the womb, up the fur of the mother and into the pouch...by itself. There it attaches itself to a mammary gland and continues to gestate. We call this type of animal a marsupial."

Bikaropin went back to the scroll. "We'll just leave that fourth sex as a Mammary or Pouch. That's what the Mukgat call it. Number 65 are the Needia. Very rare, dark brown skin, 17 decimeters...and infuriatingly invisible eyes. Number 66 - the Neksheth-Or. They had a metallic bronze exoskeleton. They're now extinct. Number 67 are the Nogah-Ayin. Common, yellow skin, 16 decimeters, unpredictable and they can't hide in the dark...their eyes glow. Number 68...extinct. The Noga-Or. They had fluorescent skin. Number 69 are the Opoteeve. Common, bright green skin, very nasty attitude, 18 decimeters. Number 70 are the Orek-Karaw. Common, light tan skin, nasty people standing over 19 decimeters... and almost two thirds of their height...their legs." He grinned real big. "Number 71 - the Owlam." He stood up and bowed left, right and front. He sat back down. "Number 72 are the Ozen-Ageel. Uncommon, pale green skin, 18 decimeters...extremely long earlobes...usually hanging below the shoulders. Number 73 are the Ozen-Pawthak. Rare, 18 decimeters, rather nice people, and tremendously large ears that are large in every aspect - up, down... and to the rear."

Upton brought a picture of an elephant up on the monitor. "Anything like those ears?"

Bikaropin stared at the picture a moment. "Not quite that

big…but very close. Number 74 are the, now extinct, Parash-Zanab. They had a tail that they could whip the *peewodon* out of you with that thing. Number 75 are the Parenk. Gray skin, abundant population, 16 decimeters and brilliant green hair. Number 76 are the Perek. Dark tan skin, 15 decimeters, very nasty attitude and they have retractable claws - both hands and feet. Number 77 are the P'Lalfan. Common, pale brown skin 16 decimeters, nasty people… who spend most of the time in the water because they have flipper like hands and feet and can out swim most fish. Number 78 are the Plyskenlil. Pale brown skin, 16 decimeters, nice attitude, and they have one horn…that sticks out of the center of their forehead." He looked at Upton. "You got any animals that fit that description?"

Upton gave him a helpless smile. "Only in mythology."

"Really!" He grunted and went back to the scroll. "Number 79 are the Pok-To. Very rare, pale green skin, 11 decimeters, nice but they're pranksters…they are all hunchbacked. Number 80 are the Pryato. Rare with ebony skin, 13 decimeters, rotten attitude…their genetic marker…is hair that is blue on top and purple on the sides. Number 81 - now extinct - are the Perfor. They had shimmering blue skin. Number 82 are the Radli. Very common, dark brown skin, 18 decimeters, unpredictable…and they have a four decimeter long snout, with a BIG mouth and many sharp teeth."

Upton brought a picture of a crocodile up on the monitor. "Is their mouth anything like that?"

Bikaropin nodded his head from side to side as he thought. "Close…but not reptilian."

Upton and Montalvo both got a giggle out of his comment.

He went back to the scroll. "Number 83 are the Raffa. Very rare, light tan skin, unpredictable…and they stand about 22 decimeters. Number 84 are the Ragal and they are very similar to the Raffa, except they are about 23 decimeters in height."

Emerson could not help himself. "23 decimeters…that's…" He raised his right hand way above his head. "…about here!"

Bikaropin nodded with a smile. He went back to the scroll. "Number 85 are the Rahanan-Sar. Common, yellow skin, 19 decimeters, nice people, light green hair. Number 86 - now extinct

- Rakab-Rosh, had dark shiny green skin and mammoth arms. Number 87 are the Rasixer. Very rare, pale gray skin, 14 decimeters, nice people who have these large eyes that allow them to see...even in the darkest areas."

Upton brought several pictures of owls up on the monitor. "Anything like these eyes of these birds?"

Bikaropin nodded. "Very similar." Back to the scroll. "Number 88 are the Roistee. Most people can't tell them from plants. Very reclusive and very hard to figure out their overall population. They're about 16 decimeters. Number 89 are the Room-Ozen. Uncommon, caucasian, 17 decimeters, unpredictable...and their ears go straight back and droop. Number 90 are the Saraff-Or. Rare with dark tan skin, 17 decimeters, and they have reptilian skin. Number 91 are the Sayba-Or. They're about 16 decimeters, abundant population. Their skin is...mottled different colors of brown. Number 92 are the Shan-Ad. Abundant, brown skin, 19 decimeters, very nasty attitude...and they have both fangs and tusks. Number 93 are the Shan-Karoot. They're common, dark tan, about 17 decimeters...they use sign language to communicate...because they have very large, very sharp pointed teeth that usually tears their tongues to shreds...as babies. Number 94 are the Shan-Kawdar. Very rare, ebony skin, about 17 decimeters...no teeth at all. They have carapace like lips...that are very sharp. Number 95 are the Shann. Uncommon, pale green skin, 18 decimeters...no external ear. Number 96 are the Shekem-Rakab. Very rare, pale green skin, 10 decimeters in height, rather nice people...the widest part of their bodies is their...awkwardly wide shoulders. Number 97 are the Skirteer. Common, 15 decimeters, totally unpredictable and they have bright purple skin. Number 98 are the Smameers. Very rare, caucasian, 15 decimeters, unpredictable...half of their height is long legs...which they use to hop. They don't walk. Number 99 are the - now extinct - Sodle. Jet black skin, 17 decimeters and they had multi-faceted eyes. Number 100 are the Soof. Uncommon, orange skin, 17 decimeters and a rather nice attitude. Number 101 are the Taychon. Very rare, bone white skin, 17 decimeters, rather nice... and a very, very, very wide mouth. Number 102 are the Tekaylath-

Sar. Rare, 13 decimeters, Ebony skin, ebony hair, ebony eyes... ebony everything. Number 103 are the Teeve. Rare, milky green skin, 16 decimeters, nasty attitude...and green eyeballs. Number 104..." He got a scowl on his face. "...those wretched Teltermak. Thank the makers, the Teltermak are extinct! Number 105 are the Tendixive. Very common. Ebony skin, 12 decimeters in height... rotten attitude...and they can spit venom...very accurately. Number 106 are the T'Mor. Rare with dark tan skin, 17 decimeters...and they don't have mouths, they have beaks. Number 107...were the - now extinct - Towlayaw-Or. 7 decimeter high, scarlet skinned garbage. Number 108 are the Towlayaw-Sar. Very rare, pale gray skin with crimson hair and about 14 decimeters. Number 109 are the Towtoo. Rare, dark brown skin, 12 decimeters, and they have multi-jointed arms and legs. You don't ever want to try wrestling one of these people. Number 110 are the Tsaylaw-Ozen. They are very common, pale brown skin, 11 decimeters, nasty attitude...with long ears that have...poisonous spikes on the end. Number 111 are the Tunkatil. Very common, caucasian, 14 decimeters, good attitude and horns that stick out the sides of their heads and go straight out. Number 112 are the Turgon. Unfortunately they are common - we think – they're about 19 decimeters in height...they now have animal-like intelligence, they are covered in brown fur, wear no clothing and are carnivorous canine like creatures. Number 113 are the - now extinct - Twakon. They had a metallic exoskeleton. Number 114 are the Untarba. Very rare, black exoskeleton that's rather difficult to penetrate with just about any sword, 16 decimeters, and a good attitude. Number 115 are the Weesak. Common, tan skin, 19 decimeters, nasty attitude...nine fingers and one opposable thumb on each hand. Number 116 are the Wokig. Common, caucasian, 18 decimeters, nice people...they have a bushy yellow mane that surrounds their entire head...even the females. Number 117 were the - now extinct - Yagalom-Ayin. They had shiny brown skin and... some very nasty poisonous fangs. Number 118 are the Yahan-Ayin. Very rare, pale green skin, 14 decimeters...and four eyes that can all look in different directions at the same time. Number 119 are the Yathar-Sar. Rare 18 decimeters, with long thin body fur all over.

Number 120 are the Yazeemay. Common, dark yellow skin, 19 decimeters, nice people with purple eyeballs. Number 121 are the Zaberd. Very rare. Very attractive aqua skin. They stand about 16 decimeters...and have a nasty attitude. Number 122 are the Zaneb-Orek. Common, light brown skin, 15 decimeters, nice attitude...but they have no arms. Instead they have these...whip-like appendages. They use them to pick up and carry, and whip the *peewodon* out of you. Number 123 were the - now extinct - Zee-Altha. Neon green skin." He sat there with a smug smile for a moment. "Number 124 are the Zerowa-Mashak. They are uncommon, ebony skin 19 decimeters... and their entire bodies are covered in quills! Makes you wonder how they...procreate...without causing all kinds of grievous damage to each other. Anyway...number 125 - finally - are the Zer-Sar. Rather common, caucasian, 17 decimeters...with incredibly large, oversized feet." He falsely panted several times. "Other than the Heyyah, that is all of the...sentient types on the planet."

Montalvo looked a little stunned. "Do you...mean that... there are other...races...who are not...uh...humanoid...that are... sentient?"

"There're a few...who hide in the northern wastelands," said Soolchakan. "They are very reclusive, they don't come out very often and they look like some rather large reptiles. Several are capable of flight. The thing that makes us believe that they are *not* any form of *true* reptile is that...just about every other reptile on the planet is cold blooded and couldn't possibly survive in that bitter cold."

Montalvo started getting a little excited about this new information. "How much do you know about them?"

"Not much, really," said Bonarain. "They've never bothered us...so we've never bothered them."

Soolchakan snickered and looked away from Bonarain.

Bonarain looked at him in a hurtful way. "What?"

"Nothing," said Soolchakan in a rather guilty way.

She let out an angry grunt. "WHAT!?"

He glared back at her. "Nothing!"

"It is not nothing," she said angrily.

He glared at her. "Drop it!"

She turned her head away from him, blinked her eyes twice and sniffed. She looked momentarily confused.

Montalvo tried to steer away from that issue. "You said that you have destroyed...completely...all that warred against you. Are there any...who are still living, who never attacked...again...before you started the genocidal attacks on enemies?"

All five Owlam bowed their heads and looked a little sorrowful.

"Excuse me," said Bikaropin - and he disappeared.

Soolchakan gritted his teeth. "We...had...a traitor! One of our own."

Montalvo bit his lip and cleared his throat. "Uh...what... happened - if you don't...mind talking about it?"

Soolchakan looked at Montalvo grimly. "She betrayed...and murdered several of...her own race. She had this grand scheme...of becoming Drey Sssorg and...possibly taking over...the entire Milky Way. First she had to eliminate...all Owlam who were older than she. She had to kill...665 Owlam...in order to obtain her goal. She murdered several that were younger...I guess that was to throw us off the track. We caught her...and banished her...to a place of complete solitude."

Montalvo frowned. "But...you're all able to move from one dimension to another...at will...how...uh...how did, or can you stop her from...moving...somewhere else?"

"By the power of Drey Sssorg. I commanded her, by the power, to not use the dimension shifting capability...ever again. I commanded her, by the power, to stay where she is...no matter what."

Milch was flabbergasted. "So again, you are saying...that this power of yours...is that strong! You can order someone to do something, completely against their will, and they are 100% obligated to obey?"

Soolchakan moved his grim stare to Milch. "That is a fact. The power of Drey Sssorg...is absolute. If I tell one of my children to do something...without using the power...they can do as they like. If I tell them...by the power...to do something...they will do it...*no matter what."*

Emerson cleared his throat. "Most of the different races that we've come across...the act of treason...is usually a capital offense. The offender is...executed."

Soolchakan leaned back and stared down at the table.

Bonarain looked up at Emerson. "She begged to be executed. She said that she preferred...death...rather than hanging around... obeying the power of Drey Sssorg...with someone else having the power. Banishment was a more fitting punishment because it was what she didn't want."

Emerson shook his head a little. "How do you know that she's still there...wherever there is?"

Soolchakan grinned and let out an evil chuckle. "We keep track of her. She doesn't know that we're watching her...but we do. We don't communicate with her, we don't let her know anything. We just watch her."

"Wait a minute." said Doctor Lewis. "If you have her...in some exile prison...some place...what's to stop her from committing suicide? She said that she preferred death to...living in a prison... how?"

Soolchakan let out another chuckle. "By the power of Drey Sssorg. I commanded her to be incapable of harming herself. She sits alone...contemplating her crime...for as long as there are at least twenty Owlam who are older than her, are alive, she is not to be harmed. If it gets down to there being only twenty Owlam, or less, who are older than her...then she *will* be executed. The four of us, here, are all over 14,000 years old. Shalam, the oldest of all of our children, is not yet 6,000. Her age is...under 2,300 years. She is going to be imprisoned for a long, long, long, long time. I really don't care how much it hurts her...she betrayed her own and that's all that matters as far as her permanent punishment is concerned."

8

The ship had been orbiting 'Heart' for six days so far. Milch was in the sickbay, getting one of his scheduled regular checkups. Doctor Randolph was running the medical scanner over him. He noticed that she seemed just a little bit distracted. He cleared his throat, placed his hand under her chin and lifted her head. "Lois, is there something...bothering you?"

She looked rather surprised. "Uh...no...uh...well yes!" She sighed. "I'm the mother of two children...and I never...saw anything like that...in my life."

Milch rolled his eyes. "Huboy! What new...*thing*... happened here at this strange planet of Heart...or should I wonder about anything strange...in regards to these...Owlams?"

She put the medical scanner down. She puffed her cheeks out as she blew air out while thinking. "I gave birth to two children. Both times I had the assistance of our modern technology and... anesthetic capabilities...and a few other little gadgets and gizmos that we use...for medical reasons. Yesterday, however, I witnessed the birth of an Owlam baby. It was...so incredible! I never thought that...I would ever see anything...like that."

Milch snickered a little. "Are you telling me that there's another new surprise, in regards to our unusual hosts?"

She snickered back. "The capabilities that these people have...it's so unbelievable...what they did."

"Okay...WHAT!?"

She was slightly surprised by his abrupt irritation. "Uh... the woman that was giving birth...they had her flat on the table. They were...doing that thing that they do...when they communicate telepathically. They were, probably, all three communicating."

Milch cocked his head to the side. "All three of whom?"

She closed her eyes and put a hand to her forehead. "The woman giving birth, of course, and two female attendants. The pregnant one was sweating and looking a little uncomfortable. They pulled her pants off and just a few moments later, her water broke. She lay flat...and the two attendants...their forearms disappeared. They moved their arms...I guess, into her abdomen. The pregnant one held her breath...and the two attendants lifted their arms. A moment later...their forearms reappeared and...and...they had a newborn...cradled in their hands. The mother's stomach flattened... just a little...after they pulled the baby out. When the mother gave birth...it was little over two minutes from the time the water broke, till the baby was out of the womb. They used that crazy dimension shifting to...get the baby out...without any pain for the mother. I would have loved to have had that...advantage...when my babies were born."

He was sitting there looking shocked. "They...reached through those dimensions...grabbed the baby...pulled it into another dimension...and then pulled the baby out...and brought it to this dimension..." He went through several different thoughts as he contemplated what he had heard. He looked back at Randolph. "From the look on your face, there seems to be another shoe... waiting to fall."

She chuckled nervously. "Is it that obvious?"

"You have a *certain* longing look in your eyes."

"Yes, Sir. I have a question...that I've been thinking about... for some time. I'd love to be able to find out something that's been bothering me about what they've said...and didn't say."

"Gimme a hint."

She sighed loudly. "They say that they're over 14,000 years old...but the oldest of their many, many children is...about 5600." She shook her head. "Why didn't they...worry about any form of procreation...for over 8000 years?"

Milch now felt the same confusion that was bothering Randolph. He shook his head. "That...is a...rather personal question...and a very, very interesting one...as well. I hadn't thought of that..." He opened his eyes wide in wonder. "...over *8000* year hiatus...from the bomb to the babies."

Randolph smiled expectantly. "Do you think that I could ask

them?"

Milch sighed. "So far…they've been very open. They've answered all of the questions, candidly, that we've asked."

She scoffed. "Yeah, but most of that was to the anthropologists, the botanists, the geologists, the zoologists, the oceanographers…all of the sciences. This is…"

"…Part of anthropology," said Milch. "Do you want to be the one to put the question to them…or should we have Montalvo ask the question?"

She smiled. "It is my question…I'd like to be the one who does the asking."

"Okay," he chuckled. "We'll have you in on the next session… with the first generation." He crossed his arms and looked at her a little sternly. "Can you finish my exam now?"

She giggled as she picked up the medical scanner.

Another meeting in the conference room started. This time, Lieutenant Commander Lois Randolph was attending…to ask her question. All four Owlam stared at Randolph with suspicion in their eyes.

After the roll call was entered into the minutes of the meeting, Soolchakan looked at Milch with a bit of a smirk. "What questions do you want answered today?"

Before the anthropologist, Montalvo, could monopolize the conversation, Milch gave Randolph the floor. "One of our doctors has a question about your family. Specifically…well I'll let her ask."

Randolph smiled. "Thank you, Sir." She turned to Soolchakan. "I've been trying to think of some way to ask this question. I guess the best way is to just…blurt it out." She licked her lips. "You said that those nasty bombs went off…some…uh…how long ago was it?"

"Just over 14,600 years ago," said Soolchakan flatly.

"Yes…okay, 14,600 years…but, no children were born…until less than some 6000 years. Why did you wait so long…to procreate?"

The three Owlam women looked around - at anything. Soolchakan looked at the women and grunted in disgust as he realized that they did not want to give the answer to this question.

He took in a deep breath and let it out slowly. He turned back at Randolph with a sad look in his eyes. "We didn't…really know…that we…*could…procreate*…for a long time. Right after the bomb went off…none of the women had any ovulation periods, none of the men could…perform the act." He looked down and sniffed. "It was…an accidental incident…" He gave Bonarain a sideways glance. "…that occurred…where we found out that we…were able to…procreate."

Bonarain sat there, staring at the ceiling, tight lipped as her face turned a little red.

Soolchakan continued: "We have these…strange looking reptilian scales on the back of our necks. For centuries, we… excreted…what we call *Mushoshk*." He looked back at the women and they all were still staring at the ceiling. He cleared his throat and shook his head. He smiled at Randolph. "We did not find out…until the year 15 ATUT what it is. Again, as I said, it was somewhat of an accident." He gave Bonarain a bit of a disgusted stare. "Someone decided to go against, an unwritten law, where we cleaned this *mushoshk* off of our necks…in private. Bonarain decided to be nasty and she got a handful of her *mushoshk* and wiped it in my face. That was the first time that any Owlam wiped their *mushoshk* on another Owlam. For the first time…in over 8000 years…I got an erection." He gave Bonarain a nasty look. "I had a burning in my…body… and it was rather difficult to fight it. For some reason…I'm not sure why…I returned the favor, just to be facetious, I suppose, and wiped some of my *mushoshk* on her face."

Now Bonarain's embarrassment was in full bloom. Her face seemed to be glowing a bright red that rivaled the color of Soolchakan's shirt.

Soolchakan smiled at Bonarain. "I know what I felt. Why don't you tell them…what you felt?"

She gave him a dirty look. She wrinkled her nose at him. She looked at Randolph with a strained smile. "I had a…" She looked up. "…burning feeling…in my body…and especially my…female organs." She looked back at Randolph. "I had an incredibly strong and irresistible desire…to have sex. It was still my understanding, after 9 millennium, that Owlam men were…incapable. I didn't know that he was having an equally strong drive for sex…until he dropped his pants." She blushed again. "When I saw that he was…in full bloom, my pants went down and we…did the deed." She snickered. "We went at it for…quite a while. When we were finished, we both collapsed…in complete exhaustion." She leaned back in the chair. She looked up as if contemplating. "We slept for quite a while, and… after we woke up…I did a mental…search of my body. I knew…I don't know how I knew…I knew that I had conceived." She looked at Randolph with a blank expression. "I knew that I had conceived, I knew that for the first time since becoming an Owlam Elf, I was pregnant…and I knew that the baby was a boy." She sighed. "It was during my pregnancy that I found out…how we can…mentally manipulate the child…in order to get rid of any…defects…in the child." She looked at Soolchakan. "In the year 16 ATUT, the first ever Owlam baby was born. My son Shalam…the first Owlam Elf baby…ever."

Soolchakan turned to Randolph. "86 years later, she had a second son. His name is Monaha. It took a few more years to convince Kiyalee and Chyning…that procreation for them was possible as well. Bonarain gave them all of her…knowledge of how to correct any defects in the unborn child…in order to make sure that the child has a chance at a normal life."

Kiyalee chuckled a little. "In the year 111 ATUT, I gave birth to a girl. Her name is Aya. She became Shalam's first wife."

Randolph looked horrified. "But…that…that's incestuous! You could come up with all kinds of…horrible mutations…and defects."

"Remember," said Chyning. "We can use our mental powers to repair any defect or mutation…while still in the womb. In the year 116, I gave birth to my first child: Zina."

Soolchakan spoke up. "In the year 5575 ATUT, Xachool was born. He is the firstborn…of the 23rd generation." He looked at Randolph. "23 generations of Owlam and we have not had one single child born…with any defects or mutations."

Doctor Lewis was looking rather confused. "Are you saying that the only time…that any of you…have, or can have sex…is when you wipe your…what did you call it - musk - on each other's face?"

Soolchakan gave Lewis a dirty look. *"Mushoshk!"*

Lewis cleared his throat. "Thank you…for the correction," he said with a guilty look on his face.

"The answer is - yes," said Soolchakan. "None of us…of any generation, have ever been able to…have sex or conceive…unless we share our *mushoshk*."

Chyning grunted in a disgusted manner. "That was one of the things that we were hunted for. Some of those monsters that… hunted us down and killed some of us…they got our *mushoshk* for the purposes of making, and selling, a powerful aphrodisiac."

Gomez sat there laughing. "Are you telling me that this… stuff…that comes *only* from an Owlam…it affects other races…as an aphrodisiac?"

All four Owlam glared at Gomez.

"Excuse me," said Upton the zoologist. "It does seem a little strange that a substance, that's peculiar to Owlam, would affect other species in the same way that if affects you."

Soolchakan and Bonarain looked at each other with an evil grin on both their faces. Both disappeared. Kiyalee and Chyning both giggled. Soolchakan reappeared next to Upton and wiped some mucilaginous excretion on her face, just below the nose. Bonarain appeared next to Gomez and wiped a similar substance on the lower part of his face. Soolchakan and Bonarain disappeared again - they both reappeared in their seats…wiping something off of their hands with rags.

Gomez and Upton were both panting heavily with strange looks on their faces. They both tore all of their clothing off and headed for each other. Without any care for who else was in the room, they immediately began having mad passionate sex, right there on the floor, with no concern for whatever or whoever else was in the room.

Milch looked at the four Owlam in horror. "How long… uh…are they going to…keep doing that?"

Soolchakan sat there with a smug smile. "Until they pass out, or the *mushoshk* wears off."

Milch tried to avert his eyes from the activity. "Which do you think will happen first?"

Soolchakan just shrugged.

Milch shook his head with his eyes shut. "Let's reconvene somewhere else. Right now, let's give those two...some privacy." He looked at the four Owlam. "Please join us...in recreation room...4."

The four Owlam disappeared.

Before everyone could get up Milch snarled at Randolph. "Okay, Lois, this was your idea. You stay here and watch them."

Randolph looked mortified. "For...what?"

"To make sure that they don't kill each other...sexually."

"I'll stay," said Doctor Lewis.

Milch looked at him angrily. "I told her to stay."

"I'll stay...as well," said Lewis.

Milch grunted in disgust. "Who's going to represent the medical staff...in the meeting in the rec room?"

"We can send Dodge," said Lewis.

"Dodge is an RN," said Milch. "I want a doctor."

"All right," said Lewis. "The only other doctor, on board, is our pathologist - Schmitz...and he's part of this group anyway."

Milch sighed. "Fine!"

Schmitz gave the nervous laugh. "Uh...whose going to represent the main science section...now that Gomez...is... occupied?"

Milch closed his eyes in disgust. "Someone call Riley. He's the second in science after Gomez."

Yeoman Aua looked around. "Uh...who should we get...to represent the zoology section?"

Milch opened his mouth. He looked over at the *pair*. He looked back at Aua. "Tough! We won't ask any zoological questions... until later." He looked back at the pair. "*Much* later." He thought for a moment. "Either that or we keep it to the ornithologist...what's-her-name?"

"Lt. Maxine Veach," said Aua.

"Fine, let's go," said Milch.

After four hours of questions and answers in recreation room 4, Milch was getting rather concerned. "Look, I know that they probably deserved this...sexual shake up...as a lesson...but...no human being can go this long...without some detrimental problems resulting from it. Is there anything that we can do...to stop their... insatiable...desire?"

Soolchakan chuckled. "Have a woman clean his face off and have a man clean her face off. That way, whoever is doing the cleaning, won't be affected...themselves."

Milch called to Lewis on the intercom. "Did you hear that?"

"Absolutely," said Lewis. "We're on it...right now!"

"Let me know what happens," said Milch.

"Yes, Sir," came the response.

After several fretful moments Milch was hailed on the intercom.

"Go," said Milch.

Lewis came back. "They've both completely collapsed in exhaustion. We examined them and their respiration and blood pressure have gone back to normal...but they're both in a complete state of physical collapse."

Milch looked at Soolchakan, a little perturbed. "Take them to their quarters. No point in trying to wake them up...maybe for several days."

All four Owlam giggled.

"We're getting them to their quarters now, Sir," said Lewis.

"Thank you," said Milch. He looked back at Soolchakan. "Okay, let's get back to those...very *large* blue birds in that country you call...Lower Oosam."

Three of the Owlam looked at Kiyalee. She smiled and gave them, what she knew, about the birds.

Two days later, Gomez tried to attend the conferences. After his head slammed down, with a very loud bang, on the conference table...from falling asleep where he was, he decided to give up and go back to bed...for a while longer. He got up from his chair - and fell flat on his face. One of the security personnel gave him assistance getting back to his quarters.

Upton woke up. She looked up to see one of the nurses at her side. "Hello, Francine," she croaked. She tried to move. She could not. "Can you get me some water…I'm parched…and starving."

Lieutenant Berg smiled back and went to the food dispenser. She came back with a tray containing a very large breakfast. "As long as you've been out, I figured that you might be a little hungry." She put the tray on the nightstand and helped Upton sit up. She moved the tray into position for Upton to eat.

Upton made a few feeble attempts at feeding herself. She whimpered helplessly as she gave up. "I can't…"

"That's all right," said Berg. "I was expecting this. You've been out for some time now." She picked up the glass of water and placed the straw in Upton's mouth. "Drink it slowly, Honey."

Upton sucked in a few mouthfuls and swallowed quickly, then looked up at Berg. "How long…have I been…out?"

Berg looked at her scanner. "According to this…74 hours, 11 minutes and 19 seconds."

Upton looked up in horror. "Seventy…four…hours?"

Berg took a fork and scooped up some scrambled eggs. "Eat now, Honey. You can get all of the particulars…later…after you get some strength back."

Upton chewed slowly and swallowed. She looked up at Berg and opened her mouth for another morsel.

After another day of rest - for both Gomez and Upton - both came feebly staggering into the conference room.

Milch looked at both of them. "Gomez, do you think that you can stay awake…this time?"

"Yes, Sir," said Gomez. "I'm doing fine now. Maybe not up to 100%, but, I'm at least at…80%."

Milch grunted approval. He turned. "Upton, how're you feeling?"

She gave him a tired smile. "I can make it, Sir." She went to her place and gave out a squawk of surprise as she sat down. She gingerly adjusted her position in the chair and looked up at Milch. "I can make it, Sir."

Bonarain snickered. "Uh...Doctor Lewis...why don't you examine her?"

Lewis looked confused. "For what?"

Bonarain rubbed the lower part of her abdomen. "What do you think?" She gave him a haughty smile.

Lewis grunted, got up, went to Upton and turned on his medical scanner. He scanned from the top down. When he got to the lower part of her torso his eyebrows went up. He cleared his throat. "Congratulations, Joyce...you're pregnant."

She glared at him. "That's impossible! It ain't my time of the month." She looked thoughtful for a moment. "Not for...at least another five days."

Lewis leaned closer to her. "There *is* a zygote, a fertilized ovum...in your uterus. You *are* pregnant."

Upton's jaw went slack. She turned and looked at the Owlams.

Bonarain had a friendly smile on her face. "Male Owlam *mushoshk* will make a female...*any* female of any species...ovulate."

Upton went limp in her chair and shook her head.

Lewis cleared his throat. "You can make any important decisions...later. For now, let it be known, that you know that you are definitely pregnant.

Upton looked at Soolchakan showed her teeth and snarled.

After one of their conference meetings, Doctor Lewis again wanted a little private conversation with Milch.

Milch decided that it should be done in his office, next to the bridge. "Okay, Doctor, what's on your mind?"

Lewis sat down after getting a cup of coffee from the food dispenser. "I've been...forbidden by the Owlam...to do any more scans. Okay, for the sake of diplomacy and harmony and all of that good stuff, I stopped. The only thing that I could go on, for a closer look, was the scans that I had already accomplished." He sipped his coffee. "What I found...is...I know you won't like it, but I found another mystery...in regards to our hosts."

Milch groaned and put his hands over his face. He took in a deep breath. "Okay, give it to me."

Lewis chuckled nervously. "These people...have an extra organ that I...just have not been able to figure out. They have a liver that functions very much the same way that ours does. They, however, have...what appears to be an extra liver, just below the normal one. Everything that I see about it, shows that it is definitely a liver...but it does not...act the same way. Our liver helps to filter the body and create over six billion different chemicals that our body needs, daily. This extra liver of the Owlam...it only creates...one enzyme. It does absolutely nothing else. Their systems are, daily, flooded with this enzyme. I have tried to analyze it...but...the only way that I could do a comprehensive analysis...is...an autopsy. I don't think that...any of them are willing to die for our...curiosity."

"What about...a biopsy? Do you think that they'd go for that?"

"I...would have to dig...too deep. I would have to go around, or through a couple of other organs...and I don't know...if I'd have the right place. I don't know...how much it might hurt them."

"So...this one has to remain a mystery."

"I'm afraid so, Sir. I wish I could find out more, but with this I can't. We have established a good relationship with them and I certainly don't have any desire to do any damage to that. The results could be very..."

"Yes, they could be...very...."

For two years the ship orbited the planet of the "Heart". When they departed, they had a wealth of information about the star system and all of the indigenous, life forms, sentient or otherwise.

Milch sat in the conference room pondering. He sipped a cup of hot chicory coffee. He looked out the observation window and sighed. "Captain's log, computer annotate the time. The...Heart system is inhabited by a...sentient species...that guards this system with an iron fist. They are an autocracy...but not an oligarchy. If anyone decides to visit this system...I absolutely suggest that you come here as a friend. Come here as an explorer and not a conqueror.

Be polite, be truthful and be friendly. Your lives absolutely depend on it. The Owlam can be kind to…polite visitors. They *are* incredibly harsh…to the…impolite. According to what the Owlam are telling me…this ship is the first one…to have a round trip voyage, in regards to this system. All others…who came here as conquerors…lost everything that they sent in. They stopped smashing the…enemy ships…into the moons, over 3000 years ago and started dumping them into one of the five gas giants that are in this system. No telling how many…crash sites there are in those planets…the Owlam didn't count them. I repeat…be very polite and be completely truthful." He licked his lips. "End of entry, log and save."

What you have read so far is what the Owlam told the out-world people. Read on…let's go back 14,600 years ago and find out what really happened.

9

Soolchakan had been sleeping…until someone grabbed him by the back of his belt and bodily tossed him out of the Tram shuttle car. He landed hard on his shoulder. He looked around bleary-eyed through his hangover. He turned back to see the Tram door close as it departed on the rail for the next station. He struggled up and tried to chase the Tram. He got to the end of the high platform where he was forced to stop running, or staggering. He stood there helplessly rubbing his sore shoulder.

"Hey!" He shouted at the occupants, even though, he knew that they could not hear him. "I'm supposed to get off at…uh…" He looked down at the palm of his left hand to see what he had written there. He blinked twice to try to focus on the writing. He looked back at the retreating Tram. "…station 585, you…you…" He snarled in frustration. "This one is…" He turned and looked up at the sign at the top of the platform. "…it's…uh station…" His shoulders sagged. "…585." He turned back to the Tram. "Thank you very much… you…" He gave them an obscene gesture.

He started stretching some of the kinks out of his body. He attempted to dust the dirt off of his regular black uniform. That sore spot on his shoulder might have a bruise on it, however his main concern at this time was whether or not the shirt had been damaged. He looked back down at his hand and gasped. There was a time annotated there…he was supposed to report to station 585, no later than…he looked up at the clock on the landing and let loose with a stupid giggle. He was actually early. That wretched supervisor would not be able to give him any grief about being late…today…at least… for once. He carefully felt the back of his left shoulder, looking for any frayed material. He sighed with relief, when he found nothing wrong.

He scratched his buttocks and felt the flask in his back pocket. He chuckled. He was early getting to work…today…good reason to celebrate, with a drink. He pulled the flask out, unscrewed the lid, put it to his lips and raised it, ready for the burning of the liquor in his throat…only there was nothing but air. He frowned as he pulled the flask away from his lips. He knew that he had filled it before leaving his quarters. He wondered if he had drunk all of it… before getting to 585. Then he noticed a crack and a small hole in the bottom. He clenched his eyes and teeth in anger. This flask that had served him well for so long…was now worthless. He threw it as hard as he could, off into the weeds that surrounded the platform. He started checking his pants for dampness and found none. He rubbed his hands on his pants below the pocket and smelled his hands. If the liquor had leaked out and dried up, the smell would still be there. He stood there looking at his hands, contemplating in complete confusion. The flask was empty, his pants were dry and there was no smell. That could only mean that the flask had been broken in his quarters and he had tried to fill a broken flask…and there was a puddle of that expensive liquor…on the counter…back in his quarters. He stood there just shaking his head. He was going to have to survive the entire night…without a drink.

He turned to go to the elevator. He belched. Something lumpy and foul tasting was in his mouth. He went back to the edge of the platform and spat the nasty stuff out onto the Tram rails. He spat several more times trying to clear his mouth, while wondering what he had eaten that could taste that bad…coming back up.

He sighed and had a feeling in his bowels. He raised his right leg and pushed. A rather loud noise escaped his rectum and he grimaced. "Oh no," he moaned. "That was juicy." He could feel several "lumps" in his pants. He awkwardly waddled to the trash can on the platform. Maybe there was something in there that he could clean out his pants. He looked in and growled in anger. The one time that he needed to use some of the garbage…to get garbage out of his pants…someone had done their job and emptied the garbage. He was going to have to sneak into the work area and hope that he could get to the bathroom…before anyone noticed that he was there. Good luck to that hopeless plan.

He walked over to the elevator and angrily punched his

control number on the keypad. The pad came out and he licked it. He turned away from the automatic sliding door and rubbed his head to try to think of what to do. He leaned back so that when the door opened, he would know without having to watch it. The problem was that as he turned, the door opened and he fell backwards into the elevator…banging his already sore hung-over head. He snarled as he got up. The door closed, he punched his secondary code onto the keypad and the elevator doors closed and it started the automatic descent.

The door to the elevator came open and standing there was the on-duty Red Shirt. So much for trying to sneak in.

He sighed. "Officer Grade 5 Soolchakan, reporting for duty, Sir."

The man standing in front of him sniffed twice and wrinkled his nose as he stared at Soolchakan. "I'm Officer Grade 3, Whallek… and I'm wondering…did…you…?"

"No, Sir," said Soolchakan. "I got off of the shuttle and…found out…the hard way…that some…animal got up on the platform… and dumped. I wasn't expecting anything like that…and that's why I didn't notice it…until after I stepped in it."

"How could that have happened…those platforms were built high…to avoid that kind of thing?"

Soolchakan rolled his eyes. "How should I know? I wasn't there when…whatever animal did it…did the deed. Don't worry though, I cleaned it up."

"Well, you didn't get your boots completely cleaned. Get to the bathroom…before you stink up the whole office."

"Might be too late for that," he chuckled nervously as he headed for the bathroom.

He stopped by the emergency closet. They always had extra uniforms in there…for any unseen emergency. Usually the emergencies that had been planned for did not include someone *soiling* their own garments. He got lucky. There was a pair of pants in the closet that was his size. He grabbed it quickly and almost ran to the bathroom.

He pulled his pants and underwear down. He growled at

himself. He had forgotten to get some new underwear. Too late now, just get it later on another bathroom break. He cleaned himself off and threw the 'soiled' garments into one of the bags that was supposed to be used for burning classified out-of-date documents. He sealed the bag, got dressed, discreetly headed out of the bathroom and got to the burn bag storage vault before anyone noticed what he was doing. He tossed it into the vault and breathed a sigh of relief.

He went back to the main office, to find the Red Shirt.

"Again, Sir, Officer Grade 5, Soolchakan, reporting for duty. Which color am I wearing today...Yellow or Green?"

Whallek looked at him and smiled. "Today...Officer Grade 5, Soolchakan...you are the Red."

Soolchakan looked at Whallek dull-eyed. "Huh?"

"The personnel in this area have been minimized...for this evening. It seems that Kalash has started some...new major offensive against Galsino. Our high command is not expecting any attack from Galsino...aimed at us. They're going to be too busy defending their city against the Kalash offensive."

"So what's going on with minimization here? Is there maximization somewhere else?"

"There are numerous reports of Axswain activity, to the north."

"Oh...so...right now..."

"Most eyes are looking north...at Axswain."

"What's to stop the Axswain from coming around...here?"

Whallek closed his eyes and grunted in frustration. "Are you familiar with this part of the perimeter?"

"No, Sir, I've usually been assigned to...oh...somewhere between station 108 and 167."

Whallek shrugged. "Okay." He took in a deep breath. "Just north of here, around station 590, there is a huge gorge. There's no way that the Axswain could get there artillery across the flimsy bridges that cross that gorge. The outside farmers all use small carts, in order to get their merchandise across. They're usually praying that the things don't collapse as they cross. I don't think that the Axswain would, or could, use those bridges to mount any form of an offensive here. It would take just too long to get any sizeable force across."

"All right, Sir, so I'm the Red Shirt. How big is the...staff that's going to be here?"

"You, one Blue, one Yellow and one Green."

Soolchakan stammered in shock. "But...just...four... people...for the whole operation...all night?"

"As I said: Total minimization...for this area...tonight."

Soolchakan just shook his head. He looked up at the clock. "So, where's the rest of my team?"

"Hopefully, they'll get here soon and we can get the shift change done. Right now, go get your Red."

Soolchakan smiled as he went to the closet. He checked the sizes of the Red Shirts as he slowly looked them over. Tonight...he was the big shot. Yes, there would only be three others, however, he would still be in command. He found the correct size. He pulled it off the hanger and slowly put it on. He stared at himself in the mirror, grinning as he adjusted the shirt. He headed back to the main room.

"Officer Whallek, who are the personnel in my...minimized staff, tonight?"

Whallek looked at the roster. "Your Blue Shirt, tonight is Officer Grade 6, Bonarain. The Yellow Shirt is Officer Grade 6, Kiyalee and your Green Shirt is Officer Grade 7, Chyning."

Soolchakan wanted to run. "Bonarain? Chyning? It's a bad enough thought...having to put up with...just one of them...all night. Both of them?! That's..." He covered his face with his hands and growled. "Somebody hates me!"

"Kiyalee ain't nothing to be proud of either," chuckled Whallek. His demeanor changed radically. "But then...neither are you," he said angrily.

Soolchakan just snarled back at him.

At that moment the elevator door opened. In walked a brown haired woman...who was wearing just way too much makeup.

Soolchakan closed his eyes. "Bonarain," he muttered sullenly.

"Really?" Whallek followed her to the closet.

Bonarain was flipping through the Green Shirts for her size.

Whallek tapped her on the shoulder. "Are you Officer Grade 6, Bonarain?"

She glanced back and looked at him through bloodshot eyes. "Yeah!" She turned back to the shirts and then jerked her shoulders up in fear. She turned back to Whallek looking up at him in fear. "I…mean…yes, Sir…Sir." She turned her face away grimacing.

Whallek cleared his throat. "Tonight…Officer Grade 6, Bonarain, you are the Blue Shirt."

Her shoulders sagged down and she looked up at him astounded. She opened her mouth and tried to say something. She looked around in confusion for a few moments. "Me…uh…me…a…Blue…?" She closed her eyes and shook her head. She looked back at him. "Me…a Blue Shirt tonight?"

"Yes," he said lackadaisically. "The vast majority of the personnel are currently looking to the north at the Axswian. The west side…has been drastically minimized."

"Oh," she said. She swallowed. She looked up at him and gave him a helpless chuckle. "Blue?"

"Yes, Blue."

She clasped her hands together beneath her chin and smiled. "Thank you…Sir." She headed for the closet where the Blue Shirts were kept.

Whallek went back to stand near the elevator door.

Soolchakan joined him. "I hope that the one who gets the Yellow is just as happy."

"We'll see."

The elevator door opened. Two women came out of the elevator, one with flaxen hair the other with black hair.

Whallek immediately confronted them. "Which one of you is Officer Grade 6, Kiyalee?"

The flaxen haired woman shrank away from him with terror in her eyes. "I…just got here…I didn't do anything…did I? I mean…I'm on time…I didn't…what'd I do?" She glanced up at the clock and then back at Whallek.

"You haven't done anything wrong, I'm just informing you,

that tonight, you are the Yellow Shirt."

It took a moment to register. Her expression changed from fear to confusion to a big smile. "I…I'm a…Yellow…tonight?"

"Yes," said Whallek looking a little disgusted.

The black haired woman looked up at Whallek, totally perturbed. "Do I get any good news…or is it the usual…Green Shirt?"

"You're a Grade 7…the one and only Grade 7 on the shift. Everyone else outranks you…what do you think?"

Chyning's shoulders sagged. She mumbled a very insincere congratulations at the elated Kiyalee and headed for the Green Shirt closet, grumbling all the way.

After checking her make-up (for the third time since arriving), Bonarain went to the food vendor. "Nothing like a good hot mug of kwatha to start the shift," she said merrily as she pulled the steaming mug out of the slot. She got a spoon and sifted in the hot brown liquid, looking for one of the tasty, big lumps to chew on.

"We may have a big new re-write on Regulation number 3," said Whallek.

Soolchakan yawned. "Oh really, and why's that?"

Whallek leaned close to Soolchakan. "It seems that a certain young…Officer Grade 7…named…Chyning…keeps consuming kwatha, somewhere near a console…and has spilled it on the console…and ruined about eight consoles. If she gets some kwatha… make sure that she doesn't get anywhere near a console…with the food."

Soolchakan looked at Whallek in shock. "Wouldn't there be…some notice in the briefings about that?"

Whallek let out a grunt of frustration. He went to the supervisor's console. He hit a few keys and pulled up the shift briefings…from the last 84 days. He turned to Soolchakan looking a little facetious. "Why don't you catch up on the briefings? Maybe you can get your…crew caught up as well."

"Uh…I can't…get on that console. I've never…been a Red Shirt before. I don't have a password," said Soolchakan helplessly.

Another grunt from Whallek. "Tonight, you have been

assigned as the Red Shirt...by High Command. Tonight, you have the capability to get information...on this console. There's still a level of security that says you can't get...certain information, but you're still the supervisor...tonight and have the capability to use *this* console." He punched a few keys and the monitor showed that Whallek was logging off. "Try it!"

Soolchakan sat down and fed his identification and password into the computer. A few seconds later the greeting came up on the monitor: Welcome, Red Shirt Soolchakan. He sat there stunned (with a stupid grin on his face). Confirmation that tonight, he *was* the boss.

"Now, call up the briefings," said Whallek flatly.

Soolchakan chuckled. He tapped in the dates that Whallek had put in and the computer responded, showing that he was on page one of the briefings from the last 84 days. He was on page one...of 277 pages.

Whallek leaned close to Soolchakan. "Looks like you've got some reading to catch up on."

Soolchakan stared at the screen in horror. "I guess... it will help...to pass the time...without...complete boredom."

"Just keep Chyning away from any console...with kwatha." He cleared his throat. "Are my people relieved from duty yet?"

Soolchakan swallowed. "As soon...as my...Blue and Yellow... are fully briefed and satisfied...yes, you and your people can go." He felt a little giddy over the thought of being in command. It was a new feeling that made him apprehensive as well as glad.

Whallek stood up. "Green Shirts...relieved! Blue and Yellow, brief your relief and you can go!"

Soolchakan started reading. He prayed that some of this stuff would be interesting...so he would not nod off and have to read it...over and over and over and over...till the shift was over.

Whallek leaned down again and spoke softly. "I suggest that you start with today's briefing. Once you've got that out of the way, you can go back...and get caught up."

Soolchakan chuckled nervously. He went to the end. Today's briefing consisted of six items. He scanned them quickly at first. Then read them. Boring, boring, boring, boring...slightly interesting... and boring. He felt sick. If the other 83 briefings were...even close to this...it was going to be a very, very long night.

Three of the swing shift personnel, wearing Blue, went to the closet. They tossed the Blue Shirts into the laundry and retrieved their own possessions.

Chyning was slowly walking past, with a fresh steaming mug of kwatha.

"Don't go near any consoles with that food," said Soolchakan sternly.

Chyning looked back at him a little angered. She headed over to the break table, sat down and sipped slowly while sulking and giving Soolchakan some dirty looks.

He hit the key to look for "key words". He punched in Chyning's name. There were nine references. He went to each one and found that all nine were admonishments for Chyning causing a huge amount of damage to consoles and how she was being forced to pay for all of them. He coughed a few times, attempting to try not to laugh out loud. He knew that the consoles were expensive and if she was paying for nine consoles...she did not have much money left for entertainment...or living, especially at the salary of a Grade 7.

"Okay, you can go...thanks," said Kiyalee.

Two women wearing Yellow Shirts headed for the closets and changed.

Whallek waited for the last of his crew and headed to the elevator with them. Just before the door closed, he exchanged salutes with Soolchakan.

While Bonarain and Kiyalee were watching their monitors and Chyning continued sulking, Soolchakan decided to check up on his crew. He did a "key word" on Kiyalee. There were nineteen entries. He frowned as he saw it. He called them up and started reading. He was horrified when he saw that all nineteen were safety write-ups on her...in regards to the incorrect handling of firearms. There was a special entry on her that stated that she was forbidden to get anywhere near one of the big, energy pulse cannons.

He decided to check on Bonarain. She had fourteen write-ups…on her attitude. Very bad attitude…and spending too much time on doing her makeup. He looked up and saw that she *was* currently paying more attention to the makeup than her console.

He looked around the room fearfully. He did a "key word" on himself. There were 67 entries. He closed his eyes and let out a long sigh. He knew that he had a few blemishes on his career, however, 67? He pulled them up and started reading. He felt a little sick. Admonishments and letters-of-warning in regards to slovenly appearance, drunkenness, tardiness and bad attitude. He reached for his flask and…gritted his teeth in disgust as he remembered where the useless flask was now.

He sighed as he realized that here at 585 was the worst leader of a crew of the worst of the worst. Leading was a drunken slob. Following was a megalomaniacal make-up queen, a walking safety hazard that was considered most likely to kill friend than foe and a clumsy fool that seemed quite capable of demolishing the entire station with just one mug of kwatha.

High Command had decided that 585 was the least likely place to be attacked and had dumped the garbage here.

He pulled up today's briefing. "Heads up!" He read off the boring and redundant information. "Any questions?" He saw three blank stares. "Today's briefing is over." He went back to page 1 of the 277. He went to the food vending machine and got his own mug of kwatha, gave it a few sips and started reading…hoping that he could stay awake.

Bonarain grunted in disgust. "I know about all of you losers. I've heard about you." She let out another huff of disgust. "The reason I'm here, is because…I didn't spread my legs for one of the Senior Officers at that party."

Kiyalee laughed. "What? You think you're better than any of us? Guess again!"

Bonarain looked back at her angrily. "I refused to go on a date with Nakalak. He's married! He came up to me during a party…and he asked me on a date. I reminded him that he *is* married, refused to go out with him…and I've been in the dump ever since."

Soolchakan growled back at her. "I was at that party. I

remember that incident. The only reason he asked you on a date was because he lost a bet. As I recall, he was very relieved when you said no."

Bonarain glared back. "Oh, don't give me that nonsense!"

"I was there too," said Chyning. "Being a Grade 7, I ended up being one of the food servers. Whenever you're in that position, the upper crust tends to talk freely in front of you...like you're part of the décor...and ignore you. I was carving pieces of meat, while Nakalak, Jahong and Booxo were arguing about something. I forgot what they were arguing about when they bet on what they were griping about and said that the loser had to ask for a date from the most useless woman there. They all three saw you, looked at each other and laughed. I watched them go over to Pultairn and ask for confirmation of what they were saying. After a short conversation, Nakalak was hanging his head while the others were giggling. Then he went over and asked for the date." She showed a big toothy grin. "He *was* very relieved when you said no. He swaggered back to the others with a big smile on his face. They all had sour looks on their faces, because he didn't have to...pay off...and waste his time on you."

Bonarain looked hurt. "You...you made that up!"

"No she didn't," said Soolchakan dryly. "I was there too. I heard the bet."

Bonarain looked back at her monitor. "Well...at least I'm not paying for a dozen ruined consoles," she muttered bitterly.

Chyning stood up and spat back. "NINE! It's not twelve it's nine!"

Kiyalee snickered. "You're not so holy. You're paying for a console too. I was there...I remember. You were so busy re-re-re-redoing your makeup when the motion detector beeper went off on your monitor. You spilled something...pinkish...on the console, it shorted and burned out." She giggled. "Nearly caused a fire."

Chyning looked off into space and muttered. "I wish I was the one who was selling you all of your makeup. I'd have all nine consoles paid for and I'd be able to retire...soon."

Soolchakan had heard enough. "SHUT UP, ALL OF YOU!

You can't bellyache and watch your monitors. You can gripe at each other later…after this shift is over."

Bonarain gave him a nasty look. "Don't get sanctimonious on us. We all know your record."

"Maybe so," he snarled back. "Tonight, though, *I am* the Red Shirt. I don't have to worry about being sanctimonious, I'm in charge. Get back to your monitors and shut up."

Bonarain and Kiyalee both snarled as they turned back to watch their monitors.

Chyning was giggling in the break area…when she suddenly spilled her kwatha…all over herself. She gasped as the hot liquid soaked through her pants.

Soolchakan was grateful that she was not on a console at the time. "Clean it up!"

Now it was Bonarain and Kiyalee who were giggling.

Chyning made an awkward walk to the bathroom, still letting out little gasps of pain as she tried to hold the hot, wet fabric away from her body.

When the door closed to the bathroom, the three remaining people laughed out loud.

"She is clumsy," said Bonarain through her giggles.

"Keep her away from the consoles…with kwatha," snickered Kiyalee.

'Keep her away from any more kwatha,' thought Soolchakan. "Just keep your eyes on your monitors," he said through his chuckles. "Every now and then, we'll give you some relief." He sighed. "With only four of us…it is definitely gonna be a long night…and we'll all probably leave in the morning…with bloodshot eyes."

Bonarain sighed and leaned back as she watched the monitor. Kiyalee hit a few knobs, doing some adjustments as to where she was focusing her attention.

A short time later, Chyning came out of the bathroom - wearing nothing but her underwear. She looked up and saw that all three were staring at her. She muttered at them angrily. "Are you enjoying the show?"

"Finish getting cleaned up," said Soolchakan dully. "Then go clean up your mess in the break area."

Bonarain and Kiyalee started giggling again as they looked back at their monitors.

Chyning grunted and found something to wear in the spare uniform closet. She took the shirt and pants and headed back to the bathroom. Several moments later she came back out of the bathroom. She had a look of disdain on her face. "Did you want to do an open ranks inspection?"

Soolchakan shook his head and sighed. "Just go clean up your mess."

She sighed as she got out a clean Green Shirt and then went to the utility closet for a mop. She came back out with the mop and bucket.

Soolchakan saw what she had. "Aren't you forgetting something?"

Chyning looked confused. "Huh?"

"What about a broom?"

She wrinkled her nose at him. "The mug didn't break. It landed in my lap."

"Oh," said Soolchakan flatly.

Bonarain and Kiyalee both chuckled again.

After the cleanup, Chyning was putting away the mop when Bonarain gasped. She leaned closer to her monitor. "Did you...see that?"

"I saw something," said Kiyalee in surprise.

Soolchakan and Chyning both headed for vacant monitors. If something was spotted, all personnel were to be at the monitors - for any emergency that might come up.

Soolchakan looked at his monitor. "What's going on?"

"A stampede," said Bonarain. "One group of those herding beasts...they're stampeding...for some reason."

Chyning got her monitor focused in the right area. "There... behind the herd...one of those big carnivorous predators...it's ripping the throat out of...the one who ran the slowest."

Kiyalee saw the bloody attack and gagged. She put one hand over her mouth and the other on her stomach.

Soolchakan growled. "If you're gonna puke…don't do it on the console!"

She leaned over, pulled a trashcan out from under the desk, put her face in the can and threw up.

Bonarain huffed in disgust. "Take that…mess…somewhere else…in the bathroom."

Kiyalee got up, hugging the trashcan in front of her…waiting for another heave. She walked slowly with her face aimed at the trash can - just in case. She went into the bathroom and closed the door.

Chyning chuckled. "She wouldn't last very long in the offensive forces…not with that weak stomach."

"That's probably why she's a defensive watcher," said Bonarain.

"No," said Soolchakan. "If she ever gets her hands on a weapon…it's more likely that she'd shoot a friend rather than a foe." He huffed and shook his head. "She's as clumsy with weapons as Chyning is with kwatha."

Chyning snarled at Soolchakan.

Bonarain shook her head. "Has anyone ever bothered to name all of those wild creatures out there? I've often wondered why we call all of them…almost the same thing."

Soolchakan sighed. "If…one day…all of these wars cease… maybe then we'll be able to sit down and name all of them. It's possible that…a long time ago…someone did give them some kind of name. With all of this fighting, between all of the City-States, who cares what those things…any of those things…are called?"

Kiyalee came out of the bathroom drying her hands on a towel. "Is that…horrible spectacle…over?"

"No," said Bonarain. "The big nasty just ripped that herd beast's stomach open."

Kiyalee gagged, clapped her hands over her mouth and ran back into the bathroom.

"Cut the nonsense," said Soolchakan growled angrily. "Quit watching that messy feeding and look out for any Galsino forces."

Bonarain and Chyning immediately adjusted the search zones on their monitors…with tightly clenched lips.

Soolchakan went to the bathroom door and knocked. "We're back to looking for Galsino and not animal carnage."

Kiyalee opened the door. She looked up at Soolchakan somberly and sniffed. "Thank you." She went back to her station.

Chyning went back to the break table.

Soolchakan went back to the supervisor's desk - and brought up the 277 pages of briefings that he needed to read.

They all sat there in silence for quite a while. The sun was giving off its last glare through the windows as it slowly sank down below the western horizon.

They all knew that it should be a very quiet night. The main clue was that now, all of the different herding beasts were calmly grazing. This gave the indication that there was virtually no threat from the Galsino forces - not tonight. Any force headed towards the city of Owlam from Galsino would spook the beasts and send them off on another stampede.

The dim night lights in the office area came on. Bonarain and Kiyalee continued scanning. Soolchakan continued reading. Chyning was sitting in the break area reading a book, waiting to relieve anyone on a monitor, for whatever reason they needed to be relieved.

Kiyalee got up and stretched. "Chyning, I need a bathroom break."

Chyning marked her place in the book and headed for the console.

"Don't bring any kwatha with you," chided Bonarain.

Chyning wrinkled her nose at Bonarain as she sat down and started checking the scans.

Kiyalee headed for the bathroom, still stretching some of the kinks out of her muscles.

Soolchakan was on page 82 when the monitor just went dead. He looked around a little surprised and noticed that everything in the big room that ran on electricity, had gone dead. "Just what we need," he growled. "A major power failure."

According to safety protocols, when all power was cut off, the locks on the armament closet would spring open and heavier blast proof shaded windows would fall into place in front of the observation windows.

All three of the people in the room were muttering some form of disgusted thought about the power failure. They wandered around in the darkness, hoping that it was just some form of a drill.

Kiyalee came out of the bathroom. "What happened, the toilet won't even flush…"

At that moment, all four were blinded by a light, coming through the small watch portals, the likes of which, none of them had ever encountered before. They all four dropped to the floor, shielding their eyes from the tremendous glare.

As the glare subsided, Bonarain got up and looked out through one of the observation holes. "Look out there!"

Soolchakan got up. "Look at…what?"

"The shadow of that tree…it's…going away from us. The sun still hasn't gone completely down. That shadow should be coming towards us. It's going the other way. There's…something…in the city…causing that unbelievable glow."

Soolchakan looked up at the trapdoor in the ceiling. "Up top! We can't see a thing in here…all of the windows are facing the wrong direction. Get a weapon and let's get up top."

Soolchakan, Bonarain and Chyning headed for the weapons locker, while Kiyalee jumped up on the desk, directly below the trapdoor, in order to open it, so they could all climb the ladder to the top of the bunker.

Bonarain looked up at Kiyalee and had just enough time to scream: "NO!" She turned around and shook her head. "You hollow-headed *bimyock!*"

Kiyalee had violated the first safety regulation, concerning the trapdoor. According to the regulation, you were supposed to hit the two releases clips, while standing in the area where the door would swing down - AWAY from you. She was on the wrong side and when gravity took over and the door (which weighed approximately eight times what Kiyalee weighed) came swinging down, slammed into her - chest level and up - and knocked her flying over a bank of consoles, onto the floor.

Chyning was on the floor, holding her stomach, laughing hysterically at the sight of Kiyalee getting knocked teacart over teakettle and flying through the air.

Soolchakan growled in disgust. He reached into the arms locker and pulled out one of the big pulse rifles. He hit the power switch…and nothing happened. He growled again, shut it off, dropped it and grabbed one of the long range sniper rifles. He checked the magazine in the gun, saw it was fully loaded and grabbed three more magazines. He put the extra magazines in his pockets. He reached down and grabbed Chyning by her collar. "Stop laughing and get a gun! We don't have time for any of this stupidity!" He dropped her down to the floor.

Chyning's head hit the floor and she sobered up… momentarily. She got up, still giggling and headed for the arms locker. She got one of the small caliber rifles and three magazines.

Bonarain armed herself with a rifle and extra magazines and then went to check on the fallen Kiyalee.

Kiyalee was getting up…with a very fat lip and a bloody nose.

Bonarain helped her to her feet. "You're supposed to open it from the *other* side you *bimyock!*"

Kiyalee looked back angrily - through crossed eyes. She steadied herself against the back of the console desk. She looked around dazed.

Bonarain huffed. "Go get a gun and get up top!"

Kiyalee looked at Bonarain angrily and tried to uncross her eyes. She started staggering towards the gun locker bouncing from the wall to the console as she made her way on rubbery legs.

Soolchakan had climbed up on the desk, under the trapdoor and pulled the lower section of the ladder down. He looked up into the pitch black hole of the shaft that went up to the top. He shook his head and grunted as he slung the rifle over his shoulder and started climbing. All of the rungs were square except for the last ten at the top. This way, in the dark, you would know that you were all the way up. He heaved a big sigh and started climbing. He banged his knuckles on two of the rungs as he was climbing and had to quickly come up with a new way of climbing…without destroying his hands.

It was slow, however, he finally found a round rung and started counting. He found round rung number ten and then the upper trapdoor. He had to feel in the dark for the five security locks.

Bonarain climbed up the ladder until she hit her head on the bottom of one of Soolchakan's boots. "What's taking so long?"

He gritted his teeth. "If you hadn't noticed, it's kind of dark in here. I have to find the locks by feel. Just shut up and let me do it…or would you rather get up here and push this heavy door up?" All he heard was an exasperated grunt. He continued searching for the locks. Once again he skinned a knuckle as he slid the back of his hand along the bottom of the trapdoor. He decided that it would be better to slide his hand slowly, again, in order to save some of his skin. "Lock one is popped," he said flatly. He continued. "Lock two, popped." For some reason the designer had put them in irregular places, just in case an enemy from the outside was trying to get in. "Lock three, popped…lock four, popped…okay, lock five, popped." Now he was going to have to use his shoulders to push the door up. This one was nowhere near as heavy as the one at the bottom. The bottom one was supposed to be able to withstand just about any kind of blast - from either a hand held bomb or a high powered pulse gun.

Before he could push the door up he thought about the rifle. If he pushed up, with the rifle over his shoulder, it could damage the weapon. He had nothing on his belt to hold the gun and the infernal passageway up was too narrow to hand the rifle down. While he was pondering this dilemma, he grabbed the sides of the ladder… and just happened to find a hook…the hard way. He grunted in pain as his right hand throbbed for a few moments. He pulled the rifle sling off his shoulder and hung it on the hook. He then braced himself, using a ladder rung, the wall and his shoulders to push up. He was extremely grateful that it was a lot easier to push it up than he thought it would be.

Remembering how bright that light had been at first, he closed his eyes, in case the light was still anywhere near the original intensity. As the trapdoor opened, he slowly opened his eyes. The glow up here was bright, however, not to the point of burning his eyes out of their sockets. He pushed the door out of the way, grabbed his rifle and climbed out.

There was a strange orange glow coming from the inner city. He looked in total horror at the spectacle in front of him. All of the city was in flames. Near the center was a huge column of dark smoke that rose up to a giant black cloud that was overhead. The cloud was easy to see from the glow of the burning city.

He stumbled several steps away from the trapdoor and fell to his knees. Bonarain was the next to exit the trapdoor and her reaction was similar to his. Chyning came up next and nearly passed out when she saw the city.

The three of them knelt there in shock looking at what used to be their homes…now in flames.

Several shots were fired from the bottom of the escape shaft from a rifle on fully automatic. The bullets ricocheted a few times in the shaft, pinging off of the steel sides and the rungs.

Soolchakan grimaced. "Did someone give her a gun?"

Chyning looked concerned. "Isn't it…proper protocol…for all of us to be armed?"

He simply snarled back at her. He crawled to the opening and hollered down…without exposing his head to the opening…in case there was any more gunfire. "Kiyalee, put your rifle on safety!"

She mumbled something. Talking through her fat lip was a little hard to do.

"Put it on safety!"

Several more bullets pinged their way up through the shaft.

Soolchakan growled at himself again. "PUT YOUR GUN DOWN!" He listened for a few moments. "Did you put that thing down?"

"Yuh," came the response.

"Walk away from it!"

"Yuh!"

He put his rifle down next to the shaft. He climbed back down the ladder to check on…whatever had happened. He found (the hard way) that at least two of the rungs had been hit by bullets and now had some rather sharp edges from the damage of a bullet penetrating the rung and creating a circular flash of sharp edges. He reached the bottom.

Kiyalee was standing away from the shaft with her head down and her hands clasped tightly at her waist. She looked like a guilty child who had been caught with her hand in the cookie jar.

In what little light there was, he checked the rifle that she had used to blast up the shaft. She had nearly spent over half of a 60 round magazine. He grunted in disgust. He took the rifle back to the ammunition locker and chose a different rifle. This was a small caliber sniper rifle, however, it did not have the capability of firing on fully automatic. Kiyalee did not move except to watch what he was doing.

He came back to where she was standing. "Get up that shaft," he muttered angrily.

"I...dun hab a gun," she mumbled through her fat lip.

"I'll carry the thing up the shaft," he snarled through his teeth. "Now, GET UP THERE!"

She crawled up on the desk and ascended the ladder. He sighed and shook his head in disgust as he followed her up.

"There's a rifle just outside the shaft up there," he said. "DON'T TOUCH IT...AT ALL!"

She grunted. She got to the top and left the shaft

He was close behind.

Kiyalee was on her knees staring at what used to be the great metropolis of Owlam. "Momma! Momma! Muh momma...is sumwhuh in dat...fire!"

Soolchakan laid the rifle for her, next to her and shook his head. "Could...Axswain...possibly have had some weapon capable...of...*that*?!"

There was a sudden brilliant glow that came from behind them. Again all four were on their knees facing away from the glow and shielding their eyes because it was so incredibly bright. When the brightness subsided, they turned and even though it was quite a distance away, they saw another giant black cloud with a column of smoke.

Bonarain let out a gasp of horror. "Whatever...hit us...they hit the city of Galsino as well. That...that cloud is...approximately where Galsino sits."

Chyning pointed off to the northwest. "There's another one!"

They all looked where she was pointing. That horribly brilliant glow was not so painful to the eyes at the distance that this one was.

Bonarain again did some quick geographical figuring in her head. "That's the city of Kalash!"

Soolchakan was finally able to find his legs. "Are...the Axswain that powerful?"

Bonarain turned her attention off to the north. "OH! Oh, my...there's another one...and it's about where Axswain should be. They just got hit too."

Soolchakan was almost in tears himself. "Who else...is close enough...for us to see...another one of those...?"

At that moment another one went off, far to the east.

Bonarain swallowed hard. "That...that's Teltermak." She turned her gaze to the southwest. "The only other one that we could see would be..." At that moment, far to the south, another one of those glows went off. She stood there staring helplessly. "...the city of Zee-Altha."

Soolchakan fell to his knees again. "Owlam...Galsino... Kalash, Axswain, Teltermak and Zee-Altha. How many...more of the...City-States are...gone...that we can't even see from here?"

Small and large white particles started slowly floating down on and around them.

Kiyalee looked at the sudden shower of white. "Is that... snow? There shouldn't be any...snow...for another three months."

Chyning caught a piece in her hands as it wafted down. "It's...ash of some type. Its ashes from the city...raining down on us. It's whatever...is burning...in the city."

Bonarain fell to her knees. She was in too much shock to cry. "Whatever...or who...ever," she said in a dead monotone.

They heard some popping, buzzing and humming start up. Emergency generators were kicking into gear, lighting up the area and turning all of the power on in the area. Soolchakan was the first to get back to the trapdoor. He went down as fast as he could.

Bonarain was next followed by Chyning and Kiyalee.

He immediately headed for the radio. There was some chatter and static going on already. He listened at first, trying to hear if there was any answers. So far it was just questions and no one seemed to have any answers. All of the chatter was coming from the perimeter Watch Sector locations. Nothing was coming in from Command Central.

He looked back at the three women. "I don't know what to say to you. This is my first command…and it may be my last. We'll just have to wait and see…until someone from…whatever is left of…the Command Section calls us with instructions…if there's any Command Section…still left."

Kiyalee looked at him with worry on her face. "What happens if you're the only Officer Grade 5 left?"

"They had to have someone…on the…northern perimeter… facing the Axswain area who…is at least a Grade 2…at the *very* least. If they don't, then we'll see what happens from there." He sat down and tried to listen to some of the chatter.

The three women sat down as well.

He looked at Kiyalee. "Uh…where is…your weapon?"

Kiyalee hunched her shoulders and grimaced. "I…go get…"

"NO!" He looked at Chyning. "You go back up and get her weapon. I don't want another…shootout in the shaft…at, or for, nothing."

Chyning looked at Kiyalee disgusted. She put her rifle down and headed for the shaft. After coming back down with the rifle, Chyning sighed and looked over at the dispenser. The kwatha was still hot. She went over and poured a fresh mug for herself. She looked back at her colleagues. "Does…anyone else want a mug?"

Bonarain scoffed. "How can you think of eating or drinking at a time like this?"

Chyning shrugged. "Go ahead and starve if you want to. It may be a…long while before we get any more of the good kwatha. I…don't wanna miss this opportunity."

Kiyalee sighed and went to pour herself a mug. She looked over at Soolchakan who was listening intently to the radio. She poured another mug for him and took it to him. Chyning poured another mug and offered it to Bonarain. Bonarain sighed and accepted it with a nod of her head. They all sat back sipping kwatha and listened to anything on the radio that might give them a clue as to what had happened and what was going to happen.

Bonarain looked up surprised. "What...did...you hear that?"

Soolchakan looked at her just as surprised. "It sounded as if...as if Nagasoom...is still alive. He must've been on the northern perimeter...he was watching the Axswain...himself...just in case they did try something crazy."

"Master Officer, Neenatha is still alive as well," said Chyning. "I heard her responding to Nagasoom."

Soolchakan let out a growl of anger. "That was Master Officer, Jahong! That...man is still alive."

"I just heard Officer Leader, Wymini," said Bonarain. "It seems that there was a whole bunch of high ranking officers on the northern perimeter." She sat back and let out a long breath. "It seems that most of our high command is still...very intact...on the northern perimeter."

A warning light went off on one of the consoles. Soolchakan went to that console and looked at the code that was on the monitor. He read it and looked up at the trapdoor. He let a grunt of frustration out. "No one closed the top trapdoor! We're open to attack...from the top!" He glared at Chyning. He ran to the ladder and started the long climb up. When he got to the top, he was winded. He looked around to see if anyone - friend or foe was up there. No one.

He checked the keypad at the top of the inside shaft. It was on...now. He punched in his code and it gave him a menu. He hit the code for closing and locking the trapdoor. He went down three rungs as the electricity and hydraulics kicked in and the door closed. He listened as all five locks engaged. He breathed another sigh of relief and descended back to the office. Once again at the bottom he glared at Chyning.

He stood on the desk at the bottom of the ladder. He reached up to a smaller trapdoor near the big one and opened it. Another keypad - that was now functioning - was exposed. He hit the menu key and then hit the code for closing the heavy door. He watched it slowly go back up. After the locks re-engaged, he checked them just to make sure. He sighed.

10

"Ladies, are there any new developments on the radio?"

Bonarain looked up. "They're counting...whose left," she said sadly.

Chyning had a tear running down her cheek. "They figure... that everyone in the inner city...is dead. There's no way to put out... any of the fires...because...all of the emergency...responders...were in the middle of those...fires...that destroyed the entire city." She pulled a tissue out of a box and blew her nose. She sniffled a little as she threw the used tissue away. She looked up at Soolchakan. "Nobody! Nobody who was in the city is...alive. All of the younger... children...citizens...were in the inner city...for protection. All the citizens of Owlam...below the age of...20...are dead. All of the High Command...that were at Command Central...are dead. Anyone... that any of us knew...who were in the inner city...and even some of the outskirts...are..." She covered her eyes with her hand and started sobbing.

Kiyalee was just sitting there holding an ice bag on her lips with tears running down her cheeks and sniffling.

Soolchakan checked the locks on the trapdoor again. He jumped down off of the desk. He went to his station and listened to what was going on. One of the Officer Leaders was taking a roll call from each of the watch stations. He was currently up to station 299. It was going to be a while before he got to this one.

"Get back to your consoles," said Soolchakan quietly.

Bonarain huffed and glared at him. "The consoles! What are we looking for?"

"It sounds as if anyone who was in the inner city...is dead. Anyone who was not...in any inner city area...survived. We don't know...how many of the Galsino...were not in...their inner city... of Galsino." He cleared his throat. "Some of them...could be wandering...around out there...and..."

Bonarain and Kiyalee both sighed and went back to their assigned location. Chyning sat at the break table hugging her knees to her chest.

Soolchakan was not sure exactly what to do. He decided that until the roll call came to station 585 he might as well continue reading the briefings that he had missed. He was up to page 195 when Officer Leader Jeejow called out for a personnel count at station 585.

Soolchakan keyed the microphone. "There are four of us assigned here tonight, Sir. Red Shirt, Officer Grade 5, Soolchakan. Blue Shirt, Officer Grade 6, Bonarain. Yellow Shirt, Officer Grade 6, Kiyalee. Green Shirt, Officer Grade 7...Chyning...all personnel at this station...present and accounted for, Sir."

Jeejow did not respond, he simply continued the roll call to station 586.

"Only eleven more stations to talk to," said Chyning in a dull manner. "Has anyone been listening...or adding up...the numbers of...whoever is left?"

"It wouldn't really be an accurate number," said Bonarain. "It would just give us...the head count of...whoever was on duty... when that...thing happened. There's probably a few people who... were still in the Trams...when it happened. There's probably a few people in the outer farm areas that are still alive. It might be several days...before any...accurate count can be finished."

A bell went off as a new message came across the Supervisor's monitor. Soolchakan read it and sighed. He hung his head for a moment.

"Well!" shouted Bonarain. "What is it?"

Soolchakan looked up. "Surprise, surprise...we are under emergency conditions. As a result of this emergency condition... it is unknown...at this time when any of the personnel who are in the watch stations...will get any relief. We are...*stuck*...here...until further notice." He hung his head.

Bonarain stood up with her teeth clenched. "What about... those of us who didn't live in the inner city? I can walk to the perimeter Tram rails...in just a short time. I need to check my quarters...to see if anything is left."

"I live just across the street from the rails," said Soolchakan angrily. "I don't know if my place is intact, but I'm pretty sure that it is. I'd like to go back and check...but we have our orders! Sit down and do your job!"

"But...but...my things...I need to know!"

"If there is anything intact, considering the situation, it just might be confiscated for whatever purposes that High Command can think of!"

She huffed as she sat down and turned to her monitor.

Kiyalee took the ice from her mouth. "What's that...strange glow off to the west? The sun...it's gone down...but there still seems to be some kind of...twilight...just off to the west."

Soolchakan grunted. "That glow...is the city of Galsino in flames. That glow is...a reflection off of the upper clouds...from the fires."

Bonarain pounded her fists on the desk. "That's another reason to go check my quarters. Maybe those fires...that they can't put out...haven't reached my quarters...yet. Maybe I can save... something."

Chyning laughed out loud. "The only thing that you care about is your wretched makeup kit. You've got most of that here with you. What could you possibly have back at your quarters that's more important, to you, than that?"

Bonarain started heading towards Chyning with a look of rage in her eyes. Chyning stood up ready to accept the physical challenge.

Soolchakan slammed his fist down on his desk. "SIT DOWN, BOTH OF YOU! We don't have time for any stupid little petty squabbles. Don't start acting like those demimondaines near the..." He stopped himself and sighed. "...the demimondaines that...are probably nothing but charred remains...now that that section of the city...is...completely gone."

The two women still glared at each other. Bonarain gave Soolchakan another nasty look and went back to her console. Chyning sat back down and glared at Bonarain.

Soolchakan looked back at his console. There was a new

message on it. He turned to Chyning. "Since you're the only one who is not busy, I need you to inventory our food stores…here at the station. Again, we may be here for…quite a while…and the higher ups want to make sure that we've got plenty of food."

Chyning looked up and shook her head. "There's usually an emergency supply in that big locker off to the side. There's always enough food in there for ten people for thirty days. Inventory complete!"

Soolchakan glared back at her. "What's in the NON-emergency food stores? They want to know that as well. They also want to know any count on the extra…emergency stand-by clothing that we have in those lockers. They also want a count on any weaponry that we have available here…pulse weapons, projectile weapons, ammunition and caliber. Go count it…count it all…and it better be accurate."

Chyning sighed and hung her head. She got up, and walked slowly to another desk. She picked up a pad and stylus and began slowly counting all of the non-emergency, day-to-day rations that were in the hot and cold food storage units in the break area.

Soolchakan went back to the briefings.

The large room was very quiet for a while as Bonarain and Kiyalee continued their scans, Chyning was counting and Soolchakan was reading.

Bonarain sat back and stretched. "Has anyone checked the bathroom…since *she* went in there…barfing?"

Soolchakan realized that he had to go. "I'll check," he said dully. He got up and went in, remembering that she had said that the electric flusher was not working…at that time. The smell hit him as he walked in. He stopped breathing through his nose as he looked around the room. He shook his head as he walked over to the toilet, pulled some paper off of the dispenser and raised the seat. He relieved himself. He was grateful when he hit the flusher and found that it was now working. He straightened out his uniform and left the bathroom. After closing the door, he took several deep breaths. He went back into the main part of the room to where Kiyalee was still scanning. "Kiyalee, you need to go clean up your mess."

She looked up confused. "But…didn't you…flush…yourself? I heard the flusher."

"I flushed…that which was *in* the toilet. When you went in there and…purged…your aim was…even worse than your aim with a gun."

Both Bonarain and Chyning made groans of disgust.

He leaned down closer to Kiyalee. "GO into that smelly bathroom and…clean up YOUR mess…Now!"

She got up with a look on her face as if she might just lose it again. Soolchakan sat down and continued monitoring on her console. She walked towards that bathroom. Her walk was like that of a condemned prisoner headed to the execution spot. She got to the door and opened it. She let out a disgusted "Oh!" as she turned her head aside and walked into the bathroom…leaving the door open. Several times while she was cleaning, she came out to get a breath of fresh air.

"Thank you," said Bonarain quietly.

"You're welcome," said Soolchakan just as quietly.

While she was in there cleaning, they heard the flusher go off at least a dozen times.

They did not see anyone at all for the next four days. All communication was through the main intercom. They were not allowed to leave the office area so they did not know whether or not the Trams were still running. If they were, no one was getting off or on at station 585.

Soolchakan desperately needed a drink. He had not gone without any liquor, or any alcoholic beverage for that matter, for more than one day. Inside he was a mess. Outside he did not look much better. There was absolutely nothing anywhere in the station that could satisfy his craving for alcohol.

Bonarain was constantly complaining about how she had run out of some of the different stuff she used for her makeup and how she was having to substitute things that just did not go together.

Kiyalee kept on grieving about her mother. It seemed that after all of this war time that these four had gone through, she was the only one that, at that time, still had a living relative. Now, like the other three, she was alone. Her upper lip finally healed in that time and the other three were the only ones who knew about her bad encounter with the trapdoor.

Chyning had finished the inventory, after two days, and was taking it to Soolchakan. On her way, her clumsiness hit again and she dropped the electric pad that contained all of the information. The part that held the battery in place came off and the pad shut down. She looked at it in horror. She picked the battery up and put it back in. The screen gave erratic readings for several moments and then shut down completely. She let out a growl of frustration.

Soolchakan sighed. "Did you back it up as you went along?"

She looked up at him angrily. NO...I didn't think it was necessary!"

He sighed and hung his head. "Do it again."

She gave each one of her colleagues a nasty glare as Bonarain and Kiyalee sat at their monitors chuckling. She went to a desk, pulled out another one of the electronic pads...and set it on an automatic hookup with one of the, currently unused, consoles. She went back to recounting all of their current supplies. Twice during this inventory, she dropped the pad again. One of those times, the screen shattered. She had immediately run to her working console and was very relieved that the counts were constantly being sent to the console and she did not have to go back and count any of the past ones again.

The watch stations had not been set up for this kind of emergency. There were no shower facilities. Each one of them had to take turns going into the bathroom and taking a sponge bath. While one was in the bathroom, the other three just had to...grin and bear it...for a while.

Soolchakan pounded on the bathroom door. "What's taking you so long in there? You're taking longer than any two of us combined!"

"I'm doing my makeup," shouted Bonarain.

Kiyalee and Chyning both groaned.

Kiyalee was sitting at a watch console with her hands on her thighs and her legs bouncing with a look of desperation on her face.

Chyning had both fists in between her legs, pushing against her crotch and her breath was noisily going in and out of clenched teeth.

Soolchakan growled. "You can do all of that...*chokwad* makeup and primping, out here in the hallway mirror. Don't forget that there are others of us...who need to use that toilet!"

A moment later, a comment from behind the door: "I'm not dressed!"

He grimaced as he pulled his fist back as if he were going to punch the bathroom door. He dropped his arm down and opened his eyes and his mouth in thought. "Nobody is interested in that right now. All we want to do is get to that toilet. You can finish dressing and primping out here. Now, you either let us in there, or YOU are going to have to be the one who cleans up three puddles of pee out here!"

"Give me a moment," shouted Bonarain.

"You've had too long a moment already," snarled Soolchakan. "NOW!"

A few moments later, the door was unlocked. Bonarain came out, with her makeup half done, looking at him, rather angry. She was wearing her underwear and a Blue shirt. She was carrying the rest of her clothing and her makeup kit.

He pushed passed her, closed and locked the door and headed for the toilet. He stood there with a stupid grin on his face, sighing with relief as he urinated. He let out another sigh of relief as he flushed. He went to the door and opened it. Both Kiyalee and Chyning were standing there looking up at him angrily. They both ran in after he came out and locked the door.

He stood there in shock for a moment. He headed for the watch consoles as he was trying to consider the logistics of what was going on in there. He could see two men, standing on either side of the toilet, relieving themselves. 'Two women...if they...no that wouldn't work...unless they...' He decided that he really did not want to know - how or what.

Several minutes later both women came out. They both

scowled at Bonarain as they passed by her. She snarled back and went back to her applications. The two women went to the watch consoles, rubbed their eyes and went back to the "duty".

After checking for any updates from High Command...for the third time and finding very little that was useful, Soolchakan looked back at the hallway where Bonarain was still checking her makeup. He grunted in exasperation and headed into the hallway. Bonarain ignored him as she continued doing...whatever she was doing. He looked down on the floor at the huge bag that had been opened up and spread out. He saw bottles, tubes, brushes and several other things that he could not even identify. He knelt down, scooped up the entire thing, folded it up and headed for the trash chute. Bonarain screamed at him as he did the scooping and moving. He ignored her ranting completely.

Bonarain screamed at him. "Do you know how expensive all of that is?!"

He turned back to her. "Do you really want to know how much I don't care?"

She looked at the closed door of the chute and back at him. "The bag alone cost me..."

"DON'T CARE!"

"But...all of that makeup..."

"DON'T CARE!"

"What...am I supposed to do?"

"To begin with, you can stop wasting time with all of that *hoolyach*! The other two women, currently at this station, don't spend one tenth of the time that you do, primping. Second..." He held out his arms questioningly. "Who are you dolling yourself up for? No one here...cares! Third, once they are able to relieve us...there won't be any parties to go to...for quite some time...while we're trying to figure out...just how to survive."

"But...I..."

"No one cares!"

She looked as if she was going to cry. "You don't understand...!"

He straightened up and folded his arms across his chest. "Okay, explain it to me."

"But...I..." She waved her arms erratically trying to think. "You...I...but it just...I...have to look good."

He looked at her dull-eyed. "For whom!?"

She had her fists down at her sides and let out a very angry and frustrated squawk.

"Now, put your pants and boots on, quit worrying about makeup and get to one of the consoles. It has been quite some time since either one of them was relieved."

She looked up at him dejectedly. Then with a sulking look she reached down and grabbed the pants. She put them on, while glancing back at him, angrily. She reached down and put her boots on. She gave him another angry glance just before she headed back to where the consoles were.

He followed slowly.

Kiyalee and Chyning looked up and saw her "partially" done makeup job. Both turned back to their consoles and started giggling.

Bonarain bared her teeth and claws and was ready to advance into a maelstrom.

Soolchakan grabbed the back of her shirt and tugged hard. He got his face up close to her left ear and angrily whispered: "Don't even think about it! We need to get along...for an undetermined length of time."

She looked back at him with clenched teeth. She turned back, closed her mouth and her eyes. She dropped her arms and sighed. She slowly walked to one of the consoles with her head hung low. She turned it on and started scanning.

Soolchakan walked up behind her and checked which watch she was doing. He went to another console and turned it to the other scan. "Yellow and Green...you're relieved for chow," he said quietly.

Kiyalee and Chyning got up and headed for the break area.

Bonarain sighed. "I hate you."

"You don't need any of that stuff now," he answered back quietly. "Besides...no one will be manufacturing that stuff...for a long time. It has now become...totally superfluous."

"That's why I hate you...you're totally right. There won't be any...of the parties now...for who knows how long. No more of the equinox celebrations…the solstice celebrations…or probably even the special anniversaries. We won't have any…parties or celebration…" Her thought just wandered off. She sniffled a little.

Every now and again, while the two of them were watching the monitors, she would pull out a tissue and wipe some of the makeup off. Better none than just partial.

The seventh day came. Nothing new to report. The four of them were sitting quietly looking at monitors. They were all startled as they heard the elevator turn on and start whirring as the mechanism was being utilized.

Kiyalee headed for her rifle.

Soolchakan chased her down and grabbed her. "NO! Not until we know who it is! We don't need any…accidental friendly casualties."

She huffed at him and stood there glaring.

He went to the armory and pulled out a heavy caliber automatic rifle. He went to the elevator door.

Bonarain pulled out a pistol and stood next to him.

Chyning was not very sure what to do.

The elevator door came open. There were three men standing inside. One Officer Leader and two Officer grade 4.

The Officer Leader looked down at the rifle aimed at him. "Good day, I'm wondering…did you…NOT get the alarmed message?"

"Uh…no…Sir," stammered Soolchakan. "No…alarms…of any type."

One of the Grade 4 went to the command console. He typed a few keys, watched the monitor and then looked up. "The alarm… its dead, Sir."

The Officer Leader sighed. "I see." He looked back at Soolchakan and smiled. "I'm Officer Leader, Xadorm. I sent a message…ahead…that I was coming around to the stations. I come in peace. You may put the weapons away."

Soolchakan flushed a little as he lowered the rifle. "Yes, Sir. Anything new to report to us…we haven't really heard anything…

in…ever since that…attack."

Xadorm looked around. "Shall we all sit down and have a nice civilized discussion?"

"That would be very nice, Sir," said Soolchakan.

Xadorm looked at one of his Grade 4. "Sheekog, why don't you go watch the scanner, while I update these people?"

"Yes, Sir," said Sheekog as he headed for the consoles.

All the rest of the personnel in the station headed for the break area.

Xadorm looked at Soolchakan in surprise. "Your… machine…you still have some…kwatha?"

Soolchakan chuckled. "There's only four of us here, Sir. In order for us to eat all of that kwatha, we would have had to have been eating it all day and night. There are other things to eat, Sir."

"Yes," said Xadorm. "Well I am *not* going to pass this opportunity to have a mug of that brew…right now." He went to the dispenser and savored the aroma with his eyes closed as the thick brown kwatha drained into the mug. He picked up a spoon and started looking for the big lumps. He popped a lump into his mouth and chewed slowly. "Wonderful!" He sat down at the table in order to have a few more mouthfuls before starting the briefing.

The other Grade 4 came up to Xadorm with a pad. "Here's the current inventory for this station, Sir."

Xadorm looked at it as it was laid near the mug. "Thank you, Shkor." He took a sip of the kwatha. He started looking down the inventory. He frowned. "Uh…did you have some kind of…military action here?"

Soolchakan was momentarily taken aback. "Uh…what, Sir, do you…uh…what do you mean, Sir?"

"According to this inventory, you're short…28 rounds of ammunition. What happened to them? Was there a…minor confrontation with an enemy?"

Soolchakan closed his eyes and let his breath out slowly. He clenched his lips, then huffed. "No…Sir…uh, no, Sir, there was no… any type or military confrontation. There was…an accidental… discharge of a weapon."

Xadorm sat there wide-eyed. "Accidental? 28 rounds... accidental? Someone accidentally discharged a rifle...on fully automatic?"

Soolchakan cleared his throat. "Uh...yes, Sir...that's...exactly what happened. An accidental discharge...on fully automatic."

Xadorm laid the pad on the table. He looked at the four members of the station 585 team. He shook his head. "An accidental...discharge on fully automatic! The only *bimyock* that I know of, stupid enough to do that, is that idiot, Kiyalee."

Kiyalee flushed. Chyning went into gales of laughter. Bonarain turned her head to the side and snickered with her hand over her mouth. Soolchakan sniffed and cleared his throat again.

"Uh...yes, Sir," said Soolchakan. "It was...Kiyalee that did it." He pointed to Kiyalee. "She's right there...and she's the one who did it." He leaned back and looked up at the ceiling in a feeble attempt at trying not to laugh himself.

Xadorm looked at Shkor, who was fighting a losing battle at not laughing as well. Sheekog was snickering at the console. He had heard what was going on in spite of having to watch the scanner. Chyning's laughter was becoming quite contagious. A contagion to all except Kiyalee. Xadorm and Soolchakan were losing control of themselves as Chyning continued with her laughing as she laid her head on the table...while still laughing.

Kiyalee slammed her fists on the table. "ENOUGH!" She looked around at everyone as a tear trickled down her cheek. "It was...an accident. No one got hurt. No damage...absolutely no damage to the station." She covered her face with her hands.

Chyning was rubbing the side of her head that had been on the table when Kiyalee hit it. Apparently there had been a bit of a shock wave through the table and it had been effective - somewhat effective. Chyning was still giggling a little as she rubbed her head.

Xadorm gave Kiyalee a disgusted look. "Were you outside... upstairs already...before the accidental discharge?"

"No, Sir," said Kiyalee red-faced.

"Then...how could there be absolutely no damage to the station?"

"I…was going up the shaft…and had the gun…aimed up the…escape shaft…when it went off."

"Was the door on top open?"

"Yes, Sir."

Xadorm did not look convinced. He looked at his aide. "Shkor, go take a look in the shaft. See if there…is *absolutely* no damage…in the shaft."

Chyning looked over at Xadorm. "Would you like Kiyalee to show how she opens that door?" She again dissolved into another fit of laughter.

Kiyalee's face, again, turned bright red. She clenched her eyes and teeth…and backhanded Chyning. Chyning reacted immediately by pulling Kiyalee's hair, pulling her backwards on her chair and both of them went to the floor fighting. Soolchakan grabbed Chyning and pulled her back while Shkor pulled Kiyalee back.

Xadorm stood up and pounded a fist on the table. "STOP IT! Both of you, stop this nonsense. I don't care what problems you have with each other, we don't have time for this. We have an enemy out there who has killed millions of the citizens of Owlam. Now, BEHAVE!" He sat back down glaring back and forth at the two women. "Sit! Both of you…now!"

The three of them went back to their seats.

"NO!" Xadorm glared at them. "You…Red Shirt…sit between those two…until they can behave."

Soolchakan shoved Kiyalee to his right and sat down in the chair that she had previously occupied. Chyning was still standing there glaring at Kiyalee. Soolchakan reached up and grabbed the back of her Green Shirt and yanked her down to her seat. Now she was glaring at him.

"Thank you," said Xadorm patronizingly. "Can we now act like adults and get back to business?"

"Yes, Sir," said Soolchakan. "You said that…millions…are…gone?"

Xadorm looked down sadly. "Yes…the people who were… near the wall…or in the stations…are the only ones left."

"Uh…how many…Sir?"

Xadorm looked up. "Twenty-eight thousand…and sixty-four. That's all that's…left…of this…once proud, sprawling metropolis."

Everyone sat there in silence for several moments. Bonarain and Kiyalee sniffed a little trying to keep from crying. Soolchakan just shut his eyes and hung his head. Chyning looked up at the ceiling, while biting her lower lip.

"Unusual thing…" said Xadorm. "Three fourths of the… survivors are women. Not really surprising…since most of the survivors…were the defensive watchers." He let out a heavy sigh.

Soolchakan looked up at him sadly. "So…what of…the offensive forces?"

Xadorm closed his eyes and shook his head. "Now…we are the defensive…and offensive forces."

Bonarain cleared her throat loudly. "So…what do we do? I mean…if all of the offensive forces are gone…how are we supposed to…defend a city the size of Owlam?"

"We all have to learn…how to do both," said Xadorm flatly.

Bonarain's jaw dropped. "With…just twenty-eight… thousand?"

"Nothing's been taken off of the table…yet," said Xadorm. "We are trying to…figure out…any alternative…that we can."

Chyning regained a little composure. "What about the inner city? Does anyone know…really if anyone is still alive… somewhere…in there?"

Xadorm shook his head. "There has been no sign…of anyone coming out of the…inner city…alive. From the vantage points that we can look from…there is no activity at all…in the inner city… except for a few fires that are still burning."

"Still burning!" Kiyalee looked stunned. "Seven days and… there are fires…that are still burning?"

Xadorm looked at her. "There are over a dozen…major lumber yards in the inner city." He sighed. "That's our best guess… at what is still burning…after all this time."

Soolchakan swallowed and cleared his throat. "So…what… if any, is the immediate plan? What are we doing…for now?"

Xadorm clicked his tongue. "For now…the plan is to split up

into Teams of fours…all over the city. Since we have exactly three women to every man…that is the setup. Each Team will be one man and three women."

Soolchakan nodded. "Have the Teams been chosen yet, or are they still working on…who is with whom?"

"Yes," said Xadorm. "We have your assignments." He looked up at Shkor. "Got the assignment pad?"

"Yes, Sir," said Shkor. He pulled a pad out of a pouch on his side and handed it to Xadorm.

Xadorm took it and looked back at Shkor. "Have you checked that shaft yet?"

"Uh…no, Sir, I was helping…break up a fight."

Xadorm grimaced. He glanced back and forth at Kiyalee and Chyning. "I believe the fight's over. Go check the shaft."

"Yes, Sir."

Xadorm turned on the pad. He hit a few places on it with the stylus. "Your name is…Soolchakan, Grade 5...and let's see." He stared at the small screen for a few moments. "Okay, here it is…you are teamed up…" He looked a little startled for a moment. "Uh…this is your Team…here!"

Four jaws dropped and four sets of shoulders sagged.

"But…NO…it can't be," said Bonarain fearfully. "You can't put me…with these…" She looked at the other three in horror.

Soolchakan gritted his teeth a little. "Why the four of us together? Is it because we are…here together…already?"

Xadorm closed his eyes and shook his head. "Nope!" He opened his eyes. "The four of you…are together…because no one else…wants any of you on their Team." He looked at Soolchakan. "An alcoholic!" He turned to Bonarain. "A megalomaniacal makeup diva!" He turned to Kiyalee. "The clumsiest *bimyock* that ever touched a firearm!" He turned to Chyning. "The clumsy computer destroyer!" He leaned back and clasped his fingers together. "No one wants you…any of you…probably even *you* don't want you. Tough! High Command has assigned the Teams…so get used to it. Your designation is: Team 7016. You four are one of the, over seven thousand Teams…that are left of the city of Owlam…to defend the city of Owlam."

The four members of Team 7016 looked at each other with some disdain and disgust. They were the outcasts and as a result, they were numerically designated as the *last* Team. Number 7016 of 7,016 Teams.

Shkor came back to the table.

Xadorm looked up at Shkor. "Report!"

"There are several…ricochet marks going up the shaft. There are two rungs…where bullets pierced them…from the underside. Other than that, no apparent damage. The upper door must have been open…when she blasted the shaft. There are no marks of any type on the door."

"It was open," said Soolchakan flatly.

Xadorm looked puzzled for a moment. He was scrutinizing Bonarain very closely. "Now I know why I didn't recognize you - you've taken all that massive amount of makeup off. I remember those celebrations that you came to. At the Great Holy Festival, you were wearing more makeup than any of the children." He shook his head. "You look…so…different…when you don't have a gross of makeup on your face."

Bonarain looked away totally embarrassed and irate.

Shkor chuckled. "For the first time…we're actually seeing your real face."

"From now on," said Xadorm, "the four of you will actually live together. All Teams have to live with their specific Team members. You will or can be called upon at any time…depending on what High Command wants your Team to do. Now, before the… firestorms…I need to know…where you lived. Where were your quarters?"

"Mine…gone," said Chyning sadly. "I lived in the tower section. Tower 45, apartment…"

Xadorm held up his hand. "The apartment number is… irrelevant. None of the towers…are standing. That is one thing that we are *very* sure of…from what we can see…from our vantage points."

Kiyalee hung her head and started sniffling.

Xadorm leaned forward. "Did you live in one of the towers?"

She shook her head without looking up. "My mother...and I lived on Dwyloo Street. It *is* close enough...to the towers..." She covered her face with her hands and started sobbing.

Xadorm looked at Bonarain.

Bonarain gave him a dull-eyed stare. "I live on Yanalak Street." She sighed. "I live in the 1600 block."

Xadorm nodded. "Yanalak? That's practically perimeter. That should still be there...intact." He looked at Soolchakan. "You?"

Soolchakan was staring at Bonarain. "I...live in the 1500 block...of South Perimeter Road."

Bonarain looked at Soolchakan in shock. "From my quarters...that's only..." She looked off disgusted again. "I actually live that close to *him*," she muttered.

Xadorm smiled. "That's actually convenient. You are one of the very few Teams that has a choice as to where you will be quartered. As soon as you make the decision where you're staying, you will inform High Command. Don't think that you will be using both of them for quarters. When you are called on to act...there will be no stops on the way. The four of you *will* dwell in the same quarters. Any questions?"

The four members of Team 7016 all gave each other more disgusted looks.

Xadorm stood up and hollered angrily: "Do you understand?!"

"Yes, Sir," muttered Soolchakan.

The three women just gave weak, but angry, nods.

"All right," said Xadorm. "Now...in a little while, there will be a Team coming here to pull the supplies out of this station. Take as much as you each can carry. Take what you need and what you want. This station is one of several that are being abandoned. The stations that are not being abandoned will be doing extra work... covering the unmanned stations. You will also be doing some training in offensive capabilities...just in case they're...needed. So... start packing." When he finished, he immediately picked up his mug and headed for the kwatha dispenser. "You might want to take some of *this* with you. It's getting rare and this machine has some really good kwatha."

Shkor grabbed a mug and got himself a portion of the brown mixture.

Sheekog came out of the computer area. "All of them are shut down now. The watchers in the other stations are informed. We can clean this one out…completely."

"Go ahead and bring in the chests," said Xadorm. "I'm sure that these people will be needing…or wanting something, from here, to help supply their needs at their quarters."

Sheekog headed for the elevator.

Soolchakan looked at Xadorm. "Should we be helping him?"

"There won't be enough room in the elevator…for two people and all of the chests," said Xadorm as he spooned a big lump out of the kwatha. "He'll need help getting them out of the elevator…down here."

Soolchakan got another mug full of kwatha from the dispenser. He went to the elevator door with his mug to wait for Sheekog.

After Chyning got herself a mug of kwatha, she was admonished by Xadorm to stay away from the computers. She was no longer in the mood to enjoy her kwatha, however, she ate it anyway.

Soolchakan was half way done with his kwatha when the elevator door opened. There were several stacks of chests, banded together, in the elevator. Seeing as how all of the chests were empty, the stacks were rather light. Moving them out of the elevator was very easy.

"Remember," said Xadorm. "We're going to clear everything out of here. Take what you can carry…or drag. Use as many of the chests as you want. I will suggest that each one of you takes a weapon…except for Kiyalee. Someone else will carry that for her."

Kiyalee's face, again, turned bright red. She turned away mouthing some obscenities.

"I suggest that you don't take any of the pulse rifles."

Soolchakan looked at him rather puzzled. "Uh…why not?"

"That…city-wide power failure that occurred…just before

that flash and the firestorms...somehow...the pulse rifles, all over the city, were damaged. A few of them have been turned on and the results were...not good. Until we figure out what's wrong with them...stick to the projectile rifles."

There were three sizes of the chests. Soolchakan picked one of the small ones and put a heavy caliber rifle along with 200 rounds of ammunition. He picked a smaller caliber of rifle for Kiyalee along with 200 rounds of ammunition and placed this in the same chest.

All four of them took a large and placed as many of the uniforms in them that would fit. At first Bonarain was a little upset about getting the larger uniforms, however, once convinced that they could be altered, she had no problem cleaning out the closets of anything larger than what she normally wore.

They each took five or the "rank" shirts - for later use. The Owlam military depended heavily on being able to see this ranking system from a distance, it was very necessary to keep a good supply of them on hand.

They were advised to take a good supply of the emergency packaged rations with them as well. It was not known how soon they would be able to set up any kind of commissary for new rations or fresh food.

By the time the four of them were finished with their legalized ransacking of the station, all three women had filled two large chests each. Soolchakan had two large and one small. The one small was the one that was holding all of the weaponry so it turned out to be the heaviest of all of them.

They marked their individual chests and dragged them into the elevator. The door closed and the 'up' button was punched. They all heard the elevator motor straining under the weight that was currently in the elevator and the ride up was a little nerve wracking. It took longer and the noises they heard were all unusual. When it finally reached the top and the door slid open, they all gave off a loud sigh of relief. Then they dragged all of the chests out of the elevator.

Each one sat down on one of the big chests, puffing and panting from the exertion. The elevator door closed and they heard the motor kick in - without any of the strange noises that they had heard on their way up. They turned their attention to the railway, looking for the next Tram car that would come along.

The elevator door opened again. Xadorm and Shkor came out.

"As stated earlier," said Xadorm. "The four of you *will* live at the same address. Since there are two of your addresses that should still be intact, the four of you will have to decide which of those addresses you will be quartered. You will inform High Command, as soon as you've made the decision."

"It will probably be mine," said Bonarain smugly. "I don't see any reason why we would be moving into a...hovel that's been... neglected by a single man."

The two other women giggled. Soolchakan just gave her a dirty look.

Soolchakan stood up and rubbed his back. "Officer Leader, how soon will we know...anything...of what's going on or what's happening...or a new duty schedule?"

Xadorm hung his head. He sniffed and looked back up. "Nothing like this...was ever...looked over or even dreamt about... in the planning area. We...are having to...plan as we go...and see what we've got. That's why we need to know...as soon as possible... where your Team is quartered."

"There's a Tram car coming up," said Shkor quietly.

When the Tram car came up to the stopping point, Soolchakan used the small heavy chest to block the Tram door in the open position. The six people on the platform fought the heavy chests into the Tram and once again sat there huffing and puffing from the effort. The small chest was pulled in, the door closed and the Tram moved out. When the Tram car arrived at station 586, Xadorm and Shkor quietly departed.

The door closed and the Tram car started moving again.

Bonarain huffed. "Again...we'll probably use my quarters. The place that you live in...probably reeks of stale armpits and booze."

'Just my bedroom,' thought Soolchakan. He gave Bonarain a stern look. "We *will* look at both...before making any final decisions."

Bonarain placed her fists on her thighs. "We don't need…"

Soolchakan interrupted her, shouting as loud as he could. "WE WILL LOOK AT BOTH…NO MATTER WHAT!"

Bonarain sat back, crossed her arms, looked out the window and pouted for most of the rest of the trip.

It was a long silent trip to their final destination. No one else got in or out for the duration. It was a solemn reminder to the Team as to just how many of the citizens of Owlam had died in the flash and the firestorms.

11

Kiyalee shook Soolchakan. "Wake up...oh great and all powerful leader. We need to know...which one is the stop we're supposed to get off at."

He stretched a little and rubbed his eyes. "I wasn't really sleeping...just resting my eyes...uh...where are we now?"

"We just crossed the bridge after the Kiynon stop."

He stood up and stretched again. "Two more...two more stops and we're there."

Bonarain stood up with her mouth wide open. "What?! You mean you get off at the...Vondor stop?"

"Yeah, so what?"

She flung her arms out. "That's my...we both live in the same area?"

"You did say that you lived in the 1600 block of Yanalak, didn't you."

"But...we get off...at the same stop?"

"We've never had the same schedule before. That's probably why we've never seen each other...there...before."

Bonarain shook her head with a disgusted look on her face. She sat down with sagging shoulders.

"So," said Chyning. "Which place do we check first...and where do we leave our...baggage?"

Soolchakan sighed. "My place is closer. I live just across the street from the stop. We'll put the stuff in my place, take a look, and then go look at hers. We'll only start dragging all of this stuff over to her place...*if* it's more suitable. Otherwise, we'll stay at mine and only have to move all of this...stuff...once."

The correct stop came up. Again, he used the heavy armory chest to hold the door open while they dragged the other eight chests out. Once all of the chests were out, they once again sat down on them to regain some strength.

"So, great leader," said Kiyalee. "How far is it?"

He pointed across the empty street. "Right there…on the second floor…above the *Wonder House Tavern*."

Bonarain clenched her eyes shut. "It figures! You live directly above a boozer." She huffed in disgust. "If we live there…we'll never get any sleep."

"Right now, I don't think that that's a problem," said Soolchakan sadly. "Most of the regular clientele…is probably… charred to a cinder." He heaved a sigh. "It's usually open…this time of day. I don't see…any…activity…of any type…right now. I don't hear…anything. No birds…no bugs…very little wind…and nothing else."

All four of them looked around. The silence was incredible. There was a slight wind. There was a barely audible electric buzzing coming from the Tram rail mechanism. No sound of any people or stray animals yipping or yowling. A Tram car was coming up the way. It stopped and the door opened. There was one man, wearing the rank of Officer Grade 6, on board. He looked up and gave a bit of a sad nod to the people on the platform. They gave him a nod back. The Tram door closed and it moved on to the next station.

Kiyalee sighed. "Please tell me that there's an elevator…or some kind of lift to the second floor."

Soolchakan chuckled. "There's a freight elevator in back. The tavern owner…if he's still alive…stores a lot of things…on the fourth floor."

Chyning stood up and moaned. "There's no time…like the present. We might as well start moving our treasures across the street."

"Let's get one person on each end of a chest," said Soolchakan. "Seeing as how…there doesn't appear to be…any looters around, and the tavern is just across the street…I don't think we have to leave anyone here on the platform to…guard the stuff."

Bonarain paired with Kiyalee and Soolchakan with Chyning. They randomly picked two chests and lifted them. Soolchakan lead the way, directly to the front door of the tavern.

"I thought you said that there's a freight elevator…in back," said Bonarain.

"There is," said Soolchakan.

"Then why are we headed to the front door of the boozer? Why aren't we headed to the side...to go around?"

He grunted and set the chest down. He turned back to Bonarain. "Take a look! If we head off to the right, we have to go around three buildings to get there. If we head off to the left, there are two buildings. There's no alley in between. If we go in the front door, all we have to do, then, is just go to the back...of the boozer...to the elevator. Pick a route!" He glared at her.

Bonarain snorted. "Okay, straight through."

Kiyalee looked confused. "You...got a key...to that front door?"

"Yes," sighed Soolchakan. "The owner trusts me."

Bonarain scoffed. "Not very bright, is he!"

He ignored her and leaned down to pick up the chest. Chyning lifted it up with him and they continued across the wide street. They got to the sidewalk and then up to the door. He put the chest down to get the keys out of his pocket.

"Hey," said Kiyalee. "You're...leaving footprints...on the sidewalk."

He looked down confused and noticed the prints.

Bonarain looked horrified. "What is that stuff...that we're leaving our...prints...in?"

"Ash," said Soolchakan softly. "You...remember that...ash rained down on us...right after the...attack. That big cloud...up there...the fires that we saw...and then...the ash. No one...has been here...to sweep it up or...walk through it...for that matter...since the attack."

The four looked around and realized that their footprints were the only ones in the area. No sign of any other man or beast. Just the fresh footprints of the four standing there.

Kiyalee looked as if she was going to cry. "But...it's been... how many days...since the attack...and no one...?" Her voice drifted off as she bit her lip.

Bonarain cleared her throat. "Yeah, it has...hasn't it? Here we are, standing in front of a tavern…that no one has been to…" Her shoulders sagged. "This is getting depressing."

Soolchakan stuck the key in and unlocked the door. He pushed the door in and looked inside a very dark room. He walked in and felt his way to the light switch. Several garish neon lights came on and lit up the room. He sniffed and scratched his chin. He went back out to move the chest. "Let's get all of them inside the door…before we go check her quarters."

They moved the two chests inside.

After setting the chest down, Bonarain went to a table and ran a finger across it. She turned to her comrades with a concerned look on her face. "This is not ash. It's dust. Was this place open… the day you reported for duty?"

"Yeah," said Soolchakan solemnly. He sniffed. "It was…real lively that…day."

They all stood there silently, pondering the possibilities. Here was a tavern that had been outside of the blast and firestorm perimeter. All of the buildings on this street were intact and showed no signs of damage from fires or looting. The wondering of what exactly happened bothered all of them.

"Let's go get the other chests," said Kiyalee sadly.

They moved all of the heavy chests into the business area of the tavern. After the effort they decided to just sit for a while and regain some strength.

Off to the right of the main door was a large alcove where there was a gaming area. There were all kinds of tables set up for different kinds of bar competitions. On the back wall of the gaming area, there were the normal signs, indicating where the public toilets were located. Off to the left was the main drinking area. Directly ahead, after going around several tables, was the main bar. Behind the bar were all of the glasses and large bottles of different types of liquor, ale, wines and other assorted alcoholic beverages. To the right of the main bar was the access to the area behind the bar. That hallway area continued back to the back of the building. The hallway wall, just like all of the other walls were cluttered with pictures, murals, drawings and even some graffiti. Directly behind the main bar there was one set of double doors, centered behind the bar. Off to the left, behind the bar, was a single door.

Bonarain scoffed. "Ya think that maybe there's anything to eat here? It is a boozer, but they might have some actual food."

"They always have fruits, fruit juices and vegetables that they use to make mixed drinks," said Soolchakan flatly as he stared at one of the bright lights that had started blinking. "There's a cooler... somewhere behind those double doors over there."

Kiyalee looked around a little spooked. "Maybe...if we look around this...entire place...we can figure out what happened...to the owner. This entire area was spared...from the fires...so where... are the people who lived and worked here?"

Soolchakan shrugged. "So...let's do some exploring and checking."

"It might be a good idea to lock the front door," said Bonarain.

The other three looked at her as if she were crazy.

"Someone might see our footprints out there...and do... who knows what? If there is some...looter, or any of the criminal element, that has been exploring this area...waiting for someone to show up...to rob, our footprints are a complete giveaway."

Soolchakan sighed. The thought of some scavenger, lurking about the premises, gave him a bad feeling. He closed the front door and locked it. He turned back to Bonarain. "Are you happy?"

Bonarain just shrugged.

They all got up. Kiyalee headed for a door that was on the left side of the tavern, just in front of the main bar, while the other three were heading to the other end of the main bar to explore what was behind it.

Soolchakan saw Kiyalee and stopped her. "That's the door to the stairs. That just takes you upstairs. We'll look into that after we know what all is down here...on the first floor."

Kiyalee sighed and followed the rest of them to the hallway on the other side of the bar.

Bonarain went to the double doors behind the bar, Chyning headed for the door at the far end of the bar. Soolchakan and Kiyalee headed down the hall. Near the end of the hallway, there were three doors. One large door on the left, one door straight ahead and one on the right.

"That big door on the left is the freight elevator," said Soolchakan.

Kiyalee mumbled a response. She went to the door that was straight ahead while he went to the one on the right - that was standing slightly ajar.

Kiyalee unlocked and opened the door. Her shoulders sagged. "It just leads to another street in back of the boozer." She looked down. "There's no footprints in the ash out here...that I can see...from here."

"That's Tokton Street," said Soolchakan. He pushed the door open where he was looking. It led to a dark echoing room that had a smell of a vehicle garage. He felt along the wall just inside the door to the left and found a light switch. He turned it on. It was a very large garage that could store two large vehicles. He wandered in the room with his mouth agape. "No wonder those guys aren't here."

Kiyalee followed him in. "What...d'ya mean?"

"Look around you," he scoffed. "This is the parking garage for a fire fighting team, with their trucks. All of this equipment... along the walls...it is spare supplies, for a firefighting team. Choshki and his tavern employees...they were an emergency response team. They could close the bar and respond to a fire." He went up to a picture on the opposite wall. "That's them! They're all in this picture. Choshki, his bouncers, and all the other people who worked here. They were *all* one team."

"So...where are they now? Don't you think...after all of this time they should have come back...for more firefighting supplies?"

Soolchakan hung his head and his shoulders sagged. "If they haven't come back...by now...it's a...horrible possibility...that they aren't coming back. They could have been responding...and... who knows...what disaster fell on...or burned them...to death." He looked up and sniffled. "I don't think...they're coming back."

She cleared her throat loudly. "Uh...do you...think that there's anything in here...that we can use?"

He shook his head. "Maybe...I don't know...and I'm not

going to make any decisions on that…at the moment." He wiped his nose on his sleeve. "Let's…go see what the others have found."

They headed back to the bar area.

Bonarain pushed through the double doors and nearly gagged at the smell. She felt along the wall until she found a light switch. She was now staring at a very large kitchen. Some of the food that had been in the middle of preparation, at the time of the attack, was still on some of the counters, showing different levels of decomposition and decay. She held her nose as she explored the back area where there were several storage areas and refrigeration units. The food in these areas was still good. There was a large area where they had enough burners to cook enough food for an army - or a tavern full of hungry drunks. She headed back out of the kitchen. She was amazed at how the doors were capable of keeping, all of that stench, confined to the one room.

Chyning came out of the room she had been exploring. "What was in your room?"

Bonarain looked over at her. "Kitchen…BIG kitchen! There's a lot of extra food in there. I don't think that…our Team 7016 is going to starve…any time soon. But we will need to do some cleaning…if we stay here. What'd you find?"

"It's storage. Some boxes of extra booze, kegs, glasses, mugs, plates, flatware…a few chairs and tables are stacked in there as well." She looked beyond Bonarain as Kiyalee and Soolchakan came back from the hallway. "Did you find anything…usable?"

The four of them exchanged information for a few minutes.

"This is a four story building," said Bonarain. "Your apartment is on the second floor…what's on the others?"

Soolchakan shrugged. "Let's go find out."

They went up the stairs to the second floor. There was a landing where there was only one door. The other part of the landing simply led to the stairs to get to the third floor.

Bonarain looked around in confusion. "How…many apartments…are on this second floor?"

Soolchakan shrugged. "Mine."

"How big is it?"

"It's...uh...five bedrooms...a dining room, living room, three bathrooms...and a kitchen."

Now all three women were looking at him in shock.

Bonarain sputtered a little. "How...does a...Grade 5...rate a...FIVE BEDROOM APARTMENT?"

He sighed. "As you clearly pointed out - it is directly above a tavern...and right across the street from a very..." He hung his head and cleared his throat. "...used to be...a very busy...Tram stop."

Kiyalee shrugged. "Okay, let's take a look. We have to compare it...to Bonarain's place...and see which one we want to live in."

Soolchakan opened a very small door next to his front door. He exposed a small keypad. He punched his code in and the door unlocked.

Bonarain chuckled. "Were you able to do that when you were drunk?"

He looked at her angrily and balled up his fist as if he was going to punch her. He let out a low growl, dropped his fist and pushed the door open. A light came on automatically. He walked in followed by the three women.

"Yup," said Bonarain. "It smells like an apartment where a single man lives."

"I wouldn't know," said Chyning in a chiding manner. "I've never been in an 'unmarried man' apartment before...like you."

Kiyalee giggled.

Bonarain snarled at Chyning. "Watch it, you *bimyock*! I'll..."

Soolchakan could not let things get out of hand and he interrupted. "DO NOTHING!" He glared at all three women angrily. "We have to get along...and work as a team...let's try to avoid any...petty squabbling."

Bonarain and Chyning both backed down after each giving the other a rather dirty look.

Chyning took a look around at the living/dining area. She sighed. "It's going to need a lot of dusting...and some of that..." She wrinkled her brow. "...furniture..." she said in a questioning manner. "It...just has to be replaced...with something...a LOT more…suitable to living."

"You mean - less smelly," said Bonarain in a demeaning manner.

They explored the rest of the rooms (except for his bedroom, where he refused to allow them in) and decided that they would need a lot of better (cleaner) furniture, before moving in here.

The Team continued their exploration on the third floor. This was an unexpected shock. Someone had been attempting to do some upgrades and repairs on the third floor. It was all one big room with all kinds of tools, lumber, paint and other building accessories scattered around - all covered with months of dust.

They went up to the fourth floor. This area had definitely been used for storage. There were a lot of tables, chairs, mugs, glasses, plates…and liquor stored up on there.

Soolchakan fell in lust with the supply of liquor that was stored up here. He found fourteen cases of *the* most expensive brand of alcohol that could be found in the city of Owlam. Fourteen cases, with twelve bottles to the case meant one hundred sixty-eight bottles of glorious benders. He wondered how many more of the bottles of *Golden Age Liquor* were in the storage room on the first floor.

Bonarain sighed. "I think…we'll be living here."

Kiyalee looked at her incredulously. "Uh…why…how can you be so sure…when we haven't even looked at your place yet?"

Bonarain stared off into space. "All I've got is a one bedroom…tiny apartment. I don't have any…access to any of the other…apartments in the building. Here…we have…food, space, more storage space…and a big garage…if they assign a vehicle…of some type, any type…to this Team."

"Fine," said Chyning. "So we stay here…and try to find some decent furniture."

"I'll need…a little help," said Bonarain. "I…have a few things…at my apartment that…I'll need here."

Kiyalee stood up tall and placed her fists on her hips. "I am NOT gonna help you move ANY of your *chokwad* makeup!"

"Neither am I," said Chyning.

Soolchakan chuckled. "I may be strong…but any attempt at

moving all of your…makeup…is beyond anything that I'm capable of."

Bonarain snarled back at them. "I'm talking about more clothing, a few pieces of furniture - like my bed - and some *cleaning* supplies…along with some very badly needed AIR FRESHENERS!"

Chyning grunted. "How are we gonna get…a bunch of furniture up to that second floor?"

Soolchakan rolled his eyes. "Through that freight elevator I told you about!"

Kiyalee sighed. "Okay, let's go see what we need now…today. I didn't see any beds in your…*extra*…bedrooms…and we will need some beds…to sleep on."

Soolchakan grunted. "I haven't been getting very much sleep lately."

"Neither have I," said Bonarain despondently. "Maybe if I get my own bed back…things'll…change."

Soolchakan shrugged. "Okay. I saw a nutting truck in the garage. It has a bunch of fire extinguishers on it. "I guess we can leave those behind and use the truck to…move…your necessities."

They descended the stairs in silence. They went into the garage area and found that there were two of the nutting trucks. This was going to make things a lot easier to move any needed equipment. They moved all of the extinguishers off of the trucks.

Soolchakan put several tools on the trucks. "You never know what we might need…once we get there."

Kiyalee looked at him and shook her head. "Sledgehammer? Fire Ax? Screwdrivers? Pry bar?"

Chyning and Bonarain just shook their heads.

"I hate to break up our merriment," said Soolchakan, "But, on the remote possibility…that there are some looters in the area…I think that we better arm ourselves."

The three women all sighed.

Bonarain stood there with her arms folded. "Who carries what and who pushes what?"

He looked at Bonarain. "You and I will carry rifles. Chyning and Kiyalee will push a truck."

Kiyalee looked hurt. "Don't we get guns?"

"Chyning can carry a side arm - I don't want you touching a gun."

Chyning went into another one of her giggling fits at this comment. Kiyalee was ready to backhand her again, however, Soolchakan saw the look on her face and got in between before Kiyalee could strike. She backed down, frowning and red faced. Then Soolchakan turned around and backhanded Chyning. Now Kiyalee was giggling and Chyning was surprised and red faced.

They armed themselves and headed for the big garage doors. Soolchakan hit the switch and the big garage door started going up.

Kiyalee watched the door go up. "How are we gonna get back in? If you close this door...when we leave...how do we get back in?"

He took his key and tested it in the door that led to Tokton Street. It worked. He looked back at Kiyalee. "Any other questions?"

Kiyalee sniffed contemptuously as she pushed the nutting truck out of the garage.

Soolchakan looked at Bonarain. "Lead the way. The two trucks are in the middle and I'll watch the rear."

"You'll be watching *our* rears," said Chyning with a snort.

He scowled at her. "Move out!"

Bonarain led them to the left. She got her rifle ready for business. She looked everywhere as she headed for her quarters. Kiyalee was pushing the first truck, Chyning the second.

Soolchakan followed and looked around at any and all windows, searching for anything that might seem untoward. He was thoroughly disgusted at the thought that he might have to defend himself and his Team, from another citizen of Owlam. Every few moments he looked down at the ground. He shook his head in despair. The only prints in the ash belonged to his team and the cargo trucks. No other tracks of any type in the ash could be seen.

They got to the end of Tokton Street and Bonarain turned right. They were now going down a connector street, on the way to Yanalak Street. They passed by Saksan street. Still the only sounds that they heard were the wheels of the cargo trucks and the wind. The next street was Yanalak.

Bonarain stopped. "Oh help," she said in a somewhat desperate manner.

Soolchakan took a quick look around. "What's the matter?"

"The...buildings on...the north side of the street...they're mostly burned out! It looks like the fires...completely gutted everything...from Amdeeg street...and everything north of there."

"Where did you live, north side or south side of Yanalak?"

She cleared her throat. "I...uh...south side."

"Then hopefully, your place is intact."

"Yeah."

"Then let's go!"

She turned right. She was not looking for any threats now. She was staring at the buildings on the north side of the street. All were partially or completely charred façades that were full of broken windows. Looking through the windows on the upper floors, the sky could be seen, indicating that the back of the buildings had collapsed. There were numerous pieces of burned items littering the street that were covered with white ash. A few wisps of smoke could be seen coming out of some of the windows. "How far...did your friends have to go...to find a fire?"

He had a little trouble finding his voice at first. "This area... may have burned...later...after the initial blast. There was no one... left to put out any fires. They just burned...until...the wind stopped them...or there was no more fuel...of any type."

"I don't think it's very safe here," said Kiyalee. "Any one of those gutted...places could collapse."

"I agree," said Chyning.

"So, keep to the south side," said Soolchakan. "And let's get out of here...as soon as we can."

Kiyalee looked at Bonarain who had stopped walking and was still staring at the north side of the street. "Where we goin'?"

Bonarain turned to Kiyalee. "Uh...next...door. It's the next one." She spun around and headed for the indicated door, while wiping tears from her eyes. She went to the keypad and hit her code. Nothing happened. "I don't...know...what's going on...it should work."

Kiyalee scoffed. "Do you hear that on-and-off crackling sound?"

"Uh…yes."

"Try your code when it's noisy. That means that there's some kind of current going through it."

Bonarain listened for the sound. It took three tries before she was able to get her entire code punched in, while the electricity was indiscriminately buzzing. "It's open…now. Not gonna do much good, though. The door automatically closes after a few moments. There's nothing we can do about that. I can't depend on the electricity to come on, with enough time, to keep opening it."

Soolchakan growled. He picked up the sledgehammer and motioned the others to stand back. One hard swing with the hammer destroyed the locking mechanism on the door. Another hard swing destroyed the mechanism in the door frame. "Now, there's nothing to lock." He dropped the hammer back onto a truck. "Where's your quarters?"

Bonarain sighed. "Second floor."

Chyning hung her head. "You mean we gotta bring things down…here from the second floor?"

"It's all *down* stairs," said Soolchakan. "Back at the bar, we've got an elevator."

Kiyalee looked around. "Should we keep someone down here…just in case?"

"Yeah," said Soolchakan despondently. "We really…don't know anything…as to who might be anywhere near here…or what their attitude or motivation is." He shook his head. "I'll take the first watch, while you go upstairs and start moving…necessities."

Chyning looked at Bonarain. "I hope it isn't a keypad up there."

Bonarain waggled a chain from around her neck. "No, it's a key."

The three women went up the stairs. They got to her door and Bonarain sighed as she unlocked the door and opened it. She walked in and headed for the bedroom. "We're going to need to get all of the clothing. We're all close to the same size, so that gives us more to alter…as needed."

Kiyalee and Chyning walked into the bedroom and glanced around suspiciously.

Kiyalee leaned close to Chyning. "Where's all the makeup?"

Chyning shrugged.

"Let's just get as much clothing as we can and get out of here before we get infected with over indulgence in makeup."

Chyning looked off to the side of the living room. "What's that door go to?"

"Nothing," said Bonarain without looking. She did not want them digging through her makeup in her makeup room.

Chyning and Kiyalee both grabbed an armload of clothing out of the closet. They noticed that Bonarain was getting some linens together, including taking the sheets off of the bed. They headed out the door. The trip downstairs was a little unnerving, seeing as how they were going down blind with a major obstacle of full armloads of clothing. They dumped the clothing on one of the trucks and stood there puffing and panting.

"Take a turn of your own," said Kiyalee. "I'll watch for a moment."

Soolchakan grunted. "One load…and you're tired already?" He shook his head in disgust.

"Her clothing is heavy," complained Kiyalee. "Don't worry, I'll keep watch. You can trust me."

He looked at her dull eyed. "With a gun?"

She clenched her fists down by her sides. "What's the problem?"

"I seem to remember a hail of bullets…doing a little ricochet dance up that shaft…remember?"

She let out a disgusted grunt and headed back up the stairs.

Chyning was giggling during the entire conversation. She wiped her eyes and followed Kiyalee.

Bonarain was putting several different things into a box. "I don't know how much we'll be able to take on this trip…but we should try to take as much as possible."

"That's only part of the problem," said Kiyalee.

Bonarain and Chyning looked at her confused.

Kiyalee sighed. "You have a bed. He has a bed. Neither of us has one. What are we supposed to do tonight...double up with you...or him?"

Bonarain scratched her head. "I don't know how much those trucks can carry, but I think they can hold three beds."

Chyning was trying to pull some more of the clothing out of the closet. She peered out. "What? Where are the other two beds?"

Bonarain sighed. "We may have to...do a little...looting of our own. If no one has been back...in any of these...other apartments...in the building, then...well...they just might not... need them anymore. We do."

All three women pondered that thought for several moments in silence. Chyning huffed and started pulling more clothing out of the closet. Bonarain continued her box stuffing. Kiyalee went to the kitchen to look for any food that they could take with them.

Chyning took her load downstairs. She dumped the clothing on the pile that was already there. She slowly walked up to Soolchakan. "Our Team member...who lives...lived here... suggested that...in order for Kiyalee and I to have beds...we should take them from some apartment that is..." She cleared her throat. "...currently unoccupied." She turned away with a pained look.

Soolchakan hung his head. He looked up and shook his head. "The very thing that I'm defending this stuff from...we're gonna end up doing just...that. This stinks!"

"You...got that ax...and could use it to...bust down a few doors."

He sighed. "Yeah, yeah, yeah." He handed the rifle to Chyning, picked up the sledgehammer and headed for the nearest door on the first floor. Three hard swings and the door gave way. He headed for the next door.

Bonarain and Kiyalee came running down the stairs.

Bonarain turned when she heard another hit from the hammer coming from another part of the hallway. "What...whatsat?"

Chyning shrugged. "You suggested that we look for beds." She chuckled. "He's...opening some doors." She cocked her head and grinned.

"Why down here?"

Chyning scoffed. "If there's beds down here, then we don't have to carry any down from upstairs."

Bonarain looked at Kiyalee. "That actually makes sense."

Kiyalee nodded agreement.

Soolchakan came back wiping some sweat off his forehead. "Okay, there's three apartments that we can look in. Once we find some beds for you...all of you...we head back to get them set up."

Kiyalee looked confused. "Aren't we...gonna clean those places out...of anything that we need?"

He dropped the hammer onto the truck. "One step at a time, please. We need to get...at least the bare necessities...and report in...to the new Command Center, and give them our location."

Bonarain put her fingers to her forehead. "Didn't you...tell them already...about the bar?"

He sighed. "No, because until I destroyed these doors... it wasn't really decided that the tavern would be our...Team 7016 Headquarters."

"Let's find some beds," said Kiyalee flatly.

Bonarain was happy to get her own bed. The other two women had to settle for "stolen" property from the apartments with the destroyed doors. They were able to get all three beds, with frames, on one truck. They scavenged some more food from all four apartments and started their march back to the tavern. They saw no tracks other than their own.

They were able to fit both nutting trucks into the large freight elevator at the same time. Once they got to the apartment, they chose bedrooms and started moving the big chests and putting beds together.

Once he had helped them get all of their possessions to their rooms, he found the main intercom set in the firehouse garage and used it to report in. He punched in the number and waited for a response.

"*This is Command Central, Officer Grade 3, Sunteth, to whom am I speaking?*"

"This is Officer Grade 5, Soolchakan. Team Leader of Team 7016 reporting in."

"*Already? You're saying that you found a place...already?*"

"Yes, Sir, we have a place that's fully intact, plenty of room for us, sufficient food, close to a Tram stop, and close to a watch station."

"*Copy! What is your exact location?*"

"We're just across the street from the Vondor stop. We're quartered in...what used to be the *Wonder House Tavern*. Any further instructions at this time?"

"*Negative! We'll contact you...either by courier or intercom, uh...what's your code there.*"

He gave them the code. He ended the call and headed back up the stairs. All three women were still unpacking and putting things away.

Kiyalee saw him looking around at all of the new things they were pulling out of the chests. "Excuse me, great leader, but we're gonna need some chests of drawers for our rooms. Do ya think that we can pull that off...on our next looting campaign?"

He sighed in disgust. "Sure! We don't need to worry about any chairs or tables...there's plenty of that here."

"That's tavern chairs," spat Chyning. "We want something... just a little bit more comfortable than that."

He cleared his throat. "Yeah! Make a list...so we know what to get on...our next trip."

12

It was nineteen days before they were contacted by Command Central. During those days they made several trips back to the "opened" apartments. They were able to furnish the bedrooms for Kiyalee and Chyning completely.

After all of the trips they made they had decided that they were the only ones in the area and a trip back to that building on Yanalak Street was safe for one person to go alone.

It took one trip to salvage all of the canned or nonperishable foods from the four apartments. They were going to open up more apartments in the area in order to do a scavenger hunt for any and all usable food in the remaining apartments.

Bonarain took full advantage of the alone trips. It took her eight trips, with a full nutting truck, to get all of her makeup, with associated paraphernalia, back to the tavern. She set up an area on the third floor where she put her vanity and makeshift shelves, to hold all of her goodies. She then took some sheets and hung them up in order to have some privacy while doing her makeup.

The fifth bedroom in their combined quarters became an armory. The makeshift armory was the central bedroom, so that no one had to go too far in order to get to the weaponry - just in case.

Soolchakan was a little upset over the fact that the three women kept on doing a feminization to his home. He drowned his irritation in several different liquid "pleasures of the flesh" from the first and fourth floor liquor storage areas, as often as possible.

Once a day, one of the Team would go to the nearest watch station and take a look around. This was also a depressing reminder of the fact that they were the only ones in the area. The ash had not completely blown away in the mild breezes and the only footprints that they found were still their own.

On that nineteenth day, the three women were dining in the tavern area using up some of the last refrigerated perishables that they had found (so far). Someone started banging on the front door. All three of them nearly jumped out of their boots when the knocking started.

Bonarain spit out a mouthful of food (on purpose) and went up near the door. "Who…who's there?"

"Senior Officer, Nadak," came the reply.

The three women all looked at each other in shock.

"They finally remembered us," said Chyning sarcastically.

Again through the door. "We're here from Command Central to inspect the quarters and all personnel and give you some new orders."

Bonarain shrugged, unlocked the door and opened it just enough to peer out. "You said we…who all is there?"

The man standing there let out an exasperated breath. "Senior Officer, Nadak, along with my Team 19, Doctor Shurmook with his medical crew and Officer Grade 3, Shahay, with her Team 989…is there anything else you need to know?"

She gave a helpless chuckle. "Just wondering…Sir…Sir… uh…" She opened the door. "Uh…come on in…Sir…uh…Sirs…all of you."

Three men and nine women walked in looking around the room as they entered. Some of them smiled, some looked at the inner part of the tavern with a little disdain and some just looked.

Bonarain took a glance outside and noticed a large transport truck parked behind a small personnel bus. She wondered why they had not heard the vehicles approaching. That would have been a very different sound - that none of them had heard for several days.

Nadak gave the three women a top to bottom look. "I see a Blue Shirt, a Yellow and a Green…where's the Red?"

Kiyalee scoffed. "Drunk!"

Nadak closed his eyes, turned his head to the right and let out a low growl. He turned to Kiyalee. "Do you think that you could find him?"

"Yes, Sir," said Kiyalee sheepishly. She turned and almost ran to, and up, the staircase.

Nadak turned to one of the other men. "Might as well start

your examination on these two."

Bonarain backed up a little looking concerned. "Examine... what?"

Doctor Shurmook walked towards her with a pleasant look on his face. "Supreme Officer, Nagasoom has ordered that everyone get a quick checkup...to make sure that you're still in good physical condition."

Chyning had a look of concern on her face. "Do we have to get undressed...here...now?"

Shurmook gave her a comforting smile. "Only if you have an injury that is covered by your clothing that you need me to look at."

Chyning shrugged, went back to the table where they had been eating and shoved some more food in her mouth. She sat down and continued eating.

Bonarain watched Chyning and scoffed. She turned back to Nadak. "Sir...uh...can we get you...something to eat...or drink... while you're here?"

Nadak sighed. "Only if you can spare it."

Bonarain smiled. "We've got plenty."

Chyning grunted. "...at the moment," she said disdainfully through a mouthful.

They heard Soolchakan yelling at Kiyalee as the two of them came down the stairs. "What d'ya mean somen's here? Those *bimyocks* at C'mand Sntral done forgot us. Whussa joke?"

Kiyalee came around from the bottom step with a disgusted look on her face. "He's coming...like it or not."

Soolchakan staggered around the corner looking very disheveled and inebriated...with a glass of some kind of liquor in his hand. He looked around the room with an angry face that turned to shock when he saw all of the other people in the room.

Nadak shook his head. "No, we *bimyocks* did not forget you...or your Team...here at this..." He looked around the room and cleared his throat. "...booze barn. We finally got around to you...with some equipment, orders and...we have to do a quick... physical on all of you. I can see, however, that *your* mental condition is...somewhat questionable."

Soolchakan swallowed hard. He looked down at his glass, nervously looked around and then quickly set the glass down on the nearest table. He cleared his throat several times as he tried to clean up his appearance - and then just hung his head.

Nadak let out his breath in a huff. "Now that...*all*...of this Team is present...we are going to have our two doctors from Medical Team 226 examine you. Doctor Shurmook will take...the drunken fool...and examine him. Doctor Aneensa, she will examine the women."

Doctor Shurmook looked at Soolchakan with a smile. "Where would be the best place...for some privacy?"

Soolchakan waved his thumb at the staircase. "Upsairs...tha be bess." He cleared his throat nervously.

Team 7016 and the two doctors went up the stairs to be examined in their bedrooms.

Nadak walked over to the glass that Soolchakan had abandoned. He picked it up, looked at it with a little disgust and then sniffed the contents. His face changed to shock. He looked at the group that had come with him. "This...this is...*Golden Age... Liquor!*" He held the glass up and stared wide-eyed at the yellow liquid. "Where...how...?"

"We are in a tavern, Sir," said Shahay. "There is always a probability of...just about any type of alcoholic beverage being present...in a tavern."

Nadak swirled the contents of the glass. He shook his head. "Oh...to the blazes with it." He took a sip of the liquor and closed his eyes tight as he swallowed and felt the liquor burn all the way down to his stomach. He took a deep breath. "Yeah, that's *Golden Age*! No wonder he's drunk. If I had a case or two of this stuff...I'd have a bender of my own...while the stuff still lasts."

One of the other personnel who had come in huffed. "Sir, did we come here to inspect the premises and personnel...or get shnockered until we hurl?"

Nadak gave him a nasty look. "As you were, Officer, Honn. We can still enjoy a few things...occasionally...while we're inspecting. And they did offer us...a drink." He cleared his throat and took another sip and closed his eyes as he felt the liquor burn all the way down to his stomach.

Doctor Shurmook took Soolchakan into his bedroom. He pulled out a pad. "Okay, let's see now…" He looked up. "Your name and rank?"

Soolchakan cleared his throat and spoke slowly. He was desperately trying to avoid any slurring of his speech. "Officer… Grade…5, Soolchakan."

Shurmook nodded. "Grade 5…yes…and who is the Team leader?"

He cleared his throat loudly again. "Me!"

Shurmook looked shocked. "Huh…you…a Grade 5…the… Team leader?"

Soolchakan nodded.

Shurmook made the annotation on his pad. "Team 7016… the Team Leader…is Officer Grade 5, Soolchakan." He scratched his chin. "All right, now I'm going to check your vitals…and then ask you a few questions."

Soolchakan nodded.

The doctor did a few of the normal things that would be expected in any examination. After making all of his annotations. He stood there looking at Soolchakan and let his breath out slowly. "There is…just no real kind or polite way to ask this. I've had to ask it of all the men that I have examined and…none of them seem to like it." He took another deep breath and let it out slowly. "Since the attack…when we had that horrid light and the resulting…fires…that gutted most of the city…have you, or do you remember having…at any time since…an erection?"

Soolchakan's jaw dropped.

"Please be honest."

Soolchakan looked horrified. "What…what kind a quesson is that? Whaddayoo care…if I got…hard?"

Shurmook hung his head. "Since that attack…so far… no man, that I have examined…can remember…getting *hard*. No man…since that attack has had any form of sexual relation…even…

masturbation."

Soolchakan was suddenly very sober. "I...thought that...we were just too...busy...to worry about...frivolities." He had a worried look as he gazed at the doctor. "Is there something...wrong with us...because of that crazy attack?" He hiccupped and belched.

"We think so. So far...no man has been able to...perform... and no woman has been willing to...participate, either by submitting or being the instigator. No one...in the city walls of Owlam...male or female...has had sex since the attack."

"Does that mean...that we're all...duds?"

"I'm not sure what's going on, however, what I would like to do...is give you some privacy and...I want you to see if you can... stimulate yourself."

Soolchakan looked disgusted now. "And if I can't...are you going to have one of my...Team...or your Team try to do something?"

Shurmook let out a disgusted groan. "No, I think we'll hold back on that...until we find out the condition of the women." He grunted. "Now, on to another question...how much sleep have you been getting...if any?"

Soolchakan looked away and his shoulders sagged. "Only... when I pass out...from...drinking...too much."

"Any sleep...other than that?"

Soolchakan shook his head sadly.

Doctor Aneensa took all three women into one room. She gave each one of them a once over in the area of checking vitals. When she finished she had all three of them sit on the bed and she stood there facing them. "We are not here to just check on your vitals. We are here...because so far there has been...a bit of a change...in all of us. We're hoping that it's only temporary...but...it might not be."

Kiyalee huffed. "What's going on?"

"Yeah," said Chyning. "You seem to be taking the long way around house."

Aneensa smiled. "Yes...I was. What I need to know from you is: When was your last menstrual cycle? Was it before or after that attack and/or have you had a cycle since the attack?"

Bonarain swallowed. "I…was supposed to have one…about nine days after the attack. I…used the pads…but…nuthin'."

"Uh-huh," said Aneensa. She turned to Kiyalee. "What about you?"

Kiyalee just shook her head. "I'm…irregular…very irregular. Sometimes I've gone five months without a cycle, other times I've had as many as three cycles in one month."

"Have you had a cycle…since that attack?"

Kiyalee just shook her head.

Aneensa turned to Chyning. "What about you?"

Chyning pulled her personal pad out. She looked at her calendar. She looked up at the doctor rather concerned. "It…should have happened. It should have happened four days…ago. It didn't. I thought…it was just nerves…or something like that."

"Unfortunately, it isn't," said Aneensa. "It seems that…no woman, anywhere in the city of Owlam, of all the women that we've talked to…has had any menstrual cycle…since that attack."

The three women of Team 7016 looked at each other a little forlorn.

"Another question, ladies, how much sleep have you been getting, since that attack…if any?"

Bonarain looked worried. "I don't…remember…the last time…I woke up…from sleeping. I can't even remember dozing off…since the attack. I can remember a lot of…laying there…bored to tears…but I couldn't…sleep."

"Same thing," said Kiyalee.

Chyning had a guilty look. "The only time…I had any sleep… since the attack…I…sampled a little too much…of the…ale…from the booze storeroom." She flushed. "Other than that…nuthin'."

Everyone was back in the tavern bar room.

"It's the same thing here," said Shurmook. He shook his head. "There's only twenty-one more Teams to check on…and I don't think that we're going to find anything different. We haven't so far."

Nadak nodded his head sadly as he stared at the floor.

Soolchakan heaved a sigh. "So…what…does all of this mean, Sir?"

Still staring at the floor, Nadak answered. "What it means is…we are the last…generation…of the city of Owlam. Once we… who are inside the walls…are all dead…there will be no more… Owlam. All of us…who are still alive were…somehow…sterilized… by that wretched attack." He looked up. "We also seem to have an epidemic…of sleep deprivation. The crazy thing there…no one seems to be suffering…from this lack of sleep. It seems to be some kind of crazy…thing…that goes along with what the medical personnel are calling…residuals."

Chyning scoffed. "So…what are we defending?" She shook her head. "If there aren't gonna be any more of us and we can't seem to sleep, then…what difference does it make what we do?"

"We are still alive," said Nadak. "Supreme Officer, Nagasoom, has given the order…that we will persevere…with what we have. We will continue to defend Owlam…to the very last. We may not be remembered in history, but, we're going to try to make everyone around us remember…NOW!" His gaze went up and he had a stern look on his face. "We will *make* them all remember that the Owlam were *here!*"

Soolchakan hung his head. "By…doing…*what?*"

"The equipment that we have brought with us…for you. You will use this equipment to…prepare to…fight back any enemy… by any method that you can use. We will make any…enemy…pay dearly for trying to breach our walls and take what we have. Is that understood?"

Soolchakan shrugged. "Yes, Sir, but…what's this equipment and what do we do with it?"

"Its thick floor mats, exercise equipment and some guidance videos. You will start by watching the videos. You will then use the equipment to learn to fight…hand-to-hand. You will become offensive soldiers as well as defensive personnel. That's what you're going to do." He looked around. "We may have to set up the equipment in this room, unless you know of a bigger room, at your disposal, where we can set it all up."

"Let's take a look at the third floor," said Soolchakan. "I... think that you'll find it more to your liking."

Nadak stood up. "All right, let's go check it out."

Honn looked around the room on the third floor. "This is excellent!" He paced off a large area of the room. "We can put the mat down here." He looked off to the other end of the room. "We can put the practice equipment over there...and no one will be crowded. I wish everyone had found...facilities like this." He gave his Team Leader, Shahay an evil side glance. "It would be *very* nice."

Shahay sneered at him. "None of the taverns, in our area, are this large. None of them have a big room like this...that was undergoing renovation. You'll have to be satisfied with your gymnasium."

Honn chuckled. "The only problem now...getting all of the equipment up here."

"That's not a problem," said Soolchakan. "We have a couple of nutting trucks and a freight elevator."

Honn stared at Soolchakan wide-eyed. "I'm liking this place even more."

Shahay snarled through her teeth. "No, we're not moving our living quarters to the southern area. Nagasoom has stated that he needs...certain ranking personnel there, on the north side...ready to take on the Axswain at any time."

Nadak turned to Soolchakan. "Let your Team get the equipment up here. I need to talk to you about some other things."

Soolchakan felt a cold chill go down his spine. He was wondering what he was going to get chewed out for now. "Yes...Sir. Uh...did you want to talk here...or...?"

"Downstairs will be fine."

"Yes, Sir."

Soolchakan followed Nadak down the stairs like a condemned prisoner. As they got into the bar area, Nadak stopped and looked down at the glass of liquor that had been abandoned. Now Soolchakan really felt like he was in for it.

Nadak got close to Soolchakan. "You got any more of that *Golden Age?*"

Now the suspicions were really going haywire. "Uh...yes, Sir, I've got a few more bottles."

Nadak had a patronizing smile. "Get one for me and I'll forget...your slovenly appearance."

Soolchakan quickly headed for the storeroom behind the bar. He had found three more cases of the expensive liquor in there. He came back with an unopened bottle. "Here you go, Sir."

Nadak cradled it carefully. "Oh you don't know...how long I've wanted to be able to get my hands on...just a glassful of this." He kissed the bottle. He placed the bottle on the table and cleared his throat. "Now, down to business! Have you searched any of the... un-scorched apartments in the area?"

Soolchakan was momentarily taken aback by the question. "Uh...just four of them...over on Yanalak Street...Sir."

"Are there any more in this area?"

"Probably...several dozen...maybe...more?"

"Open all of them. Search all of them. Find...any food that you can and store it...I guess this place would be fine for the storage. Something is happening. The crops, both inside and outside of the wall, are...wilting. They're rotting in the fields...in spite of sufficient irrigation. We don't know why, but we think that it's...some kind of residual...plague from that attack. We've noticed that a lot of the wild herd animals...and the predators are...not doing too well either. Find *all* the food you can and...store it where you know how to get to it. We may not be getting any fresh food...for who knows how long. You can survive on that food. Once it's gone...then we have nothing but emergency rations."

Soolchakan sighed. "All the apartments?"

"*All* of the buildings! Businesses, homes, storage facilities... it doesn't matter. We may have to scrounge for everything we can get. All of the manufacturers...were in the central part of the city. Nothing new is being made. Food processing, weapons manufacturing, furniture..." He looked at the bottle on the table. "...breweries..."

"Are you...going to need an inventory?"

"Only if things get...really critical."

"Are we going to get any help?"

"No, because Nagasoom has decided that the only threat to Owlam is Axswain. We've heard nothing of Teltermak to the east, Galsino to the west or Zee-Altha to the south. Kalash isn't doing very well either, and besides, they hate Galsino more than they hate us. No, our primary enemy...that's still viable...the city of Axswain."

Soolchakan pondered for a few moments. "Yes, Sir."

"When I think of what happened...it's just...sickening."

"I know, Sir...I..."

"You don't know the half of it!"

"Uh...what's...the other half?"

Nadak hung his head and sighed. He sniffled a little. He turned away and wiped his eyes and nose. "Just before...that... attack..." He cleared his throat. "...I saw a report from the census building." He heaved another sigh. "Two days before that attack... the population of the city of Owlam had just hit...five million nine hundred fifty thousand. We were only fifty thousand away from six million citizens. I didn't look...but I know that there were a great many of them who were...under the age of...nineteen."

Soolchakan felt a huge lump in his throat. "And now...we're down to...wait a moment, someone told me that we had lost... about...three million."

"I know, I know. We always lie, so that no one knows our real numbers. This way, we can always give them a bigger surprise than what they were expecting."

"What about...what's left?"

"Twenty-eight thousand and sixty-four. That's all of us that are left...that matter." Nadak gave him a rather angry looking glare. "Orders from the top...from this day forth...if anyone tries to find out our numbers...now...if you get caught by some enemy...cut the figures down...by a fourth. If anyone asks what our numbers were... before the attack, you tell them that we were just short of three million and our current numbers...just over seven thousand. Is that understood?"

"Yes, Sir."

"Now, another reason for this...search of all of the

apartments."

Soolchakan was shocked. "What else do we need, other than food and an inventory?"

"In...a few other parts of the city, there have been found... some cowards...who had hidden themselves in their quarters... and were afraid to go out...at all. Nagasoom wants these cowards found...if there are any more."

Soolchakan shook his head. "What do I do...if I find somebody?"

"Take them prisoner and report the cowards...as soon as possible."

"What's being done with them?"

"If there is an attack, by...who knows what...at this time, those cowards will be put on our front line of the attack. If they draw the fire of the enemy and get killed, it will give us...the ones who did their duty, a better chance of survival...in any attack."

"Uh...Sir, if I...may ask...how many...so far?"

Nadak looked off to the side. "Forty-six," he spat.

The two men sat in silence until they heard approaching footsteps.

Honn came down into the bar. "Sir, we have all the equipment up there, ready to go. I need to assess the personnel now."

"Right," said Nadak. He looked at Soolchakan. "Join him..." he grabbed the bottle. "...while I take care of this. I'll be up in a moment." He got up and headed out the front door with the bottle of liquor.

Soolchakan followed Honn up the stairs to the third floor. Other than the area that Bonarain had blocked off, for her private beauty parlor, the place had been turned into a working gymnasium. There was a very large mat that took up almost one fourth of the big room. There were several large punching bags and exercise machines set up off to the side.

The three women of Team 7016 were looking over the exercise machines with a little awe (and consternation).

Soolchakan was a little stunned. "Isn't this...just a...little bit extravagant and expensive?"

Honn leaned close and whispered. "Don't forget…this equipment had originally been set up for a population of almost six million. With what's left…we can afford to be…extravagant - especially with the ones who are left…who matter. As far as price… right now…money is…virtually worthless."

Soolchakan stared at all of the equipment, wide-eyed. The only thing he could do was nod.

Kiyalee motioned for the other two women to get close. The three huddled together. "They want to see us…doing some fighting. They want to watch us and determine how good we are at fighting… hand-to-hand," She gave an evil grin. "Why don't the three of us… attack our…fearless, drunken leader? Let's give them something to look at."

Bonarain and Chyning now had evil grins on their faces as well.

Honn hollered from across the room at the three women. "Take your rank shirts off and we'll pair you off. We need to see what level you need to be started at…with the training videos. You also need to remove your work boots, while you're on the mat."

With nasty looking smiles, the women took off their Blue, Yellow and Green. They hung them on one of the exercise machines. They shed their boots and walked onto the mat.

Soolchakan pulled his Red shirt off and looked for someplace to hang it.

"The floor will hold it," said Honn in a disgusted manner.

Soolchakan grunted back and flipped the shirt over his shoulder - to somewhere - anywhere - behind him. He leaned against the wall as he took his boots off and then he headed onto the mat. He did not like the expressions that he saw on the faces of the three women. He got closer and he liked their expressions even less.

Kiyalee's eyes suddenly widened. "NOW!"

All three women lunged to the attack.

Bonarain woke up, face down on the mat. She hurt, rather badly, in several different places that she could not remember injuring. She tasted blood in her mouth. She lifted her head slightly and saw a small patch of dried blood - where her open mouth had been on the mat. It took a few blinks to get her eyes in focus. She groaned in pain as she attempted to prop herself up on her elbows. There was a very nasty pain in her left shoulder. She looked around the gymnasium.

Kiyalee was sitting, off the mat, against the wall near the staircase. She had her ankles, seemingly, as far apart as she could get them. She was holding a rather large ice pack over the left side of her face. Her hair was uncharacteristically messed up.

Bonarain tried to speak and got out nothing but a croak. She cleared her throat. "Hey…whadapan?"

Kiyalee looked up out of her right eye without moving her head. "You mean…you don't remember?"

"We…jumped…that drunken *chogo*. I remember…jumping at him. I…don't remember…nuthin' after that."

Kiyalee lifted her head up and grunted. "He fought back…he won."

"He…uh…where's Chyning? Where's everybody else?"

Kiyalee took a deep breath and let it out. "Chyning is with the doctor. He's taking care of her broken arm."

"Soolchakan…busted…her arm?"

Kiyalee closed her eye and scoffed. "*She* busted her arm."

"How?"

"She tried some…fancy-schmancy elbow smash. He blocked it - with his knee. She busted her arm across his knee. Then he… mopped the floor with our faces."

Bonarain hung her head. "Crap! We're just a trio of *wuffy little poofids*."

Kiyalee scoffed. "Funny you should say that. After Soolchakan…did his single-handed act of drastically rearranging *our* attack pattern…that Officer, Honn, who *is* a professional fight trainer, took him on." She grunted in pain and rubbed a spot on her right side rib area. "That Honn…knocked Soolchakan out…with one shot. *He* called Soolchakan…a *wuffy little poofid*."

Bonarain looked up totally in mental anguish. "So…the three of us…got the *peewodon* kicked out of us…by a…*wuffy little poofid*. What does that make us?"

Kiyalee grunted in pain as she tried to move her right leg. "It makes us...*wuffier*...than a *wuffy poofid*."

Bonarain laid flat on the mat again. "So," she grunted. "Why isn't one of them doctors looking at us?"

"They already did. They decided that we would...live. The only thing that I need is this...*chokwad* ice pack. All you need...is count...your teeth."

Bonarain ran her tongue around her mouth. "They're all there."

"You seriously...don't remember...*nuthin*'?"

Bonarain groaned as she rolled over on her back. "NO! I... can't remember a thing...after jumping at him."

Kiyalee shook her head. "You're lucky! I remember...every painful shot."

Bonarain got up slowly - or at least she tried to get up. It took her four attempts before she was finally standing - on very unstable, rubbery legs. She staggered toward Kiyalee. "Should we join them...downstairs? I don't think...they want us to have...another fight session...until we've had a little practice...with those punching dummies."

Kiyalee looked up and dropped the ice pack away from her face. Almost the entire left side of her face was one big bruise. "*We* are the punching dummies."

"How did your face get to looking...like that?"

"I met his foot...the hard way."

Bonarain grunted. "Yeah. So, again, shall we go... downstairs?"

Kiyalee looked over towards the stairs. "I think...we better take the elevator. If either one of us...tries the stairs...we're gonna need more attention than what Chyning is gettin' right now."

They came out of the elevator. They stumbled and staggered their way to the bar area where everyone else had congregated.

Chyning was laid out flat on top of the bar, wearing nothing but her underwear, while the two doctors were doing final inspection on a cast on her right arm. There were several large bruises on her body. Chyning herself was "feeling no pain". She was staring off into space with half closed, glazed over eyes, singing some tuneless song with words that were totally unintelligible.

Bonarain leaned against the end of the bar. "Hey, doc… whatever you gave her…can I have some of it?"

Shurmook looked over at Bonarain. "No you can't. There's no more new manufacturing of pharmaceuticals. We have to use them…sparingly. I have to do an examination of you…now that you're conscious." He gave Bonarain the once-over looking at. "You better sit down somewhere, before you fall down - both of you."

Bonarain looked at a chair by the nearest table. "Good idea."

Both Bonarain and Kiyalee staggered to chairs at the table and sat down. Bonarain gasped and grimaced in pain as she sat and placed her hand on a very tender spot on her left hip. Kiyalee put the ice pack back up to the swollen left side of her face and slouched down with a loud sigh.

Doctor Aneensa left Chyning and came over to work with Bonarain and Kiyalee in helping them "count their marbles", to see just how many they had left.

Bonarain looked over at Soolchakan. He had a rather large bandage covering a part of his right cheek. She sighed. "Did one of us do that to his face?"

Kiyalee huffed.

"I did it," said Honn proudly. "You think that a *chogo* like you could do any damage…to anyone…over the age of five?"

Bonarain snarled back at Honn.

A woman walked up to the table where Bonarain and Kiyalee were suffering in misery, carrying several video boxes. "Hello, I'm Officer Grade 5, Shaffani. I'm one of the Fighting Instructors. You… *bimyocks* are pathetic. You will watch all of these videos while you are…convalescing. You will learn from these and…don't try taking on anything tougher than the punching dummies that we've supplied for you." She scoffed. "I wouldn't be surprised if those dummies kicked the *peewodon* out of you as well, so…again, don't take on anything tougher than the dummies."

Bonarain looked at them. There were twelve altogether. They were all marked: Beginner. She sighed in utter despondency. She looked over and saw a pile of videos in front of Soolchakan. "Why two sets...doesn't he have to look at the same ones we do?"

Shaffani chuckled patronizingly. "We saw him...handle the three of you...with *great* ease. We've looked at his record. He's already a Fifth Rank Fighter. According to your records...all three of you women...we can't find any fight training...at all. So...you're Novices." Again that nasty, demeaning chuckle.

Kiyalee looked at the bandage on Soolchakan's face. "But...I saw him get...knocked silly, by Honn. What makes him...a Fifth?"

Shaffani rolled her eyes. "Honn...is a *Fifteenth* Rank Fighter. The only reason he's a Fifteenth...is because there's no higher rank... currently. I'm at the Thirteenth Rank. That's why he's the coach and I'm an assistant. Our colleague..." She pointed at another woman, who was sifting through some other videos. "Officer Grade 5, Teetayan, is also a Thirteenth. We are checking...everyone for there fighting capability..." Again the chuckle. "So far...you *bimyocks* are in last place...absolutely dead last. Every other Team has at least three people who are either Third Rank or above. This pathetic Team has only one person who has a rank." She grunted in disgust. "As I said - pathetic."

Bonarain wanted to slap the smirk off of the face of Shaffani. She knew that if she tried it, however, she would probably be fed her own fist - along with her shoes, socks and underwear. She sighed, picked up the first video and started reading the instructions on the box.

The visitors departed - after the drugs wore off and Chyning was lucid. They were all given instructions on utilization of the training videos - with a few more sneers and jeers.

Soolchakan informed his Team of the mandatory search of all buildings in the immediate vicinity. He informed them of the cowards and all other information concerning the bleak situation.

Kiyalee shook her head. "What is all this? We have to search all of the buildings...every room. We have to look for these...

cowards…if we find any…where do we put them? Where do we store all of the food that we find? When are we going to have time to…do the fight training *and* do all of the searching?"

Soolchakan grunted. "According to the doctors…it seems that there is some kind of residual…contamination going on…from that attack. One of the…manifestations…as he called it…we, as a whole, talking about everyone who was inside the walls when the attack happened, don't seem to need any sleep. No one seems to be getting any sleep. We just lay there in bed…bored silly. They want us to record how long we go without sleep and what we're doing in all of those waking hours. We train, we search, we report…" He shook his head. "I think they just came up with something to keep us busy."

Bonarain grunted back at him. "Or it may be just what they say - get ready for any kind of military action…offensive or defensive."

"So," said Soolchakan. "For the next few…however long it takes…at night we're in our makeshift gymnasium…training. During the day, we search out and inventory…*all* of the buildings… that haven't been gutted by fire."

Chyning tapped her fingers (of her left hand) on the table. "So what about prisoners? Where do we keep them? Who guards them?"

Soolchakan hung his head. "Let's hope…that we don't find any. If we do…we'll take care of that situation…if it arises."

13

Over the next eighteen days, they did the searches of the area. They chose the ones furthest from their "headquarters" to start with. Each day they came back with one of the nutting trucks, at least half full, with non-perishable groceries. The other truck, sometimes, ended up with some kind of frivolity. They were accumulating a rather large food bank of their own.

They did see a few charred bodies, in the burned areas near the untouched buildings. They were not really sure what to do so they left them alone. There were stories of certain diseases arising out of dead bodies, however, all of these had been charred and that was supposed to kill any form of contagious microorganism. They still did not like the idea of handling any bodies.

On the nineteenth day, they were going out on their normal routine of scrounging. They had mapped out the area and were doing an orderly grid search.

"I don't understand this," said Chyning. "We've been victimized by all of this destruction...but we still have running water. How come we still got running water...and electricity?"

Bonarain, who was walking point, turned around and glared at Chyning. "Haven't you read *any* of those booklets, tracts, pamphlets or regulations that you were supposed to read? You're gonna stay a Grade 7...forever if you don't do some reading." She turned and started leading the procession again while shaking her head and letting out more "very audible" scoffs.

Chyning looked back at Soolchakan. "What'd I miss?"

Soolchakan sighed. "There are over...*were* over twelve hundred water pumping and purification stations in the city. There... were...over sixteen hundred different power stations. They're scattered, far and wide, all over the city, inside the wall. This way, no matter what happens, no matter how much destruction...there should be a pumping station and a power station that can give...just about any section of the city all the power and water that it needs. Right now, since we're getting into these buildings and shutting off all power and water, since no one is using that facility, we're preserving whatever we have, just for our area. Once we've shut down all of the other buildings, in this area, our...home...will be the only place... here...using any power or water. That's why we have plenty...and as Bonarain said - all of that information is in the *MANDATORY READING* SECTIONS of the regulations."

Chyning hung her head, turned red and continued her uneasy pushing of the truck. The first few days, with the cast on her arm, it had been quite a chore trying to push the truck. Now, she had some practice at it and was able to move the thing a little easier - with minimal pain in her broken arm.

Bonarain stopped and checked her map. She turned. "Okay, we're here. This is our target for today."

Kiyalee looked around. "But there's...buildings across the street there, why aren't we doing them?"

Bonarain held up her map. "THAT, on the other side of the cross street is the 1900 block. We've already searched the 1900 block, north and south side of the street. Today, we start our search of the 1800 block, OKAY?!"

Kiyalee flushed and hung her head. "Yeah, okay."

Soolchakan looked up at the building. "At least it's not another one of those eight-story buildings. This one only has three floors."

"Yeah," said Bonarain. "I still can't understand why some *bimyock* designed a building that tall...WITHOUT AN ELEVATOR! Apparently he wanted everyone to get, and stay, in shape."

Soolchakan handed his rifle to Chyning. "Do I need the hammer to get in?"

Bonarain tested the door, hung her head and sighed. She pointed at the door. "Get the hammer."

He picked up the heavy sledgehammer. He walked up and gave the door a quick stare down as he looked for the best place to smash the lock in. The women backed away as he prepared himself. The first hit made a hole in the door, just above the locking mechanism - and a burglar alarm went off. He growled as the irritating bell was doing what it was designed to do. It took three more hard hits around the locking mechanism before the door gave way. He walked inside and looked up at the alarm that was high on the wall. It was calling - with no one listening. One hard hit on the alarm and, after clattering in pieces all over the foyer, it was now silent debris. He rubbed his ears. He looked at the women. "The door is open...are you waiting for some special kind of invitation?"

Bonarain and Kiyalee came in and the three of them headed up the stairs. Each landing had an apartment on each end of the landing. Six apartments in all in this stairwell. On the top landing, Soolchakan readied himself to break down another door. The women waited on the stairs while he destroyed another locking mechanism. Once the door was battered in, the two women entered to start the search. He went over and bashed in the other door, left the hammer on the stairs and then joined the women for the search.

This apartment, like many others they had searched, had a rather bad smell in it. Usually it was some non-perishable food that had been left out and was, by now, thoroughly rotten. There was something that was rather unrecognizable sitting in a bowl on the dining room table. It had been decorative - at one time. Kiyalee picked up the big bowl, took it to the bathroom, flushed the foul smelling contents and rinsed the bowl.

Bonarain and Soolchakan continued down the hall and each picked a door on opposite sides of the hall for their search.

He opened his door and walked in. He started with the normal once over glance around. A large, neatly made bed, two nightstands, two chests of drawers, two overstuffed chairs, a vanity (complete with all of that garbage that women use to paint their faces) and a door off to the side to the closet. He was heading for the closet to start searching...when he heard Bonarain scream. He spun around quickly to head for that other room and cracked his knee against a piece of furniture.

Kiyalee had dropped the bowl she was rinsing when she heard the scream and was able to get into the room, with Bonarain, before Soolchakan could limp his way over there.

He limped in, ready to take on an opponent or unknown origin. Instead what he saw was both women, giggling and hugging... something that he could not see because they were covering... something.

He rubbed his pained knee. "What's going on? Wha...what is it?"

Both women turned around with joyful looks on their faces.

"This is a sewing room and...this...it's a sewing machine," said Bonarain triumphantly.

He flopped down in a nearby chair, wincing as he rubbed his throbbing knee. "SO?"

"All that sewing, altering that clothing to fit, that we've had to do by hand..." said Kiyalee grinning. "...we can use *this* to do the alterations, quickly, and save a *huge* amount of time."

"Yeah...okay," he said as he continued rubbing. "So, how do we get it out of here? It looks like, for some reason, it has been bolted to that table."

"We'll UN-bolt it," said Bonarain patronizingly. "Whoever put it in here has to have some tools...somewhere in this place."

"Fine! Good plan. Go find the tools." He stood up, wincing again and limped back to the room that he was going to search. He walked back to the bedroom, sat down on the bed and rubbed his knee again. Finally after the pain subsided, he went to the closet. It was a big walk-in closet that had male clothing in one corner and female clothing that took up more than three quarters of the hangar space. He shook his head disgusted. "Most of this...female stuff... expensive, overpriced, flashy garbage," he muttered. He looked at the male clothing. Whoever had lived here, the man was rather large...in the midsection. His clothing appeared to be the same kind of expensive show-off stuff. "Did these people have anything that was...normal?" He shook his head. Most of what he found was for showing off while attending extravagant parties.

"Found the tools," shouted Bonarain from somewhere else in the apartment.

"Oh joy," he muttered sarcastically. He headed out of the bedroom to perform the looting job on the sewing machine. "You women might like what you find in their bedroom closet."

The two women looked at him confused and then looked at each other. They both shrugged. Bonarain put a wrench down and both women headed to the room that he had just vacated. He picked up the wrench to start removing nuts and bolts when he heard ear-piercing shrieks of joy, coming from the women. He growled to himself as he started loosening a nut on the underside of the table. This place was going to give a lot of clothing for all. He wondered if this family had an equally, expensive taste, in the food as they had in their clothing. They did. There was some very expensive items in Owlam cuisine - as well as two more bottles of *Golden Age Liquor*.

He got the pleasure of lugging the heavy sewing machine down the stairs. 'If this had been going up...they would have to carry it,' he thought. He got down to the bottom of the stairs and rested there while he was panting.

Chyning looked inside the door, saw what he was carrying and gasped in delight. "A sewing machine...a professional model!"

"It's...in a carrying case..." he puffed. "How...could you... even know...what's in here?"

She grinned. "I recognize the carrier. I've been wanting one, of that model, for a long time." She walked in and touched the outer case lovingly.

"Get back to your duty," he snapped. "Time for frivolities... when we're back at our HQ."

She retreated out the door looking a little forlorn.

He lugged the thing out the door and placed it on one of the trucks. Chyning sat down next to it, with her broken arm resting on top of the case and a big grin on her face.

He turned to go back up the stairs. The other two women were coming down the stairs with huge armloads of the fancy dresses from that closet. He groaned in disgust. They heaped all of the dresses on the truck with the machine and Chyning let out a squeal of delight when she saw all of the dresses. All three of them started babbling, at the same time about their plans for the dresses.

He listened to their noises for a few moments until he had had enough. "HEY! Enough of that *h'oolyach*! Remember what we're here for! We're here…for necessities. That stuff…ain't…necessary!" He looked at their surprised faces. "Besides…where are you gonna put all…" He waved his hands at the huge pile of dresses. "…that? None of the closets…back at our quarters…are that big."

Bonarain stood up and slapped her fists onto her hips. "The fourth floor is *not* full. We can partition an area, for each one of us… including *you*…up there. We can set up the sewing machine and do all of the adjustments, stitching and tailoring up there."

The other two women agreed, merrily.

He shook his head. "Remember our priorities. One: Search out the area for necessities and any…cowards. Two: Fight training. This stuff here is…at best…last on the list." He finally felt that his strength had come back to him. "Right now…we forget about… foraging through that…luxury stuff. We go back up and look for food…NOW!"

Bonarain and Kiyalee followed him back up to the third floor, still babbling about their plans for those fancy dresses. They went back to apartment 6 and ransacked all of the non-perishable food.

Apartment 5, on the third floor, did not get them any luxuries. It did give them a decent supply of food.

Back up to the second floor. Apartments 3 and 4 were to be searched now. He smashed in the door of number 3. The women entered. He hammered the door to number 4. When it opened, he was nearly knocked backwards by the smell. He grabbed the door and pulled it shut, trying to keep from gagging.

The women came out of 3, each carrying a box full of groceries. They looked at him confused.

Bonarain cocked her head to the side. "Why you lookin' so green? Is there something in there? What could possibly be that bad?"

"Take that…food downstairs," he croaked. "Is there any more usable food…in that apartment?"

"No, we got it all, this is it," said Kiyalee.

"Take it down, then…come back up here and…you'll find out."

Both women shrugged and lugged their spoils downstairs. They came back up looking rather suspicious. He motioned for them to get closer to the door. They came closer, cautiously. He opened the door and gave them a good whiff.

Bonarain retreated into apartment 3, holding her nose. "You could give someone a warning...couldn't you?"

Kiyalee just leaned over the railing and threw up.

He looked at Bonarain. "Oh...yeah...she has a weak stomach."

Bonarain still had a look of horror on her face. "What...is that...in there that could possibly be so...foul?"

Kiyalee went into apartment 3 to find some place to rinse her mouth out - and possibly lose a little bit more out of her stomach.

"I think...that something, or someone...died in there. As long as it's been since that attack...if they died that day..." He shook his head in disgust. "Either way...we have to check."

Bonarain hung her head. She looked back up. "Hold your nose!" She followed him into the apartment.

They found the source of the smell in the bedroom. There was a couple, laying on the bed - in an advanced state of decomposition. From the amount of dried blood, all over the bed, and pooled on the floor, and a bloody knife on a nightstand, it was obvious that they had opened there veins and simply lay there bleeding to death. They had carefully placed their identification cards sitting on the other nightstand.

He quickly picked up the ID cards and retreated to apartment 3. Bonarain quickly followed and closed the door as she departed. Once in the other apartment, they heaved a few deep breaths in order to try to get some of that stench out of their nostrils.

Kiyalee was sitting in a big chair with one hand over her mouth and the other hand on her stomach.

He looked around the room. "Where's...the com setup?"

Bonarain picked up the microphone. "Here it is."

He walked slowly to where the device was. He took the microphone and then punched the code to Command Central on the keypad. The response was almost immediate.

"Command Central here, what's your designation and location?"

"This is Officer Grade 5, Soolchakan of Team 7016. My Team and I are currently searching the 1800 block of Gand Street for anything usable."

"Do you have something important to report?"

"I'm not sure. We were told to report if we found any cowards hiding in the area...we didn't find a coward, but we did find a couple that committed suicide. Does anyone care about that?"

"Stand by." They heard some unintelligible chatter coming over the speaker. *"Team 7016, are you still in that location...now?"*

"We're across the hallway...the stench is incredible."

"Understand...we need you to go back in there and report any form of insect life...that's working on the corpses."

Kiyalee and Bonarain looked at him in shock.

He cleared his throat loudly. "Is this...a joke?"

"Negative! Get in there and report all insect life!"

He sighed. "Stand by, I'll go check." He held his nose and went back to number 4. He walked slowly back to the bedroom, looking for any form of insect in the front rooms. He found none. He walked into the bedroom. He looked around and was absolutely stunned when he saw no sign of insect life in there. He went back to number 3 and picked up the microphone. "Uh...Sir...you may not believe this...but...I don't see *any* bugs of any type at all...none, Sir."

"None at all?"

"Nothing, Sir."

Again some of the muttering. *"Thank you, for that report, Team 7016. Go ahead and close the apartment and mark the door."*

"What do I mark on it?"

"That a couple of doovofts committed suicide in there, what else?"

He shrugged. "Yes, Sir...Team 7016...out!" He closed the line and looked at the two women. They had that look of anxiety on their faces.

Bonarain chuckled nervously. "Should we search that place... for any food?"

Kiyalee stood up looking at Bonarain as if she had lost her mind. "Would you want to eat...*anything*...that comes out of...that...place?"

Bonarain huffed. "Okay! So...what do we mark the door with?"

"There's got to be something...somewhere...in this apartment that can be used."

Bonarain started looking for some kind of a marker.

Soolchakan looked at his other companion. "Kiyalee!"

"What?"

"You get a towel...or something. You get down there and clean up your puke...so that neither one of us ends up slipping in it."

She gave him a nasty look and headed to the bathroom for the towel.

Bonarain found a marker and was headed back to door 4. "What're you gonna do?"

Soolchakan went back into the hallway and picked up the sledgehammer. "I'm going downstairs to open the doors on the first floor." He turned to go down the stairs. He made the special effort to avoid stepping in any of the mess that Kiyalee had made when she had lost her breakfast. "Slob," he muttered bitterly.

He looked out the door before opening the apartments on the first floor. Chyning was sitting next to, and fondling, the container that the sewing machine was in. He muttered under his breath and turned to apartment 1. When he hit the door, he heard Chyning yelp in surprise.

She came to the door. "You could at least warn somebody!"

He looked at her and smirked. "You're supposed to be keeping an eye out...in all directions. If I took you by surprise, it's because you weren't doing your job."

She started sniffing. "Uh...all of a sudden...you stink! What *is* that smell?"

He took a quick whiff of each arm. He could not smell anything untoward. It was possible that his nose had become somewhat deadened, or accustomed, after spending all that time near the bodies. He sighed. "We found a couple of suicides...in apartment 4. I guess that that smell…lingers for a while."

"Is that why…somebody puked?"

"What d'ya think?"

She looked back at the nutting truck. "You…" She turned back to him. "…didn't bring any food…from *that* apartment…did you?"

He closed his eyes and groaned. He gave her a dirty look. "We're not that stupid."

She chuckled nervously and walked back outside, waving the smell away from her face. She sat back down next to the sewing machine.

He snarled and went to the outer door. "KEEP WATCH!"

She jumped up and looked back at him angrily. "For…what?"

"Bugs!"

Her expression changed to a look of shocked confusion. "What?"

"Bugs!"

"What do you want to know…about bugs?"

"There's two dead bodies in apartment 4. There are no bugs… eating the bodies. Command Central wants to know if we see any bugs."

Now she just looked shocked. "They want…an inventory… of bugs?"

"Yes! Now, have you seen any…any at all…since the attack?"

She stood there pondering. She looked along the ground. She looked up high for any flying insects. She looked all around her. "What kind of a joke is this?"

Kiyalee had come down the stairs to clean up her mess. "He's not joking! Command Central wants us to look for bugs."

Bonarain had finished with the door and was coming down as well. "Yeah, we had a hard time believing it as well. Command Central is worried about, and wants an inventory, of bugs."

Chyning looked down at the heavy caliber rifle that was on the cargo truck. "Did they say what kind of weaponry we're supposed to use?"

He readied himself for another swing at the door to apartment

1. "We're just supposed to report any sightings." He swung and the door gave way.

Bonarain walked into the apartment. Kiyalee stopped cleaning and was following Bonarain.

"Finish cleaning up your mess," snarled Soolchakan. "It's gonna smell pretty bad, pretty soon if you don't."

Kiyalee scoffed. "Pretty soon, this whole stairwell is gonna reek. My puke ain't gonna make a whole lotta difference."

He growled and turned to apartment 2 on the other side. He was a little aggravated with the women and took his frustration out on the door. One hard smash with the sledgehammer and the helpless door flew wide open and slammed against the inner wall. He took the hammer out, dropped it on the truck and went back to search apartment 2.

They finished looting the apartments on the first floor. As they got ready to depart he stopped and looked up at the windows of apartment 4. He turned back to Bonarain. "You still got that marker?"

She looked at him confused. "Uh…no…why?"

"Maybe you should mark the outer door as well…you know… about those bodies."

She sighed and shrugged. She went back inside apartment 1. A few moments later she came out with a marker and wrote a message on the outer door, concerning the bodies in apartment 4.

They continued on to the next stairwell in the building. In their later searches of the area, they did find one more suicide - and zero insect life.

Back in their quarters they spent most of the night in their makeshift gymnasium. They would watch the videos that gave them information on the best form to use. They would then spend a great deal of time punching and kicking the big hanging bags.

Chyning, for the moment, could only work on her kicks. The cast on her arm made it difficult to punch. The healing bones made it rather painful to even think of punching with her right arm.

Occasionally they would do a few face to face confrontations, on the mat, with each other. The women were very frustrated over the fact that Soolchakan always won these little sparring matches. He was far more ready to fight and far more experienced in both offense and defense.

Seventeen days after Team 7016 received the videos, Team 989 came back to evaluate any progress. Officer, Honn knocked Soolchakan out easily. Officer, Shaffani knocked Bonarain out easily. Officer, Teetayan knocked Kiyalee out easily. Officer, Shahay knocked Chyning out easily.

After all four were brought back to a state of awareness, the evaluation that they were given was completely dismal.

Fifteen days later, Team 989 showed up again. The results were identical to the last one.

Shahay sat at a table in the bar with her recorder. "Officer Grade 3, Shahay reporting. The progress of Team 7016 is… insignificant…at best. The only one who has any excuse…for not… getting any better…is the one with the cast on her arm. Pretty soon, though, she won't have that excuse…either. If they don't show any improvement in our next visit…" She gave the members of Team 7016 a stern look. "…it is recommended that these *bimyocks* should have their status changed from active duty military personnel…to practice dummies for personnel who *are* improving." She turned her recorder off. She gave Team 7016 another look of disgust. "Team 989, let us depart and find something…worthy of our attention." Team 989 got up and left.

Team 7016 sat there nursing their bruises and feeling sorry for themselves…in complete silence…for several hours.

Two days later, Doctor Aneensa showed up to look at the broken arm. She examined Chyning in the main bar, while Kiyalee was cooking in the kitchen, for all five people in the building.

Aneensa took the cast off and examined the arm. "This is healing nicely. Have you been practicing with that rubber ball?"

"Yeah," said Chyning dejectedly. "It doesn't hurt as much as it did…at first. I can squeeze it harder too. I can keep doing it longer as well."

Aneensa nodded in approval.

Kiyalee came out of the kitchen, pushing a cart full of food that had a very welcome aroma. They all got their plates and served themselves, buffet style, off of the cart.

Aneensa shook her head as she ate. "You people are one of the most fortunate Teams…at the moment. You have a good supply of food here, you're somewhat isolated from the rest…but I'm told that if you don't start showing some…extreme improvement… in your fighting capabilities…the Supreme Officer, Nagasoom will assign this place to someone else."

Kiyalee dropped her fork on her plate. "You really know how to kill someone's appetite."

Aneensa took another mouthful of food, chewed it and swallowed. "I know that you're all hurting…and someone at Command Central came up with the idea that you're not advancing because you haven't been given any advanced videos. They sent some with me. Maybe if you look at these videos…and practice with them…maybe you'll improve." She pointed to a large black case that she had brought with her. "The videos are in there." She went back to eating.

Soolchakan got the case and brought it to the table. He opened it, took out a video and looked it over as he ate. He handed the video to Kiyalee and pulled out another one. As they continued their meal, he continued pulling out videos and passing them on. All of the videos were on techniques showing some deadly kicks and punches, as well as some better defensive and counter-punch moves.

"They need to see…some kind of improvement," said Aneensa.

Bonarain scoffed. "We don't have much of a choice, do we?"

Aneensa finished her meal and checked Chyning one more time. "I'll be back in a few days to look at that arm again." She turned to Soolchakan. "In the meantime, I suggest that the four of you do less foraging and more practicing on fighting techniques. Your futures…in this home…may depend on it."

Team 7016 spent the next sixteen days studying the videos and practicing. Their foraging fell to virtually nothing. They were desperate to keep this home that they had established. All reports said that they were among the most fortunate and there were other Teams who would love to get their hands on this mansion.

The next group that came had an unexpected visitor: Supreme Commander, Nagasoom himself - along with his Team 1. He watched as, once again, all four members of Team 7016 had a dismal showing. After the four of them were dragged - semi or totally unconscious - off the mat and back down to the first floor, Nagasoom had them standing at attention in front of him. He paced back and forth looking at them with complete disgust.

He faced them and took a few paces backward. "This is your last warning," he said in a sinister manner. "I'm going to give it to you in a very loud manner, in front of witnesses…so that no one can say you misunderstood or didn't hear me, or that I didn't say certain things." He took another step back and took in a lungful of air. The voice that they heard was almost deafening. "As Supreme Officer, I am giving you a direct order! You WILL improve… or else! We are going to come back in twenty days. At that time you WILL show improvement. You WILL show us that you have learned something! You WILL be better fighters…strong arrogant fighters! If not…you lose this place. Someone…more deserving will get it, and you will be sent to Command Central, to do nothing but serve food and/or clean toilets! You WILL learn how to fight and be deadly soldiers in hand-to-hand combat…or you will be lackeys!" He stepped back again and cleared his throat several times. He smiled. "Any questions?"

"No, Sir," chorused all four of them.

"We have some more videos for you. These are some really advanced techniques. You won't have the excuse…that we didn't supply you with all the material that's available. I am giving you no excuses whatsoever for your failure. Any questions?"

"No, Sir," chorused all four of them.

He grunted, turned around, made a gesture with his left hand for his Team to follow. Team 1 left the building. Team 989 was directly behind them, however, not before Honn looked back and scoffed contemptuously at Team 7016.

After the visitors had all departed, Soolchakan finally moved.

He swallowed (what felt like) a big lump in his throat. He turned and looked at the three women. "I...I've never heard...a voice...like that before."

Bonarain took in a deep breath and let it out slowly. "How... did he do...that?"

"I don't know," said Kiyalee. She hugged herself and shuddered.

"I...wet myself," said Chyning forlornly. "Excuse me...I have to...go clean up and...change." She waddled towards the stairs.

The remaining three sat down at the table where the new videos were. "I...think that...we're going...to have to do... even less scavenging and even more practicing...if we're going to succeed...in any way at all," said Soolchakan. He looked at the two women and raised his eyebrows. "Any...dis...agreement?"

Bonarain looked at him fearfully. "Let's wait until...she comes back down. We can decide which one of the videos...to start with."

Kiyalee held one up. "Maybe this one. It has my vote. According to what it says on the outside...it is five steps above..." She looked up at Soolchakan. "...fifth. That's where...you are right now...isn't it?"

He simply nodded.

They waited for a long time. They were each reading the information on the cover of each video carefully.

Kiyalee looked over at the staircase. "Where is she?"

"I'm gonna go check on her," said Bonarain. "She might have taken a shower and...gone upstairs to the sewing room."

Soolchakan growled. "Sewing is NOT what any of you...us... need to be practicing right now. Fighting...to stay...in the place that we've arranged...put together...supplied...nurtured...that's what we need to be practicing."

Bonarain ran up the stairs. She came back down in a very short time. "She's in the apartment, watching one of the 'beginner' videos."

Soolchakan shook his head. "Let's get all of these up to the apartment. We'll watch them up there...together. Hopefully we can learn something…anything…useful."

Chyning was sitting in a chair hugging her knees to her chest. She was intensely watching one of the beginner videos.

Soolchakan walked up to the video machine and hit the eject button.

"Hey," Chyning looked up at him angrily. "I was watching that!"

He pulled the beginner video out and placed the advanced one in it. "We are no longer novices." He looked at her sternly. "They don't pit us against novices. They have us go against…hard professionals. We need to step up our training. We're not going to get there with these…beginner videos, okay?"

Chyning looked at the other two women. "Sound like a good idea to you?"

They both nodded.

Chyning shrugged. "Put it in. Let's watch it."

They watched three videos. They watched each one twice.

Soolchakan stood up and stretched some of the kinks out. "Shall we go upstairs and punch the *peewodon* out of some practice dummies?"

Chyning looked up with a pained expression. "My arm still hurts. I can't punch…with any force…or…I don't know."

He leaned closer to her with his teeth clenched. "Then KICK!"

All four spent the entire night punching, kicking and, in some other ways, mauling and brutalizing the dummies. They returned to the apartment where they all took showers and then returned to watch more videos. Once again, they went to the gym and mauled the dummies. Another shower and more videos.

Not one of them complained about the rigorous workouts. They all felt that they needed to continue, however, they did not know exactly what it was that was driving them to continue learning and brutalizing the dummies. They continued with this course of action for several days, being driven to continue and excel - and they did not understand why. They just could not stop. They would watch a video - twice. They would practice the technique taught in that video until they were nearly exhausted. They would take a shower, dry off - and watch another video, repeating the cycle, over and over, until they finished all of the videos.

They were involved with one of the training sessions when Chyning let out a yelp. The other three looked at her, first with disdain and then with surprise. She had been complaining about the punching. She could not do it until her arm healed completely. She had been told to practice kicking and do any and all punching with her left. They saw her, on her back on the floor, with her foot still up on the hanging punching bag. They all walked over to her, somewhat confused.

She looked up at them. "I...kicked a hole in it. My foot's... stuck!"

Bonarain helped her, by pulling her foot out of her shoe. She then twisted the shoe slightly to get it out of the hole.

"That's interesting," said Soolchakan. "I've been told...that it's possible to kick...or punch holes in these things. I've never seen it happen. I've seen some of these...that were repaired, with tape." He examined the hole. He looked down at Chyning. "I'll get some tape and cover this...damage." He looked back at the women. "Get back to your practicing. I'll fix the hole...and continue my punches on this bag."

It took several coats of heavy duty tape, however, he was able to get the bag back to some semblance of usefulness. Then he started brutalizing it, seeing if he could knock another hole in it.

The day of the test arrived. Team 7016 decided to be a little facetious. They pushed all of the tables and chairs, in the bar, off to the side in the gaming area. They brought the big mat down to the bar area. The match would take place here, on the first floor. They would not allow any of their opponents to tour the facility - unless they were the victorious ones.

Supreme Officer, Nagasoom arrived with the larger entourage. He came with Team 1, Team 226 Medical, Team 989 and Team 3706. He walked in and looked around. "You've...changed things." He looked at Soolchakan. "Any particular reason?"

"Yes, Sir," said Soolchakan flatly. "If some *wathoot fovok* wants to take this place from us…they don't get to see any more of it… unless they win. If they don't win…they don't get to go upstairs…at all."

Nagasoom chuckled and nodded with a big grin on his face. "My, my, my…aren't we the…*bold* one." He looked at the others that had come in. "Let me introduce you…" He looked back at Soolchakan. "…to the ones who wish to claim this place…as their quarters." He pointed to a woman. "This is Officer Grade 4, Yandeeki. She's the Team Leader of Team 3706. The rest of her Team…Officer Grade 6, Bozlek, Officer Grade 6, Chondee and Officer Grade 6, Tasa. They don't like the place that they're living in, right now. I told them about this place and they decided to move in here. They would like to look over the entire place…first."

"Excuse me, Sir," said Soolchakan through his clenched teeth. "This is *our* home. If those *chogo* want to look at the upper floors… they're going to have to get past us…first! They don't go upstairs… unless *we* are defeated. If *they* are defeated…they leave…having seen only this part of OUR home."

Nagasoom looked at Soolchakan with wide eyes. He chuckled again. "Yes…you are in your home. I can understand the…desire… for privacy. Very well! We'll honor your…rules…in your home."

Bozlek scoffed and turned to Nagasoom. "That's not what we were promised, Sir. We were told that we could have a look at the entire building, prior to knocking these *bimyocks* around. Why are we changing that now?"

Nagasoom replied without taking his eyes off of Soolchakan. "In a military setting…I'm in charge…of everything. This is…a little different." He smiled. "This is a home! You respect the wishes of the home owner - even if your military rank is above theirs." He turned to Bozlek. "That's something that is called…mutual respect." He smiled. "If you want someone to show you respect - you should show them some respect…as well."

Bozlek looked at the rest of his Team. "I guess we'll have to flatten these *wuffy poofids* first. Then we get the grand tour of our new abode."

Soolchakan huffed. "That's a lot of empty talk...from a *chogo*."

Bozlek shook his head and showed a sinister grin. "I'll *chogo* you!"

Soolchakan scoffed. "More empty talk. If you think you're so good, then why haven't you advanced? Don't let anything but FEAR hold you back...*chogo*!" He felt a little awkward with his threats. He remembered that one of the philosophies was to rattle your opponent, mentally, before the first blows are struck. He also remembered that Nagasoom had ordered them to be arrogant.

Bozlek crouched and started advancing slowly. He was chuckling with a sneer on his face. He suddenly rushed at his opponent with his fists ready for just about anything - almost...just about anything - however, not everything. He was staggered when he received an open palmed uppercut to the bottom of the chin. He stumbled back awkwardly and caught a fist, right between the eyes. Blood flowed freely out of his broken nose. He was a little stunned by the blow and retreated a little, in an attempt at recovering and countering. Soolchakan never gave Bozlek the chance. The last thing that Bozlek saw, prior to being knocked unconscious, was the bottom of a foot, as he was walloped in the face by a spinning back kick.

Doctor Shurmook was on the mat immediately when he saw Bozlek spin around and go down like a rag doll. He held up his hand for Soolchakan to stop. He went down to one knee and heard Bozlek choking on his own blood. He turned the man over to let the blood flow out of the mouth instead of down the throat.

Soolchakan snarled in a loud manner. "That *chogo* is bleeding on *my* mat!"

Shurmook looked up and grunted in disgust.

Nagasoom chuckled. "Please, Officer, Soolchakan. This is not supposed to be a death match."

Soolchakan gave Nagasoom a threatening look. "If someone is trying to take my home away from me...I'm *not* going to be polite."

Nagasoom nodded. "Good point...but please...no fatalities."

Soolchakan turned back to his Team. "All right…try to remember that statement: No fatalities." He looked back at Nagasoom. "No promises, but they'll try."

Nagasoom looked down at the fallen Bozlek. "Doctor, can you get him off of the mat?"

Shurmook looked up. "Yes, I suppose we can move him… without any further damage. If the sparring must continue…he needs to be…out of range."

Nagasoom smiled and nodded in agreement. He turned back to Team 7016. "Officer, Chyning…why don't you spar with… Officer, Tasa?"

Chyning came up close to Soolchakan and whispered to him. "I still can't use my right arm."

He turned his back to the others in the room and glared at her. He whispered back. "The other day, you KICKED a hole in one of the punching bags…you don't need your fists…you've got your FEET! You also need to remember that he did tell us to be arrogant."

Her eyes widened and she grinned. "You're right." She looked over at Nagasoom. "Which one of those *chogos* is my victim?"

Tasa walked onto the mat sneering at Chyning. "I'm gonna mop up Bozlek's blood with your face."

After three direct kicks, to the midsection, the chest and the face, Tasa was the one being dragged, semi-conscious, off of the mat by Doctor Shurmook.

Chondee (the one who had been chosen to face off against Bonarain) walked onto the mat. She looked back at Honn. "They don't seem to be as bad as you said they were."

Honn just shook his head in confusion.

Chondee turned back to Bonarain and laughed. "Just think… when we throw you out of here, we get to keep everything that… WAS yours. It will all be ours now. I'm not even gonna give you time to kiss any of it goodbye."

Bonarain thought of her special makeup room - with all of her makeup and her blood began boiling with adrenalin.

Chondee just smiled. "Are you ready?"

Chondee was dragged off of the mat by Doctor Shurmook…

with a shattered jaw and two black eyes. Bonarain became an out of control warrior, when she was hit with the thought of having to give up ALL of her makeup as well as her special vanity. Chondee never had a chance. Bonarain was merciless.

Shurmook again intervened. He had gone to Chondee, knelt down and inspected the damage. "Need I remind you? There's supposed to be ZERO FATALITIES!"

Chondee mumbled some gibberish and fell unconscious.

Shurmook sighed. He looked up at Nagasoom. "Team 7016 is three for three," he muttered in disgust. "Must this…nonsense continue?"

"I can see that," said Nagasoom with his eyebrows raised. "Very interesting…they have…improved…drastically." He turned to Yandeeki. "Well…Team Leader…you've lost the overall competition…are you going to make it unanimous…or are you going to try to get back…some kind or pride for your Team?"

Yandeeki looked at the three fallen members of her Team. She scowled. "Who's my victim?"

Kiyalee strode forward with a menacing grin on her face. "*I*…am not the victim!"

Yandeeki raised her fists and approached. "Guess again!"

Four punches later, Yandeeki was flat on her back, looking up at a spinning ceiling, completely unaware of where she was. Kiyalee reached down to a patch on the right shoulder of Yandeeki's uniform. She ripped the patch that showed the Team designation of 3706, off of the shirt. She held it up victoriously.

Kiyalee snarled at all of the people on the other side of the room. "Supreme Officer…Sir…who has earned the right to live here?"

Nagasoom snickered. "It sure as thunder, is NOT Team 3706. It is, at the moment, Team 7016."

Bonarain walked to a place, just to the left of the main entrance. She grabbed a rope that was hanging on the wall. She pulled it. A banner, that had been made, with their new sewing machine, unfurled. It had been made from a large, dark blue blanket that she had found during their apartment searches. A large number

- 7016 - had been stitched on the blanket, in bright scarlet threading.

Kiyalee walked over to the banner with the 3706 patch. She picked up a knife that was sitting on a small ledge below the banner. She held the patch up against the wall, directly under the banner, and stabbed the knife through the patch, pinning it to the wall. She turned back to Nagasoom with a haughty expression. "Team 3706 is defeated!" She looked around the room at the others. "NEXT?!"

Honn looked at Nagasoom in anger. "They...they played us...me! This is not right. They acted like they were silly little goof offs! No one could..." He glared at Team 7016, then turned back to Nagasoom. "...it's just not possible."

Nagasoom shook his head. "So...they played you. Very well, they played you. So? What are you going to do about it? They did earn the right to keep this place. Are you going to challenge them?"

Honn closed his eyes and clenched his teeth. "Not...yet, Sir. I have to think. I'm...too...angry right now."

Nagasoom laughed. "If that's the case, then you can calm your anger by helping the good Doctor Shurmook and his Team in assisting the vanquished ones...out of their 'hall of defeat'. I'm sure that the victors would like to clean the place up and continue with their duties. Meanwhile, you can think about somebody... anybody that you think is more deserving of this building...as the headquarters...for their Team."

Honn snapped back. "I can think of at least a dozen...off the top of my head!"

"Not today." Nagasoom stood up and cleared his throat. "Team 7016! You have proven yourself today...and you did follow orders. I find no reason to...admonish you. You played your enemy. You knew your enemy and made them think that you are weak. Nice ploy! Unfortunately it probably won't work again. Next time you'll have to be...better prepared."

Soolchakan was a little angered. "Sir! Do you mean that we're going to have to do this nonsense...again?"

Again that chuckle. "You have a very nice place here, Team 7016. There are others who want it. Since the attack, there are not many...*really* nice places. Not many...with this kind of space...or..."

He looked toward the kitchen area. "...facilities." He smiled. "Good day, for now, Team 7016."

The Team snapped to attention and saluted. Nagasoom returned the salute and headed for the main door. Team 226 and Team 989 assisted Team 3706 in limping and staggering away.

Thirty-one days later, Bonarain walked up to the wall with the banner. She had a shoulder patch from the Team that 7016 had just clobbered. She picked up another knife off of the ledge and pinned this patch to the wall. She turned back and looked at Honn with a big grin. "That makes twenty patches in all, in the victory trophies that we've taken. Are you still going to bring more people here...to be clobbered?"

"I'm wondering that myself," said Doctor Shurmook angrily. "This is getting out of hand." He looked at Nagasoom in desperation. "I can understand being ready...to face any enemy, but...this has gone beyond ridiculous. All you're doing is getting your own people hurt. Twenty challenges against this Team 7016. All of the challenges have been won...handily by Team 7016. Meanwhile, back at my hospital, I've got four fractured skulls, six shattered jaws, three broken sternums, along with numerous broken and cracked ribs, two broken arms and one broken leg. Let's not forget the fact that there are two people who are going to be spending an inordinate amount of time getting their mouths put back together by the oral surgeon. I think, Sir, that Team 7016 *has* proven themselves. How many more Teams are going to be...deactivated medically...before you admit that Team 7016 has earned what they have?"

Honn snarled at the Doctor. "There's going to be one more challenge. Team 989 is challenging Team 7016...for this Team HQ... and for the right to claim who is the best...at fighting hand-to-hand."

Nagasoom shook his head. "Do you really want to do that?"

Honn snarled again. "We...Team 989...we outrank these people. Yet they have one of the best personal facilities...that's left in the city. YES, I want to do this." He looked at his Team members. "Wouldn't you prefer this place to...our cramped quarters?"

The rest of the Team nodded in agreement.

Nagasoom took a look at the faces of everyone in the room that was still awake. "I'll...think about it. For the moment...Team 7016 has proven themselves...and earned the privilege of living in this place...for a while longer." He stood up. "Now...we depart and leave them in peace."

After the visitors left, Team 7016 walked up to the wall and gloated over their trophies.

Soolchakan started reading them off. "Team 3706. Team 2956. Team 6188. Team 882. Team 1654. Team 5593. Team 4948. Team 1423. Team 3997. Team 3812. Team 937. Team 4519. Team 6617. Team 1383. Team 5002. Team 2904. Team 4444. Team 5017. Team 4141. Team 1892. Quite a display, isn't it? I wonder if anyone else has this kind of setup."

Eight days later Team 989 showed up ready to fight. Honn was aggravated over the fact that he had been made to look like a fool. He really was not that concerned with the facilities as he was trying to regain his status as the best fighter in - what was left - of the city of Owlam.

In a very short time, Team 7016 now had trophy number twenty-one hanging on the wall. A patch from Team 989, from the shoulder of Honn himself was now pinned to the wall beneath the big blue and red banner of Team 7016. Nagasoom decided that there would be no more challenges against Team 7016.

14

Team 7016 was visited again. This time it was peaceful... therefore welcome. Supreme Officer, Nagasoom, with his Team, and Master Officer, Jahong, with his Team - and for some reason, Doctor Shurmook, with his Team, also in attendance. Jahong was the Commander of the Southern Region of Owlam, therefore Team 7016 was in his chain of command.

Nagasoom sat down at a table in the bar area. "I see that you've moved the mat out of here and reestablished this as an entertainment area."

"Yes, Sir," said Bonarain with a smile. "That mat did detract from the overall appearance of the room. We like to think of it... now...as an area to entertain our guests...rather than spending all of our time beating the *piddleeyanks* out of them.

Jahong looked around the room. "I understand that this establishment also has a garage. I'd like to see it...especially since we are distributing some battle vehicles to different Teams around the city."

Soolchakan looked at Kiyalee. "Why don't you show, our esteemed guest, the garage?"

Before Kiyalee could get up, Jahong motioned her to remain seated. He turned to Soolchakan. "I'd rather that you be the one to show me."

Soolchakan cleared his throat nervously. He was not sure he could make it to the garage without stumbling. He had spent most of the morning drowning reality, with three bottles of wine (and a shot or two of *Golden Age* Liquor). He got up and steadied himself by leaning on the table. "If you insist, Sir."

"I do," said Jahong. "I like to get to know my...Team leaders."

Soolchakan sighed. "Yes...Sir." He looked back at the hallway and motioned to Jahong. "Back...there...Sir."

Jahong stood up. "Lead the way."

Soolchakan wavered a little as he got started. He blinked his eyes and took a deep breath. He smiled at Jahong and then started a weak attempt at not wobbling as he staggered slowly down the hallway.

Jahong had a smirk on his face. "How is it that a tavern has a garage?"

"Uh…it seems…Sir, that the ones who worked here…were also uh members of a furfoting…" He closed his eyes and cleared his throat and tried to talk slower. "…a first response team that fights fires."

Jahong had a bigger smile on his face. "What happened to them?"

Soolchakan stopped and looked as forlorn as possible. "They have not been seen…since that…attack. I think…they went out to answer a call…and…use your imagination."

Jahong nodded thoughtfully, however he still had a bit of a smirk on his face. "So absolutely no one has been trying to claim ownership."

"Sadly…enough…correct…Sir."

"Were you acquainted with them?"

Soolchakan cleared his throat and hung his head. "I knew all of them…very well, Sir."

Jahong nodded. "My condolences. We all…lost friends… and family."

Soolchakan nodded a thanks. He continued down the hall. He opened the door to the garage and motioned for Jahong to enter the garage first.

"Oh my," said Jahong as he looked around. "This…place could handle…*any* of the trucks that are available."

"It looks as if it was…initially set up for…one of the really big fire trucks."

Jahong turned back to Soolchakan. His demeanor changed to one of being stern. "So, now, my friend…what should I do? Should I set you up with one of the better vehicles…or one of the most rattletrap jalopies that I can find?"

Soolchakan was taken aback by the change. "I…uh…don't

quite unner...uh...untruh...uh...get what you're saying...Sir."

Jahong got cocky and had an evil grin on his face. "I can get one of the top-of-the-line vehicles in here...if you help me. Or...if you're not willing to...be polite...you get junk!"

Soolchakan was having a bit of a tough time with his bladder. He swallowed hard. "I'm...lissnin."

"This place *was* a tavern."

"Yessir!"

"Taverns have all kinds of...spirits."

"Uh...Yessir!"

"Usually everything from the top liquors to the lowest form of rot gut grog."

"Yessir!"

Jahong got close to Soolchakan. He had a bit of a menacing look in his eyes. "Don't try to tell me that you don't have any...I can smell it on you."

"Smell? Uh...what...Sir?"

"*Golden Age Liquor!*"

Soolchakan had to clinch tighter. "I...gotta few...bottles... Sir." He was wondering what to do. The count of the number of bottles of that fabulous liquor had fluctuated. In the searches throughout the area, he had been somewhat fortunate in finding several more bottles in some of the apartments. He knew that he had several unopened cases still sitting up there in the fourth floor storage room. That room had been partitioned off and his portion contained all kinds of spirits, while the women had mainly extravagant clothing in theirs. None of the women had been interested in the type, or count, of the different spirits. Just how many bottles did Jahong want - and for what - actually?

Jahong got closer and spoke, just above a whisper. "I want fifteen bottles of *Golden Age Liquor*." He cocked his head. "I also want a keg of that *Chasaga* beer." He chuckled. "I know that you have to have *some* beer here - I'm hoping that there's at least one keg of *Chasaga*...that you can...spare."

Soolchakan cleared his throat. He looked around nervously and sniffed loudly. He was getting ready to answer, however, he had to turn his head to the side - when he belched. He looked back at Jahong.

"That's *Golden Age*," said Jahong with his eyes closed. He cleared his throat. "I'd recognize *that* smell...as well."

"How about...eight bottles...Sir?"

"Fifteen!"

"Uh...ten bottles?"

"FIFTEEN!"

"Uh...case?"

"FIFTEEN! Either that or you get the crappiest junker that can be found in the inventory."

Soolchakan cleared his throat and swallowed. "Yes, Sir... uh...how do you plan on gettin'...fifeen bottles of liquor anna keg... out of here...wiffout parading it pass Nagasoom...and have him wonering where his share is?"

Jahong chuckled. "I drove my vehicle...to the back of this building. It's parked right outside your garage door. We move the stuff through here and my Team, each thinks that they are getting one bottle - just like me - without knowing that I'm getting extra. They will know about the keg though. NOW, where's the booze?"

"I...I'll have to go up...to the fourth floor...where it's stored... to get it and...bring it back down here."

"Can you bring it back here...without parading it in front of Nagasoom?"

Soolchakan sighed. "By usin' the elvator...yes, I can."

"Good!"

"What...is your...jusification...going to be for giving...one of the lowest ranking Teams...a top vehicle?"

Jahong chuckled. "A top of the line vehicle...for the Team that has beaten the *peewodon* out of every Team that they've faced off against. I can easily say that you've earned it...plus you obviously have the facilities to take care of it...here in this huge garage."

Soolchakan nodded. "You've...thought this through."

"Yes."

"Open your...vehicle. I'll go get...the suff."

Jahong smiled. "Thank you."

Soolchakan went to the elevator. He hit the switch for it to go up. As he was headed up, he was thinking of reporting Jahong to Nagasoom. No, that would not work, because then Nagasoom might confiscate all of the… He grimaced in pain. Nagasoom might confiscate ALL of the alcohol, not just the *Golden Age Liquor*. He snarled at himself. He hated being caught over a barrel like this, however, there was very little he could do. He sighed as he thought about waving goodbye…to fifteen *unopened* bottles, of the finest liquor, ever manufactured in Owlam.

He got the goodies on a two wheeler, designed to move a beer keg and headed back down. Placing a full case and a partial case of the liquor on top of the keg was no problem. He looked outside of the elevator, to make sure that no one was watching what was being done, on this end of the hallway. He saw Jahong standing in the doorway to the garage, with a huge grin on his face. He crossed the hall to the garage.

Jahong had already opened up the big garage door and had a storage compartment opened in his truck, in preparation of moving the booty in a stealthy manner. The three loose bottles were placed in the passenger compartment. Another bottle was taken out of the case and placed in the passenger compartment as well. The other eleven bottles were hidden in the storage compartment. It took both men to lift the keg up into another storage compartment in the truck.

Soolchakan looked at the distribution of the bottles. "Uh… scuse me, Sir…but…why…four in there?"

Jahong chuckled. "My Team thinks that we are each getting one bottle of *Golden Age* and the keg. They won't know about… *the rest.*" He leaned closer and the smirk changed to a malevolent look. "…and they better not find out…about the rest…if you want to keep…what *you* still have."

Soolchakan smiled. "I…unnerstan…completely…Sir."

Jahong chuckled. He closed up - and locked - the compartment with the eleven bottles. "Let's go back and join the others."

"Yes, Sir," said Soolchakan with a smile. 'You conniving thief,' he thought.

They walked back to the bar area. They saw that the visitors had all been welcomed with a bottle of one of the better wines from the stock room behind the bar. Soolchakan was relieved that no one had opened up...the really good stuff.

Jahong walked up to Nagasoom with a big smile on his face. "Yes, Sir, that garage is absolutely large enough to handle anything. I think...that we should give this Team...one of the newer 161's."

Nagasoom had been smiling and now his expression changed to shock. "What...a...161...here...for this Team?"

"Oh, yes, Sir. That garage is more than adequate."

"There...there's that much space...in *there*?"

"Absolutely, Sir. That garage was originally designed for one of the big *first responder* fire trucks. Those things are much bigger than a 161."

Nagasoom looked thoughtful. "Yes, they are." He looked back up at Jahong. "Okay, so the garage is big enough...now, how do we justify...a top-of-the-line assault vehicle, for...*the* lowest ranking Team...in the city?"

Jahong smiled. "They may...uh...are the lowest ranking, however, think back to the competitions, Sir. How many other Teams can boast of being undefeated in twenty-one face-to-face, full-contact competitions?" He leaned forward. "How many of the other Teams can say that in individual, face-to-face matches, that they are undefeated in eighty-four fights?" He stood up straight. "I think... Sir, that they've earned the bragging rights...and a top vehicle."

Nagasoom leaned back in his chair and clasped his hands across his stomach. He shook his head. "It's...very hard to argue with that." He nodded, cleared his throat and smiled. "Team Leader, Soolchakan! Which one of your Team is going to be the primary driver?"

Without hesitation, he answered: "Officer, Kiyalee, Sir."

Kiyalee had been taking a sip of her wine...and now spit it back into the glass in surprise. She looked up at Soolchakan in shock...with tightly clenched lips.

"Yes," said Soolchakan with a smile. "I think that it would be best that she do the driving. I've seen pictures of the 161, and it has several turrets to shoot from...and we wouldn't want any bullets -

accidentally going up the shaft…would we?"

With that remark, Chyning started coughing (in a feeble attempt at disguising the fact that she was laughing). "Scuse… me…have to…visit the…restroom." She got up and continued the coughing, all the way to the bathroom.

Kiyalee was sitting there glaring at Soolchakan, with a *very* red face.

Soolchakan looked back and forth from Kiyalee to Nagasoom. "Yes, Sir, I think it would be best that she's the primary driver."

"I've never driven anything that big," snapped Kiyalee.

Soolchakan glared back at her. "Learn!"

"I'm not a mechanic either."

"LEARN!"

"But…I…" She tried frantically to come up with something else.

Nagasoom had heard enough. He leaned forward and glared at Kiyalee. "You will stop arguing and you will make yourself ready to go get a 161. You will learn to drive the vehicle and you will study all of the instructional manuals and you will become a mechanic for that 161, and you will take very good care of the vehicle…is that understood?"

Kiyalee stared at Nagasoom wide-eyed. "Yes, Sir," she said in a shaky voice. "Immediately…Sir!"

He leaned back in his chair. "Good! When we leave, you can go with us to collect the vehicle. You'll learn the route back to this place."

She looked concerned. "Route?"

"Yes, we've had a few Teams out there…clearing a path… through, what's left of…the inner city. We have a north-south and an east-west route…that's cleared out…now. Burns less fuel than attempting a circuitous route around the perimeter."

"Yes, Sir," said Kiyalee sheepishly. "Uh…where…am I supposed to fuel it up…Sir?"

Nagasoom looked up at Jahong with his eyebrows raised.

Jahong shook his head. "Uh…there's a…fuel station…just east of here…that's still functional." He looked at Soolchakan. "Did you miss that, while you were searching the area?"

Bonarain chimed in. "We haven't gotten that way yet, Sir. We started at the far west…of the non-charred area and we've been working our way east. This is a rather large area, for four people to check on, and between our fight training, checking the watch station…and again the size of this area…it's taking longer than we thought…Sir."

Jahong nodded. "Okay." He turned to Kiyalee. "You *will* familiarize yourself with the location of that fuel station."

Kiyalee smiled helplessly. "Yes, Sir."

Nagasoom picked up his glass of wine and sipped it. He shook his head. "Is it possible…that you have another bottle of this wine…that I could have?"

Bonarain smiled. "I'm sure that we could spare a bottle… maybe even two, Sir."

"That would be greatly appreciated," he said as he took another sip. He looked around at the other people in the room - and frowned when he caught Soolchakan's gaze. "Is there…something wrong…Officer?"

Soolchakan shook his head. "Uh…Sir…if I may…be… blunt?"

Nagasoom chuckled. "The toughest Team in the south…or possibly all of the city of Owlam? Yes, I'll allow it."

"Sir…why…did you dye your hair…gray?"

Nagasoom looked affronted. "I did *NOT dye* my hair…any color. When I was young, my hair was light brown. When I turned fifty, my hair started changing from brown to gray. By the time I turned sixty-five, my hair was completely gray. What makes you think I dyed my hair?"

"The…uh…brown roots…Sir."

He stared back at Soolchakan as if he were completely crazy. "I don't have…any brown roots!"

Doctor Shurmook had been sitting quietly, off to the side sipping wine. "Sir…I'm afraid he's right. I can clearly see…brown roots…under your gray hair."

Nagasoom huffed. "Are all of you insane?" He got up and

walked over behind the bar to the huge mirror that was back there. "Brown roots - BAH! My hair turned gray...and now this drunk thinks it's going back. You people are going to pay for this idiotic prank." He went to the mirror behind the bar and started mussing his hair to see the roots. He froze in shock as he saw that that it was true. He turned back and looked at Shurmook. "Is...this...no it can't be real!" He looked back and forth, from mirror to the doctor. "Can it?"

Shurmook came up to the bar. "I told you, Sir, that since that attack, we've been seeing...new and residual manifestations. Livestock, both in and outside of the wall...they're dropping dead... for no apparent reason. The crops are wilting in the fields...in spite of the fact that they're getting sufficient fertilization and irrigation. Wild animals are dropping dead - again for no apparent reason. There is an incredible and inexplicable lack of insect and avian life. Now...we see that your hair is changing color. This could be...one of those strange manifestations."

Nagasoom turned back to the mirror, pulled his picture ID card out of his pocket and compared it to what he saw in the mirror. He turned back to Shurmook. "Am I getting younger as well?"

Shurmook shrugged. "You do...seem to have less... wrinkles...on your face." He looked at his reflection. "For that matter...so do I!" He almost ran around the bar to get a closer look at his reflection. He shook his head. "This...is...astounding!"

"What...that you have less wrinkles?"

Shurmook looked at Nagasoom in shock. "No!" He looked back at his reflection. "The top...of my head. For several years... nothing...but shiny skin. Now...I see...new hairs...coming up out of the...completely bald top...of my head!" He started feeling the fuzz that was growing on top of his head. "Maybe...we are... getting younger...or...healthier. I don't know, I'll have to...study this phenomenon...carefully."

Bonarain sat there with a nervous smile on her face. "Would that...uh could that mean something...as to why...Kiyalee's hair has...brown roots?"

Kiyalee snapped at Bonarain. "I don't have brown roots! My

hair is naturally blonde!"

"Not anymore," snickered Soolchakan.

Kiyalee ran up to the bar and started checking her roots. "NO! This...this is...impossible! How...does hair...change from blonde to brown...naturally?"

Nagasoom shook his head. "How does it change from gray to brown...naturally?" He went back to searching the roots all over his scalp.

Shurmook shrugged. "Again, just like that strange gray blotch, that everyone seems to have appearing, on the back of their necks...some unusual manifestation...as a residual, of some kind, from that attack."

Everyone looked at Shurmook in a strange manner. Several of them chorused, together: "Gray blotch?"

Shurmook looked at all of the people staring at him. "You mean...I haven't mentioned that before? Are you telling me...that none of you...not one of you noticed it...on someone else?"

Several people started rubbing and feeling the back of their necks.

"I don't feel anything strange," said Nagasoom.

"Neither do I," said Jahong.

Shurmook shook his head. "No, there is no...roughness or anything else. It's just...a place on the back of everyone's neck, where part of the skin is turning gray. No one has experienced any discomfort of any type...it is just a...strange manifestation."

Several of the women looked at the doctor with some anxiety, disbelief and a little trepidation.

One of Nagasoom's Team members, Officer Grade 1, Tooloola spoke up. "If this is true, how come none of us women have noticed it?"

Shurmook rolled his eyes. "Pull your long hair off to the side and have someone look at your neck. Come on, there are twelve women here...I don't see any of you with short hair. It's no wonder that none of you women have noticed it." He stood there looking at a collection of gawking women. "Well...take a look at each other. None of you can see the back of your own neck, you have to have someone else tell you what's back there."

At that moment Chyning came back from the bathroom. She had composed herself...somewhat. Bonarain went up to Chyning, spun her around and checked the back of her neck.

"What..." Chyning turned back around. "What're you doing?"

"I'm looking at the back of your neck," scolded Bonarain.

Chyning slapped Bonarain's hands away. "Stop feeling my neck, what's going on?"

Bonarain huffed. "According to Doctor Shurmook, everyone inside the city walls of Owlam, is developing a big gray blotch...on the back of their neck. I was checking you to see if you had it as well."

Chyning backed away with a suspicious grin on her face. "What's the joke?"

"No joke," said Nagasoom. He turned around and pointed to the back of his neck.

The other three men in the room all turned their back to Chyning and showed the back of their necks. Several women turned around and pulled their hair out of the way.

Bonarain stood there with her fists on her hips. "Now, will you let me see the back of your neck?"

Chyning changed from suspicion to fear to horror. She slowly turned around and pulled her hair off to the side.

Bonarain chuckled nervously. "Hey...Doctor?" She looked around the room. "What would you say...if I told you...that our black haired Chyning...has brown roots as well?"

Chyning spun around angrily. "What? What...are you talking about?"

Shurmook walked up to her, looking carefully at her hair. "It seems that...everyone...in the city of Owlam...their hair is changing. Everyone's hair is changing...to dark brown...no matter what you were born with."

Chyning scoffed. "That's a load of *h'oolyach!*"

Bonarain pointed to the big mirror. "Go check...if you don't believe us. Maybe you'll believe your own eyes."

Chyning walked over to the bar. She was still suspicious that there was some prank that was about to come down on her. When she saw no one move, she cautiously walked to the mirror. As she started pulling hair aside to get a good look at her roots, she was eyeballing everyone in the room, waiting for something to happen. Nothing did and she finally turned her attention to her hair - and her jaw dropped. "My hair...is turning..." She turned around and looked at the doctor in horror. "...brown?"

Shurmook gave her a pleasant smile. "You see? No one was trying to fool you. For some reason...since that attack...there is some kind of...weird residual...*something*...going on. These changes are subtle...and painless. No one is suffering any...ill from any of it. We are just...*changing*."

Soolchakan had sobered up completely while listening to what was going on. "Turning...into...what?"

Nagasoom flopped down into one of the chairs. "Maybe... some of those reports...that we're getting...are not fabrications."

Jahong looked at him shocked. "Reports? What reports?"

Nagasoom clasped his hands across his stomach. "Everyone have a seat. This may take a while...and I don't want anyone falling down."

Everyone complied.

"Several Intelligence Personnel have come to us...from the City-States...that are closest. According to the people off to the west...the citizens of Galsino...have turned into these...*things*... that have pasty white skin and bulging red eyes. They have clawed hands...and they all seem to be about seven and a half *taja* tall. Reports from the east tell us that the citizens of Teltermak...their ears are growing...longer each day. The ears are growing straight out...to a point. To the north...the Axswain! They have developed a lot of fur...all over their body...or at least what can be seen of their bodies. This fur is...red and white striped. They have also seem to have grown...to a height of...over eight *taja*. Then...the reports from the south! These reports of the observations of the city of Zee-Altha. The people there have...green skin! *Neon* green skin. They can be seen...on top of the walls at night. They glow in the dark." He looked at Shurmook. "Do you think...that we are...developing into some freak…like our surrounding neighbors?"

Shurmook shrugged. "It's entirely possible. I need to know… more about…what ever that…weapon…was that was used. That horribly intense light, followed by an umbrella of a fire cloud, with firestorms wreaking havoc on the city. What was it? What, if any, are the residual effects? All that I have, at this time, is more questions… and very few answers. I can guess, but…that still gets us nowhere… without some solid facts."

The guests all departed, with Kiyalee in tow, to the north side of the city.

Soolchakan was a little upset over the fact that Bonarain had been so generous with the wine. Nagasoom had departed with a full case of some very fine wine. That was less booze for Soolchakan and he did not like the fact that his supply was dwindling faster than he could find new bottles in their searches.

The three remaining Team members decided to do some searching, while it was still daytime. They could practice their fighting after the sun went down. They knew that they had soundly defeated all challenges, however, they still felt a tremendously strong desire to continue beating the stuffing out of their practice dummies.

They ransacked eight apartments before it started getting dark. They headed home with all of the canned food they could find, along with a few bottles of liquor that he found. They also had some more cosmetics that Bonarain could not live without. Chyning had absconded with some rather expensive crystal statues. All were happy with their finds.

They were beating up their dummies when Chyning stopped and started listening intently. "Hey, what's that noise?"

Bonarain stopped her kicks and looked at Chyning while panting. "What noise?"

Soolchakan listened intently. "That…sounds like a vehicle horn. I think Kiyalee is back…with our…transportation."

They all ran to the elevator and took it down. At the bottom, they heard the horn coming from behind the building.

Soolchakan chuckled. "I guess she wants to park it inside our garage."

Bonarain looked puzzled. "Will it fit?"

Chyning grunted in disgust. "That garage held one of the big 'first responder' trucks. I can't think of one single military vehicle that's larger."

Soolchakan walked into the garage and hit the automatic garage door opener. As soon as the door started opening, Kiyalee finally let off of the horn. As the door went up, the rest of the Team got a good look at their new, dark green assault vehicle that already had the 7016 designation painted on the two front doors.

Bonarain shook her head. "I never thought it would be something that...*big*."

Chyning chuckled. "What were you expecting...one of those showy little Staff cars...that they give to the upper ranks?"

Bonarain shrugged. "I didn't...know what to expect. I just didn't think...of anything that...*big*."

The truck was big and heavy. It had dual tires in the front and dual tandems in the back. On each side, there were four steps going up to the front doors. It had eight headlights on the front (of which only two were on at this time). The vehicle was armored from front to rear. There were numerous slots on the sides and rear where someone could fire out, with relative safety inside. On top there was a turret where a large weapon could be placed for additional firepower.

They all watched as Kiyalee backed the vehicle into the garage. As soon as she got it inside, the engine was turned off. The driver's door came open and Kiyalee looked out (with a black eye and a smile). "It's not as hard as I thought it would be to drive," she said merrily.

Soolchakan stared at her eye a little in shock. "Uh...what's with the new..." He pointed to his eye as an example. "...bruise?"

She chuckled. "It seems that another Team wanted this specific truck. I had to fight for it."

Bonarain smiled. "And...you...won!"

"Yup," said Kiyalee proudly. "This one is *the* newest 161 in the fleet. It's been driven less than any of the others and..." She sniffed loudly. "…it smells…*real* new." She reached into her pocket and pulled out a patch. "This is the newest of our trophies…for the wall under the banner." She handed it to Soolchakan.

He took the patch and chuckled. "Team 167 is now added to our list of vanquished foes."

Bonarain looked at the others. "Should we take this monster for a test drive?"

"No," said Kiyalee. "It's late and I need to look at the manuals on it. We can all take a ride…tomorrow when I take it over to get it fueled up."

"That sounds good," said Soolchakan. "We'll be able to get a better look at it in the daylight."

Kiyalee nodded in agreement. "Right, put it to rest for the night. Besides, I've been driving it, all the way from the north side, and my butt is totally sat out."

Soolchakan gave the truck another once over. "Are there any instructions for us?"

Kiyalee looked at him confused. "Huh?"

"Is there anything about this truck, or any orders from Command Central that we need to know about?"

She sighed. "As far as the truck is concerned, I'll let you know, as I find each of the instructions, in the manual…that you need to know about. As far as Command Central…I've been told to tell you that…in case we go on the offensive, before we head out, we have to pick up Teams 6598 and 6638. They've been assigned to ride along with us…on any offensive." She dug in her shirt pocket, pulled out a piece of paper and handed it to Soolchakan. "Here's a list of the names of the people on those Teams. It also tells where they are…so I can pick em up."

He looked the list over. "The only one that I'm familiar with is this Officer Grade 7, Kiymee."

Kiyalee nodded. "I got to meet the two leaders, Heelitha and Nanchee." She giggled. "Neither one of them are happy over the fact that they both outrank you, but this is our vehicle."

He shrugged. "You can't always get what you want…or like."

"Yeah. They had to give in, because they don't have a garage… at all."

15

Morning came way too early for Soolchakan. He had spent quite a while in the gym, punishing one of the practice dummies. He had then gone to the fourth floor and obtained three bottles of different spirits, which he liberally drowned himself in for the remainder of the night. He was still drunk when the sun came up and it was time to get their first familiarization trip, with the truck, as a Team.

The women had each beaten the tar out of a practice dummy as well. After a good hot shower, they, as a group, went up to the fourth floor and took turns with the sewing machine. Each one had two new outfits done, by the time the sun came up.

Everyone headed to the garage. The women got there first and were ogling the truck. When Soolchakan staggered in, all three women made squawks of disgust.

While waving the smell away from her face, Bonarain snapped at him. "Did you take a shower after your workout last night?"

"I think that stink is both sweat and booze," said Chyning.

Kiyalee got directly between Soolchakan and the truck with her arms folded across her chest. "You are NOT getting in my truck, smelling like that! If you wanna get in *my* truck...you take a shower first."

He looked at the three women. "I'm...cmnder of this Team, and I say when..."

Kiyalee flattened him by pushing him backwards. "I told you that you're not getting in this truck smelling like that. Go take a shower first. After you shower...make sure you put on a clean uniform. I'm not sure which stinks worse...you or your clothing."

It took him three attempts at getting back on his feet. He saw the scowls on the faces of the three women and figured that they were too mad and he was too drunk to argue. He staggered out of the garage to the elevator. The three women followed. He looked at each one, a little confused.

"We're gonna make sure that you get to your room and get some clean clothing," said Bonarain adamantly.

He snorted at her. He tried to hit the "up" button and missed.

Chyning snarled in disgust and hit the button for him.

Once on the second floor, the women pushed him towards his bedroom. He was getting a little disgusted at the treatment he was getting, however, he could not figure out a way to stop them.

As they entered his bedroom, all three women let out another squawk of disgust, at both the smell and the extremely messy appearance of the room.

Bonarain started unbuttoning his shirt. "You girls find...see if you can find something that's clean. If you can't...we'll have to postpone our trip until his...stuff has been run through the washing machine." She shoved him into his bathroom. "Finish undressing yourself and...get cleaned up!" She shook her head in disgust as she headed back to the other two women.

"The only thing, in this room that's clean, is the inside of these booze bottles," said Chyning as she held two of them up.

Kiyalee looked around the room at the clothing that was strewn around. "What do we take...for cleaning?"

Bonarain snarled. "All of it! Take...everything! We can't tell, because of the smell...what's clean and what isn't...so...we'll run all of it through...just to make sure."

"Probably the first time in months...that any of his stuff has been near a washing machine," said Chyning disgusted.

They opened up the two windows to the room in an attempt at airing the premises out. All three of them stood at the windows for a few moments, clearing out their sinuses by breathing deeply.

Kiyalee looked back at the room. "How can anyone live like that?"

"He's too drunk to tell," said Bonarain. She shook her head. "Slob!"

After a long shower, he finally came out with two big towels wrapped around him. He was cleaner, however, he was still drunk. He looked around the room. "Where's all my clothes?"

Bonarain shook her head. "I notice that you looked on the floor, for your clothing. Did you bother to check the closet?"

He glared at her. "Why?"

Bonarain hung her head.

Kiyalee huffed. "Do you ever put anything away…in any of the closets…where you're supposed to put your clothes?"

He growled at them and went to the closet. All that he found in there were his boots. He looked back at the women. "Where's my clothes?"

"Being WASHED…for the first time…since you first got them," said Kiyalee.

He shook his head and started for the bed, to sit down. "Where's my sheets…and blankets?"

"Chyning took all that stuff outside. She set fire to all of it," said Bonarain. "We can save your uniforms, in the washing machine. Your linens…were beyond hope."

He sat down on the bed. "So when are we goin' on our truck ride?"

"As soon as we have a complete set of clean clothing for you to wear," snapped Bonarain. She saw him looking around. "What're you looking for now?"

"I need a drink," he said sullenly.

Kiyalee covered her face with her hands and groaned.

"No you don't," said Bonarain flatly.

Chyning came into the room with a set of clean linen for the bed. She wrinkled her nose at Soolchakan as she dumped the sheets on the bed. She walked away without saying anything.

Kiyalee shook her head as she looked around the room again. "Is anything in the drying machine yet?"

"Yeah," said Chyning. "Just started it."

Bonarain headed for the door. "He can't get any drunker… right now. We've cleaned all of the bottles out of the room."

The other two women followed.

He sat there on his bed feeling a little irate. "Women! What a pain!"

The three women sat in the main room.

Chyning looked at Bonarain. "Do we really have to wait for him? I mean, can't we just…take the truck…for a short ride?"

Bonarain sighed. "He is…the Team leader," she said dejectedly. "We have to…have him there…no matter what."

Kiyalee sat there looking at her nails. "Is there…a complete outfit, of some sort…in the dryer?"

Chyning rubbed her eyes. "There's two uniforms, three pairs of socks and…some…*stained* underwear."

Bonarain looked at her in horror. "Didn't you clean the underwear?"

Chyning sighed. "The stains are permanent. They won't come out. At least there aren't any…*chunks*…in them…anymore."

Kiyalee gagged. She turned her face to the side and waved her hands wildly as if to signal that Chyning should stop talking.

Bonarain shook her head with her eyes closed. "Slob!"

They sat there quietly until they heard the dryer shut off.

"Time for the moment of truth," said Bonarain.

They went to the machines. Chyning pulled all of the stuff out of the dryer and shoved it into a basket. Kiyalee pulled the load out of the washer and threw it into the dryer.

As Bonarain put a new load into the washer, she looked at some of the stuff that had been transferred. "You didn't put any of our clothes in with his, did you?"

Chyning looked at her in horror. "Are you crazy?" She shook her head and took the load to Soolchakan's room. She opened the door and kicked the basket inside. She closed the door.

Kiyalee looked at the other two. "You think he's gonna get dressed…on his own?"

Bonarain rolled her eyes. "Even he isn't that stup…" She looked at the door and back to the other two women. She walked to the door and banged on it several times. "Are you getting dressed in there?"

"Of course," he shouted back angrily.

Kiyalee flopped back down in a chair. "I guess that there is… some part of his brain that…somehow…is still working."

A while later he came out of his bedroom. The uniform

looked a little rumpled, however, the women did not mind that. At least it was clean. He started looking around the room.

Bonarain stood up and stared at him confused. "What…are you looking for?"

Without looking at her he just hollered. "I need a drink!"

All three women were up, with their arms folded across their chests.

"No…you…don't," scolded Bonarain.

"You get in the truck, without booze," said Kiyalee.

He growled. He glared back at them. "Let's go."

Kiyalee opened up the rear door. "Before I start it up, I want to show you some of the things inside here." She climbed in.

Bonarain and Chyning stood a ways back - just in case he fell - as he tried to get in. They were both a little surprised when he made it up the four step ladder and into the truck - on one attempt. They then followed.

The interior was high enough for them to be able to stand. The entire back of the truck was an armory. There were twenty rifles that were in racks - ten on each side. There was a huge central container that had over 3,000 rounds of ammunition in it. There were also ten pulse rifles, complete with extra power packs on racks.

Soolchakan was staring at a storage rack that was near the top turret. On each side of the truck was a large pulse cannon, complete with twenty power packs. "It has been years…since I handled…one of these things. You can knock down a…big building…with one of those." He looked at Bonarain. "Have you ever fired one of those?"

She shook her head with her mouth hanging open. "Uh-uh."

He looked at Chyning. "How about you?"

She looked at him stunned. "I…didn't even know…that they made any of…those things…that *big*."

"A long time ago, I test fired one of them," said Kiyalee.

Soolchakan looked at her shocked. "How many people got killed?"

She raised her fist and clenched her teeth, as if ready to knock him out. She snarled as she spun on her heels and headed for the driver's seat with both fists clenched at her side. She sat down. "Somebody open the door!" She turned the engine on.

Chyning jumped out of the truck and opened the big door. She waited while Kiyalee pulled out of the garage and hit the automatic button to close the door. Then back into the truck.

"Hold on," said Soolchakan. "I wanna know…how you get this pulse cannon…set up…to fire. This thing…is way too large for a person to carry it…on their own."

Kiyalee looked back at him scowling. "Have you got the power pack out of it?"

He looked at the back of the cannon. "It hasn't been installed…yet."

"Good," she said facetiously. "I wouldn't wanna blow your big mouth off." She got out of the driver's seat and came back to the cannon. "First, you release the front and back straps."

Kiyalee released the front one while Soolchakan hit the rear one.

Kiyalee now hit a release on the central part of the roof of the truck. She then slid a round door back and they could see the sky. "Now, it's gonna take all four of us to move it into position."

Kiyalee and Chyning were on the front while Soolchakan and Bonarain held the heavy weapon in the rear. Kiyalee pushed the front of the barrel up through the opening. She looked back. "Okay, slowly, come forward." The other three started moving the gun forward. As they moved Kiyalee kept pushing the gun up until it was perpendicular to the floor. She then pushed the gun against a u-shaped bracket. It clicked into place. "Okay," she said. "Now, it can be handled by just one person."

Soolchakan took hold of it. "Okay, so the bracket holds it. How do you aim it at the enemy?"

Kiyalee knelt down and pulled two large pieces that were built into the sides, up and together. They snapped together and formed a platform for whoever was firing the cannon to stand on.

Soolchakan snickered. "My, my, my, what will they think of next?" He stepped up onto the platform and pushed the cannon up as he went. The base of the bracket did a 90 degree turn as he pushed up. He stood there holding onto the cannon. "It won't move anywhere. How're you supposed to fire at an enemy that's off to the side?"

"You haven't pushed if far enough forward," said Kiyalee.

He shrugged and pushed a little more. He heard a loud clang and grimaced in fear because he thought that he had broken something.

"Now you're there," said Kiyalee.

He opened his eyes and breathed a sigh of relief. He started swiveling the cannon. It moved very easily in any direction. He also found out that it was now on some kind of runner that allowed him to move the bracket in a complete circle around the opening. He grunted an approval. "Okay, that's how we put it up here. How do we get it down?"

Kiyalee showed them the procedures, which basically turned out to be a reversal of setting it up. After getting the cannon back in its brackets on the wall, she went back to the driver's seat.

"Uh...scuse me," said Bonarain. "Why...is there a steering wheel on each side?"

Kiyalee looked back. "That's in case the driver gets...disabled. Someone else can be sitting in the other seat and take over the duty, while the disabled person is pulled out of the seat and someone else takes over."

Chyning huffed. "But...with that...huge windshield...the driver...er both of them are totally exposed...to any enemy fire!"

Kiyalee looked back at Chyning as she hit a big red knob. As soon as she hit it, large metallic, accordion shields came down and covered most of the front, and side windows, leaving just a small hole for the driver to peer through. "The windshield is made out of some kind of stuff that can stop most calibers of bullets. The metal shields can stop *any* bullet."

Chyning smiled. "That's much better. Makes me feel a little safer."

Kiyalee grabbed a knob in the middle of the dashboard. She started pumping it and the shields slowly raised back up. When they finally clicked back into place, she rubbed her right bicep and shook her right arm. "That's a lot of work!" She repositioned herself in the seat. "Does someone want to play second driver…while I take this baby to the fuel station?"

Soolchakan sat down in the back. He had found a manual on the big pulse cannon and decided that he wanted to re-familiarize himself with the big weapon.

Bonarain shrugged and took the other seat. "Can I help steer or…is it only one at a time?"

Kiyalee snickered. "You can take hold and help. You can get used to it that way…just in case." She reached over and hit the starter button. The big engine fired up and growled loudly as it idled. "Everybody ready?"

"Let's go," said Bonarain.

"Ready," said Chyning.

Soolchakan just gave them a hand signal as he continued to read the manual.

Bonarain giggled. "Can we drive it around a little…just to get some of the familiarization with it?"

"We better fill it up first," said Kiyalee. "We're below one eighth of a tank."

Bonarain nodded. "Okay, where's this fuel station?"

"We got to get to Perimeter road and turn east. That's where they told me it was."

"Okay," said Bonarain.

Bonarain found out that it was not really a truck that was made for driving on city streets. It was not very maneuverable when it came to sharp 90 degree turns. You had to pull hard on the steering wheel and go very slowly in order to keep from hitting a wall.

Chyning chuckled. "If these streets were any narrower, we'd have a *real* problem."

Fortunately, once they were on Perimeter road, it was a straight line to the fuel station. Bonarain let go of the wheel and let Kiyalee steer the truck up to the pumps. Kiyalee stopped the truck and turned the engine off. She slumped in the seat and let out a loud "Whew!" The three women got out. Kiyalee was getting ready to show them how (and where) to fuel the vehicle.

Chyning looked back up at the truck. "Where's…his majesty?"

"He's still reading," said Bonarain.

Kiyalee huffed. "What? He thinks he's too important to learn how to feed, and care for, this big monster?" She went to the rear entrance and climbed up. "Hey, Great Leader! I gotta show you what to do out here."

He looked up from his reading. "You go ahead and show the others. I'll watch later. Right now, I'm trying to find out about this nasty new weapon."

Kiyalee snarled. "What's so special? You've fired a four-five-six cannon before!"

He looked at her disgusted. "*This* is *not* a four-five-six. *This* monster is a four-five-*nine*! Until I saw this manual, I had never heard of a four-five-nine. This thing is…more powerful and has a much greater range than any four-five-six."

Kiyalee looked at the two cannons. "Wow!" She turned to the other two women. "They didn't tell me that! All they said was that the guns were new."

"Oh, they're new all right. *Very* new!" He went back to reading.

Kiyalee climbed down. She looked at the other two women and shrugged. "For now, I'll show you. We can show him later… after he finds out about those new cannons."

Bonarain looked up into the interior. "Did I hear him say… four-five-*nine*?"

Kiyalee nodded as she headed to the side of the truck. "The fuel nozzle is over here." She showed them eight step procedures on fueling.

Chyning growled. "Why'd they have to make it so complicated?"

"In case the truck gets captured," said Kiyalee. "This way, if you do any of the steps wrong…the truck just dumps the fuel on the ground…as soon as someone, who's not familiar with the truck, tries to fuel it up and drive it off."

"Anti-theft safety mechanism," said Bonarain dryly.

The truck was driven around the area for almost half the day. All four got some time at the wheel. They all agreed that it would be much easier driving the thing out in the countryside. They would not have to worry about any (or at least not very many) sharp turns. They took it back to the fuel station and filled it up again before taking it back to the new garage for the truck.

They were in the gymnasium beating up on their practice dummies. They had received new dummies because they had destroyed all of the other ones that they had been given originally. No one seemed to be able to figure out why this Team was so destructive to their practice targets. No one else had needed to replace more than one dummy.

There was suddenly a loud klaxon going off. The four of them froze and listened to the noise for a moment as they looked at each other in fear.

Chyning was the first to speak: "Who…who's attacking us?"

"I don't know," said Soolchakan as he rushed to the second floor to get to a communication device. The alarm on the communicator was going off as well. He picked it up and responded through his panting. "Team 7016…reporting…in…Team Leader… Soolchakan…reporting." He took several deep breaths trying to slow his breathing. "What's the situation, Sir?"

The response came back. "*All Teams, get to your trucks and report to the north side assembly area, immediately. Those who are supposed to pick up other Teams on the way - do so and report as soon as possible to the north side.*"

Soolchakan swallowed hard as he looked as the rest of his Team. "I…don't know where…to report."

"I do," said Kiyalee flatly. "They showed me, when I got the truck. Come on, we've gotta get all of this sweat off of us and then pick up Teams 6598 and 6638. Let's get changed!"

They all stripped their sweats off and headed for the showers. After a quick shower, they got in uniform and headed for the truck. Kiyalee and Chyning were up front at the twin steering wheels while Bonarain sat in the back checking her makeup and Soolchakan took a few more hits from a new flask that he had found.

They headed out for what was going to be, for the most part, a long and boring drive. Kiyalee had a map that showed where the two Teams were. Instead of heading for the road that went due north, they had to follow the Perimeter road, going east. The two Teams that they had to pick up were on the way, at different spots on the perimeter.

They reached Team 6598. They got to meet the Team Leader, Officer Grade 4, Heelitha. The members were Officer Grade 5, Tetta, Officer Grade 7, Hoolton and Officer Grade 7, Kiymee. They were waiting by the side of the road, armed to the teeth, along with a few other supplies.

Soolchakan looked over all that they had with them. "What are you doing with all that? There's plenty of weaponry already inside the truck."

"We're supposed to bring this, according to the mandate from Supreme Officer, Nagasoom," said Heelitha. "I understand that there's some ammunition and weapons in the truck, but we're supposed to bring this with us and use the trucks equipment as spares. We also brought the extra rations."

Soolchakan felt embarrassed. "I…didn't see…any mandate… like that." He turned to Kiyalee quickly. "Does this thing have any rations in it…for us?"

"The compartments under your seats back there," Kiyalee snapped back at him.

He turned back to Heelitha.

Heelitha gave him a dirty look. "That's because *you* have the truck. *That* weaponry is there for you…initially. We bring ours as our initial weapons…and the other as our food supply."

Soolchakan shrugged and sighed. "Hand the stuff up here… we'll find somewhere to put it."

Team 6598 relayed eight pulse rifles, eight regular rifles, 1,000 rounds of ammunition and sixteen power packs for the pulse rifles and almost 100 field ration meals. Then they climbed up in the vehicle. As each one entered they gawked at all of the weapons that were already in the vehicle.

"I see what you meant," said Heelitha. "There's enough here… we didn't really have to bring…anything. You…got enough…for all of us."

Soolchakan shook his head. "We already had enough for you and us…and we've got enough for that other Team that we're picking up as well. If they heard that same mandate…we're gonna get awfully crowded with weapons…and food."

Heelitha sat down. "Uh-huh!"

Soolchakan sat down next to her. "Maybe while we're driving towards the next pick-up point…you might check out this pulse cannon that we've got here."

She snorted. "I and my Team are very familiar with the 456."

He snorted back. "These ain't any 456! These two cannons are the new 459!"

She looked at him angrily. She looked down at the cover of the operational manual and her expression changed to surprise. "45…9? When did that come out?"

"I have no idea. All I know is that this truck came armed with two of those highly destructive machines."

"Uhm…do you have another copy of this manual?"

"No, the truck only came with one copy."

She let out a grunt of annoyance. She looked at her Team. "Hoolton, why don't you come over here and read the manual…on the cannon?"

Hoolton smiled weakly. "Did I hear you call it a…45…9?"

"Yes," said Soolchakan flatly.

Hoolton chuckled nervously. "If that thing is a bigger, better weapon than the 456…you bet I'd like to know more." He moved to where he could sit next to Heelitha and the two of them read the manual together.

They were about three quarters of the way through the manual when Kiyalee pulled to a stop at the next pick-up point. She looked back. "Get ready to make room for a lot more weaponry… and other assorted stuff."

Bonarain groaned. "Yeah…just what we need. More guns and ammunition…like we don't have enough in here already."

Team 6638 consisted of Team Leader, Officer Grade 4, Nanchee, Officer Grade 5, Choog, Officer Grade 7, Natoy and Officer Grade 7, Ee-Ema.

Eight more pulse rifles with sixteen power packs and eight more regular rifles with another 1,000 rounds of ammunition, and 100 more field ration meals.

Kiyalee looked at her map. "I wonder if it would be shorter, just to take the Perimeter road…all the way to the assembly area."

"No, it wouldn't," said Heelitha. "If you take a good look, you'll notice that the perimeter makes a long turn to the east and then a big wide bend before you're in the northern area. That road that goes to the west…it is the shortest route."

Kiyalee sat there shaking her head. "It's depressing…going through all of that rubble…that used to be…such a big, beautiful city."

Her comment was met by silence. Everyone in the truck hung their heads thinking of what used to be and just how much had been destroyed in the firestorms.

She put the truck in gear and on they went to the assembly area.

There were a few tears and sniffles as they drove through the rubble and fire-gutted buildings. There were no landmarks, of favorite places to go, that were left. Nothing was recognizable. Several of the people in the truck stopped looking out the front windows and just hung their heads.

The ten big towers, where the elite of the city had lived were gone. Before the attack, you could see those towers from anywhere on the perimeter wall. Now, no one could even tell where they had been as they drove through the one cleared street.

Soolchakan looked at all of the melancholy passengers. "Have any of you…been in this part…since the attack?" He glanced at all of them. "Anyone?"

"I have," said Kiyalee. "Just to drive the truck…home. That's the only time…I've been…here."

Most did not respond. A few just shook their heads.

It was a rather long, quiet drive to the assembly area.

They finally arrived at the assembly area. Most of the people in the truck were astonished at how many vehicles were there - not to mention the fact that there was an area this large, with no rubble on it.

Kiyalee burst the bubble of the survivability of this area. "This area was covered with debris," she said. "It took a lot of the people, who are living on the northern perimeter to clear an area this big. Otherwise, we'd be spread out for quite a distance on the northern perimeter road." She continued driving to a check-in point.

"We're probably last," said Heelitha.

Nanchee, the Team Leader of 6638 shook her head. "Don't be such a pessimist. So what, if we're last. We had a long way to go… to get here."

Hoolton stretched his legs. "Yeah, a long way to go…for some silly drill that the higher ups decided to have."

"It's awfully expensive for just a drill," said Nanchee. "Think of all of the fuel that was burned…just getting all of these vehicles here…and no one is refining any new fuel…yet."

They reached the check-in point. Kiyalee stopped and leaned out her window. "Teams 7016, 6598 and 6638 reporting in, Sir."

The woman at the point looked down at an electronic pad and checked off the three Teams. She looked up and pointed off to her left. "That woman there will guide you to your staging point."

Kiyalee looked forward and saw a woman with a small green flag raised high. "Thank you, Sir." She put the truck in gear and headed for the green flag. When she reached the woman with the flag, that woman climbed up to talk to Kiyalee as she guided them to their spot. She spoke only loud enough for Kiyalee to hear. As soon as the truck was parked, Kiyalee shut the engine off.

The guide woman leaned in the truck. "All Team Leaders need to report immediately to that big building over there with all of the area banners on top."

Everyone got out of the truck and started stretching muscles. Soolchakan, Heelitha and Nanchee headed for the building.

"So," said Nanchee. "What dya think?"

Heelitha looked confused. "About what?"

"This drill...if it is a drill."

"Like you said...it's an awfully expensive drill. I hope that they have a good reason. I'd hate to see all of that fuel being burned for nothing."

"We'll know when we get the briefing," said Soolchakan nonchalantly.

The building that they were headed for had flags for each of the four City Commands: North, south, east and west. Soolchakan, Heelitha and Nanchee were all part of the south.

They found that they were going to have to report again. They were checked off by an aide to one of the four area commanders. They were instructed to have a seat and wait for the Supreme Officer to make his announcement.

Soolchakan yawned. "How long do you think we'll have to wait?"

The aide gave him a dull look. "As soon as all of the Team Leaders are here. There are still nineteen that haven't arrived yet."

"We weren't last," said Heelitha.

"No," said Nanchee. "But we came awful close."

They left the vestibule and found themselves in a large auditorium. There was more than enough seating for all of the Team Leaders. The trio found a place to sit, as close to the front as they could get, and still be together.

Soolchakan wanted to take a drink from his flask, however, he did not think that it was a wise idea. He looked around to see if anyone else was using a flask. No such luck. He would have to stay dry during this meeting.

Nanchee kept looking back at the entrance. "Two down, seventeen to go."

He was glad that she had started at nineteen. He was not sure that he could take a countdown that was much longer than that.

She kept looking back and counting down. Finally the last one came in. She faced front. "Okay, Supreme Officer, whatcha got to say to us?"

Heelitha grimaced. "Don't say that too loud. You don't want

to be the first one slapped down at a big meeting."

Nanchee just chuckled.

A few moments later, Nagasoom made his entrance. The four area commanders followed him out onto the stage. Everyone did their proper protocol of standing and rendering a salute. He returned the salute and they all sat down.

Nagasoom gave the congregation a once over. He smiled. "My fellow citizens. Today...is going to be a day that will be remembered by all the citizens of Owlam...for as long as there is at least one of us, drawing breath. Today...we are going to attack and extract vengeance on the city of Axswain, for the attack on us that killed millions of Owlam citizens."

There was a rumbling of voices that almost echoed through the big room. All four of the area commanders were gawking at him with shock on their faces.

"Yes," he continued. "We are going - all of us are going. We are going to attack the Axswain people and...do even worse to them...than what was done to us...nearly a year ago. Think...of all of the friends you lost. Think...of all of the family you lost. Think... of what this city used to be and what it is now. That should give you the proper motivation to spring to the attack and wreak havoc on the city of Axswain."

Master Officer, Plothok, the North Commander could not sit still. "Sir, that...it...just not possible!"

Nagasoom turned and glared at him. "What? Why not?"

"Sir...we just...don't have the...facility...or personnel...to carry out an attack of that magnitude."

Master Officer, Kodge, the commander of the western area stood up. "Sir, we all know...that it would take at least 500,000 well trained troops to mount an offensive like that. Today...here...we have less than 30,000. What do you...hope to gain?"

Nagasoom looked even angrier. "VICTORY! Victory over an enemy that has been a big enough pain, for FAR too long."

Neenatha, the Eastern Commander stood up. She was holding her fists up to her chest and clenching her teeth as she talked. "Sir, we don't even know who it was that attacked us...using that...

whatever it was they used. How can you be so sure that it was the Axswain?"

Each one of the protests from the Master Officers was met with a chorus of agreements from the people in the seats. The noise was getting a little louder with each protest that was raised.

Nagasoom lost his composure completely. "ENOUGH!" He looked at each of the area commanders and then out into the auditorium. "I have made my decision! We are going to attack! We are going to attack...TODAY! I am not going to listen to any more of these...inane protestations. My guts tell me that the city of Axswain was behind that attack and nothing that I've heard has convinced me otherwise."

The room was strangely silent while he was talking. No one had the courage to interrupt or protest - any more.

He was still angry. "You will now go to your vehicles and you will explain to your Teams. I will make an announcement over a loudspeaker, to all of them. One of my aides has already given your Teams the orders to get your vehicles battle ready. They are complying with this order at this time."

No one was able to protest any more. No one had a look of shock on their faces any more. They all sat there staring at him with the same grim determination that he had. The city of Axswain must be punished for what it did to the city of Owlam. No questions asked.

Nagasoom glanced around the big room waiting for another protest. He seemed rather surprised that he was not getting any - anymore. He cleared his throat and straightened his tunic. "I will be leading the attack. We have intercommunication in each of the trucks, so I will be able to move vehicles as I see fit, in order to assure our victory. We will leave with just enough fuel to get us to the enemy city..."

Neenatha, the Eastern Commander, stood up. "A suggestion, Sir?"

He turned and glared at her. "What?"

"Sir, if we go with just enough fuel to get there...what happens after we breach the wall. We'll be sitting there with no transportation.

We'll have to go through the breach...on foot..."

"Your suggestion is...?"

"Fuel up all of the vehicles to the maximum. Have each vehicle carry a supply of fuel cans lashed to the outside of them..."

Kodge, the Western Commander, jumped up. "If they have all of that fuel on the outside, they'll just help us die faster, if they get hit!"

Neenatha turned to him angrily. "Hear me out!"

Nagasoom held up his hand. "Let her finish, Master Officer, Kodge."

Neenatha gave Kodge a nasty look. She turned to Nagasoom. "Thank you Supreme Officer." She clasped her arms behind her back. "Just before we get within range of the wall, we stop, pour all of that fuel into the fuel tanks and jettison the empty fuel cans. This way, when we hit the wall, we can drive right through the breach, without having to worry about somebody running out of fuel in the breach, requiring us to create another breach for the vehicles blocked outside."

Nagasoom looked at Kodge. "Do you still have a protest to that plan?"

Kodge licked his lips. "My apologies to Master Officer, Neenatha. I acted too...hastily. I find no...argument with that plan."

"Neither do I," said Nagasoom. He signaled to one of his aides. "Leelkiy, get out there and get the word to all of them to get their vehicles fueled to capacity and start the distribution of extra fuel cans."

The woman jumped up and ran out a side door.

Master Officer, Jahong, the Southern Commander stood up. "Do we...retrieve these cans...on the way back home? It would seem a bit of a waste of our limited resources to just...leave them there to rot."

Nagasoom smiled. "Yes, we'll retrieve them. At this time... we cannot afford to waste any of our resources. Once we're able to get some manufacturing going on again..." He chuckled. "Possibly using any surviving Axswain citizens as slave labor, then we'll see what we can get rid of permanently...other than our enemy...the city of Axswain."

A screen came down behind and above the commanders on the stage. Nagasoom went over the logistics and tactics of the attack. Everyone listened intently without argument. For some reason, no one could think of a way to argue against. All suggestions were those that would enhance the attack.

By the time they were finished with all of the plan of the attack, the sun was going down. All of the Team Leaders were headed back to their vehicles.

Soolchakan, Heelitha and Nanchee were looking for their transportation among the over 6,400 vehicles parked in this area.

"It's a 161," said Soolchakan. "It's one of the big ones."

"The 195's are the really big ones," said Heelitha flatly.

"Yeah, but there's only about ten of those monstrosities," said Nanchee. "The 161...there's probably about a hundred of them."

"Look for the big designator of Team 7016," said Soolchakan. "Remember, there's only seventeen Teams that start with a seven."

Heelitha snarled. "They all look the same. We should be able to mark them...somehow, so we can find our vehicle...in this ocean of trucks."

Nanchee giggled. "Just think if you were assigned one of the 74's. Those small little vehicles that can move fast, hit fast and escape fast...I've counted over one hundred of them...just in this area."

Soolchakan shook his head. "You'd be looking...forever. The 74's and the 104's...hundreds of them."

"There it is," said Nanchee as she pointed off to the right.

Soolchakan was ready to say no, however he saw Kiyalee, along with two other people, on top, doing something with one of the 459 cannons. "Why'd she mount the thing? It's gonna take all night...once we leave the city in order to get to the Axswain wall. What do we need that thing up there for?"

"We'll ask her when we get there," said Heelitha with a shrug.

"Wait a moment," said Nanchee. "When we went inside... none of these vehicles had their big guns mounted...outside. Now... they all have them...ready to go."

They reached their 161.

Soolchakan climbed up the outside. "Hey, Kiyalee, what's with the mounting of the gun?"

Kiyalee turned to him. "One of the 'higher ups' gave us the order to mount and secure the 459. So, I taught everyone here how to mount and secure a 459. If someone gets hurt...we don't have to guess who can help get the other one up here...if this one gets damaged."

He looked at what had been done. The cannon was mounted on its swiveling turret bracket and had four other brackets, hooked to the top of the vehicle that kept the cannon from bouncing around.

He looked at each one of the four brackets. "How do we...get ready quickly...with that thing tied down like that?"

She sat down on the top of the truck and sniffed. "The quick release for each one of the braces is on the inside. The cannon can be ready to arm and fire in about three heartbeats."

He looked at all of the fuel cans that were lashed to the outside, and on top of, the truck. "I certainly hope we don't have a fire."

Chyning scoffed. "If we do, we'll suffocate long before we feel the heat. We won't suffer much at all."

He felt his stomach rumbling. "We were in there too long. I need something to eat...and I've gotta hit the bathroom."

Kiyalee giggled. "Over there," she pointed. "They got a few thousand of those outhouse facilities set up. After you get rid of something, we'll get you a field ration."

He headed for the outhouse. He was not thinking of any food. What he needed was a drink. He had not brought any bottles of liquor with him, because he did not think that he was going to be away from his supply that long. He got to an unoccupied outhouse, walked in and closed the door. First things first - he pulled his flask out and got ready for a good swig. He growled in frustration. There was just enough left in the flask to wet his tongue - now there was nothing in there but air. He closed the cap, put it back in his pocket and did what was normally done in an outhouse. After relieving himself he went back to the truck.

Chyning was waiting for him with a selection of different field rations. He looked at the labels and grunted. One large lump tasted just like another large lump. It did not matter what was written on the outside, they all tasted the same - bland. He picked one, shook his head as he opened it and started eating.

Nagasoom came out on top of the meeting building. He stood looking up at the four sector banners that were fluttering above him. There were several people who were setting up a microphone and loudspeaker system for him. He waited patiently for them to finish. He looked out over the mass of vehicles that were parked in neat rows on the huge lot. Finally they finished and he stepped up to the microphone. There was a bit of a din going through the thousands of Owlamites that were milling about among the vehicles. It did not quiet down until he started talking.

"My fellow citizens of Owlam. Today, will be one of the greatest days in our history. Today…we are going to wreak havoc on the ones who destroyed our beautiful city."

Soolchakan, Heelitha and Nanchee stood there quietly. They knew what was coming.

He continued. "Today, we are going to attack and destroy the city of Axswain."

One of Team 6638, Ee-Ema looked at the others around her in shock. "Has his brains turned to *h'oolyach*? He can't be serious!"

Her sentiment was shared by many thousands of others who had not been inside the auditorium and they did not hesitate to complain.

Nagasoom heard the protestation and became angered. "STOP ALL OF THIS INFERNAL COMPLAINING!"

The entire area was suddenly very silent. There was that strange loud voice that they had heard inside.

He glared out at the multitude. "As the Supreme Officer, I have decided that it is time to stop stalling and attack! It will take us almost all of the night to get to the city walls of Axswain. The sun will be coming back up when we get there and that's when we will attack. I know that you will all be awake, because the doctors have informed me that no one has had any real sleep since the attack. That is our ally. We don't sleep, therefore we will not be tired when we get there. Your Team Leaders have been informed of the manner of our attack. You will follow their orders completely. I will be in communication, over the vehicle intercoms, if I see anything that needs to be changed in our attack. Now, if by some chance, you are taken prisoner, by those *doovofts*, you will not reveal any of our numbers. If they want to know about how many of us there are…cut the figures by one fourth. Tell them that we started with only 7000 in our army and not the 28,000 that we do have. This is a tactic that we will use, as long as there is any citizen of Owlam, that is still breathing. Never tell anyone of our total numbers." He stepped back and took a breath. He smoothed his hair back with his hands and went back to the microphone. He now talked in a normal manner. "Never forget this day, my fellow citizens of Owlam. Now…mount your vehicles and let's move out."

16

The vehicles were started in shifts and driven through a tunnel to the outside of the great Owlam wall. As soon as they were marshaled to their spot in the movement, they cut their engines, in order to preserve fuel. As soon as all of the vehicles were outside the wall, Nagasoom punched a code into a box on the outside of the tunnel. Huge metal doors went into place to close the tunnel. The city could now be labeled as abandoned. There was not one single sentient creature that they knew of, inside the wall. All of them were on the outside preparing to attack the city of Axswain.

Nagasoom turned on his intercom. "Now, my fellow citizens, we will go forward and rid the world of the Axswain pestilence. When the sun comes up, we are going to kick the piddleeyanks out of our enemy. I am going to enjoy this. Death to the Axswain. All vehicles…start your engines and let's move."

A great roar was heard as all of the vehicles started up. Nagasoom's truck was the first to move. All vehicles followed.

Kiyalee was in the main driver's seat. Chyning was in the secondary.

Soolchakan went up to Chyning and whispered in her ear. "Did you wet yourself that time…like you did the last time he talked like that?"

She turned her head and snarled at him. "No, I didn't! I've heard it before…and it…doesn't scare me…anymore."

Chyning turned back to the steering chores. On this uneven ground, Kiyalee was having a few problems keeping the truck moving in a straight line. As they drove along, any sapling that they came across was no challenge for the big truck. The larger trees, were something else. There, they had to break the line and move around.

Heelitha looked out the front of the vehicle. She could only see what was in the headlights of all of the vehicles, however, because of the number of trucks, the forward area was rather well lit. "Why is...everything...so brown? It almost looks like winter is coming on...but...that's months away. All I see...are dead trees and...plants."

"I don't know," said Nanchee. "It must be some of that...residual stuff that the doctor was talking about. I'm wondering where all of the animals are."

Soolchakan scoffed. "With all of the noise that we're making, with this many trucks...any animal, if there are any, in our path, they're running scared...somewhere."

"This is the first time...I've ever been outside the walls of the city," said Ee-Ema.

"Same here," said Chyning.

"I wish it was daylight, so I could see," said Tetta.

"Not much else to see," said Hoolton.

The rest of the trip was very boring. Five times, during the trip, Nagasoom got on the intercom and asked if anyone was having any mechanical problems. He asked if anyone had seen anyone stop because of mechanical problems. He seemed to be very worried about some of the vehicles not making it to the attack. Somehow, they all did.

When the light started coming over the horizon, in the east, Nagasoom ordered a full stop. At that time, they got out and started pouring all of the fuel from the cans into the fuel tanks. There were several stacks of the cans left behind as they started the engines and again began their advance towards the city of Axswain.

At a certain point, everyone turned all of their headlights off. No one knew why, they just simultaneously all turned them off.

Nagasoom was sitting in his truck gloating over how he had brought the military of Owlam to this level. It had been almost fifteen years since Owlam had initiated any major offensive against the hated city of Axswain. Now, under his leadership, there would be an attack that no one would forget.

Finally they saw their goal in the distance. The great wall that surrounded the city of Axswain came into view. It was mainly the upper portion that they could see through clearings in the leafless trees. It was no less ominous than the wall that surrounded Owlam… and would be just as hard to breach.

Below, much closer, they saw some people in fruitless farmlands running towards the wall. The attack was no longer a complete surprise. These people would most assuredly warn the city of Axswain of this attack. Nagasoom hoped that the propaganda about how bad these people were at battle would take over the minds of his people and they would fight on bravely. His hope was total victory.

There were ten of the big Type 195, Lead Heavy Assault Vehicles. They had sixteen personnel in each one, there were two of the big 459 pulse cannons sticking out the top and four doors on each side that could be opened for someone to shoot, with little personal exposure, at the enemy. They were big slow moving vehicles that were capable of maximum fire power and maximum damage.

There were one hundred and nineteen of the Type 161, Heavy Assault Vehicles. Soolchakan decided to be the first one to man the upper 459 cannon while the other people in the truck opened the six side doors on this truck. These vehicles were not as big as the 195's, however, they were capable of inflicting some very heavy damage of their own.

There were two hundred and sixty-five of the Type 109, Medium Assault Vehicles. They also had an upper cannon, however, it was the smaller 456 cannon. They had one door on each side for shooting at the enemy. They helped support the bigger assault vehicles.

There were 3,061 of the Type 104, Light Assault Vehicles. They had only the cannon up top, and no side doors. They were faster and much more maneuverable. They had the 456 cannon. Their job was to look for smaller pockets of enemy and quickly destroy them.

Finally there were 3,004 of the Type 74, Small Sprint Attack Vehicles. Faster and even more maneuverable than the 104's. The driver sat in the middle, while there were shooters on each side in the front and one up top with a medium range pulse cannon. They were built to hit fast, move fast and get out of the way. Do some quick damage and then allow the heavier assault vehicles to come in and smash anything that was left with conventional or pulse weapons.

The last vehicles to come up were the big Type 48, Medical Vehicles. Nagasoom did not like the idea of wasting twelve personnel in each of these eight vehicles, however, he did realize that there was the need for medical assistance for anyone…as long as the medical personnel took care of the Owlamites first…and foremost.

Over 6,400 vehicles were advancing on Axswain - and no one had any idea of how many enemy they would be facing. They just knew - for some inexplicable reason - they were compelled to continue with this attack - with no fear of death or injury.

Soolchakan looked around and was a little surprised to see some three-wheeled vehicles move up to the front. He had not seen these vehicles before. Each had one rider who had to steer and shoot at the same time. They were armed with pulse pistols. The range was very short and the rider had no armor between themselves and any enemy gunfire.

The Sprints and the Light Assault Vehicles moved to the front as they kept grinding their way through trees, heading for the wall. The three-wheelers moved up with the lighter vehicles and then started pulling ahead.

So far, no hostile fire had come from the Axswain. There was still a hope that they had actually pulled off a surprise and that the city would not be prepared for any type of assault like this one. Some were wondering if the attack on Axswain had been real and not faked as Nagasoom had intimated. If they had been attacked, in the same manner, with whatever weapon they had, then Axswain might possibly be in the same condition as Owlam. That thought was secondary - to all others. The primary thought was: Kill Axswain and all inhabitants.

They arrived at the edge of a large tree line (of dead leafless trees) and were looking at the farms that were closest to the walls. Here, just like back at Owlam, all of the crops were wilting, or completely dead, in the fields. They could not even see a healthy crop of weeds. Here and there, they could see one or two green weeds. There were no crops. There seemed to be no plants that were thriving after the attacks that had decimated all of the cities in the area.

Without any command from Nagasoom (that was spoken), all of the Sprint vehicles suddenly spun their wheels and kicked dirt all over the vehicles behind them. They sped towards the wall, looking for any form of resistance that was within their range. If any of them came close to a house or a barn, they opened fire and caused grievous damage to the structures. Others just churned up the dirt on land - where crops should have been growing. The three-wheelers sped along just ahead of the Sprint vehicles.

The Sprints were less than a third of the way to the wall when the Light Assault Vehicles spun their wheels in the dirt and took off for the attack.

At that same moment, the Sprints changed their attack pattern. They broke up into thirds. One third taking the lead, one third slowing to half speed and one third stopping altogether. After the lead line was far enough away, the second line increased their speed. After the second line was far enough, the third line began advancing again. Now all three lines were spread out and had plenty of maneuvering room for each vehicle as they fired and were ready to attempt dodging any shooting that would be raining down on them from the top of the wall.

The three-wheelers did not change their tactics. They stayed slightly ahead of the front row of Sprint vehicles.

The Medium, Heavy and Lead Assault vehicles moved up slowly, spacing themselves as widely as they could, in order to do as much damage, to as wide an area on the wall as they could inflict - with what they had.

When the Light Assault Vehicles reached the area where the Sprints had split up, these vehicles did the same maneuver. Now there were six rows of vehicles heading for the giant wall.

Just after the split of the Light vehicles, all of the heaver vehicles, in the rear, started forward. There would be only one line of these vehicles seeing as how each of the front six lines had over 1,000 vehicles in each of their lines and there were only 394 of the large assault vehicles.

Finally, the front line started receiving enemy fire from the top of the wall. They all started a zigzag pattern to avoid allowing any one to zero in on them.

The front row of Sprints and the three-wheelers started returning fire. The pistols on the three-wheelers had virtually no effect on their targets. The 456 small cannon was doing some damage of blasting chunks of concrete out of the top of the wall. It did not seem to be cutting down on any of the enemy fire. They were still being bombarded with pulse and conventional fire from the wall.

Soolchakan was watching as the shooting took place in front of him. The beams from the pistols and rifles all appeared to be white. The beams from the 456 cannons was orange. He wondered if the beam from his 459 was a different color. Just to test it out, he aimed at an area on, the top of the wall, where a lot of concentrated enemy firing was coming from. He pulled the trigger and got one of the biggest shocks of his life. A large red beam shot out of his 459 and hit the wall - or blasted it - from where he was. The 456 cannons had to get closer. The front two rows of Sprint vehicles were within the effective range of the 456 cannons, meaning that only the front two lines could do any damage to the wall. This nasty weapon he was firing was doing damage from the seventh line of attack. When the cannon operators on the other big vehicles saw that they could hit the wall from back where they were, all of them opened fire. Huge portions of the top of the wall were coming down under the onslaught of over 400 super cannons.

Nagasoom's truck lurched forward. He wanted to be in on any kill and the fact that there were two of those big 459 cannons mounted on the top of his truck and they were accurate and effective from here, he wanted to get even closer to see if short range could increase the damage. None of the other Medium or Heavy vehicles followed his tactic. They stayed back and stuck to this new plan. They did, however, continue blasting large chunks out of the top of the wall.

Then something happened that changed the entire scenario. A huge beam came out of the middle part of the wall. It was round and yellow and the beam had a circumference that was larger than any of the Sprint vehicles that were up front. The beam was aimed at the harassing vehicles in front. As it hit the ground, four Sprint vehicles and several of the three-wheelers went flying through the air and there were vibrations that they could feel coming through the ground, even from Soolchakan's area. The brown vegetation in the blast area was all engulfed in flame. The beam only lasted for a moment, however the devastation was incredible.

Nanchee looked up at Soolchakan. "What was that?"

"I don't know," said Soolchakan in a shaky voice. "I...I've never seen anything like that!"

"That must be one of those *Heelmashk* weapons," said Heelitha. "I heard that our science divisions were working on something like that...but they hadn't finished it. Looks like Axswain already has it."

Nanchee almost looked panicked. "So what...do we do?"

Heelitha grabbed Soolchakan's leg. "Try to aim your fire... where that beam originated! You've got to take that thing out or... we don't stand a chance!"

Nanchee was still rattled. "Why...haven't they fired again? They blasted an area...and then...nothing!"

"It takes a while to warm up...and it takes a while to recharge between blasts," said Heelitha. "Didn't you read any of the scientific updates?"

"Not on that thing," said Nanchee.

Soolchakan took his best guess as to where the beam had originated. He fired several blasts in that area. He was tearing up a lot of concrete, however, he could not see that he was hitting that horrid weapon, or anything else that mattered. Another beam came out of the middle of the wall and he saw that he had been way off to the left. This time the beam had a direct hit on one of the Sprint vehicles.

"It *is* a *Heelmashk* weapon," screamed Heelitha. "Look at the vehicle it hit...blasted to pieces...and the metal is...burning. You've gotta kill that thing!"

Soolchakan moved where he was targeting the wall. It took four bursts from his cannon and the results were devastating. A deafening blast rocked the entire area. Concrete was flying everywhere as the *Heelmashk* weapon exploded, in an interior part of the wall. There were several small pieces of concrete that pinged off of the truck that Soolchakan was in. Once the dust cleared, they could see numerous, very large pieces of concrete, laying around in the battlefield, that all of the vehicles now had to avoid. There was a huge gaping hole in the wall and from the top of the vehicle, he could see all the way through the wall.

"I think I made a mess," said Soolchakan. He was a little stunned at the amount of damage.

Heelitha looked up at him. "You silenced that big *Heelmashk* cannon! That's what matters!"

Soolchakan did not really feel that good about what he had done. "Yeah, but...there's several overturned vehicles...and the survivors...of the crashes...are running back to us...and their being picked off by snipers...at the base of the wall."

Nanchee snarled at him. "Let the forward Sprints take care of the snipers. You keep watching...in case those *Melafathan Fovoks* have another one of those cannons. They'll do more damage than a few snipers."

Heelitha grabbed his leg again. "Can't you shoot at the snipers?"

"I'd have to fire...directly through *our* vehicles. Hitting an area...up high on the wall is no problem. Those snipers are at the base of the wall."

Heelitha went back to her side door to look out and see if there was anything that could be done.

Another jolt hit as one of the *Heelmashk* weapons fired. This one was off to Soolchakan's right. He saw that it had had some devastating consequences for the vehicles in that area as at least five Sprint vehicles were spinning through the air.

Nanchee was almost in tears upon seeing the carnage. "Shoot that thing!"

"It's too far away," said Soolchakan. "Hopefully...someone over there can...kill that one the way I did...the first one." He then saw four red beams, all aimed at approximately the same area, start chewing holes in the wall.

Then another earth shattering jolt as the second one suffered a direct hit and now there was another gargantuan hole in the wall. Being able to observe from the side, instead of directly in front, showed even more how immense the blast was as chunks of the wall, large enough to crush the vehicle that Soolchakan was in, were spinning through the air as well.

Then they started hearing some strange whistling sounds and after each whistle there was a loud explosion as one of the conventional types of weaponry was coming at them.

Heelitha scoffed. "Those things can't hurt *us*. Those things are supposed to take out infantry. We're all mobile." She sneered. "We don't have anything to fear from those things."

At that moment, one of the whistlers scored a direct hit on one of the Light Assault vehicles. There was the initial blast and several residual blasts as some of the weaponry inside the vehicle detonated.

Soolchakan looked down from where he was with the cannon. "Any more stupid observations you wanna make?"

Heelitha glared at him. She looked up at the spare 459. "Can't we use both of these cannons…at the same time?"

"No," said Kiyalee. "The only ones that are designed to use two 459's at the same time are the big *Lead* Heavy Assault vehicles. We can only use one at a time."

Heelitha grunted in frustration. "And these *chokwad* rifles don't…have anything close to the range that we need…to take out any enemy…yet!" She turned to Kiyalee. "Can't this thing go any faster?"

Kiyalee looked back and shouted at Heelitha. "I'm not supposed to go any faster…unless it's ordered by Nagasoom! He went forward…that's his business! We keep advancing slowly…until further orders are given…from the Supreme Officer!" She turned back and clenched her teeth as she kept her speed constant with the other heavy vehicles on each side.

Soolchakan looked for Nagasoom's truck. It was not hard to spot, seeing as how it was one of only ten Type 195's. It also had Nagasoom's flag flying off of the rear. He had caught up to, and was passing, the lines of the Light Assault vehicles. The twin 459's on top were firing away at different areas near the base of the wall as they attempted to stop the snipers. Between Nagasoom's 459's and the 456's on the Sprint vehicles, it appeared that the vast majority of the snipers were now inactive - either dead, wounded...or hiding.

Soolchakan went back to concentrating his fire at the top of the wall. He could not understand how so much damage had been done and yet there was still hostile fire coming from the rubble at the top. He saw the huge holes that were the result of the *Heelmashk* weapons being blown up, however, the bottom of the holes were still at least eight stories up. There was no way to drive any of their vehicles through the holes - without some massive ramps.

Nagasoom reached the front lines of the Sprint vehicles. His 459's were having all kinds of devastating effect on the snipers at the base of the wall and the ones on top of the wall.

Then another jarring jolt. This time the giant yellow beam came out and Nagasoom's truck was the main target. His vehicle had been going in a straight line and thus made an easy target. In the aftermath of that shot from the *Heelmashk* weapon, Nagasoom's truck just sat there burning helplessly. Anyone inside had been killed in the blast or was being baked alive. There was no reason to look for survivors in that truck.

At the moment Nagasoom's truck was hit, everyone on the battlefield had virtually the same thought: Pick up any running Owlam survivors and get out of here - NOW. Several of the Light Assault vehicles sped forward to assist in picking up anyone that was running. The personnel with the 459's kept firing at anything they thought was hostile fire from Axswain to cover the rescue of the runners. Then all vehicles - as one - turned around to their right and headed away from the wall as rapidly as they could.

All vehicles sped away to that big tree line, where they would all be out of range of any of the Axswain weaponry. They stopped, turned and watched for any possible stragglers that might have been missed. During the time they were waiting, six more injured stragglers made it to the Owlam lines.

The eight Medical vehicles were very busy taking care of

numerous broken bones, burns and other injuries associated with crashes.

The four Master Officers all met at one central location to try to decide how long they would wait for any more stragglers. Unfortunately they could not, at first, decide who was in charge. All four had each unilaterally decided that they were the one who was now in total command and not one of them was ready to relinquish command...yet.

The argument ended when Master Officer, Plothok got a little angry and shouted in a voice that no one had ever heard him use. The only time they had ever heard that voice before was from Nagasoom. "I, Master Officer, Plothok, am now the Supreme Officer. I was the ranking one, a year ago, I was the ranking one a month ago, I was the ranking one before this pointless attack started and I am the ranking one now! Not to mention the fact that I am also the eldest. Any questions?" The other three stopped talking and gave him blank stares. Plothok looked at each one with an angry glare. He took a deep breath and let it out slowly. "Now," he said calmly. "We will wait...until midday." He looked toward the enemy city. "If by then...there are no more stragglers...we go back home." He looked back towards the home city. "I just pray that...while we embarked on this...this idiotic adventure...no one moved in to Owlam...and is leaving us all...homeless." He looked both ways up and down their lines. "Make sure that all weapons are aimed at the enemy...just in case they try some...counterattack."

In preparation for a counterattack, Soolchakan looked at the power pack on his cannon. It showed that it was down to 8% power. He knelt down in the vehicle. "I need a fresh power pack for my monster."

Bonarain opened a storage cabinet and pulled one out. "Where should I put the spent one?"

He looked around. "Somewhere...where we don't get it mixed up with any of the full ones."

She nodded.

After the initial six late-comers had showed up, they saw nothing moving on that field of carnage. Not at first.

Someone shouted a warning. "Here they come!"

Soolchakan had not been paying attention. He had been fidgeting a little because he desperately needed a drink. The rations that had been passed out did not help his need at all. It put something in his stomach, however, he was aching for some kind of alcohol. He looked up in surprise when he heard the warning.

Several large vehicles and at least 2000 infantry were advancing slowly. An order came over the intercom from Plothok. *"Don't let those vehicles of theirs, get anywhere near us...they might have one of those Heelmashk weapons mounted on those things and I don't like what I saw happen because of them...all of the 459's...open fire!"*

Soolchakan carefully aimed the cannon and started shooting at the closest vehicle that he could see. He noticed that there were three other red beams hitting the same vehicle. At first he did not see that the concentrated fire was showing any effect on the big truck. Then the enemy truck stopped. A portion of its front started glowing red hot and all of the personnel inside the vehicle, jumped out. Moments later - Boom! The explosion sent several of the infantry personnel flying helplessly from the blast.

All of the Axswain personnel started firing. The Owlam personnel found that they were out of range of the conventional and the hand held pulse weapons.

He heard several more explosions to his left and right as the Axswain trucks were being super-heated and exploding from the 459's. Right now, he was very glad that the Axswain did not have any 459's of their own - the results could be disastrous.

Since all of the Axswain vehicles had been blown up, before they could get within range of their own weapons, the Axswain personnel went into a full chaotic retreat back to the city.

Everyone in Soolchakan's truck let out a sigh of relief. The Owlam army had lost the attack, and won the counterattack. As usual, a wretched stalemate.

Once again the intercom started buzzing. *"If there had been any other stragglers...the Axswain would have killed them...on their way here. Since I see no hope of any more...who were lagging behind...*

people of Owlam…let's go home."

Soolchakan could not help himself. He had a sudden urge to use this powerful cannon against the retreating infantry. He aimed and held the trigger down as he swept the cannon back and forth across the field. He saw several, in his line of fire, throw their arms up as they fell. Several just went limp and fell.

Some of the other people who had 459's started doing the same. The Axswain seemed to be getting heavier casualties in their retreat than they had suffered in the attack. These infantry personnel had no place to hide - especially since the concentrated fire of the 459's started grass fires in the dead vegetation on the battlefield.

All of the brown vegetation caught fire quickly and the Axswain medical personnel were not able to go back and help any injured. There was not much wind, so the Owlamites did not have to worry about a flash fire chasing them…so far.

The intercom started buzzing. *"Enough of that! Cease fire and let's go home."*

Soolchakan looked down at his new power pack. As he figured, holding down the trigger had been a major drain on the power pack. In just that short time, the pack had gone from 100% to 48%.

Kiyalee started the big engine. She put it in gear and started the long trip back to Owlam. Soolchakan, along with all of the other personnel that were manning the 459's kept watch with the cannons aimed to their rear - just in case any of the Axswain people got brave…or mad enough…or crazy enough to come back.

On the way back, they retrieved all of the empty fuel cans that had been jettisoned. In times like this, when no new manufacturing was going on, you could not afford to waste anything.

The sun was going down when they finally got back to the sanctuary of their own Owlam wall. Plothok opened the big gate to the tunnel. All of the smaller vehicles went through first, while the bigger ones with those big mean 459's kept watch.

Finally it was Kiyalee's turn to move her big 161 through the tunnel.

Now, Soolchakan could finally get some rest. He could hardly wait to get back home and drown himself with some of his collection of spirits.

They pulled through and everyone was assembling at that big parking lot. No one was going home…yet.

Soolchakan nearly panicked. Was there going to be another meeting? Would they have to sit there through a liturgy of lectures and debriefings? He groaned as he lowered himself down into the truck and then out the door.

Once all of the vehicles were parked, Plothok went up to that microphone that Nagasoom had announced the attack from. He sighed as he looked around at all of the Owlamites in front of him. "People of Owlam, our…former leader…Nagasoom…got his wish. This will be a day…that both we and the people of Axswain, will not forget, very soon. We suffered a lot of casualties…so did the Axswain." He stood there shaking his head for a moment. "Unfortunately…this day is not over." He looked around again and licked his lips. "All personnel…go back to your home. We will be doing a…roll call…of all of you. We have no idea…at this time… how many we lost. If the numbers are small…it still doesn't matter. We lost people. I don't know about you, but…I never felt good about this attack. I remember the tacticians and strategists telling us… that it would take at least 500,000 well armed troops…to mount a significant attack…on Axswain. As you all know, we have less than 30,000…and now…even less than before, because of…those that we left behind." He closed his eyes and leaned his head back. He shook his head. "I can't really think of anything to say…that could possibly make anyone feel any better about what…took place…today. All that I know is…I…no I'm not going to say it. I…do not want to dishonor the dead. Thank you all for being so brave…and now…we can go back to our homes and mourn. Again, we will be calling all of you to find out who and how many…we lost today." He once again scanned the crowd. "Go home, get some rest and…do your regular routine of being vigilant. We don't know if…one of the other cities is going to mount some…attack like the one we just…did. Go home." With that he walked away from the microphone.

For a few moments, it was very quiet in the area. No one spoke as they all headed for their vehicles. At first there was the sound of one vehicle starting up - then another and another. Soon it was the noise of several thousand vehicles all running. They slowly started heading out to their destinations.

Kiyalee and Chyning were in the front seat of their truck as she pulled the big 161 out. They all rode in silence as Kiyalee drove.

They got to the first stop, to drop off one of the rider Teams. That Team got out, collecting their weapons and food. They nodded in silence and headed for their home. When the other Team was dropped off, it was just as somber.

When they got back to the fuel station, close to their home tavern, they took all of the spare fuel cans off and left them at the station. Kiyalee filled up the tank and then they went home.

Soolchakan headed for a bottle (or two or three) of his prized stash of *Golden Age Liquor*. Bonarain headed for her private area with her makeup. Kiyalee stayed in the garage for a while, checking the truck over thoroughly for any damage or wear. Chyning headed for the watch station to check on any activity that may have been recorded on the consoles.

They all knew that it was going to be a long wait until the roll call got to them. The roll was done in numerical order and this was number 7016 of 7016. They all knew, in their hearts that it would no longer be 7016 of 7016 teams. There were no longer 7016 teams. They just did not know how many until the final tally came out.

It was four days before all of the figures came out. Seventy-one Teams were obliterated. Twenty-six Teams no longer had all four of their personnel. Ninety-four vehicles destroyed and lost. Two hundred twenty-nine vehicles damaged, but reparable. Of the 7,016 men, 78 had died. Of the 21,048 women, 248 were dead. The total population of Owlam was now 27,738.

Fourteen Teams had lost one individual. Eight Teams had lost 2 people. Four Teams were no longer a Team - just one individual. Plothok was going to make a decision - later - what to do with the incomplete Teams.

One thing that was not really on the roster was those three-wheelers that had been in the attack. Nagasoom had been upset with the people that had been found hiding. The cowards were the ones who had been put on those three-wheelers - on the front line - without any armor of any type around them. 59 had been found and 59 had gone into the melee at the front. 10 came back. Plothok was equally unimpressed with the fact that they had initially hidden in fear. He still did not know what had made them go straight to the front, however, he was still angry with them because they had hidden, after the attack, in the first place. Those ten survivors were not really considered part of the remaining population and they would never be allowed on any established Team because of their original cowardice.

17

It was decided, by the wisdom of the ones in charge that the four Teams that had only one surviving individual, would combine with one of the Teams that lost only one individual. The eight Teams that had only two personnel would combine to make four Teams. This left nine Teams with only three personnel. It was decided that they could still be a viable Team, on one of the Sprint vehicles, with three as well as four.

When it came to the fact that there were nine Teams with only three and there were ten of the surviving Cowards, Plothok was adamant that the Cowards would not be allowed to wear any Team designation nor would they be recognized as any part of the count of the Owlam survivors. They just exist and they would be sent - first - to any trouble spot, on their three-wheelers. They had to scrounge off the land or glean what they could from areas that recognized Teams had not confiscated all nonperishable goods.

Meanwhile at Command Central, there was a discussion going on between all of the top ranking officials.

Master Officer, Plothok had assumed the title of Supreme Officer. Since he had been the Commander of the Northern Command, someone had to be assigned to take over his station. He decided on Senior Officer, Nakalak, the Team Leader of Team 6.

The meeting consisted of the new Supreme Officer, Plothok, and the four Command Officers: Neenatha - Eastern Command, Kodge - Western Command, Jahong - Southern Command, and Nakalak, the new Northern Commander. The others at the meeting were the Vice Commanders of each of the four Commands.

"Something strange happened out there," said Plothok. "Something strange happened...here as well. I can't put my finger on it...but...it seems that Nagasoom had some kind of power over us...and now...I seem to have it. I know it sounds odd, but, how else do you explain what happened on that battlefield...and back here at the city?"

Neenatha looked at him puzzled. "What *are* you babbling about?"

Plothok scowled back at her. "Consider that attack pattern… when the Sprint vehicles broke out in front and then broke into three ranks…on their own. Did we discuss any sort of tactic like that… before we departed? No."

The others looked at him and silently shook their heads.

"Then," he continued. "At the very moment of Nagasoom… getting charred to death, by that…whatever weapon it was that they used…I was thinking…in my head…we need to get out of here now…after we rescue the ones who have escaped from destroyed vehicles and are on foot." He closed his eyes and shook his head. "THAT…is exactly what happened. We never discussed any rescue of…*those now on foot*. We never discussed the three lines by the Sprints, or the three lines by the Light Assault vehicles. They…just did it and…while it turned out to be…rather effective…we were beaten back because that wall…was just too daunting."

Jahong was a little upset over that observation. "Why do you think the wall was…daunting? There were two massive holes in it… we just didn't get there."

Plothok shook his head. "How high up were those holes? We would have had to build a ramp up to them…or use our 459's to blast smaller holes in lower section. Then…we would have had to drive through those holes over…who knows what kind of rubble. I don't think that the Sprints could have made it. Even if they could…what was on the other side…waiting for us…that we couldn't see? We have no idea. We have no reconnaissance. We could have been… blasted to oblivion…on the other side."

Kodge scoffed. "Then why did we follow…Nagasoom to… what we know so little about?"

"Precisely my question," said Plothok. "What made us… all…go into that attack…so unquestioningly?"

Neenatha clicked her tongue. "I think…that this might be… one of those strange…manifestations that our good doctors have been talking about."

The other people in the room all looked at her as if she were insane.

"Think about it," she continued. "A lot of times...a high ranking officer gives a command. Many times...that command is questioned...by some...not all but some. We heard Nagasoom, on a few occasions, start talking like he had...some form of hidden amplifier in his mouth. Every time he got angry...and used that...*voice*...no one questioned it. We all obeyed...everything, without question, when he used that...*voice*. I even heard you use it...when you decided that you are the one...in total command. You used... that *voice*...and we all shut up...not one of us said...no."

Nakalak was trying to grasp the thought. "Are you talking about...what some of the ancients called...'*The Voice of Power*'?"

She took in a deep breath and let it out slowly. "I...think I am."

Plothok chuckled. "So...how should I test it? Do I tell one of the people to...go commit suicide...or murder someone else?"

Neenatha grimaced. "I don't think that we should go that far."

Kodge smirked. "Why not? We still have ten of the Cowards. Why not use them to do something dastardly or even lethal...to themselves."

Nakalak chuckled. "Good idea! It won't hurt any of us...to lose a few more of the cowards."

Jahong nodded. "It might explain...why the cowards...went straight out to the front...after hiding in fear...from the firestorms."

Plothok sneered. "It was either that...or they were attempting to get back some real status...after their act of cowardice."

Kodge shrugged. "So...what do we do? How do we test it?"

"Call out," said Neenatha. "Call out to them...from here... using that *voice*. See if it's long distance...or if you have to be within ear range of them."

"They could be anywhere in the city," complained Kodge. "It might be...tomorrow before they answer this call."

Plothok nodded. "It still sounds like a good idea. The way to test it...is to do it...and give them a limitation. I will call out...and order them to be here…at midday, tomorrow. If all ten show up…at the appointed time…then there is some kind of truth and reality to what she says."

"So…do it," said Neenatha.

With a bit of a smirk, Plothok stood up. He drew in a deep breath. "All ten of you cowards…wherever you are…you will be here at the Command Headquarters…tomorrow at midday. You will not question this…you will come…be here at that time… without fail." He cleared his throat and gave Neenatha a smug look. "Is that what you were referring to?"

Neenatha was staring at him wide-eyed. "Uh…yes…Su-Sir…that is…exactly…what I was talking…about."

"Do you think that will work?"

"We…we'll see…Sir."

He looked at the people in front of him. "Then…let's reconvene, shortly before midday…tomorrow and…see if they show up."

Everyone in the room nodded.

"Good," said Plothok. "Meeting adjourned until tomorrow. Dismissed!"

They all left the room, shaking their heads. Plothok was shaking his because of skepticism. All others looked a little physically, as well as, mentally shaken.

The next day, Plothok walked into the conference room. All of the Commanders and Vice Commanders were there, ready for whatever was going to happen.

Neenatha stood up. "Sir, I informed the guards…that if the cowards show up, they…have been summoned…by you, Sir."

Plothok snickered. "Do you actually think that they will show up?"

She looked up at the clock. "We'll know shortly, Sir."

While they were waiting for the correct time, they discussed a few redundant activities that were being implemented in an attempt at regaining some form of normalcy to the city.

Senior Officer, Momasee, the South Vice Commander,

started giggling. "Excuse me, Senior Officer, Neenatha...but I don't see any..."

At that moment, all ten of the cowards walked in. The only one who was not gawking in shock at the arrival was Neenatha. She sat there looking rather proud of herself.

After a stifled chuckle, Neenatha turned to Plothok. "What do you say now, Sir?"

Plothok stood there slack-jawed. He turned to Neenatha. "Is it really possible that...I could communicate...in this manner...and give these completely unquestioned commands?"

Neenatha looked at her fingernails. "How else could you explain it, Sir?"

Kodge regained some of his composure. "How far...do you think this...*voice*...can go...in controlling...whoever it controls?"

Plothok looked at the Cowards. All ten were here, at the time commanded of them. The cowards did not look confused at all. They stood there looking as if no one had a better right to be where they were.

Plothok turned his back to the cowards. He sighed. He closed his eyes very tight and cocked his head to one side. All ten of the cowards, simultaneously lifted their right leg up and held them there. He opened his eyes, looking at his Staff. "Have any of them... lifted a leg?"

"All of them...Sir," said Jahong.

Plothok closed his eyes again. All ten of the cowards started hopping on their left leg. "Don't tell me...I can hear them." At that moment they all stopped hopping, however, they were still standing on one leg. He turned back to the cowards. All ten lowered their right leg. "Did...that...really just happen?"

"It most certainly did," said Kodge.

Plothok nodded. He slowly walked to the left end of the line and faced the first man. "What is your name?"

The man swallowed. "Supreme Officer, Nagasoom...took away my name, Sir. I am now...Coward...Number 36, Sir."

Plothok looked a little puzzled. "Nagasoom named you... Coward Number...36!"

"Yes, Sir."

Plothok moved to the next man in line. "Your name?"

"My name is Coward Number 40, Sir."

Plothok gave him a blank stare and a nod. He glanced back and forth from 36 to 40 and back. He closed his eyes.

Number 36 pulled a knife out of a scabbard on his belt and rammed it into the middle of the back of Number 40. Number 40 gasped and slowly sank to the ground. He died rather quickly.

The other cowards stared in shock at what had just happened. All of a sudden, all of them snapped to attention, with a somewhat stunned look on their faces. Just as quickly as they had been shocked at the murder, they now looked calm.

Plothok took three steps back. He took in a deep breath. "This man, Coward Number 40, he suffered some wounds in the battle at the Axswain wall. He did not tell anyone. He tried to be brave. He just succumbed to those wounds." He looked at Number 36.

Number 36 knelt down, pulled his knife out of 40's back, wiped the blood off and put it back in the scabbard.

Plothok took another step back. "Take this dead body and… bury it somewhere. You are dismissed."

The remaining nine cowards picked up the body and carried him out of the conference room.

One of the Aides came in looking very surprised. "Sir, what happened in here? They…I mean…what happened?"

Plothok calmly looked back at the Staff and then at the Aide. "It seems that that man…was injured at the Axswain wall…in the battle. He did not tell anyone. Just a few moments ago…he fell dead…from those wounds." Plothok pursed his lips. "Very strange fellow."

"Yes…Sir," said the Aide. "Very strange…indeed." He bowed his head as he backed out of the room, closing the door as he departed.

Plothok turned back to the Staff. "What did you people see?"

"It seems," said Neenatha, "that you ordered a man… to murder another man…in cold blood. You then ordered all of them…to believe a line of *h'oolyach* that you invented. They believed it…and…"

"And I have…a very dangerous…power." He leaned his head back with his eyes closed. "Why…me? How did…Nagasoom get this power and…why did it transfer to me…on his death?"

Kodge was typing information into a computer. He was looking at the console very keenly. "I'm trying to figure that out, Sir. Hopefully we can find out…what you two had in common… other than being the ranking individuals…who survived that flash-firestorm."

Plothok stared at the ceiling. "I am not going to use this… this power as I give this order. I am just going to give this order… to all of you as the Supreme Officer: Find out what…Nagasoom and I have…uh…had in common. Why was it his power…and now mine? Find out anything you can. I don't care how…even remotely absurd it sounds…find out!"

Neenatha smiled at him. "Anything else, Sir?"

Plothok took a deep breath. "No…meeting adjourned."

It was three days before the Staff was called back to the conference room. Everyone came in, one at a time. They all gave Senior Officer, Jahandi, the East Vice Commander a dirty look. She was the one who had called them all in - and did not tell them why.

Plothok made sure that he was the last to arrive. He came in keeping a blank look on his face. He sat down at the head of the conference table and pondered for a few moments before addressing Jahandi. "So…what is this important information that you think you have?"

Jahandi stood up and cleared her throat. "I think that I may have solved the mystery of who gets this strange power."

Plothok looked a little skeptical. "All right, let's hear it."

"I looked at several different factors…and then came across the fact that…Nagasoom was the oldest, of all the citizens of Owlam to survive that attack. He is the one who originally came up with this…*voice.* Since he passed away, you now have it."

"So…Nagasoom was the eldest survivor…and I am the

second eldest."

"Actually, Sir, you're the third eldest to have survived...the firestorm."

"Then...why did this...power...bypass the second eldest and come to me?"

"Because the second eldest was Officer Grade 1, Tooloola. If you remember, Sir, she was a member of Nagasoom's Team. When his vehicle, and everyone in it, were incinerated...Tooloola...died with him. She never had a chance to obtain...this power, but you did."

Plothok looked around the table at the rest of the Staff. "Interesting." He drummed his fingers on the table a few times. "So...if something happens...to me...who is...next?"

Jahandi looked away from Plothok to Neenatha. "That would be Master Officer, Neenatha. She is the next eldest...after you, Sir."

Neenatha looked stunned. "I don't want this kind of power. It's almost...as if you can...it IS a power where you can...make someone murder someone else...and then make them forget that they committed murder...and...it's HORRIBLE. I don't want it!"

Plothok smiled and shook his head. "It may not be your choice, Neenatha. I didn't ask for it. I don't know if Nagasoom was really aware of it. I didn't understand any or all of the ramifications of it...until that experiment with the cowards. We still don't know what it is...or where it is manifested from."

Neenatha shuddered and hugged herself. "Still...I don't want it!"

Plothok looked up at Jahandi. "I take it that you studied the list a little further? Can you tell us who would be next...after Neenatha?"

"Yes, Sir." Jahandi looked at her pad. "After Neenatha, it would be Master Officer, Jahong, then Master Officer, Kodge, then Senior Officer, Nakalak, then Senior Officer Ellyee, then Senior Officer Holla." She looked at Plothok rather concerned. "The one factor that I don't have here...is the cowards. I have...no idea... where any of them are on this list. I have the names of the forty eldest surviving Owlam...but I know nothing about any of the cowards...until we get their original name and date of birth. For all we know...all nine of them...could be in the top twenty...and if something happens to you...one of them could have...this power... and take over and...extract vengeance, for being treated the way that they are being treated...at this time."

Plothok nodded with his lips clenched. "So...I need...to call them back and have them...inform you...uh...*us*...of their age. They might be curious as to why they are being asked this question."

Kodge scoffed. "If you can make one of them commit murder and then make all of them forget that he murdered one of his own...I think that you could make all of them answer the question and then go home, forgetting that they were asked the question...in the first place."

Nakalak grunted. "So, what happens if one, or more, of the cowards turns out to be older than Neenatha?"

Plothok raised his eyebrows. "Let's...fight that battle...when it comes. No...preemptive strikes...yet." He turned to Jahandi. "Give me your intercom number and I'll...use the power...to inform them to contact you...and give you their real name, their date of birth...and their...coward number designation. Do you have your recorder on...in case you're not there when they call?"

"I always have it on," said Jahandi with a smile.

"Good, keep us informed." Plothok looked around the table. "Anything else...new?

There were no responses.

"All right! We are adjourned...until something else comes up."

Three days later, Jahandi sent a report to Plothok on the nine surviving cowards as to their age and where they stood in line from the top.

The next day, there was another Staff meeting. At that time, Jahandi reported, to the entire Staff, that of the eight surviving cowards, the eldest one of the eight was well over 6,500 down the line from the eldest Owlamite.

The Staff all wondered why Plothok acted a little strange. All they could remember was him repeating the message that this *Voice of Power*, was a very dangerous thing.

Kodge looked around at his colleagues. "Other than the news that none of the eight cowards can possibly get this...power... any time soon, do we have any other business?"

"Yes," said Plothok. "We are going to start searching through those charred buildings...in the central area...and look for any more survivors."

Neenatha scoffed. "Are you crazy? It's been over a year... since that attack. Who could have possibly survived...in those charred remnants of buildings...for this length of time?"

"I don't know," said Plothok. "It took quite a while to find all fifty-nine of the original cowards...that participated in the attack. Who knows...how many other cowards have been hiding... somewhere in the rubble...and are now definitely too afraid to show their faces?"

"They would have starved to death by now," said Nakalak. "There isn't...even a slight chance of there being anything...edible... still left in that rubble. No one could have survived this long...in there."

Plothok stood up. "We're going to do it! We're going to look. We have no idea how...creative a coward can get at hiding. We ARE going to make sure...that there are no more cowards hiding anywhere, in the inner city!" He cleared his throat. "Any questions?"

Surprisingly, there were none.

"Fine...get the order out. We'll look at all of the results... as they come in. If there is a coward...who is still hiding and hasn't been found, there will be some kind of...hidden dwelling place. We find these dwelling places, we find any other cowards that might be out there. Meeting adjourned."

The next few months were spent in everyone going through rubble. The doctors were kept rather busy, tending to sprains, strains and a few broken bones. It was not until they had been looking for two full months that one new female coward was found in the northeast section of the rubble. This new one received the new name of: Coward Number 60.

Another meeting of the Staff was called.

"I told you that there were more out there," Plothok said smugly.

"Yes, you were right," said Jahong. "One thing about this situation, though…I think that we've been going about it the wrong way."

Plothok glared at him angrily. "You mean you don't like getting your hands dirty?"

"No, Sir, that's not it…we have…you! You have that *Voice of Power*. If you want this silliness of finding more hiding cowards, who are still able to avoid us…why don't you use that power…and… make them…come to you? I remind you that you did say that… some of these cowards…could be very creative in the way they hide. It appears that…no Owlamite can hide from the…*Voice*."

Plothok's face went blank. He looked at all of the faces of the people in the room. "That…is a…*very* good idea. Why didn't any of us…think of it before?"

"You would have to word it…rather specifically and correctly," said Nakalak. "Otherwise…all of the cowards will be back here."

Plothok looked thoughtful for a few moments. "All of the citizens of Owlam…who have not already shown themselves… you will come forward now! If you have reported in…before and are on one of the Teams, or already have a Coward Number… you do not need to show yourselves at this time. Only those who have been hiding and are still unknown to myself and this Staff need come in. You will be at the headquarters building…no later than midday…tomorrow…no matter what it takes to get here." He looked at Nakalak. "Do you think that's sufficient?"

Nakalak smiled. "Hopefully, yes, Sir."

"I'll notify the others in the building of your order," said Ellyee. "No telling what they would think…if another scruffy looking Owlamite shows up…unannounced."

"So…once again, we have a short meeting," said Plothok with a smile. "Maybe it will be another short meeting again…tomorrow."

Kodge stood up smiling. "What about the order…to continue searching the rubble? With the order, that you just gave, I don't think that we need to do anymore…rubble searching. The doctors have been kept busy…with too many accidents…from finding…holes the hard way."

Plothok looked thoughtful. "The search for cowards and any other survivors…in the rubble is ended. All those of Owlam, who are not cowards, may go back to duties that are more productive…to our survival." He cleared his throat. "That should do it." He chuckled. "We will meet again…just before midday tomorrow. There we will wait and see if there are any more…new visitors."

At midday, the next day, two women showed up at the conference room. They were wearing rags and were both very dirty and unkempt. Once Jahandi got their "original" names and birth dates, they were given the designation of Coward Number 61 and Coward Number 62. They were also given duties to perform as was befitting their new status (whether they liked it or not).

Plothok again addressed the Staff, leaning back in his chair with his feet propped up on the conference table. "What was the original count…of the cowards…male and female…I mean?"

Jahong looked over the figures. "There were originally twenty-three men and thirty-six women. Now, because of the three that have showed up…late, that makes a total of thirty-nine women. Since that battle…there are now…six men and five women…in the coward status."

Plothok chuckled. "And as a reward for their cowardice, they will be given the most menial of tasks. They will always be the first sent into a battle area…and no one will grieve over their deaths."

Several more months went by as the surviving Owlamites were doing everything that they could, with their small forces, to keep track of any form of outside interference with their lives.

Soolchakan had been grieving over his dwindling supplies of liquor, until he found a liquor store, in the local area, that, for some inexplicable reason, he had not known about. Once again, he had a wonderfully large and diversified assortment of spirits. He would now be able to regularly drown his sorrows, without running low, for quite some time.

He was heading back to the home tavern, from the hidden supply, with four new bottles under his jacket, when he felt a huge jolt come through the ground. It nearly knocked him off of his feet. He had not felt a jolt like that since...those nasty *heelmashk* weapons at the Axswain wall. He nearly panicked. Had someone - inside Owlam - invented one? The other alternative was that Owlam was under attack - from someone else who had one of those horrid weapons.

He ran the rest of the way, not caring that two of the bottles kept clanking against each other as he ran. He came through the front entrance. The three women had gone to the main room on the first floor and were listening intently to the chatter coming over the public wires. Several voices were overlapping and it was almost complete gibberish. They were so intent on listening, trying to hear anything comprehendible that they did not notice him come in. He ran up to his bedroom to hide the four bottles and returned to the main room.

He arrived, back in time, to hear the private intercom start buzzing. He picked it up and answered. "Team 7016, Officer, Soolchakan here!"

The response came back: *"Team 7016, there's been an attack on the west side. It appears that those Galsinos are attacking us, on our west side."*

The women were now at his side listening to this conversation.

"Uh...yes, do you want Team 7016 to respond?"

"Of course, we do. You have a vehicle with a 459 on it!"

Soolchakan closed his eyes. "Copy, we'll go pick up Teams 6598 and 6638, on our way."

"Negative, 7016! Those Teams are in the wrong direction! They are east of you, this attack is on the west side. Proceed to the closest wall ramp, just west of you, and get your truck on top of the wall. We have informed Team 5694 to meet you on top of the wall.

They are west of you and they can get to the wall and assist you in the counterattack. Your regular partner Teams will have to use the Trams. We need you there...NOW!"

Soolchakan shook his head. "Team 7016 copies...out!" He turned to Kiyalee. "Is that monster fueled up?"

She snapped back at him. "Of course it is! I always keep my baby fueled up. We don't know when we're going to need it, so..."

"All right, all right...everyone to the vehicle...now!" He was going to have to grit his teeth again and go through another attack... sober. Hang the luck!

The women got in the truck. Soolchakan hit the button to open the big door. Kiyalee started it up and drove out. He hit the button to close it. They did not wait for it to finish closing before they took off.

Kiyalee maneuvered the truck to the Perimeter road and turned east. "Where's this ramp?"

"It's just past the Tram's Thalwa stop," said Bonarain. "Don't worry, you can't miss something that big."

"I hope you're right," said Kiyalee with concern in her voice.

Bonarain chuckled. "She'll see."

They passed two other Tram stops before passing Thalwa. There was a road crossing just after the Thalwa stop where she was able to get the big truck on the other side of the Tram rails.

Then she saw the wall ramp. "That...thing is *huge*! You could drive five of these trucks...side by side...up or down that ramp!"

Bonarain giggled. She looked at Chyning. "I told you she couldn't miss it."

Kiyalee hit the ramp at full speed. "Where's this other Team that we're supposed to pick up?"

"Don't have a clue," said Soolchakan. "I don't think that there's gonna to be too many Teams...up here on the wall, waiting for us, though."

Kiyalee shrugged. "Hope you're right."

Chyning looked out the front window. "First time I've ever been up here. I didn't realize how wide this wall is."

At that moment, two of the Light Assault Vehicles sped past

Team 7016.

Bonarain scoffed. "Can't you keep up with them?"

"NO!" Kiyalee clenched her teeth. "This thing is nowhere near as fast as those buggies. They're designed for speed and maneuverability. This one is designed for heavy firepower."

At that moment, a Sprint Vehicle almost flew past them.

Bonarain sat back and sighed.

Soolchakan looked up at the 459, on the left, sitting in the storage bracket. "When we get to…Team 5694, we're gonna get that thing in its place. I don't want to have to wrestle it in place…while moving."

"There they are," said Kiyalee. She started slowing.

The others looked out the front window and saw four people holding up a banner with 5694 printed on it.

Bonarain held on as the truck slowed. "Why don't ya wait until you get to them to slow down?"

"Because it takes a while to slow this monster down."

Bonarain just rolled her eyes and held on.

The big truck finally stopped. Soolchakan opened the rear door. "Officer Grade 5, Soolchakan, Team 7016 here, welcome aboard!"

A woman started climbing up. "Officer Grade 5, Chanda, Team Leader of 5694. They told us to bring our pulse rifles and give you some new instructions."

Soolchakan looked at her startled. "New…orders?"

"Yeah, now, you're supposed to pick up Team 4432 as well. They're just a short ways further west."

"Oh, another Team, well that's fine. This rig can hold it."

The rest of 5694 got on board, with weaponry: Officer Grade 6, Tay, Officer Grade 6, Skoss and Officer Grade 6, Wedanee.

After getting the 459 into ready position, they were off again, speeding along on top of the wall. Before they got to Team 4432, four more Sprint vehicles sped past them.

Team 4432 consisted of: Officer Grade 4, Setska, Officer Grade 5, Pandee, Officer Grade 6, Holshook and Officer Grade 7, Otee.

Team 4432 had their pulse rifles and ten cans of extra fuel for the big vehicle. Apparently, headquarters did not want this vehicle running out of fuel at any time during the battle.

After pouring the fuel from five of the cans into the main fuel tank, they were on their way again.

The drive up on top of the wall was not as bad as driving through the streets of the city. The wall was smooth and wide on top. There were no sharp turns so they could go at full throttle the entire way.

They listened to some of the chatter on the intercom as they sped along. Apparently, the Supreme Officer along with the Master Officer of the Western Command and the Vice Commander of the West were all there at the battle front. They heard a report that the wall had been breached and that the Galsino troops were pouring in through that breach. The Owlam troops that were there desperately needed reinforcement. Kiyalee was pushing the truck for every bit of speed that she could get out of it.

After an eternity, they finally were able to see the battle area in the distance. The wall had been breached, however, the huge breach was full of rubble, from blowing the wall to pieces, and it made for some very precarious footing for anyone trying to climb through. Anyone attempting to climb through the breach could not get up to the top of the wall, because the rubble area had collapsed the wall well below the top.

There was a large enemy vehicle that had, somehow, been able to drive over the rubble. It was a big tractor pulling a flatbed that had a huge conical device mounted on the bed that covered the entire thing.

They heard a report on the intercom that there was another truck, identical to the one inside the wall that was approaching the breach from the west. There was also a report of thousands of enemy troops, dressed in long gray hooded robes, coming along with these two vehicles.

Outside the wall, off in the distance, there was another line of vehicles that was apparently a second wave. They were back there waiting for…only the enemy knew.

Soolchakan started warming up the power pack for the 459 cannon. The two other Team Leaders were using their binoculars to get a good picture of what they were facing.

Chanda was looking at what was going on inside the wall. All of a sudden she let out a loud growl. "I can see Plothok's truck. It's one of those big Lead Assault trucks. He's down there, coming in, straight at that cone device. He's got his two 459's going, but…they got some kind of lousy aim."

"They're shooting the supporting infantry," shouted Soolchakan. "They don't seem to be interested in…whatever that thing is…on the truck."

At that moment, a large yellow beam came out of the big part of the cone. The beam engulfed Plothok's truck and the entire truck burst into flame just moments before it blew up.

"Those Galsino *Fovoks* have a *heelmashk* weapon as well," screamed Chanda. "Even the metal was burning on Plothok's truck…just before it blew."

Soolchakan leaned down into the truck. "Kiyalee, get closer to the edge of the wall!"

Kiyalee screamed back at him. "What…which edge?"

"The inner edge! I can't get a clean shot at it unless you get to the edge!"

Chanda gave him a strange look. "Do you actually think you can hit that thing from here?"

"Yes," said Soolchakan angrily. "We did it at the Axswain wall. This 459 cannon has an incredible range."

Chanda shrugged and went back to observing with the binoculars.

Kiyalee shook her head. "How close to the edge…do you wanna get?"

Chyning was sitting on the right side of the vehicle as second driver. "Trust ME, girlie, I'll watch this side."

Kiyalee shook her head and started slowly steering closer to the edge.

Soolchakan aimed his cannon and fired a steady beam at the big cone device. A rather large piece of the cone fell off, however, it did not seem to do much damage other than that.

Chanda grabbed Soolchakan's leg. "Aim at the workings at the back of the cone. The cone isn't the weapon, that's just the barrel...those computer panels at the back...that's what controls that thing!"

He switched his aim to the rear of the cone. A second red beam started hitting the device from another truck that was on the wall, just north of the breach. Between both of the beams, the personnel who were at the panels, on the truck, started abandoning their posts. The entire rear workings of the cone device started glowing orange - then red - then BOOM! The explosion was almost the same kind that they had seen at the Axswain wall when they had blown up the *heelmashk* weapons there. The ground shook and the air was full of dirt, smoke, body parts and other miscellaneous debris.

Kiyalee made a bit of a hard turn to the left, away from the explosion. Soolchakan held on tight where he was. Most of the people inside were thrown against the right inner side of the vehicle. There were several grunts and curses as they resituated themselves, rubbing a few bruised areas of their bodies.

Small and large chunks of dirt were landing on top of the wall. The smoke engulfed them for a few moments and Kiyalee had to stop completely because she was totally blinded by the smoke.

Soolchakan was just praying that he did not get hit by some of that flying debris. He could hear some...things...landing around the truck.

The smoke cleared rather quickly. Since there was no residual fire, burning anything down there, there was no new smoke.

Soolchakan looked at where the *heelmashk* weapon had been, inside the wall and saw nothing but a massive crater surrounded by debris. He had remembered seeing, what he estimated as well over 2000, infantry troops around that vehicle. Now, he could see no one...or anything else moving around that area. He leaned back down into the truck. "Get over to the other side! Someone said that there was another one of those things out there...coming this way!"

Kiyalee rubbed her eyes and let out a quick breath. She

grabbed the gear shift, throttled it and the vehicle lurched forward as she gave it a hard left turn towards the outer edge of the wall.

Soolchakan watched closely as they neared the edge, looking for another one of those big cones. He finally saw it - aimed in his direction. He made a quick check on his power pack. It was still at 79% power. He shook his head, thinking that it had only taken 21% of his power and another 459 to kill that other *heelmashk*. He aimed and started the concentrated fire at the control panels at the rear of the cone.

Kiyalee and Chyning both screamed as they saw the big yellow beam coming out of that cone - aimed directly at Team 7016 and their big truck. Soolchakan nearly lost control of his bowels as he saw the beam. The lucky thing for them was that the beam dissipated, long before it got to the wall. They did not see any damage to the wall or anything else around them.

Soolchakan let out a loud sigh of relief and started firing again. The results were identical to the first one: Orange glow, red glow...BOOM!

This time, the wind took the smoke away from them. They were able to see the gigantic crater a lot sooner this time.

They were also able to see, again, that a tremendous amount of infantry troops that had been surrounding the *heelmashk* weapon, were nowhere to be seen.

They heard gunfire and pulse rifles being fired off to their right.

Chanda was, once again, the one with the best vantage point. "There's some enemy...still in the breach. They didn't get hit by the blast and our people are making sure that they don't get any closer to invading the interior of Owlam."

Soolchakan leaned down. "Come on, Kiyalee, get over there!"

Kiyalee growled, geared down and throttled. Again the truck lurched forward.

Soolchakan looked over at the other Team Leader. "Setska, what about that bunch at the tree line...are they doing anything?"

She looked through her binoculars at the enemy line.

"They don't seem to be. I think they're just as shocked, about the devastation, as we are."

"Okay, but, keep an eye on em."

"Right!"

He turned his attention to Kiyalee. "Don't get too close to that edge that's been damaged. It might be a little unstable and I don't wanna see this truck hitting a weak spot and collapsing it."

She slowed down quite a bit. As they approached the breach, they noticed that there were some bodies on top of the wall. They were not dressed in the familiar black uniforms of the Owlam military. They were wearing dark gray, full length hooded robes.

Setska saw the bodies and snarled. "Stop this truck! Let's check and see if any of these enemy troops…are possibly still alive. If they are…we either kill em or take em prisoner."

Kiyalee stopped the truck. Bonarain and six of their passengers, from the other two Teams, got out and started investigating the bodies of the enemy that had been thrown up on top of the wall, by the tremendous explosions of the *heelmashk* weapons.

They got their first look at the changes that had occurred in Galsino. These people no longer looked like any Heyyah that they had ever seen. Their skin was bony white. They had huge bulbous red eyes. They no longer had normal hands. They had huge sharp claws instead of hands. None of the ones who had been thrown up on top of the wall were alive. Either the concussion of the blast, or the hard landing had killed them.

Soolchakan looked over the damage that he could see from his position. The two craters had formed a natural barrier. They no longer had to worry about the breach in the wall because the craters made it impossible for anyone to get to the breach and get through the rubble.

He also noticed that several Sprint vehicles had arrived, inside the wall and they were chasing down some of the Galsino infantry that had not been blown apart by the blast. He chuckled to himself over the fact that they were able to take a few prisoners.

Setska shook her head. "The ones that are way out there…

they've seen enough. They're all turning and leaving. They know that they've been whipped."

Soolchakan spun the 459 to the back position. He secured it in place and sat down inside the truck. "So…did we win…this battle?"

"I think so. It all depends on…the count of the dead. Who lost the most? Who still has the most?"

"I'll leave that up to the higher ups to determine."

She grunted in agreement.

Soolchakan sighed. "I wonder how often we're going to have to do something like this…"

**OTHER BOOKS BY
DARA J. CARR**

The Semi-Dragon Tale
Revenge Cometh Forth
Here Are My Shorts (a collection of short stories)
Volunteer…Spy?

www.ingramcontent.com/pod-product-compliance
Lightning Source LLC
Chambersburg PA
CBHW051636050726
47502CB00011B/528

* 9 7 8 0 9 8 6 1 2 8 5 6 1 *